ISABELLA HAMMAD

Enter Ghost

VINTAGE

1 3 5 7 9 10 8 6 4 2

Vintage is part of the Penguin Random House group of companies whose
addresses can be found at global.penguinrandomhouse.com

Penguin
Random House
UK

First published in Vintage in 2024
First published in hardback by Jonathan Cape in 2023

Copyright © Isabella Hammad 2023

Isabella Hammad has asserted her right to be identified as the author of this
Work in accordance with the Copyright, Designs and Patents Act 1988

penguin.co.uk/vintage

Printed and bound in Great Britain by Clays Ltd, Elcograf S.p.A.

The authorised representative in the EEA is Penguin Random House Ireland,
Morrison Chambers, 32 Nassau Street, Dublin D02 YH68

A CIP catalogue record for this book is available from the British Library

ISBN 9781529919998

Penguin Random House is committed to a sustainable future
for our business, our readers and our planet. This book is made
from Forest Stewardship Council® certified paper.

for my parents

I

I expected them to interrogate me at the airport and they did. What surprised me was that they didn't take very long. A young blonde female officer and then an older, dark-haired one took turns in a private room to ask me about my life. They particularly wanted to know about my family links to the place, and I repeated four times that my sister lived here but that I personally hadn't returned in eleven years. Why? they kept asking. I had no explanation. At points the exchange seemed to come bizarrely close to them insisting on my civic rights. Of course they were only trying to unnerve me. Why does your sister have citizenship and you don't? Right place right time, I shrugged. I didn't want to bring up my mother. They unzipped my bags, investigated my belongings, opened every play, flipped through my appointment diary with its blank summer months, and the two novels, one of which I'd finished on the plane, then led me into a different room for a strip search. Surely this isn't necessary, I said in a haughty voice while a third woman officer ran her detector over my bare flesh, as though I might have hidden something under my skin, and dawdled over the straps of my bra and knickers, which I had matched in preparation, blue lace, and as she knelt before my crotch the laughter began to quiver in my stomach. I put my clothes back on, surprised by how hard I was shaking, and ten minutes later they called me to a booth, where a tall man I hadn't seen before gave me my passport and told me I was free to enter, Welcome to Israel.

I passed a seating area and recognised two glum-looking Arab men and a young Western woman in red lipstick from my flight, still waiting to be questioned. Their eyes followed me to the automatic doors, and as the doors sighed apart I checked the time on my phone and saw only an hour had passed. This left me two more to kill, since my sister Haneen wouldn't be back in Haifa until half past six. I made a snap decision and asked a taxi driver to take me to Akka. I had an idea I should see something beautiful first.

My adrenalin faded slowly in the car. As it did, the shadow of my bad winter returned, and I watched the passing farmland, the hills of the Galilee, through its darkness. My whole life I'd been aware of Haneen's stronger moral compass; it made me afraid to confide in her until the very last moment, until I absolutely needed to. I also wanted to resist her, the way a child resists a parent and at the same time absorbs their wisdom; I wanted to sulk in her second bedroom and feel better with the secret muffled gladness that someone was holding me to account.

I may not have locked eyes with this fact yet, but I wasn't only here for Haneen. After an hour and a half signs appeared for Akka, and my blood thumped a little harder, and then we turned off the motorway and drew up by the arches of the old city. I paid the driver and wheeled my suitcase down an alley, and when I saw the blue sky burning above the sea wall I stopped. I stared at the ancient stonework, at the dazzling water. I hadn't prepared myself for this bodily impact, the memory of my senses. A few red chairs and tables were arranged beside the pier. I approached the wall, leaned my bag against it, and stayed there a moment. The sun heated my face, my hands. My armpits began to sweat. I reached for the top of the wall and pulled myself up onto it.

Some forty feet below me, the water crashed against the parapet, foaming and jolting back. Where the wall curved on my right, a group of boys stood in a line. All elbows, hands on hips, shifting their weight from leg to leg, watching each other, waiting. Two were small and skinny, barefoot, with brown sunlit shoulder blades. Most of the older ones wore sneakers that left dark marks on the stone, and necklaces of drops fell from the seams of their shorts. The first in line took a running start and leapt, knees up. He seemed to fall for a long time, his body unfolding. Then he cracked the water and disappeared. When his head bobbed up again, the other boys didn't react. I guess I was expecting them to applaud, or something. The diver flicked his hair and swam for the rocks.

I had a vision of my own body flipping down from the boundary.

My thin cotton trousers ballooning, stiffening on the air like sails, receding as my figure plunged to the water. I both saw and could feel the wall scraping my forearms through my shirt. Legs parting, one hand reaching out, smashed in an instant and bloody on the rock.

The boys gathered closer together and were talking, eyeing me where I sat. Down below, the water drank the stones, leaving black circles dilating on their surfaces. In the distance, tank boats cut through the waves. The sea noise calmed me. After a while I jumped back onto the ground and dragged my bag away to hail another taxi. Could you take me to Haifa please? I asked in English for some reason. Maybe because I couldn't be sure he was Palestinian, not even in old Akka, or maybe because only two hours ago I'd been emphasising my Englishness in the hopes of smoothing my passage between the border police. The car was stuffy with the old day's heat. The radio was playing an Arabic song. A string of cowrie shells hung from the rear-view mirror.

'Wael Hejazi. You know him?' said the driver.

'No. Is he famous?'

The driver laughed. He sang along for a bit. 'Holidays?'

'I'm visiting my sister.'

'Jewish?'

I pretended I hadn't heard. I think he had guessed I was Arab or I doubt he would have asked. I didn't like these dances between drivers and their passengers, testing origin, allegiance, degrees of ignorance. In the final move before the jingle of change he would probably burst out with some story of loss and political alienation. I resisted the idea of being bonded to this person. I put a hand up to where the window permitted a hiss of air, the words on my lips to ask him to open it wider, but then if I spoke the language one thing would lead to another and I didn't feel like getting into it with – *Layth*, said the licence in Latin letters beside the Hebrew, under its cracked lamination, suspended on the taxi wall. A young photograph, a little smile, the moustache black, grey in the mirror, where his eyes flicked again to me and back to the road.

'Would you mind opening the window?' I said in English.

The breeze sliced through the taxi. Palm trees spiked the road-sides. Pine forests. Pylons.

The idea of coming to Haifa had arisen in January, in London. Haneen had come over for Christmas and when, a few days into the New Year, she dragged her bags back down our father's staircase, it struck me that she and I had not spoken all holiday, not properly. It was starting to rain. I handed her my pink umbrella and opened the door, gripped by guilt, and by a panicked sense that I needed her and it was too late to tell her so. We waved her taxi off and then I confided in my father, playing it down so I wouldn't agitate him. Why don't you visit her in Haifa? he said, he who had not himself been back to Haifa in just as long.

'Why don't we both go?' I suggested. 'A Nasir family trip.'

'Oh, no no no,' he said, picking up his newspaper and disappearing into the kitchen.

On the verge of turning seventy our father had finally retired, and was getting used to passing the time at home, in East Finchley. The house was on the opposite side of the city from me, and I'd arranged to stay there while Haneen was over so that the three of us could spend the holiday under the same roof. Throughout October and November I'd been playing Arkadina in *The Seagull*, and I was still riding the high after the run ended when Haneen arrived in December. There weren't many auditions happening then; instead it was parties I was preparing for, returning in the small hours and creeping up the stairs to sleep in my childhood bedroom. The theatre Christmas-bash circuit was not exactly my usual scene but I was having an affair with Harold Marshall, the director of *The Seagull*, and it was his. I spent a month drunk on subterfuge, hyper-aware of his large figure across full rooms, his rumbling voice, the black mane swept perilously back. He was the first person I'd felt strongly about since my divorce, and although I knew it was too early to call it love I can't pretend I wasn't using that word in my mind. The whole thing hadn't yet turned but I sensed it was going to and I was in denial. No doubt that added to the strength of my feelings.

Meanwhile, Haneen had covered our father's kitchen floor with boxes excavated from his attic, making piles for rubbish, organising paperwork and photographs into box-files, her reading glasses holding back her hair, which was greyer than the last time I'd seen her. I cut a path through the mess in the mornings to make coffee, waving hello, bleary from lack of sleep. When my father looked at the chaos he threw up his hands and announced 'it's hopeless'; Haneen rebuked him as though he were her child, which for some reason he didn't seem to mind. In the afternoons they walked on the Heath, and sometimes I joined and listened to their conversations. I was under the impression I was keeping up a good act. We spent New Year's Eve together, toasted his retirement and crooned along to some of his favourite old songs. After a few more days, Haneen hauled six full black bin bags onto the kerb and left for the airport.

I retrieved my own little suitcase to return across the city and came to say goodbye. My father peered over his glasses.

'You have not been yourself,' he said.

Rain was tittering on the kitchen roof. I wanted to deny everything. Then I saw his lips pursed in his white beard and found myself saying, yes, I could sort of see where he was coming from.

A few months later, my relationship with Harold ended, and I wrote to Haneen suggesting a visit. I couldn't leave London immediately because I taught an acting class on Wednesday nights and a movement class on Thursdays, which, along with an advertisement I'd starred in a couple of years prior, were currently my principal sources of income. I booked a flight for June, after the end of term. The prospect gave me solace.

'You look very tanned,' said Haneen, between kisses.

'Must be the light.'

Ceiling-high windows stood along one side of her apartment, dull with early evening, full of trees. In the kitchen a strong bulb in a coloured glass shade dropped a complex beam across the floor.

'This is all your stuff, is it?'

She wheeled my bag somewhere out of sight before marching to the kettle and filling it from the sink. The kitchen was immaculate: no magnets on the fridge, no stray envelopes. Not even a newspaper.

'How was the airport?'

'They kept me an hour and a half, ish.'

'Lucky you. But you've been waiting for me, then. Why didn't you call?'

'I went to Akka.'

'That's nice. How's Dad? If you're hungry.' She placed a bowl of fruit in front of me. The lightshade was giving her a red moustache.

'He's fine. Swimming a lot.'

'We'll call him. Everything else, how's work?'

'Slow season.'

'Right. Right.' The filament drummed through the silence. 'I'm really glad you came. How long are you staying, again?'

'I thought a few weeks. But if you need the space I can easily—'

'No no, stay as long as you like. I'll be in and out. Some nights I stay in Tel Aviv, especially if there's a faculty meeting.'

'Right.'

'But you're welcome, of course, as long as you like.'

The kettle clicked off and breathed up the tiles. I stared at her. Something was wrong. She lifted her glasses and drew her thumb and forefingers over her eyes, pinching them together. Not the gesture of a woman who wore mascara. I set my elbows on the kitchen unit and tried to emit warmth.

'How are things at the university?' I said.

'To be honest with you, it's a pain. Increasingly. I feel like I'm dodging bullets. I don't know how to, how to *be*. I'm thinking about moving to England.'

'What?'

She leaned over her phone, stroking and tapping the screen, then placed it between us.

'Don't go back to England,' I said. 'England is awful.'

'Hi, Baba!' She met my eyes but the smile was for our father.

'Hi!' came his voice at a slight delay.

'Hi, Baba. This is Sonia.'

'Habibti, al-hamdillah 'asalamtik. How are you? Did you see the house?'

'Not yet.' I laughed. 'I just arrived.'

'They gave you a hard time?'

'Not too bad. It's good to be here in Haneen's beautiful place! I can see there's a great view. I feel nostalgic. Everything is good with you?'

'Take photos please, and some videos. I'm fine, I'm fine. I'm watching a film about Vietnam.'

'I hear you're swimming a lot,' said Haneen.

'Yes.'

'Front crawl is better than breaststroke, be careful with your back.'

'Okay, Haneen. Okay.'

'So we'll speak to you tomorrow, Baba.'

'Bye. Bye, my life. Bye, Sonia my love.'

It took me a long time to fall asleep that night. I drifted, thinking about our grandparents' house. I thought about climbing the stairs, which automatically brought to my nose the smell of overripe fruit wafting in through the windows from the garden, where, disobeying my father, I used to walk barefoot until my soles were sticky with fallen plums and had to be scrubbed with a nailbrush. Sore and clean, I stand wet on the tiles of the bathroom, and then in the old shower, and then rubbed dry with one of the blue bath towels, which shrank each year until they were too indecent to wear in the corridor, and I see the arches of the windows, and can feel the breezes off the harbour. And lying on a bed, on a sofa, on a floor, reading in the heat. The room we shared, Haneen's bed on the far side, mine near the door. I'd wake early and find my grandfather downstairs, reading a big book with tiny writing by the window. They always said Jiddo was where Haneen got her brains.

My strongest memories of Haifan summers, though, were less of specific things or events than they were of certain feelings, and of daydreaming, which was an activity I looked forward to when we packed our picnics and went to the beach. Stretched out on a towel, listening to my Walkman, playing out the drama of my life in my mind's eye, while the world around us remained boring and violent. And then, when I hit puberty, indulging in illicit, confused fantasies about the Israeli boys I spied by the water's edge, their silhouettes of muscular ease like sun marks on my closed eyelids. I compared them with our cousin Issa, his friend Yusef, bow-headed and unpowerful.

I woke late with the sun on my face. There were no curtains or blinds but I'd still managed to sleep in and it was almost quarter to twelve. I shuffled into the kitchen in a pair of hotel slippers Haneen had left by my door. The windows were bright and full of trees. Beyond them, the industrial port, the water. I felt heavy with oversleeping.

'Morning,' said my sister from the sofa. She was balancing a laptop on one knee and a stack of papers on the other. 'We've got tickets to the theatre tonight. Mariam has two extra. You remember Mariam?'

'What's the play?'

'*Al-Moharrij*, The Jester. You know it?'

'I don't know any Arabic theatre.'

'Apparently it's famous.'

I didn't know what to say. I had come here specifically to escape the theatre. She bent towards her screen. I poured cold coffee into a mug and considered heating it up in her microwave.

My career had had its ups and downs, like those of most actors. At drama school I'd been one of two in my cohort with potential ingénue looks, and though at five eight I was on the tall side I had a marketably unusual appearance, or so they said. It's the kind of pronouncement that makes vulnerable young women atomise their features, upon which so much seems to depend. Mine: long asymmetrical nose, lips with high crests, heavy eyelids, curly dark auburn hair that lightened at the ends in the sun. My profile was slightly harsh; my instructor used the word 'striking'. Age softened me some, for which I was grateful, although on the other hand I was worried about losing out on character roles. Anyway, theatre is cruel to actors no matter how striking they are.

Auditioning had a painful addictive quality, made up of so much loss and at the same time the seeming constant spectacle of great roles happening to others by chance or circumstance. I landed a TV job straight after graduating and then spent the majority of my twenties in a repertory group in London doing Shakespeare and Ayckbourn and Stoppard, taking jobs in detective serials, turning up tirelessly for auditions on the West End and occasionally being cast, accepting other quick telly jobs for the money and what I hoped was exposure. I did several gigs for a performance artist named Nile Banks, who created a series of walk-through pieces in and around art galleries in London and Manchester. I took a part in a TV series as a Yemeni spy and another as an Arabic-speaking extra in a documentary about Sykes-Picot, but Arab roles didn't come up often and when they did I usually lost out to someone with black hair, regardless of whether she could even roll an R. By the time I landed a job in *The Seagull* I'd been working for almost two decades. I'd had my share of high moments. *Noises Off* at Trafalgar Studios, an RSC production of *Les Liaisons Dangereuses*; one year I played Fanny in *Mansfield Park* at the Royal Court. These moments passed; they did not accumulate. Most of my female friends in the industry had switched roles entirely, some moving behind the camera, or to script editing. They had babies, became teachers, housewives. One retrained as a barrister. Two women, *two*, out of all those I'd befriended at university and drama school and the early years, were still working: one was vaguely famous, by sight if not by name; the other had regular parts at the RSC. I had neither vague fame nor regular work of any prestige, and yet I hung on, powered by what? Vanity? Some outrageous lasting confidence in myself, propped up by a horror of what it would really mean if I gave in. Part of the reason I'd stopped spending summers in Haifa in my mid-twenties was a fear that too much time spent away from the universe of English theatre would injure my chances. I'd also met Marco, and embarking on my new life with him helped me push Palestine from my mind. Haneen was doing it for all of us, I was committed to the cause by proxy, I didn't need actually to visit. Besides, the second intifada was still going on and after Jiddo and Teta died it didn't feel like there was much point in coming back anyway. Han flew over to see us often enough. Ten years passed, during which time my marriage ended, and I stumbled on seemingly unable to right my wheels, still auditioning, still getting parts, if fewer and farther between. I tried out for *The Seagull* with such low expectations that I addressed my speech to the director himself with a knowing look. Harold Marshall was considered up-and-coming even though he'd been around for a while. I saw his eyebrows quiver as I turned to go and the next day he called to say I had the part.

That play revived in me a dangerous joy, made worse by the fact that, in the final three weeks of rehearsal, a special energy emerged among the cast, thirteen-strong, in which none, miraculously, was an egotist; an energy that reflected a glow back on the director, whom we took, wrongly of course, to be its author. When reviews singled me out for praise, I felt nervous, like I was breaking my cast-mates' trust – but then was moved to find them backstage smiling on my behalf. My father, who never gushed about anything, beamed at me and called it 'a very *sensitive* performance', and Harold suggested that I'd make an excellent Gertrude in his production of *Hamlet*, which was going to be at the National, a significant step in his own career.

I showered, dressed, checked my email. I read a few pages of a book, cooked pasta, called our mother. When my phone ran out of battery, I left it inert and black on the sofa. Looking at the sea in the window, a flat stripe of soothing blue, I could feel my Internet addiction, the urge to click and scroll, nag at me like an insect bite. I sat cross-legged on the floor and did a breathing exercise followed by a twenty-minute meditation. Haneen must have been watching me because the moment I stirred, a radio burst into life, a British accent, BBC, *A five-storey apartment block in the town of Torre Annunziata, near Naples, has collapsed, with five or six people trapped inside.* Haneen began cleaning the surfaces around the sink and then she swept the floor.

After the sun had left the windowed side of the apartment to a late-afternoon shade, the buzzer sounded.

'I think that's her,' Haneen shouted from another room.

'Who?'

'Mariam.'

'Oh, yes.'

'Will you let her in?'

'I'm actually feeling pretty tired, Han,' I said, pressing the button.

My sister appeared, pulling a T-shirt over her head. 'You don't have to come if you don't want to. Although you could have said something earlier.'

'Sorry.'

She opened the door. 'Hello-oh.'

Over her shoulder I saw a head of thick dark curly hair in the hall.

'Hi, habibti.'

'Hi, hi, hi. You remember Sonia?'

Mariam sauntered in. She wore a long sleeveless blue dress and ankle boots, which she slipped off before sitting at the counter. I had a vision of a potbellied girl in a bathing suit, running down the beach.

'We met when we were children,' I said. 'Mansour.'

'I remember. You used to come here a lot.'

'Every summer.'

'Welcome back.'

'Thanks.'

'Tea?' said Haneen.

'Thank you,' said Mariam, before asking me, in English: 'You just came from the airport?' She spoke slowly, and with long curving Americanish vowels, as though she had gone to an international school.

'Yesterday.' My own vowels sounded angular, perhaps in reaction.

I guessed this woman must be at least six years younger than me. The Mansours had lived on the same street as our grandparents, and sometimes, as part of a group of families, we would go off to the beach together for an evening barbecue. I remembered Mariam as a bossy child, always badgering us to play. Age levelled everything off and six years meant nothing now except that she was still more or less on the threshold of her thirties while I was on my way out.

'Al-hamdillah 'as-salameh,' she said. 'You must be tired.'

'Sonia hasn't been back since the second intifada,' said my sister.

'You're joking.' Mariam gazed at me. 'Welcome.'

'Okay, here we are.' Haneen handed round three identical turquoise mugs. 'How's everything going?'

'It's okay, it's okay. I mean, we've almost finished casting. The funding stuff is dragging its heels, you know with . . . and everything.' She exhaled and forced a smile, apparently conscious of me. I assumed she didn't want to bore me with the details; it wouldn't occur to me until later that she was probably unsure whether to trust me with them.

'Mariam is putting on a production of *Hamlet* in the West Bank,' said Haneen.

I laughed. 'No shit.'

'Haneen says you also work in theatre.'

'I act. Some television as well.'

'I direct.'

'Theatre?'

'Mm.'

There was a prolonged silence. Internally I rolled my eyes. Mariam sipped her tea and squinted.

'Have you ever thought about acting in Palestine?'

'Not really.'

'You should.' She paused. 'It's bad when all the talent gets away.'

'You don't know if I'm any good.'

'Can I ask you something? What is it you like about acting?'

I laughed again, more loudly. Mariam, unperturbed, awaited my reply. Even Haneen was watching me with interest. The heat of Mariam's sincerity felt like a sunbeam on my face. She irritated me. At the same time, I found her curiously appealing. As she grabbed her mug I noticed she had large hands and bendy thumbs. My mind relented to her question and I thought of Arkadina. I thought of that rare, marrow-deep sensation in the rehearsal room.

'I've been acting for twenty years,' I said.

Mariam looked at me serenely. My answer was incomplete and she would wait for me to finish it. I didn't know this woman; there was no need to answer truthfully. And it was true that there had been times in my life when I felt my work had saved me, transcending its function as a trade in a way that seemed, embarrassingly, to concern my soul. I didn't know if that was what I *liked* about acting. But the occasional glimmers of something that looked like meaning had obviously played a role in keeping me going. There was no way I could say this aloud, although I suspected it was the sort of thing she was after. I could tell she had an American-style ease with matters of the heart. Or maybe I should say a thespian's ease. Something which, presumably, I myself had once possessed, and lost somewhere along the way.

'I don't do it because I like it,' I said. 'I do it because it's my profession. Haneen, could I have a glass of water?'

My sister put her fingers under the tap, and the sound of running water turned off the subject.

'So why haven't you been back since the intifada?' said Mariam.

'It's like the Land of Interrogations. You know, it can be hard to leave a place when you're working. Not everyone can afford to go on holiday.'

'Right.' She gave a deliberate, private smile.

Haneen chuckled. If I could have embodied a black wind, I would have swept through the kitchen and whipped my sister against the counter. She passed me my glass of water. There was an interlude in which no one spoke. I had been too sharp. Mariam sipped her tea and looked at the dark window, where we three were blurrily reflected, gathered around the counter under the light.

'Mariam has just returned from America,' said Haneen.

'Were you working there?'

'I was. I trained there, as well. But I've been coming back and forth. I never stayed away for long.'

I blinked. 'We were not born here, you know.'

'What?'

'It's not really a question of return, for us. We came here for the holidays, to see our family.'

I thought Haneen flinched but I couldn't be certain.

'I'm not criticising you,' said Mariam. 'I said, Welcome back.'

After all of this, there was no way I could spend the evening alone while they went off to the theatre. Exhaustion was no longer an object: I'd been challenged and I hadn't come off well. Or, perhaps – and though I didn't experience it like this at the time, it seems plausible in retrospect – I liked Mariam's attention, and wanted to keep it a little longer.

The car had a stale smell, like old biscuit crumbs, and sitting beside her in the front seat I wondered if she had children. I looked at her soft upper arms and her capable veiny wrists as she shifted gears. We veered downhill and then, rounding a corner, upwards again. I'd forgotten the crammed feeling of this city, the way the houses stacked along the rises forced cars into zigzags.

The name of the theatre, AL-NAHDA, was written on the canopy in a column of Arabic, English and Hebrew, in white paint. A crowd stood smoking outside, mostly young people, in leggings and Birkenstocks. We took our seats in the auditorium, which was small, a black box with raked seating. No curtain, the set visible: stage left, the awning of a café extended into view, two wicker-back chairs and a table holding a coffee cup. The backdrop was a blue sky with clouds.

The stalls gradually filled and the houselights went down. Stagelights up with a recorded rooster crowing. Distant drums and cymbals, some indistinct singing, getting louder. The recorded noise died as a car with furniture strapped to the roof was pulled on by two men in headdresses and leather boots. A front tyre hissed flat; the driver's door fell open and a man jumped out, holding a microphone dangling a severed wire.

'O generous customers, generous audience!'

From the wings, and from the aisles, more performers appeared in pyjamas and bathrobes, one man in a suit, several of them carrying bits of food, cups and saucers.

'Peace upon you!' they replied, in a clumsy canon.

'And upon you,' said the man with the microphone.

'Good morning!' shouted a man in pyjamas, waving a piece of bread.

'And good morning to you, welcome. The theatre has remained—'

'A little early for Art, isn't it?' said another. He set a pile of notebooks on the café table and took a seat.

'And what is it you want this early in the morning, then?' said the microphone man, rounding on him. 'Beans with oil? Hummus with onions?'

'Ignorant,' another actor muttered loudly, thudding a chair down before the car.

'Backwards,' added the microphone man. He returned to the 'audience' who had assembled downstage, sitting, crouching, leaning on each other. The energy was good, the rhythm was precise. The microphone man announced a performance of *Othello*.

'Brothers, my brother citizens . . . because we are in the age of speed, and time is money—'

Someone snored loudly. Someone else took a long bubbly pull on his nargileh pipe.

'And because our time is gold, we are not going to present the entire play. Rather we will have to suffice with only one act, the act which relates to jealousy.'

Spotlight on the first actor. According to the programme, this was the Jester of the title. The Jester straightened up, twitched, and began to walk stiffly, as if he had no joints.

'O Night! O Day!' he said. 'O Afternoon, O Evening! Bear witness to my love for Didimona! Help me bear the separation from her as I head into battle. Cassio, Cassio!'

Soon Cassio was accusing 'Didimona' of infidelity, drawing a handkerchief from his breast pocket. 'Here is the proof.'

'Thus was Othello,' said the microphone man, striding over and indicating with an open hand, 'this brave Moroccan hero, preparing to go to war, for the struggle against colonialism. The enemies of this nation were unable to find any but this cheap way, the way of jealousy, to divert him from his duty. Look at this brave Moroccan knight—' He pointed again at the Jester as Othello, now carrying the limp body of the single female actor offstage. He wailed loudly. 'See how he was transformed from a valiant leader who feared not death, into a crushed being, incapable of anything.'

'Long live the heroic Moroccan people's struggle!' someone shouted.

'But who is responsible, my brothers, for this painful fate which befell this brave Moroccan hero?'

'Shakespeare!'

'Yes, my brothers,' said the microphone man, swinging his body round and speaking into his device in the manner of a talk-show host. 'It is Shakespeare. He is the one responsible for this tragedy which befell our immortal Arab hero Othello. And yet we must ask, who stands behind this Shakespeare? Who is the power that props him up and stands behind him?'

'Britain!' another customer shouted.

On the other side of Haneen, Mariam was laughing.

'Down with Britain! Down, down, down!'

'Yes, it is Britain, my brothers,' said the microphone man, almost wearily. 'And yet we must also ask, who stands behind this Britain?'

'America! America!'

'La ilaha illa Allah,' cried various audience members. The boy sitting in the aisle stood up and whistled, applauding.

'Yes. America, my brothers,' said the microphone man. 'Nuclear bases and Phantom fighter jets.'

'Down with NATO!' someone cried.

There was no interval. I rearranged my weight in the plastic seat to relieve my left buttock, which was going numb. At the end of Act One, the actor playing Othello was interrupted in the middle of a slanderous impersonation of the Arab founder of Muslim Spain, Abd al-Rahman, aka 'the Falcon' of Quraish, by a telephone ringing offstage. Someone emerged from the wings with an iPhone to say the Falcon wished to speak to the Jester.

By the end of Act Two, the Falcon – a slender bearded man in a turban – had been dazzled out of anger by his amazement at the Jester's phone, earphones, car and shoes, and, upon learning that his territories had much diminished since the eighth century, resolved to save the Arab world and liberate Palestine. The third and final act began with the Falcon being stopped by the Jordanian border police because he didn't have a passport.

It seemed to me that only the first act had been thoroughly rehearsed. As the play went on, energy flagged, and the performers seemed uncertain whether the more political lines should be delivered earnestly or as satire, which mostly resulted in a kind of hammy gravity. Laughter from the real audience was petering out by Act Three. I started to feel very tired, and, assuming for some reason that the entire audience felt the same, began to pity the actors. Nevertheless, at the curtainless curtain call the crowd rose unanimously for an ovation. Haneen and I clutched our programmes to our laps and stood in tandem. I tapped the heel of my left hand with the fingers of my right, looking around. Houselights came up. To my further surprise, the audience tipped down the aisles and onto the stage, and the room was soon full of the dull roar of talking. Mariam led us at a graceful pace into a sea of wagging arms.

'This is Sonia,' she said.

I found myself face-to-face with a familiar-looking man, but only once he was shaking my cold hand with his sweaty one, Mariam saying, 'Fantastic performance, Bashir,' did the features of the principal actor, perceived from afar, the Jester who had played Othello and then insulted the Falcon, rearrange before my eyes. His height and build were diminished by proximity and he was actually shorter than Mariam. Bashir smiled, said: 'Nice to meet you,' then turned away, shrieking as the café owner punched him playfully.

'They're all going to a bar,' said Mariam. 'But I don't know, I don't think, you would prefer to go home, right?'

'Mm,' I said. 'Yes I think I'll have to skip the bar this time.'

'I'll drive you. But I'd like to introduce you to someone else first.'

Mariam swam before us through the crowd. By the front row of seats we reached a young man who had not, so far as I could tell, been in the play. He was well groomed and handsome in a teenage way; his hair high on the top, cut close on the sides. His teeth were very white.

'This is Wael,' said Mariam. 'He's going to play Hamlet. He's my cousin.'

Before I could say anything, Wael was already responding to this introduction of himself. 'Really nice to meet you,' he said. Every part of him was polished, from the hair to the high cheekbones to the prominent Greek nose. Yet his face also had an unfinished look, the chin receding abruptly beneath a shadow of stubble.

'This is Sonia. She's the sister of Haneen, my friend – you remember Haneen?'

'Yeah of course, how are you Haneen, what's up?'

'Sonia's an actress.'

'Great, great.' Wael folded his arms, the smile fixed. There was a loud silence.

'Shall we go?' I said.

'Okay. Yalla,' said Mariam, wrapping her scarf. I detected disappointment. 'Are we ready?'

The exhaustion really hit me in the dark of the back seat. I closed my eyes, opened them. Rain was falling. The engine thrummed, tyres hissed, a distant horn blared. I glanced at the dashboard and saw 15:17 in green digits, which was way off. It must have been close to midnight. I didn't have a watch and my phone was still dead back at the flat. My sense of time was going awry. Yesterday already felt like weeks ago, looking down at the water in Akka.

'Everyone knows everyone,' said Mariam. 'That's the problem with this place.' Her hand slid down the steering wheel as we turned onto the main drag. The hand lifted, became a twisting shadow puppet against the glow of the dashboard, then descended to jerk the gearstick as we moved uphill. 'We don't have a normal reviewing structure, and there's no system of accounting for quality. You see what I mean?' She was looking at me in the mirror. 'I go to your play. You go to mine. I direct him, he directs me. Everyone in each other's pockets, hanging out in the same cafés. It's very nice, like you know it's a nice group of friends. But it doesn't make great art, exactly. Except maybe when people go abroad, on tour, all that.'

She wanted a rapport with me. Or perhaps to make excuses, to separate herself from this substandard artwork, asserting her aspirations to Great Art.

'I don't know,' I said. 'I quite enjoyed it.'

'And then we have someone like Wael, someone who made it big.'

'Yeah?' I said.

'Outside, naturally, in Egypt, in Dubai, you know. But this is pop culture, anyway, it's different.'

'Was this the theatre that had its funding pulled?' asked Haneen.

'That's the other one,' said Mariam. She addressed me in the back: 'The bigger theatre here did a show about a political prisoner. The Israelis said this was disloyal to the state. So, voilà, they cut the funding.'

It was a long moment before I was aware that we'd stopped moving. The engine was going, but Mariam was looking out of her window with her arms folded. The wipers slashed down across the pane and squeaked upright.

'There it is,' she said.

'There's what?'

Haneen turned in her seat and frowned. 'Jiddo and Teta's house.'

'Oh.'

I wiped the mist from my window, veined with drops on the outside. Across the road, a house stood in the dull green of a street lamp, flickering in the rain. Alone in a recess, with a freshly pebbled path. A column of arched windows down the centre, the lowest of which was the entryway, a small portico before the door. Two rows of balconies with white railings of curled iron. I stood on the second balcony in my mind and held the railing, the iron black and rough under my fingers. A light came on in an upper window and I noticed a maroon SUV parked in the driveway.

'Haneen said you wanted to see it,' said Mariam. She switched on her indicator and turned the car into the road, pausing before the traffic.

'Yes, I did. I do.'

She parked us in front of the house, leaving the indicators ticking.

'Who's living there now? Is that Aunty Rima's car?'

The house loomed and flickered. Received by neither woman, my question hung in the air. I looked up at the windows again and then, as if standing in a gallery of my mind, gazing down at the stage, waited for my emotion to begin. It was like entering a church and expecting awe and holy feelings, except that now I was waiting for grief. In its absence another feeling crept upon me, a kind of exhausted despair.

'Oh God,' I said.

In the lit upper window a shadow moved. Mariam put the car in gear and reversed back onto the road.

'Why didn't you tell me?'

'Tell you what?' said Mariam.

'Haneen?'

'What?'

'Why didn't you tell me they sold the house?'

I looked at the back of my sister's head through the maw of the headrest.

'Han?'

'I didn't want Baba to know.' She didn't turn, but spoke as at the end of a television mystery, face shaded. 'Don't tell him yet, will you?'

'I'm sure they listed it as an Arab house,' said Mariam. 'They always get more money that way.'

'Where did they go?' I asked.

'Nadia's in Canada,' said Haneen. 'Rima and Jad are in the West Bank. Haven't seen them in years.'

'What happened to all their stuff?' I said. 'Teta and Jiddo's – the furniture, the books. Did they take everything?'

'Mostly. I have a box of a few things, I can show you.'

Our grandparents both died when I was twenty-seven. Jiddo became critically ill with an infection in his lungs, and once he was taken to hospital Teta went to bed and never got out again. We flew to Haifa as soon as it was clear Jiddo might not recover. When Teta was told he had passed she said, Yes, I know. The funerals were ten days apart, their graves side by side in the Catholic cemetery. Teta and Jiddo had been a paragon of lovers. I used to tease them about the unrealistic example they set. They were cruel to love each other so much, it made the rest of us feel inadequate. They'd never even met Marco; I hadn't brought him to Haifa and they were too old to travel to London. The year after they died, I married him. And with that, one era of my life was almost entirely sealed off from the next.

Barely a week after Teta's funeral, our aunts had begun trying to convince our father to give up his share of the property. He hardly lived there, they said; and, as though they could create logic out of sheer force: he had made money elsewhere, therefore he had no right to the house. Then came the breach. He washed his hands of the property, refraining from insult, nobly I thought. The lower half of the building was given to the younger sister and the top half to the elder, who continued to live there with her husband, as she always had done. After all that, they'd gone ahead and sold it. And judging by the mood in the car, I guessed they had not sold it to Arabs.

Mariam pulled up behind Haneen's building. She kissed my sister on both cheeks, and as Haneen stepped out and shut the door, extended a hand behind to me. It was not a handshake; we touched fingers, Mariam with confidence, me uncertainly.

'See you soon, uh?' She let go, and patted the passenger headrest beside her. 'Yalla.'

2

The recorded voices sounded dusty.

Even if I cannot live in it, my soul will reawaken if there is a Palestinian state.

'Christ,' I said. 'Is that Teta?'

'Listen, listen.' Haneen pointed at the circles turning in the plastic window of the recorder.

And then, if they say there is a Palestinian state, and they say you, Sitt Aida, can live in it, if you want to. What will you say?

'Uncle Jad,' Haneen whispered.

I do not want to live in it. So what? This is my house. Why should I leave it?

But your soul will awaken.

Re-awaken.

'Wow,' I said. 'I remember this.'

'You were there?' She frowned.

And you feel there is a stronger connection now with the Dafawim?

'Yeah. So were you.'

'I don't think I was.'

'Super weird.' I sprang the stop button and began to prise the recorder open with my fingernails.

'Careful careful careful.'

'It's fine.' The cassette had a little label on one flank annotated 1994 in biro. 'Did you listen to the whole thing? I need a coffee. Does Jad know you have it?'

'It was in a box of crap they were throwing away. I guess he might have kept it if he realised.' Haneen poured boiling water into the cafetière, which smoked in the sunlight on the counter. 'What was he doing it for, do you know?'

'He often had some project going on. What else did you find?'

'Nothing, junk. Photo albums, I'll show you, they're in my office.

Oh, you know what – I had a flying dream last night. It's just come back to me.'

'That means sex, I think. Or maybe that's swimming.'

She made a disgusted noise. 'I was flying over Jerusalem.'

'I dreamt,' I said, remembering, 'I had two pet budgies. That's funny. I didn't know how to take care of them, so I . . . so I filled the bottom of the cage with bread, and the red one got buried and disappeared. At the same time there was a robbery, but the robbers didn't take anything. I was still looking for my bird when the police arrived.'

'Other people's dreams are quite boring to hear about, aren't they?' said Haneen, mock-weary. Her phone buzzed and shuffled on the counter. She picked it up. 'Hi, darling. Wait, say that again?' And walked into her bedroom.

I made myself a milky coffee and carried it and the recorder and tape into the corner where a green couch slumped beneath a window. Through the glass the trees shone, perfectly still. What I hadn't said was that it was Harold who had given me the birds in the dream, and his house that was robbed. Whenever I remembered my dreams he seemed to be there, haunting me with a faceless and yet extremely specific presence. *Dear Harold. I have decided that I would prefer never to see you again.* It was not as though he was attempting to see me. I slipped the tape back into the recorder and closed it as Haneen walked back into the room.

'Everything okay?'

'Salim's been suspended.'

I could tell I was supposed to gasp. 'Who is Salim?'

'Mariam's brother! They're talking about stripping parliamentary immunity.'

'Oh. Oh no. What's he accused of?'

'Security threat, I think. They haven't said.'

'Like, what does that mean?'

'Something like communicating with the enemy.'

I paused. 'Are you okay?'

'No. Salim's a big deal, he's in one of the major parties.'

'And he's definitely not?'

'Communicating with the enemy? What kind of a question is that?'

'I'm sorry, I don't know. I'm sorry your friend has been arrested. That's terrible. Fuck the Israelis.'

My tone was off. I needed more caffeine. I could picture the Mansour boy, a few years older than us, bookish, gangly. Haneen and I faced each other across the kitchen. She yanked the dishwasher open.

'You don't even recognise your own grandparents' house.'

'Excuse me? It was raining, and dark. Why didn't *you* tell me it got sold? I mean, how can you expect, when you leave me out of everything? It's like you want it all for yourself.'

'Oh, I see.' She pivoted, smiling falsely. 'Is that why you're here?' Her voice rose and fell on waves of sarcasm. 'You want to take it back?'

'You got me.' I clicked my fingers. 'I've come to take Palestine back.'

She didn't laugh.

'What is going on with you?' I said.

'I'm just overwhelmed. I'm sorry.' She put a hand to her face and took a deep breath. 'There's been this guy in the department.'

'Oh-ho. Okay, I see.' I laughed, relieved. We were in the same boat. 'Let's sit down. Tell me what's happened.'

'Last Tuesday we had a department meeting.' She didn't sit, but leaned against the dishwasher. 'Apparently, the previous week, the cleaners found some bags of urine in the trash in the faculty building. And in one of the bathrooms it looked like someone had been shaving.'

'That's disgusting.'

'It means there's someone living there, someone homeless.'

'Oh.'

'And it seemed likely it's a graduate student, because only they have twenty-four-hour access to the building.'

'Or she.'

'It's a he.'

'Why the bags?'

'The security cameras in the corridors at night, I think. There are no cameras in the classrooms or lecture halls.'

'I see. Yes, that's quite sad.'

'Most of the faculty started on about increasing security at weekends. To have a check-in, or stop graduate students from entering the faculty building after hours. No one was talking about the real issue, which is *why* is there a graduate student living in the faculty building? Does it not cross their mind to think, actually, this person might be in trouble? It's hard to get a word in but I piped up at the end, and a few people nodded and then Eyal, the faculty chair, returned to the question of security. The next day, he gets caught on CCTV.'

'Eyal?'

'The student. I get an email from Eyal. First of all, what I said at the end of the meeting got some of the senior faculty talking. My words *preyed on their conscience*, and they've decided to speak to the student before taking action. They've found him on one of the cameras. And he's Palestinian, though he didn't say this directly. Eyal wants me to go and talk to him.'

'Are you the only Arab on faculty?'

'There's Ashraf, but Ashraf may as well be Swedish. Anyway, I met the boy in the cafeteria the day before you came. He looked terrified. His name was Yunes. Do you remember that boy Issa used to bring over, the one who lost his parents? He reminded me of him, a bit.' She switched into Arabic. 'He says, I didn't realise you were Palestinian, and I say, Is everything okay with you? And he doesn't say anything, he just looks at me like this, like, that's a stupid question. Sort of angry, sort of wounded. I felt really embarrassed. But you know I had a job to do, and also I was trying to do the right thing, so I say, I'm a professor, you can tell me. And he laughs and says, Everything is fine, thank you, Professor.' She hesitated, then went back to English: 'It took a while to loosen him up but eventually he told me his father's an alcoholic and was just jailed for robbery. No siblings, mother died years ago. He was living at home but they took the house away because of the father's debt, and he can only just about pay tuition. He made a choice; he said he didn't want to end up like his parents.'

'Poor kid.'

'I suggested a few things, I said, Why don't you appeal to so-and-so in HR, you could get an admin position, it would take the weight off your tuition and also give you a bit extra for rent. I even said I might know someone with a spare room. And then he turned on me.'

'In what sense?'

'He looks at me and says, in this quiet voice, Why did you take this job? I was like, What? And he says again, Why did you take this job? And I don't know what to say, so I don't say anything, and then he says, You're not from here, are you. And I said, Well yes, I'm part Dutch, and I grew up in England mostly, and he goes, Why didn't you get a job in England, then? Why are you working with them?'

'Christ.'

'I know. I just sat there, I started to mumble something about, duty, I don't know – I mean, I've been teaching there for, what, ten years? Why do I have to explain myself to some student?'

'Right.'

'Then he says, You think you have an effect? And *then* he says, You know what, you're not even Palestinian. You're an Israeli. He said that in Hebrew.'

'Oh, sweetie,' I said. 'That's just stupid.'

Her eyes were glinting.

'People lash out, Han,' I said. 'The kid was homeless.'

'Yeah, yeah.'

Her face was turned to the floor. I was surprised. She was usually so self-assured.

'I don't know why this in particular hurt me,' she went on. 'Maybe because I was trying to help him.'

'The person in trouble here is him, though, not you. I think you'll just need to get over this.'

Her eyes flicked to me. 'Wow. That was unkind.'

'I didn't mean it to come out like that. I didn't mean it like that. I actually sympathise. I just think sometimes it can be helpful to think outside, a bit, of your immediate, you know, reactions.'

'How insightful.'

'What did you say?'

'It's easier for you, you just denied everything.'

'What have I denied?'

'This is real life, Sonia. This is not some play.'

My voice cracked. 'You think I don't know that?'

'I'm sorry.'

'Talk about spite.' I knew that my crack, however unintentional, was making her capitulate under the force of an automatic sympathy. Another part of me, watching myself, asked: or was that crack intentional? Maybe you cracked on purpose? Maybe, you are acting.

My sister's fists met her eyes and then her temples. 'Sorry, Sonny. I haven't told anyone else about this.'

'Not even Mariam?' The sting of her accusation lingered. 'What happened to him? The boy.'

'He's getting an administrative job.'

'Good.'

'And they're putting him in temporary student housing. She's coming over now so I'd better clean up.'

'Who is? This place is spotless.'

'Mariam.' Haneen walked over to the sofa and beat the flank of one of the cushions.

'Is Mariam sort of your best friend now?'

'Sonia.'

'A fair question.'

'You always manage to make things sound sort of insinuating.'

'What on earth could I be insinuating?'

She didn't say anything. She didn't even roll her eyes.

I took a shower. Feeling rushed, I skipped the shampoo, but finished a near-empty bottle of conditioner for damaged hair and worked my fingers through a few knots. I wore a bikini under jeans and a plain black shirt. My hair, lengthened with the weight of water, damped my back. There was no fan in the bathroom; I pushed the casement window open and secured the pin in one of the holes, and the mirror, clearing, showed a face that was all

cheekbone, my eyebrows lightly marking the ridges of my skeleton. I smeared some foundation around my eyes, mouth and nose,
smoothed the edges, dusted off with powder, and addressed my
eyebrows with a pencil. I was brushing my teeth when Mariam's
voice reached me from the kitchen. I rinsed and ran the tap, threw
one lock of hair to the other side, and entered stage right.

Mariam did not look particularly upset. She was wearing a suede
jacket. She smiled at me and kissed me generously.

'You look so much better, now you've slept.'

I ignored this. 'I'm very sorry to hear about your brother.'

'Oh.' She flapped her hand.

Without looking at Haneen, I went on: 'The security threat thing
is obvious bullshit.'

'They haven't actually announced why they're investigating him.
There's a possibility it's because he's helping me with my play.'

'Seriously?'

'Obviously we've been trying to keep it secret, but.' She wet her
lips and smiled.

'Right.' I wasn't sure how to react. I glanced at Haneen for
guidance.

'Loyalty in Culture, they call it,' said Mariam. 'They're trying to
push through a bill. Remember I told you last night,' she said directly to me, 'about the theatre that had its state funding pulled?
That's what kicked it off.'

'Where's the money actually coming from?' I asked. 'For your
play, I mean.'

'Kuwait, mainly,' said Mariam. 'But I want it to come via us here
in '48, and we have a few funders here too. That was our intention,
you know? To fight divide and conquer. This kind of . . .' She inter-
laced her fingers.

'How will you get news of him?' said Haneen. 'Can he make
phone calls?'

'The Shin Bet still have him.'

'Shit.'

Mariam overfilled her lungs with breath, which she released
dramatically.

'And now back to work.'

'Right,' I repeated, with a nervous laugh.

'My dear, if we let disaster stand in our way we will never do anything. Every day here is a disaster.'

I nodded, keeping still under a familiar wave of shame. As Mariam turned to Haneen, however, smiling and talking about the auditions for *Hamlet*, relieving me from the spotlight of her eyes, I did a U-turn. I thought of what Haneen used to say about young men striding through the streets after someone was martyred to make sure the cafés stayed shut in mourning. Resilience was not the same as detachment. Mariam was describing the guy she wanted to cast as Polonius. Her ability to switch subjects struck me as vaguely sociopathic.

'So I have been thinking I would like you to join us,' she said to me. 'My play. Will you?'

Haneen looked unsurprised.

'Your project sounds very interesting but I'm afraid I've not come here to work. This is a holiday. An important holiday.' The word holiday was awful, I dropped it. 'A break from work. I need the rest.'

'Yes, Haneen told me.'

'What?'

'She told me about your issue.'

'My issue?' I shot a spear at my sister, who avoided my eye. 'I'm very flattered, Mariam, but no thank you. I wish you the best with your production, I'm sure it will be excellent.'

Haneen shrugged at her as if to say: You tried.

'I should leave you girls to talk,' I said.

'Oh no, please stay,' said Mariam.

'No no,' I said, as if fending off a courtesy. 'I'll go and get a coffee. I have my book.'

I walked down the hill, turning left a few times and descending some stairs, until I reached a café with an outside seating area. Indoors, on the chalkboard above the bar, styles of coffee were listed in Hebrew and English; below them the Wi-Fi code: bonanza1919. I ordered an Americano and carried it on a saucer out to one of the tables. I took out *Contempt* by Alberto Moravia, gulped down some coffee, then submitted to temptation and looked at my phone. I entered the Wi-Fi password.

Harold Marshall   11:06 >
No Subject

Hi Sonia I realise we left things in sort of a bad way

My stomach dropped. The loading wheel turned and turned.

Hi Sonia

I realise we left things in sort of a bad way
And I wanted to say I'm sorry about that. When I saw you at the
audition I have to admit I was kind of thrown. You looked so
wonderful. Really Sonia I still care about you and I just wish that
circumstances could have been different
And that things could have stayed right between us. I have made
mistakes and misjudged things and I feel terribly about it all

My life is a mess right now and I'm so sorry to have caused you
pain. I still think about you all the time

I miss you
Harold

--

Sent from my iPhone

I still think about you all the time. His voice, even in the written type, brought a distinct taste to my mouth. His use of spacing was weird. The message almost resembled an apology. He used the word sorry a couple of times. Perhaps he did feel bad, in a bind, emotional, he didn't know what else to do. That was the false reading. That was the reading he wanted me to have. He wasn't really trying to apologise; he was trying to prod me.

'You stupid bastard,' I said aloud. The phrase 'You looked so wonderful' was particularly galling. Against my will my heart was responding.

The first time I'd sensed something from Harold was during rehearsals. One occasion in particular, slight in the moment, became freighted with meaning when I remembered it afterwards: he repositioned my arm for a scene with Sorin in Act Three and relinquished his grip suddenly, as though getting a hold of himself. I went on to imagine what that gesture might mean during the run, once he receded from the play's edges and I stared out at the black audience under the heat of the spot. Then, on the final night, he caught me on the backstage stairs. He was a heavy man and there was something tremendous about the sight of him rising towards me, taking the steps two at a time. 'We – we lost the enunciation in the penultimate phrase,' he said. Still giddy from the final scene I struggled to understand his meaning, until, with a sinking feeling, I realised that he was giving me notes on my performance even after the run was over. Then, before I knew what was happening, he pushed me backwards into a large cupboard that I hadn't known was there.

Harold had a wife named Renata, who had visited us after the dress rehearsal, knocking sheepishly on the door of the dressing room where we all sat separated at our lit mirrors. A sparrowish woman in a velvet dress. I should have known better. There were even signs that first night, the last night of the play. I left the communal drink early, I couldn't bear waiting for him to signal a desire to be alone with me, so I left the cast joking across the pub table of pint glasses and crisp packets and took the Victoria Line home, clopped along the dark street and without turning on any of the lights in my flat, sat down on my bed. In the quiet it struck me that the final drink with the cast had a particular function, more than simply celebration or camaraderie: it was meant to forestall this, this catapulting of the brain in the silent aftermath of applause. The eerie residual strain of the play, the lines that went on mechanically revolving, repeated and impregnated so often with new meaning and feeling, now circulating emptily, *They'll bring in the horses soon, Konstantin you don't understand him*, hanging around me like the ghost of a stage curtain as I lay back on my pillow and wondered, with the small sad glow of a delayed epiphany, if I was less an Arkadina than an aged kind of Nina.

He did call me in the morning, he did take me out for breakfast, and over the course of the next two months gave me a variety of titbits to paper over my doubt. He was starting rehearsals for a new show by a young playwright called Jackie Peters. Auditions for *Hamlet* at the National opened in a month's time. Harold had no instinct to divide theatre from the bedroom, or possibly he saw no reason to. The reality was there was little time to separate the two, since he lived with Renata and I lived in the sticks. We met between rehearsals – his rehearsals – for a quick early drink in a pub off the high street, and shared the odd cab to functions, getting out around the corner to conceal our simultaneous arrival, arranging to meet back at my place, parting at dawn. He promised again and again that he was going to tell Renata, but she was depressed, he was worried about her; the great reveal was always postponed.

The sex was like his rehearsal room: he drew me out, I waited for his approval, his adjustment, his suggestion; he the leader, I the star. I told him one evening that I wanted him to destroy me. I was shocked by the sound of that word in my mouth. He responded by becoming slightly violent, although the violence was more suggested than actual, more fleeting reminders of his physical strength. The oblivion I was asking for but did not understand persisted on the horizon of our affair like a summer thundercloud, and in the nights I ran through its long shadow as though I might reach it, while it remained there, taunting me from a distance, unbroken rain.

The days felt emptier than usual. They were not empty, however, and if I'd been more alert I might also have taken this for a sign. I auditioned, read plays, prepared for the classes that would start again after the holiday. While Haneen was there I sometimes joined her and Baba on their walks, listening as they discussed whatever it was that had happened lately, a recent spate of buildings destroyed, some diplomatic nonsense, the Palestinian leadership, questions of boycott upon which they lovingly but vociferously disagreed. Baba said we should boycott everything, including individuals; Haneen, who worked at an Israeli university, argued for what she called more nuance, she said people are produced by systems, and articulated some other more complicated ideas. I had nothing to contribute. I used the opportunity for exercise, and to be present in a family activity. Between or sometimes during these activities I fantasised, usually about my own career. One night, lying with my hands on Harold's chest, a point in the evening post-everything when, flushed with affection, I would feel warmed from the inside out with a confidence that, though not really logical, made me feel secure for the first time in a long time about my prospects – that night a contrary idea dawned on me. I might do the opposite: I might give it all up. With an unfamiliar erotic certainty a phrase appeared in my head like a quotation from something badly written – *to serve him*. An awful worn story, to become some man's creature, embarrassing even to name, but while one eye perceived the cliché the other was transfixed by the feeling it gave me, of having no power and feeling powerful. I was professionally skilled at holding two things in my mind at once and choosing which to look at as felt convenient. And not only which to look at, but which actually to believe.

Within a couple of weeks Harold turned cruel and ignored me for lengthening periods, and at a certain point I knew it would be a loss. I told myself I was making a clear-eyed decision. It was better to feel it, I thought, than not to feel it, although in retrospect this seems like the judgement of a drunk person. In any case, no amount of reasoning did anything to secure me against the pain that followed.

'I can't bear it when you look at me like that,' he said one night towards the end, in the back of a car.

Without irony I marvelled at his technique. Man Overcome, unsaddled by emotions I haplessly inspired in him. He was so good he nearly made me wonder whether I had, in fact, done it all on purpose. Or whether I possessed some power I had no control over, the same way on rare occasions one might play a part with unconscious magic ease without a proper grasp of the mechanics. I turned to face the front, where the windscreen wipers switched across the dashboard.

'Do you hate me?' he said after a moment.

I forgot myself and turning to look saw him smirk in the darkness. Yes, I did hate him. I could say nothing in reply. Say yes I hate you: Harold wins. Say no I don't hate you: Harold also wins. He put his arm around me and held my chin in an odd, coercive, upside-down way and then kissed me, very gently.

I didn't tell Haneen about Harold, but later I guessed that she must have guessed, and that her silence on the matter of my odd behaviour was a silence of disapproval. Even under the spell of it I sensed the false edge of my happiness. I was talking faster than usual and losing weight, so that my old dresses slipped on easily and people said things like, Oh my, you look different. My jaw, already hard, hardened. I've seen one photograph of myself from that winter, spiky in a green evening dress. I have a weird look in my eye and my nose looks very large. I was waking up with unnatural alertness at five in the morning and, incapable of napping, powering through the days and nights in a haze of energy apparently attractive to strangers at parties who seemed to swarm towards me. It was uncharacteristic of Haneen not to comment on my strange electric mood, but I was not in a state to recognise who was behaving according to character and who not. Besides, the only real time we spent alone together was on Christmas morning while Baba was asleep, when we called our mother and Frank in Marseille on speakerphone.

And then, what happened? A final coldness descended over Harold's features like a visor. He framed it, terrifically, as concern for Renata. The audition for *Hamlet* was excruciating.

'Your sister's drown'd, Laertes.'

The light in the room was reddish on account of an old curtain across the window. Harold sat behind the table between his producer and his casting director. One woman, silent, sat at the end with a notebook. I lifted my arm.

'There is a willow grows aslant a brook.' I locked eyes with a floorboard. 'That shows his hoar leaves in the glassy stream.

There –' My arm was like a wooden plank. I hadn't spent long enough warming up. 'With fantastic garlands did she come – of crowflowers, nettles, daisies, and long purples, that liberal shepherds give a grosser name, but our – cold – maids – do' – bravely, I met Harold's eyes – 'dead men's fingers call them.'

I caught a turning of his head towards his casting director, and a sliding of his eyes.

'Sorry,' I said quickly, 'do you mind if I try that again?'

I drew breath. The casting director opened his mouth and closed it again with a falsely awkward smile. 'Thank you, Ms Naseer,' he said, using the most common mispronunciation of my name. He shuffled his papers. The row of men rearranged themselves on their chairs, anticipating my exit.

A couple at the furthest table stood and dropped coins onto a silver dish. Nearer-by, a young man was smoking a cigarette.

'Could I have one?' I asked. 'Do you mind?'

He looked up. He wasn't as young as I had thought. Fair and slim, wearing shorts and a T-shirt, with a youthfully uncertain manner. But his face was older, forties or so. He opened the packet and extended it, allowing me to tease one out in an old-timey manner. Then he offered a lighter, flicking the wheel. I leaned back and looked away, aware of him. The cigarette was sour but had the desired effect, and within seconds I was intensely lightheaded.

'I am a tennis coach,' said the man, with a clear Israeli accent. 'I teach tennis to young people.'

'Good for you.'

'What do you do?'

'I don't do anything.'

'Are you a student?'

I gave a silent puff of laughter, crossed my legs, took a sip of coffee, tapped the ash off my cigarette into the ashtray. 'No.'

He smoked silently for a while. He was frowning. I disliked that he had made me so conscious of him.

'Where are you from?' he said.

'I am Palestinian,' I replied.

Silence. 'Okay,' he said finally.

A car passed, blaring music, and I wondered whether that was an aggressive thing to have said. I was becoming microscopically aware of his discomfort. He spread his legs a little wider, he glanced at his reflection in the café window. I looked down at Harold's email on my phone, and swiped it into the bin. 'All right?' said the man, and I bristled. Then I saw he was in fact speaking to someone else, a woman who, trying to stand, had caught her chair leg on a chink in the pavement. Did he know her? She regained her balance and turned away. He did not. Now he was pulling an exaggerated bored face, and also tugging at his socks, for some reason. No sane person made faces like that alone. I wondered what had set him off, my answer to his question about where I was from, or just the fact that I was a woman who had asked him for a smoke. I didn't want the rest of the cigarette but held it between my fingers, enjoying the echo of other people's hands holding cigarettes, elegantly. I glanced at him again, and then my phone screen flared blue. *Nabil Nasir.*

'Hi, Baba.'

'Hi, habibti, how is everything?'

'Everything's fine.'

'How is Haneen?'

'Fine. Bit of a funny mood.'

'What happened?' he said, shifting into Arabic.

'I don't know, general stress.'

'But what exactly?'

'We haven't talked properly, we've barely been alone. I think it's a university thing. Not a big deal.'

'I'll call her.'

'No, please, I don't want her to think I'm. Although to be honest.'

'What?'

'Nothing.'

'I want to talk to her anyway.'

'Don't make me regret, she's highly strung. I get the sense she doesn't exactly want me here.'

'That's definitely not true. Ask her what's wrong, please. I'm worried.' He paused before asking, as he'd asked yesterday: 'And the airport was fine, they didn't keep you long?'

'Not really. I think you reach a certain age and you aren't a threat any more. They only care about subversive young people.' I laughed. 'I don't look subversive, nor do I look young.' I trimmed my cigarette on the edge of the ashtray and put it to my lips again. The tennis coach, I noticed, had become unnaturally still, looking at the road. I shifted away from him but I was relying on the café Wi-Fi so I couldn't leave. I'd been speaking a mixture of Arabic and English; now I dropped the English. 'How's the weather there? It rained here last night and it's not too hot today, not what I was expecting.'

'Are you smoking?'

'What?'

'Or are you just breathing very heavily.'

'I'm not smoking.'

'How long are you planning to stay?'

'Three weeks? Or maybe a week, I don't know. Someone just asked me to be in a play here.'

'In Haifa?'

'No. In the . . . in the West Bank. Do you remember the Mansour family? The daughter, Mariam, directs. She and Haneen seem to be very close. She's doing *Hamlet* in Arabic.'

'You've never been in an Arabic play.'

'Oh, Baba, please.'

'Mariam Mansour, I remember her father. Isn't her brother a Member of the Knesset? When was the last time you went to the West Bank?'

'I don't know.'

'You used to love acting.'

'Mm. Thank you.' The cigarette had finished itself. I needed to get him off the phone. 'Okay, thanks for calling. Love you.'

'I spoke to Uncle Jad.'

'What?'

'Yes. I told Jad you are there. He will call you tomorrow probably. They are living in Ramallah now, he and Aunty Rima.'

I hesitated. Then I asked cautiously, conscious of my transgression: 'Do you know they sold the house?'

'Yes, he told me.'

'What? Recently he told you?'

'It was a while ago, Sonia. It's done now, it's over.'

'But Haneen just told me not to tell you. Does she know that you know?'

'Let's not make a big story. Maybe I didn't tell her, maybe I thought she knew. It slipped my mind. I forget.'

'Why does no one tell me anything? That house is important to me! It was important to me. It's part of my—'

I took an unsteady breath. In the silence, I wondered what he would say next. So important that you haven't been back in eleven years, Sonia?

'It was a mistake,' he said. 'I'm sorry. I forget things, I thought – listen, I have to go now, I'll speak to you later. Okay? I'm sorry about the house.'

'Okay fine. Bye.'

The tennis coach was writhing around a newspaper. I glanced at his frowning face then paid for my coffee and walked down to the beach.

The shore was thick with bathers, lying in and out of the shade of coloured umbrellas. Escape was never really an escape, that was the problem. You only stumbled from one thing into another. I stripped down to my bikini and asked an elderly Israeli couple if they'd mind watching my things, and then I winced over the hot sand. The water was delicious around my ankles. Someone was doing breaststroke in an old-fashioned swimming hat with appliqué flowers. A little girl paddled in the shallows with a toy baby on her hip. On the beach, lifeguards in high-up chairs dictated in Hebrew through megaphones. I did not know what they were saying. I plunged into the cold and swam for the deeper water. The buoys jumped ahead of me on the waves, and the waves rose like snow-capped mountains, crashing before they reached me.

3

Even if I cannot live in it, my soul will reawaken if there is a Palestinian state.

My grandmother's words in 1994, at the end of the uprising. That summer I was fifteen, Haneen was nineteen, and the four of us, me, Han, Mum and Dad, had been staying in Haifa since the beginning of July. Kept coolish by the stone walls, noisy fans, and an air conditioner rationed at twenty minutes per two hours, everyone spent the afternoons crowded around the television watching women done up like Barbie dolls interviewing men in formal Arabic about the peace deal. The intifada, to which no one had yet added the prefix 'first', was over. The leaders had shaken hands on the White House lawn, an initial agreement was being negotiated in Oslo, and Israeli soldiers were poised to leave selected areas of the West Bank and Gaza as a prelude to ending the military occupation and creating an independent Palestinian state. Or so we were told.

Fifteen was a restless age for me. I felt cramped and at the same time anxious about change. That year in particular I was fogged with boredom and jealousy of my sister, who, after a wild adolescence that I'd envied, was now passing into university life with a self-possession that I also envied. I imitated her mannerisms, graceful, thoughtless, the way she ran the fingers of both hands through her hair to get it out of her way, grasping the bulk and chucking it behind her. My hair was curly, hers was straight and manageable. We both tanned easily but she tanned faster. That spring I'd cut down my dancing to one class a week and I had been lonely, struggling with the new free hours after school; I was also infatuated with a pair of cowboy boots that I insisted on wearing for family outings despite the heat, which my aunts found peculiar, and which I'd sometimes fall asleep thinking about; and all these heady concerns muffled my appreciation of the events happening a few miles south.

We had done the same thing every summer since I was eight: played in the garden, gone to the beach, and watched recorded footage of West Bank confrontations after dinner in the downstairs living room. I was engaged with the political climate by default but still without the full commitment of my imagination, although that might have been too much to expect from a child. While everyone else was watching the TV, I watched the heat shimmering off the patio tiles outside the window, or tried to read. Looking back I wonder if boredom was not in some way a defence, if on a certain level I found it more stressful and confusing than I was conscious of, and my distraction protected me, keeping my mind clean from the violence. Haneen let it in much more than I did, although I wouldn't understand that to be the case until later.

With the intifada coming to an end, the television was on even more than usual. We watched the developments like the sequence of a soap opera. The song of that summer was the interminable newscast monotone, if not in the room with you then muffled through a wall or floor. Mama said the house was suffocating and campaigned for an early return to London. I habitually aligned myself with her, as Haneen did with my father, each side fierce in their partisanship, not understanding that the box of our family would ultimately not be strong enough to withstand so much rattling.

When Jad interviewed Teta, he was permitted to mute the television. In that rare silence I paid attention. Opinions my grandmother might have contributed to a normal dinnertime discussion were given a special prominence because they were being recorded. It was like watching her on stage.

JAD   *And then, if they say there is a Palestinian state, and they say you, Sitt Aida, can live in it, if you want to. What will you say?*

I can see Teta on her usual chair. And then she replies, with a falling arpeggio intonation:

TETA   *I do not want to live in it. So what. This is my house. Why should I leave it.*

JAD	*But your soul will awaken.*
TETA	Re-*awaken.*

Arthritic, dictatorial finger.

I peopled the rest of the room in my mind's eye. Haneen said she wasn't there: I erased her. Jiddo must have been, and probably my father. And Aunty Rima. Uncle Jad, who was married to Rima, had developed a kind of anthropological interest in the relations between Palestinians 'inside', our family included, and those in the West Bank. This was presumably the rationale for the interview, although I couldn't recall him interviewing anyone else in the family. He was often making day-trips to visit friends working in Nablus, or his sister who joined a women's committee in Bethlehem, and sometimes he went to Gaza, offering his medical services and returning with hearsay and descriptions of incidents he witnessed and people he spoke to. We may partly have had Uncle Jad to thank for the greater psychological allegiance of our family to the resistance than some other Palestinians in Haifa, especially those who preferred to be known as Arab Israelis, or to have the Arab part knocked off altogether, and to speak sparingly in Arabic and mostly in Hebrew. The PLO leaders had not mentioned the fate of Palestinians with Israeli citizenship. It looked like the Palestinian state they were fighting for would not include us. Include them. Include our family, I mean. I remembered a man coming over to the house one evening, he may even have been a Mansour, though also maybe not, and conferring with my father in a low tone, as though the West Bankers had their own version of the Shin Bet, and saying: 'It's not *my* intifada.' My father said nothing, as usual. Jiddo and Teta had Jewish friends, with whom we spoke English, since Haneen and I hadn't learned Hebrew, but during the summers of heightened violence these friends always disappeared.

JAD	*And you feel there is a stronger connection now with the Dafawim?*

Dafawim, West Bankers: a collective nickname derived from the *Daffeh*, the Bank. No one mentioned what the Hebrew plural ending of the word, the *im*, signified about those who used it. The only Dafawim I'd ever met in Haifa were restaurant staff or labourers.

TETA	*We are one family. Nabil knows.*
BABA	*Knows what?*
TETA	*That we are one family.*

Long crackly pause. My father's uncertainty is palpable. He has not been following. Is Teta referring to the Nasirs in particular or to all Palestinians? Must every Palestinian story be a family story?

BABA	*One family. Correct. God, it's hot.*

The rustle of a newspaper folded in half. I pictured him rising from the sofa, my grandfather sinking into the leather with the loss of his son's weight. Baba launching out of the room, pulling his jeans up by the belt loops.

RIMA	*Nabil always complains.*

Aunty Rima. Along with her colouring, I also allegedly inherited her personality. We are both known for being sharp.

JAD	*And what about you, Jiddo? Do you think relations will change with our brothers in the West Bank and Gaza?*
JIDDO	*Why change? They are our brothers and sisters. Have been, will be.*
JAD	*When was the last time you went to Gaza?*
TETA	*The last time. Take – put it in the trash. The last time was in nineteen seventy-three. I went with Nabil.*
JAD	*And the West Bank?*
TETA	*Seventy-four.*
JAD	*Where did you go?*
TETA	*Ramallah, Nablus, Bethlehem. Birzeit.*

1973. I counted. My father would have been twenty-six.

ISSA   *I don't see what they are so happy about.*

My cousin Issa dropped into my vision of the room. On a chair. Speaking with his mouth full.

ISSA   *Who do they think they are going to use those guns on?*

I assumed he was referring to the silenced television screen. I pictured a Palestinian police officer, one of the forces that arrived to replace the Israelis, posing with somebody. Kids perhaps, or an elderly woman. Muted laughter, huddling around the weapon, newly legitimised by the Israeli state; gagging for a look, a touch.

Next, with a jolt, I heard my own voice.

SONIA   *Issa, do you have a sharpener?*
ISSA   *No. Sorry.*
RIMA   *Look upstairs, darling.*

I bent close over the recorder, listening hungrily, waiting to hear more of myself. There was no more. I must have left the room. In the tape's white noise I could hear the heat, although maybe I was imagining that. I pictured a fan whooshing as it revolved, puffing out a white ribbon someone had tied to its face, pausing at the extremities. Somebody set something on the table, a jug or bowl. A woman coughed, maybe Rima. Uncle Jad started talking again. I stopped, rewound a little.

SONIA   *Issa, do you have a sharpener?*

My voice was high and teenaged and, to my confusion, strangely accented. I stopped the tape and put the recorder down. It was almost lunchtime and I still hadn't left the flat. I stood, and the movement released a slight coolness of sweat on the backs of my legs.

What was I doing that day with my blunt pencil that needed sharpening? Was I writing? Taking notes from the interview? Was I drawing? I put on my sandals, strapping the ankles. I had a memory of once sketching Jiddo asleep, his mouth open like a Greek tragic mask, but I didn't know if it was that same day. And did I go upstairs to look for one, as Aunty Rima told me to? Yes – and then, standing straight by Haneen's front door, the memory unravelled inside me like a clue on a crumpled piece of paper. I remembered very clearly. I had gone upstairs to my parents' bedroom, and caught them in the middle of an argument.

I mounted the cold stone stairs and turned at the mirror for the first bedroom, where I found my mother simmering beside the night-stand, either receding from or ready for the boil.

'What's wrong?' I said, and jumped at my father's voice behind me.

'If you could show a *little* respect, Marie,' he said, in a hard whis-per. 'Just show *some* respect.'

'Woah.'

'This has nothing to do with you.'

'Leave her alone,' said my mother.

'Yeah, leave me alone.'

My father rounded back on her. 'Why do you encourage this?'

'I don't encourage anything. Sonia is allowed to express herself.'

'Yeah.'

'Sonia, please go out. This is between me and your mother.'

'If it's bothering me, it's my business.'

'That does not make it your business – tell her, Marie.'

'Sonia, sweetie, go and find Haneen.'

Haneen was on the armchair in our shared bedroom down the hall. Her knees were up and tilted against the armrest, a book propped on her lap, her long brown hair in a plait down one shoul-der. As contained as a statue. She went on marking the margin of her book with pale chalky sounds. The television downstairs began speaking through the floorboards, followed by the dramatic music that signalled a change of news item. The heat forced its way in through the open window, and a sharp square of yellow light lay on the tiles. I stood in the doorway.

'Why are you such a bitch?'

'What?' My sister jerked into life, momentarily undefended. Then her eyes narrowed. 'What the hell is wrong with you? You're like a demon.'

I wasn't sure why I'd said that either. I could feel the fever of undigested emotions in my face, and seeing disgust on that of my sister whom I adored, I pulled my string bag from the bed and scuttled downstairs, past the open door of the living room. Only one of the faces transfixed in profile turned – Issa, looking me up and down and then away again. I stepped into the blazing sunshine.

We never went out in Haifa alone. At some point Jiddo made up his mind that, unlike our other female cousins, we who were born outside were softer and required more care. You didn't defy Jiddo. Once he got an idea in his head, it hardened against attempts to persuade him otherwise. By the time I was twelve our parents started concocting methods round this, and came up with something they called 'family days' for the four of us, under a claim of giving Teta and Jiddo a well-deserved rest. We set up camp somewhere, a restaurant in the German Colony, the beach, and our parents would let us wander off to the shops or along the cliffs. A little taste of the freedom we were used to in London to stave off the pressure of being surrounded by Nasirs the entire time. A Nasir in every corner. Doorbell rings, enter: a Nasir. Aunty Nadia, Aunty Rima, in the kitchen, on the patio, in the hall; our cousins, young and old, Rabea, Wassim, Shehrazad, Dina, Tareq and Tony, Issa, Uncle Johnny, smoking indoors, filling ashtrays with butts and cinders and watching crowds scattering at gunfire and children marching forth in school uniform, and then when the adverts came on changing the channel and lighting up again. A Nasir everywhere you looked, if not in person then in a silver picture frame in graduation robes or a wedding dress.

I went on up the hill until the house was lost from sight. My feet throbbed with an odd exhilaration. Haifa was supposed to be my hometown, one of my hometowns, and yet to be alone here, really alone, was nothing like being alone in London. My grandfather had succeeded in making me afraid. And there were other discomforts, like the awkward, objectless fear that stopped us speaking Arabic in public. I passed a middle-aged woman restraining a brown dog on a lead. The woman paused for her dog to sniff a bollard; our eyes met briefly and she smiled. I turned the corner onto another empty street and walked towards the railroad tracks, beyond which lay the sea.

I walked for perhaps an hour. To venture further to the proper beach seemed, for some reason, a bit too far; I chose a stretch near the main road where the sand was trammelled by tarmac. An almost beach, an empty, crescent-shaped, shallow bay. The sea gasped on the shore. I sat on a boulder and looked out to where the sun reclined across the water. The waves were varicose with foam, seething, changing, the white hem heaving on the sand. I had expected to have a lot of things to think over but now I was too alert in my aloneness to be contemplative. In the water a black figure bobbed up and down. I watched him for a while. When he finally stood he seemed to rise with supernatural majesty, revealing with the comic twist of an illusion broken that the water was shallow and only reached his thighs. He pulled a mask and snorkel to his forehead with one hand; in the other he held an empty net. He waded, parallel to shore. The top of my head grew hot. My pulse calmed. Under the sky, the water swooned.

A young man walked into the scene by the water's edge, in a white T-shirt and long shorts. A tattoo, half swirl, half rhombus, moved near the top of his calf. He stopped and turned and looked straight at me. He had dark skin, a round face, light stubble. He didn't smile. Something about him triggered a pulse of recognition; not that he was someone in particular, but that he was like me, blended and uncertain. There was something in his hand. I slotted the young man into one of my automatic daydreams, which were always at once erotic and chaste, according to the limits experience had put on my imagination. But as he started to approach me, whatever fantasy relation had been developing in the dark of my mind suddenly faded being brought into the light unfixed. He drew nearer and I shrugged, shrinking with embarrassment and virginity. The rock dug painfully into the underside of my thighs. I prepared to be addressed; it pulled me into focus.

He stopped a few feet away and said something in Hebrew.

'I'm sorry I don't speak Hebrew,' I said in English.

'Does this belong to you?'

His English was American-accented but not exactly. He had a muscular brow and a sullen, adolescent expression. In his twenties, probably. As he held out his hand, I saw his eyes running over my hair, which puffed out at the edges of my vision.

A split second of expectation. In his hand would be an item of jewellery, a ring or a necklace, or something else of value, perhaps a wallet. Whatever it was, it would not be mine, since I had not stood by the water. I looked with interest. Something made of metal. 'What is that?'

He turned it round to show the logo. A squashed soda can.

I returned, appalled, to his face. Everything about the walk, the question, the glance at my hair, I took for flirtatious, or at least kindly.

'No. That is not mine.'

'Okay.' He did not look abashed as he turned away. I watched him walk along the rocks towards where the road cut into the beach. He moved with a sour vigour I associated with attractive young men, his muscular legs like inert graceful weapons. He tossed the can into a large rubbish bin, and sat on a boulder further down. I waited, my indignation mounting. I wondered whether he didn't believe me, and in fact this striding overconfidently to the bin was a performance to make me feel bad. Or what if he was shy and afraid of talking to me? I sat small and limp on the rock, full of rage and something else harder to identify.

At least the rage filled a hollow and I was no longer afraid of being alone on the beach. Waves rose and crumpled on the flat sand. So far I had not spent a single thought on my family. Then I heard my name.

'Son-i-a!'

Thudding tarmac footsteps, and Haneen appeared on the roadside above. She wore shorts, a pair of very white sneakers, and a dark blue baseball cap, which belonged to me.

'Why are you wearing my hat?'

'What the hell are you doing?'

'I came for a walk.'

'Are you mad?'

The guy was watching us. That seemed to confirm something, or nothing.

'It's fine,' I said. 'What's the big deal?'

'What's the big deal? You call me a bitch and then you storm out. Teta is losing her mind.'

Too far to see, I imagined his pupils flitting at that Arabic word, '*Teta*.' Haneen climbed over the barrier.

'Look, can you come now please? Issa is parked up the road. You're such a weirdo. Tomorrow we're going to go, it's been decided—' She stopped. She too had become conscious of the young man listening. Unlike me, Haneen was not a virgin. This was something I often thought about. 'Come back. They've gone wild.'

She didn't speak as we walked to the car, and when I climbed into the back, Issa asked, 'Did you tell her?'

'Tell me what?'

'We're going to the West Bank.' Haneen sighed. 'Me and you. Tomorrow. With Uncle Jad.'

'What?'

'Yeah. Jad has to go anyway, and they want us to go with him.'

'Why are we not allowed out in Haifa,' I said, 'but we're allowed to go to the fucking West Bank?'

'Watch your mouth, girl.'

'I wish I could go.' Issa started the car. 'It's so unfair.'

4

Mariam's brother Salim Mansour was a special, quiet kind of firebrand. I gathered that much from watching the beginnings of two video debates while lying on Haneen's sofa. He wore rimless spectacles with rectangular lenses, and he didn't so much slice the air with the edge of his palm as make small indents, insisting in a soft, firm voice upon certain points of his argument like the difference between legality and justice. When his opponents made slurs against the *Aravim*, he smiled. He and Mariam had the same mouth – wide, full, slight underbite. In both videos he was asked a version of the question: how can you say this is not a democracy if we allow you to speak? In the first he replied, if you compare this to a totally undemocratic country then sure – but if you compare it to any other democratic country in the world – and he counted off a list of democratic countries on his fingers until his voice was drowned out by his shouting interlocutor. In the second video, Hebrew with English subtitles, he began answering this question with a deep breath like he was trying hard not to roll his eyes.

As for the grounds for his suspension, there was still nothing to be found on the Internet. Gagging order, said Haneen. I heard her on the phone, asking in a hushed tone about his state of mind. Everything's going to be okay, she kept saying, although it sounded like he was the one reassuring her.

Meanwhile, I was trying to behave like a person on holiday. I kept a beach towel rolled up in a linen bag with me at all times and monitored the sharpening contrast of skin colour around my groin. My hair became coarse from the seawater and humid air. I spent the days swimming, walking, drinking coffee. Haifa had changed in predictable, superficial ways, and the task of navigating this now unfamiliar city more or less stopped my ruminations straying too far into Harold territory. I didn't get a local SIM card, which meant

I couldn't use the GPS on my phone; instead I zoomed in on screen-shotted maps, lost my way and found it again, memorising this arts supply store, this Wadi Salib pharmacy, this municipal centre, orienting myself by the position of the sea, and, if I could see it, the Baha'i garden. King Faisal Street, Wadi Nisnas, Halisa, Bat Galim – the roads, the buildings, even the signs were smaller than I remembered. One morning I felt a tremor of recognition on a sloped residential street and realised I was approaching my grandparents' house. I reversed my steps. I kept an eye out for teenaged Israeli soldiers in their tight khakis, weapons clinking on their waists. I kept another out for chic young Palestinians lounging around coffee shops or on the beach. Laughing among themselves, they reminded me of dark-skinned Catalonians, or Athenian leftists, with their septum and cartilage piercings, and their hip defiance. I did not go and look at the Nasir house again.

After finishing *Contempt* I scoured Haneen's bookshelves for other reading material, and was surprised by the quantity of novels there in Hebrew. I knew she was fluent but it had never crossed my mind that she might read in that language for pleasure. I selected a few fat American paperbacks from the nineties and hauled them around with me. Submitting to their worlds was not easy. Maybe it was the subject matter. Sexual misdemeanours of middle-aged Jewish men living in Manhattan. The escapades of literary boys in Latin America. I read one short novel in Arabic, which was not relaxing, and required guessing the meanings of unfamiliar literary words from context. Another book, translated into English, I drank down in a single sitting, a novella about an angry woman with nothing to do. It was slim and went too fast, and abhorring the thought that I could only sympathise with characters that in some sense resembled me, I forced myself after that to turn the pages of all of the novels about men, sitting in air-conditioned cafés. Was it a kind of research – finding new things to learn about this obtuse other sex? Certainly it was avoidance: by never connecting my phone to any public Wi-Fi I abstained during the daytime from what I would otherwise be doing, which was checking my inbox for audition requests from my agent and googling Harold.

Press releases about Harold's production were emerging. His Gertrude was an unknown named Marissa Terrace. Younger than me. Attractive. I spent five minutes looking at Marissa Terrace's image search, drawing illogical comparisons – *I'm older but I have a better bone structure* – before turning the phone off and throwing it onto the armchair opposite the bed. Gertrude was a crap part, anyway. She had hardly any lines. Each morning I swam briefly in the sea and returned for lunch at the flat. I loitered in supermarket aisles staring at the Hebrew labels on food packets as if their meanings might spontaneously clarify. Each night I allowed myself one desultory google before leaping to my feet for a lamplit walk around the neighbourhood.

Haneen was a creature of habit. She returned from the university at half six, started cooking dinner at seven, and watched the news until ten thirty while preparing for the next day's class. Throughout the day she would have been following the latest about Salim, which she then reported to me over dinner before we watched an Arabic news channel for further developments. On Tuesday, two more Palestinian Members of the Knesset were threatened with suspension on allegations similarly lacking in detail. Then, on Thursday, armed settlers seized a temporarily vacated Palestinian home in the Sheikh Jarrah neighbourhood of East Jerusalem, shooting one of the neighbours in the leg in the process. The situation escalated. Demonstrators overwhelmed the streets around the house on Friday afternoon. Flaming tyres released a torrent of thick black smoke, wind-angled, across Haneen's television screen; tear gas streamed down like the spindly white legs of several giant spiders; women screamed, medics and journalists in labelled vests ran into the fumes, and intermittently Israeli soldiers could be seen clustering to arrest someone or disrupt something, wrapped to the hilt in armour gear and globular helmets, their long guns pointing at the sky. They looked like astronauts. Or huge insects.

With this on in the background, Haneen began marking student work, arranging piles of typed essays on the coffee table. I opened a chess game on my phone. Haneen turned up the volume.

The image on the screen was now from a phone camera. A man

lay on the ground and another man stood beside him, frantically waving. A newsreader explained that the man on the ground had been shot. His name was Nidal something. More details arrived. The shooter was a settler; they didn't have a name yet. The settler had been crouching on an old city rooftop. He or she had shot Nidal through the neck. Nidal was twenty-two. The camera zoomed in on Nidal as the group of hapless paramedics who had surrounded him allowed him to be lifted from their midst and raised above the crowd. Nidal's face was covered in blood.

'Oh my God,' I said, shielding my eyes. Haneen was watching with mad intensity, and I watched her instead of the television. I felt sick. It also distressed me to notice that the reality of this kind of news, or at least my sense of its reality, had been increased by geographical closeness. It felt like a throwback to the intifada summers of our adolescence.

'Fuck,' said Haneen. She had tears in her eyes.

'I don't understand why you choose to live here.'

It came out by accident. I expected a cutting retort. She wavered, then said: 'I don't understand it either.'

We'd hit the corner of something in this exchange. During the days that followed we edged around it with our silence, like a piece of furniture knocked in the dark. I worried that if we spoke too openly on the subject then something would disintegrate. Or maybe I was just afraid of upsetting her, and of what she might say to me if I did.

I may not have known what I expected to feel returning to Haifa, but I suppose I hoped for some circling back to my younger self. The beauty of my profession was that nothing lasted, and as a young actor, treading well-worn vinyl or wooden floors, ogling the principals downstage, this not-lasting had once approached a kind of holy truth. But life eventually taught me that some things did last, at least for some people, for some of the time they were alive. For me, not much had. Everything I'd tried to build had collapsed. Since arriving here, however, the nearest I'd come to any feeling of retrieval was this being close to a certain violence that was still anyway largely mediated by screens and closed military zones. No past continuous self showed any sign of emerging. At most I'd recovered a youthful unsteadiness and a depressing capacity for sarcasm that occasionally burst out during disagreements with Haneen, which made me feel ashamed and was not exactly rejuvenating.

In fairness, Haneen was touchy herself – about mess-making, about coasters, about maps and directions and timings. Whether I was causing the bother, or whether it was a hangover from Yunes the homeless student and her anxiety about Salim, or more generally about 'the situation', was unclear to me. Our conversations at dinnertime did not extend much further than the news of the day. Yes we were different, and yes we did not see each other frequently, and yes we had fought often and savagely as children, but usually, when we did meet, we'd have at least one meaningful conversation in which we laid bare what it was about our lives we were currently finding unsatisfying. No such conversation had transpired; if it was ever imminent one or the other of us had already botched it. I'd also anticipated meeting more of her friends, experiencing something of her social life, but Haneen, who was teaching summer classes and had opted not to take a holiday, apparently did not socialise much. The possibility that she did not want me there at all wounded me in a way I did not like to admit.

Two days later, I was searching among the toiletries in the local grocery store for some anti-frizz hair treatment when I saw a man standing near the breakfast cereals, staring into space. On account of his suit I initially took him for a businessman and would probably not have paid him any more attention were it not that an unpleasant odour, pungent and sour, like vinegar, began to disturb me. Looking again, I noticed he was so gaunt that his suit hung off him and wrinkled around the ankles. He turned. He was young. The whites of his eyes were yellow and there was a dullness in his pupils. I was so unnerved that I left the supermarket immediately.

That evening, a single settler was arrested on charges of shooting the young man named Nidal. On Sunday, the settler was released.

'How's Mariam taking all of this?' I asked, setting a load of groceries on the counter. The plastic bags crackled and wilted. The television was already on, replaying footage from yesterday's protest in Ramallah.

'Mariam takes everything in her stride. Your phone is ringing.'

No Caller ID.

'Hello?'

'Sonia!'

'Who is this?'

The voice began to laugh. 'You don't recognise me? It's Jad.'

'Oh my God. Hi, Uncle. Hi, hi.'

'Welcome back.'

Uncle Jad's voice had aged. It sounded greyer, weaker.

'Yes I – I got in a few days ago. Baba said—'

'I am calling you on Skype.' He sounded pleased. 'Sonia, I am very happy. It's been years since I saw you. I see you on the television sometimes—'

'How are things? How is Rima?'

'We are all fine, Rima sends her regards, she just went outside. So. When are we going to see you?' Before I could respond, he carried on. 'You see the problem is my health isn't very good. I don't come in to '48 very much any more.'

A tear-gas canister flew across the television and exploded at the edge of the screen.

'We are living in Ramallah now, at-Tireh. Any chance you will be coming to the West Bank?'

'Are you all right over there?'

'Everything's fine. We are in Ramallah, at-Tireh,' he said again. 'You are welcome, any time. Except, except between two and four in the afternoon. That is my siesta. Ah, see how I became old, Sonia! Okay, I look forward to seeing you.'

'Perhaps we'll make a trip this weekend, me and Han.'

Haneen shook her head vigorously.

'I would *love* that. I would love that. I have not seen Haneen in – for years I have not seen Haneen. You have made my day, ya Sonia.'

I noted down Jad's number, and as we hung up, the screen cut to a newsreader meticulously aligning the edges of a paper stack on her desk. In a singsong voice she announced an interview with a celebrated Egyptian novelist. Two men appeared in a pair of over-sized leather armchairs set very far apart.

'You don't think it's a bit funny,' said Haneen in English, 'that I've been living here for what, a decade, and neither Jad nor Rima has ever tried to see me? Then Sonia arrives, and suddenly the family is trying to heal itself?'

'Maybe it's a time-of-life thing.'

'Your life or his life? What's he even talking about with Dad? It's fishy. I don't believe in peace talks.'

'Uncle Jad always took a particular interest in me, remember.' I unloaded tomatoes into a bowl. 'Do you think it's going to be a third intifada?'

'No.'

'You're very certain.'

'It won't. We'll only have these flare-ups.'

'Why?'

She sighed. 'Lots of reasons. Too much to lose.'

I did not understand this. As far as I could see, Palestinians in the West Bank and Gaza were well on their way to losing everything. But I didn't feel like getting into a political argument with my sister, who had an easy grasp of statistics and was an actual professor. Then she received a phone call.

'Hi, yeah, yeah.' She muted the television with an extended toe. 'I saw . . . I know. I know. Hmm.'

There was a long silence. I realised she was watching me.

'Can you not just delay it a week?' she told the phone, turning her back. 'She doesn't want to. And actually I don't want her to go any more either. It's dangerous.'

I strained to listen but could only hear a dim yapping on the other end. 'What's happening?'

She swatted me away. 'You can't delay it? I don't think this is a good idea.' Pulling the phone from her ear, she said to me: 'Mariam still doesn't have a Gertrude. She wants me to ask you if you'd be willing to go along for the read-through so she doesn't have to do all the female parts. You'd be staying with her. You have every right to say no.'

'Okay.' I began to pummel the salad spinner. 'I guess, though, it would mean I could see Uncle Jad.'

'You seriously want to go and see Jad?'

'Surely I can handle it if Mariam can.'

'Sonia.'

'You're not my mother.'

'It's technically illegal.'

'How? Illegal for you, not me, remember. I only have a British passport.'

Haneen blew through her lips. She was out of ammunition. 'I was under the impression you'd come here to relax.'

This was how I found myself saying Yes to Mariam, mainly because I wanted to say No to my sister. 'When is the read-through?'

She barked the same question into the phone, and reported back: 'Tomorrow. She wants to leave here at ten.'

Haneen was gone by nine. In my hour alone, waiting for Mariam, I sat at the desk in Haneen's peach-walled office, where she had laid out three old ring-bound photo albums for me to look through.

Round-cornered photographs were suspended in wrinkly plastic windows. Most were pictures I'd never seen before. In the family snapshots our adolescent father sat slightly apart, moody, affected, a slender figure with black curls and moustache. There was Teta with her dark hair and big grin, and Jiddo in sinuous youth. Rima and Nadia in eyeliner and bikinis. One photograph in particular caught my eye: my father sitting with another young man, darker, older, a kuffiyeh wrapped over his shoulders; they were smoking, cross-legged on the ground, the short flares of their jeans lying in flat triangles over their ankles. Baba was animated, smiling mid-speech, facing away from the camera. The other man looked straight at the lens.

I chased my father through the albums, watching him and his siblings age, eat meals, go to school, go to the beach, gather in living rooms and on porches among other characters with moustaches and beehives, most of whom I didn't recognise. Two pictures towards the end of the final album showed him and my mother on their wedding day, young, shy, grinning, my mother wearing a tiara and a dress with puffy sleeves, and after that there was one more of my father with baby Haneen. He'd put on weight and his hair was shorter, he was sitting in front of a Christmas tree in a blue jumper. He looked smug, like he was trying not to smile too widely. I flipped back to the beginning again, to his younger self.

Most of what I'd gathered about the days when my father was politically active had come from our aunts, but over the years I'd caught a few bits and pieces from him directly. Sometimes he mentioned people who died, for instance. I knew he joined the Boy Scouts as a child, and the Communists as a teenager, back when the word Palestine was illegal, and I knew these organisations were covers for revolutionary activities, or at least revolutionary energies. Apparently he was also once an aspiring poet. None of the poetry was extant so he may have done no more than aspire. I knew that he left the Communists and joined the Al-Ard movement, then abandoned everything after being interrogated by the Shin Bet, an experience he refused to discuss. Whether that was out of shame at his defection or because the interrogation was so traumatic I didn't know. I knew that, uncommonly for Palestinians with Israeli citizenship, he went to Beirut in the sixties for university, then spent time in Jordan, did a Masters in Paris, and got a job in London, where he sat beside my mother at a dinner party, discovered she was the child of a refugee from the Galilee, and a few hours later offered to drive her home. I knew his sisters watched him do all this from afar, amazed, and at the end of it asked for money.

My mother, Marie, was the only child of a Dutch mother and a Palestinian father. Her parents' relationship ended before she was born and her father died when she was four, and I don't think she spent enough time with him in those first four years to leave a mark. She seemed to know little about him and we knew even less. She was raised by my grandmother, first in Utrecht and then in London.

I've never understood how she really felt about Palestine. She was known to accuse my sister and father of monomania, saying things like, There's a big world out here, my dears. My not having an Israeli passport was her doing. An act of boycott? More likely an attempt to exert control, using me to pull away. In her defence, I'm sure it was difficult, to be the child of a refugee she could barely remember, and to visit Haifa every summer as an adult with her husband. No wonder she wanted to escape the Nasirs. At times she seemed to waver between identifying as part of it and removing herself from the whole thing, and when I was young her uncertainty caused me anguish. I had an impulse to protect her. Her Arabic wasn't strong so we were often translating for her. Later it struck me as peculiar that we never tried to find her father's house – or, if it was destroyed in 1948, the place where it had stood. Perhaps she felt torn between wanting to get close to him and her fear of what she would find, or feel. Or even: not find, not feel.

By the time I was a teenager, Uncle Jad had surpassed my father as the most engaged member of the family. He didn't fit the ordinary mould of an activist and had no adolescence to compare with my father's, for example. But wasn't that the point of the intifada? It was not just for the usual types, the politicians; it was for everyone, little boys and girls, students, women married and unmarried, the elderly. Even pompous Jad was infected by the sense of possibility born of hopelessness, once people knew they had nothing left to lose. Everybody was transfixed by those scenes in Dheisha camp and al-Bireh, of schoolboys commanding battalions, and women gathering stones for their children to throw.

Although we didn't discuss it, there had been a longstanding rivalry between my father and his brother-in-law. You could see it in Uncle Jad's eagerness to control certain family situations, and also in my father's poorly disguised irritation, his readiness to opt out, break eye contact, leave the room. Jad, a doctor, had effortlessly entered the bosom of the family during his engagement to Aunty Rima and continued to bask in his in-laws' praise. His own parents were working-class Muslims from Nazareth but being a surgeon had more than offset this unglamorous pedigree. Where my dad was laconic and private, Jad spoke with a slow authority, inserting himself into conversations, pronouncing his interlocutor's name with gratuitous frequency after the vocative address, 'ya'. Ya sitti. Ya Sonia. Ya Marie. He was easy to parrot. Ya Haneen, I boomed from my bed at night. Yes, ya Sonia, said Haneen. Uncle Jad walked around the house like a child-king, back arched, kicking his legs out in front of him.

At a certain point Uncle Jad started showing an interest in me. I think at the time I assumed this was because I was the youngest grandchild – Issa, the second youngest, was two years older. Or else because I was the quietest. His interest manifested in encouraging me to speak up, which I did not take well to. Nor could I articulate why. His goading did not, in any case, actually make me speak up. Instead I'd retreat into silence and stick my hands under my buttocks on the chair. At the beginning of that year's visit, or it might have been the year before, memory blurs those summers, I remember he provoked me to a pitch of silent fury when he leaned over at the dinner table during a conversation and whispered, So, are you going to say something or not?

My mother sometimes piped up in my defence but only in the tone of a joke (Oh, *leave* her, Jad). My complaints about him were sometimes the spring of arguments with Haneen, who said I was overreacting. He's just clumsy, she would say. He means well. You're being a brat. In later years, once I'd been freed from my adolescence and its whirlpool pattern of perception, in which everything tends to the centre, I'd look back and see Uncle Jad's animus directed not at me but at my father, in the attempt to lay a kind of claim on his youngest daughter. Classic, really, that my importance in the family should be barely more than as a function of a game played between men.

'You are very naughty!'

That was all Teta had said to me when I followed Issa and Haneen through the front door. She said it again and wagged a finger, and after that I received no more rebukes for running off to the beach, apart from one long blink from my father, a characteristic look of disapproval. My misdeed was quickly eclipsed by the family decision that had occurred in my absence. Uncle Jad announced, with momentous slowness, that in the morning he would take Haneen and me over the Green Line into the Occupied Territories.

Everyone was in the room, kids balanced on the arms of their parents' chairs, assembled as in a barracks before a commander. A relative in Bethlehem had called to say that her son Rashid, just released from jail, was extremely sick. She wanted Jad, a doctor with access to Israeli medical supplies and a member of the family, to come and examine him. Apparently my father was the one who'd said to Uncle Jad: 'I want the girls to see.'

Our mother spoke, with the breathy whine of the already defeated. 'I do not want them to go to a . . .' she lowered her voice, '*war zone.*'

'There is a *peace process*,' said Jiddo from the sofa, pronouncing the double 'p' with great effort.

'Ya Marie,' said Uncle Jad, 'this is the time to encourage the children.'

'I know,' said my mother. 'But why must they be *our* children?'

'Mama,' said Haneen, with dignity.

Jiddo and Uncle Jad talked most throughout dinner, discussing the route we would take. My father said nothing. My mother gradually surrendered, though she repeatedly wondered aloud whether it was going to be safe. *Peace process*, said Jiddo. I felt the burn of my aunts' double gaze and wondered what they were thinking. We went upstairs after the meal, and my sister arranged an outfit on the edge of her bed: jeans and a button-down shirt, cardigan, scarf. Trainers. She considered the selection with her hands on her hips.

'What are you going to wear, Sonny?'

'Dunno.'

In the bathroom, I dripped toothpaste onto my pyjama shirt, spat and rinsed. Presumably Jiddo was only giving the go-ahead now because the danger was basically over. The last time Uncle Jad suggested a group trip across the Green Line, Jiddo had demolished the idea with rare, thunderous volume, continually touching a certain spot on his forehead above his eyebrow, which was surreal. Afterwards I remember telling Haneen upstairs: That made me feel kind of weird.

She agreed, it was weird. The rest of that summer, we spoke at night from our beds about the ways our family both discussed and did not discuss our relation to the West Bank Palestinians, guarding our difference under that word *Dafawim*. While Jenin was starving under curfew, Nazarenes were only twenty minutes away, watching televised footage of their neighbours 'in solidarity'. For me, these discussions felt like a milestone in our sisterhood. Like we were a team. But by the end of the summer there was nothing left to confess, and since nothing could be solved we abandoned the topic and never returned to it.

Coming back from the bathroom I found Haneen had switched off the bedroom light. I felt for my bedposts and slid under the sheet as a passing car sent a search-beam across the ceiling. Everything on the news was on the verge of becoming real. My gut turned over. I forced my mind onto other things. I flexed my feet and thought about dancing.

Haneen's alarm went off at six thirty. We dressed in silence and I followed my sister downstairs onto the sealed porch by the front door, where Uncle Jad took a final sip of coffee and led us out into the cold shadows of the new day. Haneen took the front seat, as always. Jad handed his bag to me in the back.

'Ya banat,' he said, key in ignition. 'Do we have our passports?'

We left Haifa with the radio on, lulled by the roar of the motorway. Green forests bled past the window. At the outskirts of Jerusalem, we slowed along pedestrian streets.

'So who is she, this Um Rashid?' said Haneen.

'My cousin's cousin. She's with the women's committee in Bethlehem.'

'Which organisation? WCSW?' said Haneen.

'UPWC,' said Jad.

I looked at Haneen's face in the wing mirror. When had she learned the abbreviations? All those evenings lying together in the dark, and she'd been thinking about the uprising and withholding those thoughts from me. I repeated the letters 'WCSW' to myself, and shrank into a sulk on the back seat. An empty petrol station revolved past.

After a silence, Jad said: 'Poor woman.'

'Why poor woman?' said Haneen. When he didn't respond, she asked: 'Where does she live?'

'Dheisha.'

The name 'Dheisha' was like the name 'Balata', it had the same electric effect on the mind. Famous refugee camps, famous sites of conflagration.

'And what's wrong with her son?'

'He was in a hunger strike. They were released last week and he's still very sick.'

A checkpoint appeared on the horizon. The sunlight pulled shadows from the concrete blocks down the road towards us, extending the tall legs of the tin-can lookout structure, and the figures of the soldiers walking back and forth, bulked by rifles and helmets. 'Passports,' said a soldier in English, drawing level. He was looking at Haneen in a way that made me feel sick. We gave our passports to Uncle Jad, who handed them over, and I watched the soldier's eyebrows rise at Haneen's and Jad's, both embossed with the gold menorah. Only mine was maroon with a lion and a unicorn. He glanced through the photo pages, then gave each of our real-life faces an individual blank stare. In Arabic, he said to Jad, 'Give me your telephone number.'

Jad paused. 'I am a doctor.'

'Give me your telephone number, please,' said the soldier.

This next pause was so long that I could see Haneen getting agitated. She whispered in English: 'He said he wants your telephone number.'

'I know,' said Uncle Jad. Finally, and with lordly slowness, he pronounced the sequence of digits. The soldier wrote the number on a clipboard, took another cursory look at the passports, then passed them back and waved the car through. For an instant another soldier was in the window, sitting on a graffiti-ed concrete block, and then he was gone.

We entered the Territories. My heart thrashed inside my chest. The hills seemed similar to the Galilee but dryer and rockier, less green. The road sent up a white dust.

'That is the first time I have been stopped in five years,' said Uncle Jad.

It took me a moment to register that he was still thinking about the soldier. The road bucked, lifting me off my seat. I grabbed Jad's headrest as Haneen said, 'Woah,' and he said, 'Sorry, sorry, girls,' and rapidly decelerated.

The street was strewn with rubble. We slowed beside the burnt-out tyres and the husks of dead cars astride the tarmac. Two women in long patterned dresses and headscarves picked their way around the debris, grocery bags in their tanned hands. A greyness prevailed despite the sunshine overhead. A helicopter began to chop the air.

'Look,' said Haneen.

Some distance away, two green Israeli army vehicles were creeping downhill into a valley.

'Leaving,' said Uncle Jad, 'don't worry,' as the jeeps disappeared behind a wrecked wall.

Only two hours had passed since we left the house. How close we had been, all along, to this.

'Ya Sonia,' said Uncle Jad – from habit, clearly, since what he said next was for both of us. 'We're going to take a quick drive around Bethlehem. We have a while before we are meeting Um Rashid, enough for a little tourism. Tamam?'

'Tamam,' I said.

As we turned past a building with a burnt façade, the word 'territory' rang around in my head. It comes with the territory. That's not my territory. Occupied territory. Enemy territory. Unknown territory. What exactly happened on this road to cause this mess? And where were the people standing when whatever it was had happened? What weapons had they used, had the soldiers used, how had that block of concrete ended up there, and that sheet of metal there, and who had died? And how many were arrested? Over the contents of the windowpane, a blend of television reels ran and filled the empty streets with action. If Israel was 'the inside' then that made this, the West Bank, an outside, a borderland, a neither here nor there. And yet as Jad's car descended the road to Bethlehem, opening on the right-hand side a vista of terraced fields, how much it felt like exiting through the mirror and entering the real, going deeper and deeper into the heartland.

The streets of Bethlehem were narrow and steep, and most doors were painted blue. The town had an inexplicable seaside air, like Old Jaffa.

'Over there is the monastery, beyond those fields. They make a famous wine. Now, we'll see the church.'

The route he chose was blocked with a stack of barrels. He reversed up the way we came, and wiggled down another alley.

'All roads lead to the Nativity,' he said, as we drew into an enormous, empty square. On the shady side of the church, two boys sat slumped against the buttresses. We parked beside a small wooden door and followed Jad, bowing under the lintel, into a tall stone antechamber. Then we passed through another door into the church itself.

It was cool in there and slightly damp. Two queues of columns held atop their Corinthian heads walls that were double their height. Baubles and candelabra dangled on long wires from the roof beams. Our footsteps echoed as we approached the apse. The altar was decked with ornaments and icons, blackened leathery paintings on dark walls, myriad Christs suspended from myriad crosses. Uncle Jad led the way down into the crypt, Haneen followed, but I hesitated before a framed picture of Mary holding the Christ Child. They stood together against a background of gold, with halos of battered silver, and silver hands, which made them look like they were wearing silver gloves. Jesus was more like a tiny man than a baby; cradling him, his mother looked sad and indistinctive, her head draped in red fabric. I turned away and trod carefully down the ring of slippery steps. The crypt was hot and dark. Blue velvet curtains framed a cracked section of marble floor, impressed in its centre with a many-pointed silver star. In the middle of the star, a circular vacancy.

'That is where Jesus was born,' said Uncle Jad, breathing heavily. 'You can touch it.'

Haneen knelt. A vapour of memories rose, the nativity plays of our English childhood, straw on the dais of a Hackney church, tea towels pinned with ribbon, We-Three-Kings-Of-Orientar. Peering over my sister's shoulder, I wondered whether the patrons of the church believed this worn star marked the exact spot where the baby had exited Mary's body; where, in labour, her thighs had spread and his little man-head appeared. Or whether it was vaguer than that, meaning only the birth occurred somewhere nearby. Or, more hygienic: where his parents had set the manger. I pictured the icon upstairs again as Haneen traced a reverent finger around the silver hole.

Outside the church, across the square, a woman stood hunched. Hijab, thawb, grocery bags. Uncle Jad called out to her and she crossed over, setting her bags down to kiss him four times and squeeze his cheeks. His face lit up with rare hilarity. She looked uncertainly at me and Haneen and said to Jad: 'Who are these? Journalists?'

I was powerfully flattered by the thought that I looked old enough to be a journalist. I wondered if it had to do with our clothes.

'No no,' said Jad, laughing. 'My nieces. Haneen is the dark one, and the red one is Sonia. Girls, this is Um Rashid.'

'Welcome.' Um Rashid kissed us..

'Let me help you, Aunty,' said Haneen.

We both reached for her bags. Uncle Jad walked ahead, fingering his keys.

'We had many journalists,' Um Rashid told him. 'Many many many. Before, not now.'

'I brought them because I want them to see,' said Uncle Jad. 'They never came to the West Bank.'

'Welcome,' said Um Rashid.

'Of course they will wait outside when I examine him.' He supported her arm as she slid into the front passenger seat.

'The best thing,' said Um Rashid, 'is now we can buy vegetables again.'

Jad drove slowly across the square.

'In the fighting,' she went on, 'we only opened the shops for three hours a day.' She raised the last three fingers of her hand, and held them out for us in the back to see.

A chain-link fence, six metres high, surrounded the camp. We parked by a turnstile and pushed one by one through the croaking iron. The houses of the camp stood at precarious angles. We followed Um Rashid down an alley, and the buildings drew closer together until the path became so narrow that when a pipe jutted from the wall we had to walk sideways. In a doorway, Um Rashid passed the shopping bags to two small girls and pointed us along what looked like a corridor, but turned out to be a strip of shade cast by a corrugated roof leading to a large reception room. Haneen and I sat beside each other on a scrolled sofa. A barefoot boy with pointy ears trotted in with a bowl of sugar-coated chocolates. I was very hungry and would have liked a whole handful, but Haneen only took one and I felt compelled to copy her. A red one. I sucked it to make it last. Then Um Rashid handed round sweet coffee which I pretended to drink. Out of her sight the boy lingered, peeping round the doorway at me. I stretched my face long to hide my smile.

The other half of the room was a kind of study, with a desk and table stacked with magazines. Above the desk, an old photograph of a man in a sheikh's turban; on the adjoining wall a map of historical Palestine and two framed martyr posters: both young men holding Kalashnikovs with 'Hero' written across the bottom. The martyr and Hero of Dheisha, Mahmoud Abu ar-Rish. The martyr Wael at-Tuffaha.

I stared at the posters as the sugar casing melted on my tongue, trying to ignore the wrinkling linoleum floor, the emptiness of the room, its odd decor, which spoke to me clearly of suffering and poverty. I glanced at my sister. She was watching Um Rashid with determination, and she didn't seem uneasy, at least not from the outside.

'No, it was not spontaneous,' said Um Rashid, as though responding to a question. 'Since sixty-seven we have been organising. The foundations were there. We go house to house, we get blood types, this kind of thing. We teach, we organise, this kind of thing.'

'Bravo, bravo,' said Uncle Jad.

'Not bravo.' Her lips tightened. 'It was our duty. And anyway it's over now.'

'He's still not taking food?' said Uncle Jad.

'He spits it.'

'How long has it been?'

'Five weeks,' said Um Rashid, her voice rising.

'What have you been trying to feed him?'

'Banana, I try egg, bread.'

'Water?'

'He drinks water.' She took a long breath. 'When he was arrested, I was not there.' My uncle tutted, and Um Rashid fought off his pity with another scowl: 'No, many other women were there.' She faced me and Han, waving her arm. 'We are all one family, all of us. One family. The women shouted, He is my son! He is my son! And the soldier says to Um Khaled – you know Um Khaled, khalti? Um Khaled was the loudest – and he says to her, You seem to have a lot of children. Of course, Um Khaled is always doing this, walking around claiming sons. Um Khaled says, Thank God, give me my son. And the soldier says, And this boy seems to have more than one mother. And she says, Thank God! Give me my son!' Um Rashid cracked a smile. 'I have many stories.' She set her coffee on the table and stood up. 'Yalla, girls.'

Haneen and I both looked at Uncle Jad.

'You are afraid?' said Um Rashid.

'No,' Haneen began.

'You said you wanted them to see,' said Um Rashid to Uncle Jad. 'They should see him. He is what we have become.'

Off the same tin-roofed external corridor, in the far corner of a small dark room, a young man lay on a mattress on the ground. Beside him were a stack of magazines, two big plastic bottles of water and a thin plastic cup. His blanket, following his skeleton, rose to a peak upon his chest, and even in the half-light his eye sockets were visibly depressed. His skin had a grey glow. Indents in his temples cast shadows over his fleshless cheeks, and a vein articulated down his forehead looked like a piece of string that had been plastered to his skull. A brown fuzz shadowed his chin and neck, and his hair trailed limply on the pillow. He was awake. As we entered, he half-closed his eyes at us, like a cat. In the other corner, I saw the black bulk of a turned-off television.

Um Rashid spoke in a tone that was at once assertive and muted.

'Hello, my heart.' She knelt, pouring water into a cup. 'Drink, my love, drink.'

Uncle Jad immediately knelt beside her to support the young man's back, but Haneen and I stayed near the door. The shifting of Rashid's body had unleashed a smell of decay and stale sweat. As his mother held his mouth open I looked away. When I looked back, his Adam's apple was bobbing. Water ran down the sides of his chin.

'Swallow,' said Um Rashid, touching his throat.

Uncle Jad arranged some other pillows beneath the boy's neck. One of his arms fell like a stick onto the floor.

'Come.' Um Rashid turned to us. 'Come closer. Rashid, these two girls came from the inside to see you.'

We hovered a little nearer to the mattress. His eyes rested on us. On top of his blanket someone had laid a kuffiyeh. They had dressed him like a martyr, as though he were already dead.

'The strike has been over for a week,' said Um Rashid.

Uncle Jad took a gentle but firm hold of Rashid's wrist. He pushed the hair back from Rashid's forehead with his other hand. Um Rashid opened the nearest shutter. Jad unzipped his bag on the floor, revealing implements and medicines in webbed pockets. He took out a torch and, leaning close, pressed down the skin beneath Rashid's eyes, exposing the pale pink inside his eyelid. With a blast of light-headedness I moved to step away, then stopped myself in case that would be insulting. Um Rashid had brought us in here deliberately. She wanted us to see, and she wanted her son to feel seen.

Uncle Jad shone the torch down Rashid's throat. 'Wider.' Torch off, Rashid relaxed his jaw, looking dully at the ceiling. Uncle Jad sat on his heels and spoke to him in a voice so soft that I again had to fight that same impulse to step away from a scene of extreme privacy.

'Rashid,' said Uncle Jad, 'listen to me. Look at me, Rashid. You need to be strong for us. We need you to be strong, and to eat. You are not helping anyone right now, doing this. I'm sorry to say it, but that's the truth.'

Rashid blinked.

'You will be of more value to the cause if you eat. We'll start small. Some drinks first.'

I looked at the back of my uncle's head, where a bald spot was visible beneath his hair. Crossing the Green Line and coming here seemed to have lifted a spell, for now he appeared quite differently to me. With Rashid starving before us, I could see that Uncle Jad was a kind and capable grown-up. He might be clumsy but he wasn't malicious. Haneen was right, he meant well and I was oversensitive. I felt abashed.

Rashid was staring at the ceiling. How old was he? I wondered. Was he older than Haneen? Or was he younger? His beard was thin. Somehow he looked both young and old. As I was thinking this, he turned his head and looked straight at me. His eyes were deep and large and beautiful with thick eyelashes. They passed over my face as he took me in. I gazed back. It felt like he was speaking to me. Saying what? His cheeks twitched into a smile, and we became a pair of kids in a room of adults who didn't understand us.

'Will you give him an injection?' said Um Rashid.

My connection with Rashid snapped. He jerked to face the ceiling and made a kind of lowing through gritted teeth. As though to her this sound had a distinct meaning, his mother retorted: 'Even in jail they eat salt! Even in jail—' She broke off. Her fists plunged up and down through the air. 'Don't do this to me. You are killing me.'

For the first time, Rashid spoke. Words came crisply from his lips, which startled me. He said to the ceiling: 'I don't want an injection.'

'Rashid, my dear,' said Jad, in the same gentle voice, 'why do you want to die?'

'I am not going to die.'

Another long pause. 'Then why are you not eating?' said his mother.

I watched Rashid's sunken eyes. I, too, badly wanted to hear his reasons.

'What will happen?' his mother asked Uncle Jad.

Uncle Jad looked uncomfortable. 'His hearing, eventually,' he said. 'Then his sight. Then his organs.'

There were words missing in this exchange.

Um Rashid pointed at the medicine bag. 'Give him,' she whispered.

'No,' said Rashid at once. 'I *do not want* the injection.'

'He's so weak!' said his mother, and there was spite in her voice. She did not mean physical weakness. 'They have broken his spirit. Most people draw strength from the moral, from the something, in here, from each other. Most people would stop. None of the others is not eating, Rashid! They did the strike, they got what they wanted, and then they stopped! But they have broken his spirit now, and Rashid cannot stop.' She bent over as sobs began to break from her throat.

'I don't want the injection,' Rashid repeated.

He looked at me again. To my horror, this time he seemed to be pleading with me.

'Give him the injection,' his mother almost shouted.

'No!'

'Girls,' said Uncle Jad, 'you should go.'

I left immediately. Haneen, just behind me, said my name. I turned, and we hugged each other. She stiffened in my arms before pulling away, and then I saw why. The little boy with pointed ears was watching us, leaning against the wall with his arms behind his back.

'What's your name?' said Haneen.

The boy wrapped his arms across his chest and erupted with sudden, unchildish laughter.

'What's funny?'

He shook his head and ran through another doorway. It seemed like an invitation, so we followed, but stopped at the threshold. The floor of the room was covered with mattresses; the boy was clambering over them towards the far corner. The two little girls we had seen earlier were sitting there. Rashid's small room grew larger in my memory. He had all that extra space, extra privacy, his own television. The girls trotted a pair of sticks among the blankets. On the windowsill a row of empty tear-gas canisters were lined up like toys.

We waited for Uncle Jad outside. By the entrance to the camp, shadows fell cleanly under the clear sky. The time was past midday and it was hot. We watched cars pass beyond the chain-link fence. When Uncle Jad finally emerged from the alley, pale and frowning, Um Rashid rushed out from behind him to kiss us. 'You are my daughters,' she said passionately.

In the car, Haneen asked: 'What's going to happen to him?'

'I'm sending an ambulance round tomorrow. I don't believe in force-feeding, but if he continues to refuse food he won't last long. It affects the brain, once you starve. He's clear-headed now but he won't be much longer.'

'So they're going to force him to eat,' I said.

'Yes.'

'Why doesn't he want to eat?' said Haneen.

'I don't know. There might be . . . maybe a history of other illness. Sometimes starvation itself makes you think strangely. To be honest, I can't explain it.' He sucked his teeth. 'Poor Um Rashid.'

'Isn't force-feeding what the Israelis do?' asked Haneen.

'They do it for their own purpose. You know, when we hunger strike it's because we have nothing to bargain with. Our bodies are our only battleground. The Israelis want control so they want him to live. If he dies they lose the battle. Whereas, you know, when we force-feed, and I'm not saying I like it because I don't, but when we do it we are saving his life because he's one of us.'

We travelled through a Palestinian checkpoint on the way out. A few concrete blocks. Two men in blue uniforms approached and tapped on Jad's window. One bent to look in at me on the back seat, a hand touching the gun at his belt as he might have touched his tie to stop it falling forward. His expression was somewhere between a smirk and a scowl. I glanced away. He flicked through our passports and then paused, as though contemplating whether he ought to let us through, before carelessly waving us on. Jad grunted and glanced back in his wing mirror, shaking his head with scorn.

Rashid's face kept coming back to me. The way he looked at me, as though I could have helped him. And then the way he looked up at the ceiling, as though he could see beyond it. I was enraged that they would force-feed him, I felt sick at the thought, but then what exactly did that mean he was pleading with me for? To let him die? Whose side was I meant to be on? We pulled up at a petrol station and Jad handed cash to Haneen.

'Give this to him,' he commanded her, as the petrol-station worker approached the window.

My mind prickled at his tone.

'Ya Sonia.' He met my eye in the mirror as Haneen rolled down her window. 'If you want to have authority . . . if you want what you say to have authority, in the West Bank, or anywhere in the world, you have to, in the way you speak, or the way you look, or your voice, you have . . .' He held his palm up and gently lifted it.

Unbelievable. We had barely left the West Bank and he was already at it again, instructing me, authoritatively, to be more authoritative. I stared back at his reflected eyes as they turned away, awaiting the apex of his argument in which he would specify at what precise point I'd failed to assert myself. I was almost, in my outrage, looking forward to it. He accepted the change from Haneen, and angled the car back onto the road. The landscape altered. We took a right-hand turn. I waited. Uncle Jad said nothing. Eventually, slowly, I understood. That was it: he'd given his speech in its entirety. And he was not referring to me at all. He was talking about himself. *That is the first time I have been stopped in five years.*

At the Israeli checkpoint, the soldier looked straight at me and barely glanced at our passports before directing us through.

We drove on. Uncle Jad smiled at me in the mirror: 'He thought you were Jewish, habibti.'

That night I told myself I would never return to the West Bank.

5

'Have you done *Hamlet* before?'

'No.'

'You must do a lot of Shakespeare, though? In England, I mean.'

'I've done some.'

I could feel the sun through the car windows even with the air conditioning on. An hour had passed since we had left Haifa and we were nearly at the separation wall. We had already seen it from a high ring road, curving over the landscape. Clouds shattered slowly across the sky.

For the last hour Mariam had serenely besieged me with questions. Where were you born? Have you and Haneen always been close? Where do you live now? Why don't you have an Israeli passport if Haneen has one? Where did you train? Was *The Seagull* your most recent play? What was the one before? I answered without resisting. I was not irritated, in part because the act of re-entering the West Bank for the first time since the 1990s was controlling my attention and in part because I had already decided to find Mariam's bad manners interesting. They gave her a childish air, which recalled more and more the little girl I remembered, running along the beach with a crab shell. That a person might be so consistent was wonderful, in a way.

The traffic into the West Bank was hooting and slow. Not a soldier in sight. The wall rose abruptly beside us, eight metres of grey grimed concrete, a lookout tower at the bend. My heart began to pound down into my stomach, and yet, to my surprise, I discovered that the wall was merely ugly. I was expecting to feel more shocked. The open windows of the car in front were playing a familiar percussive rhythm, followed by a tinkling jingle preceding the chorus.

'I keep hearing that song everywhere,' I said.

'That's Wael.'

'Who?'

'Wael Hejazi. My cousin, you met him the other night. I thought you might have heard of him. I guess maybe in England he's not so famous.'

'Oh right,' I said, recalling the glossy young man in the theatre.

'Wael's part of the reason we need so much funding. And also why we've got it. I mean, it's a lot by local standards. He's very, very popular . . .' She frowned and gripped the steering wheel. 'Maybe there was an incident. Or an accident, I don't know. Don't worry,' she added. 'There's always traffic. I know Haneen can be stressy.'

'I'm not worried,' I said, which was not true. Mostly, though, I was anxious because I'd had no time to look over the play, which was translated into classical Arabic. Speaking conversationally was one thing; reading a literary translation of Shakespeare aloud, in front of other Arabs, while acting, was something else. We'd gone to Arabic school as children and taken lessons in the summer holidays, and I still read the news in Arabic, but it wasn't like I practised reciting the written language any more, with its complex rhythms and grammatical structures. I told myself I was doing her a favour. Pretending to be calm before her had produced a kind of surface calm; only my legs betrayed me, double-crossed with my left foot tucked around the back of my right ankle.

From the car in front, Wael Hejazi was breaking out of the melody as the song crescendoed. I detected nothing distinctive about his voice, which had a smooth and pleasant timbre, and oscillated in the normal ornamental style – until a sudden high note allowed it to expand, delta-like, above the instruments. Somehow you could tell he was smiling.

'Wael doesn't have much experience of acting,' said Mariam. 'That's the truth, though he seems open to the challenge.' She sounded doubtful. 'And you know, he will draw in the crowds. That's the real, really, this is my aim. I want to draw in a crowd. And I don't mean that cynically, at all, you know, but . . . I hope Wael will help. Theatre might not be so alive here as it is maybe in England.'

These expressions of reverence for English theatre were

becoming familiar if annoying. I smiled blackly through the windscreen, my mind on the neon lights of the West End. That illuminated cemetery.

'He's actually from the West Bank,' said Mariam. 'I mean originally he's from al-Lydd, but he grew up in a refugee camp near Ramallah. He recently got his permit for '48, that's why you saw him in Haifa,' she added. 'Okay, you know what?' She looked in her rear-view mirror. 'We're going to take the long way round.'

With a series of hand gestures to the drivers either side of us, she manoeuvred the car cavalierly out of the jam and into the returning lane. Within moments we were speeding through the hills. At the second crossing it became clear we were not the only ones to have had this idea, and we paused in line beside a gigantic red sign.

דרך זו מובילה לשטח A
בשליטת הרשות הפלסטינית
הכניסה לישראלים אסורה,
מסכנת את חייכם
ומהווה עבירה פלילית

هذه الطريق تؤدي الى منطقة (أ)
التابعة للسلطة الفلسطينية
الدخول للمواطنين الاسرائليين
ممنوعة وخطرة على حياتهم
وتشكل مخالفة جنائية في حقهم

This Road leads to Area "A"
Under The Palestinian Authority
The Entrance For Israeli
Citizens Is Forbidden,
Dangerous To Your Lives
And Is Against The Israeli Law

'In Arabic it says "their" lives,' I noted, 'and in English it says "your".' I glanced past Mariam and saw a checkpoint about two hundred metres away, trailing a queue of cars in the opposite direction. 'Do you spend a lot of time in the West Bank, as an Israeli citizen?'

'As an Israeli citizen?' She laughed. 'Jesus.'

'Sorry.'

'Yes, I have a house in Ramallah.'

'That's legal?'

'Well . . . My mailing address is in Haifa.'

'I guess my aunt and uncle—' I said, then stopped speaking as we swerved past the sign into the West Bank.

A village hung like a bead on the string of a main road, shops bearing vegetables in coloured array, a garage with a car in-treatment on the tarmac, the sweeping automatic doors of an air-conditioned supermarket. Some of the shop signs had Hebrew translations. I wondered if they were advertising to settlers.

'I used to do more Shakespeare,' I said, as the village disappeared and a valley of interlocking terraced rises expanded below us on the left. 'Often it's something young actors cut their teeth on. And then sometimes when they become aged and esteemed they might go back and play Malvolio or something to a standing ovation.'

'Cut their teeth?'

'You know like when you're a baby, and your teeth start appearing.'

'Yeah?'

'So how come you still don't have a Gertrude? I'm surprised women aren't lining up to play Wael Hejazi's mother.'

'I know. I did have someone for Gertrude *and* someone for Ophelia, but one woman found out she had a scholarship to study in Texas and the other got pregnant. There was a third who could have made a good Ophelia but her parents weren't happy about it.'

'What's going on over there?' I pointed across the dashboard.

To the left, on a road parallel to ours, what looked like a flying checkpoint: a military van, two soldiers with heavy hardhats and machine guns, and a stopped car with green West Bank plates. One of the soldiers was shouting at the car window. A couple of metres behind him, a cameraman bore an enormous black camera on his shoulder, alongside a woman in khaki trousers and headphones, holding a boom mic.

'Is that a news crew? Are they allowed to do that?' I recalled something about it being illegal to film Israeli soldiers in the West

Bank. I wondered if I was misremembering since that sounded quite extreme.

Mariam drove slowly, looking. The soldier, apparently unmindful of the camera, was beckoning to the driver, a condescending gesture of the hand, *yalla yalla*. The car door opened and a bald man stepped out. Suddenly Mariam laughed. She picked up speed. 'They're making a movie.' We rode a crest and descended into the valley. 'They were actors.'

'Oh.' For some reason, I felt deflated.

Ramallah did not look particularly war-torn. It also felt remarkably familiar for somewhere I had only seen on television. We passed Al-Manara Square, hectic with yellow taxis and people shopping, and down a road of jewellery stores with window displays of gold chains; a shop called 'Chanel', which was not Chanel, and another called 'ZARA', which was not ZARA.

Mariam parked in the old town, outside a large building made of pockmarked limestone. In the foyer, a long-legged man with a mop of black hair drinking coffee from a paper cup nodded at her, and she responded, 'Hi, Dawud,' while pushing a heavy swing door. Dawud returned my smile. He had an uneven moustache, like a teenager.

'Let me know if you need anything!' he called.

I followed Mariam through the door onto a medium-sized proscenium stage with a raked auditorium of red velvet seats, on which I counted six men sitting. My nerves leapt in my stomach.

'Everyone,' said Mariam, 'good morning.' She shrugged a long handbag strap off her shoulder and began scraping the chairs across the stage. 'Come on, guys, let's make a circle.'

'You're late,' said a tall bald man with a smile and a crooked nose.

'I'm the director,' said Mariam. 'Okay, when you have a seat, sit. A circle, come on.'

'Hey,' said a voice beside me.

It was Wael. He was wearing a green checked shirt and slim jeans slashed and daubed with white paint.

'Oh, hello. It's good to see you again.'

'Who are you playing?' He grinned.

'Gertrude. But only today, I'm just helping—'

'Oh, hi Mama.'

I laughed. 'You're Hamlet.'

'Yeah.' He ran a hand through his hair. His cheeks were a little pink.

Over the shuffles and chatting, Mariam called, 'Sit your butts down, please, we don't have all day. We'll start by going round the room . . .'

I knitted my fingers over my crossed knee. Mariam nodded at the bearded man in glasses to her right.

'Majed,' he said. I recognised him from TV. 'I'm Claudius, and the Ghost.' In an American show, or a film; I was pretty sure he'd played a Pakistani terrorist.

'Amin, Horatio.' A younger, curly-haired man, leaning on his knees and holding his script with two hands.

'George,' said a moustached man in a T-shirt with the slogan 'LOVE HEALS'. 'Francisco, Rosencrantz, and Fortinbras.'

'Polonius, I am,' said the oldest in the room, portly, with wrinkles from smiling and a close white beard. 'Polonius. And my name is Faris.'

'Thank you, Faris,' said Mariam. 'You are also the Gravedigger.'

'Yes,' said Faris, 'that is correct. I am also the Gravedigger.'

'Wael,' said Wael. 'Hamlet.' He turned his head slightly and his lips twitched.

I said, 'Sonia, Gertrude. But just for today. I'm here to help out.' Mariam blinked a few times.

'Laertes,' said the tall bald one who had joked that Mariam was late. 'I mean, I'm Ibrahim, and I'm playing Laertes.' He had a slightly rural accent.

'And Guildenstern,' said Mariam.

'And Guildenstern,' said Ibrahim, 'and also Barnardo,' raising a finger, remembering. He laughed in a way that made me think he probably fancied Mariam.

'And I'll be reading Ophelia, for now,' said Mariam. 'Quick reminder of the plot and then we'll start. Hamlet, Prince of Denmark, sees his father's ghost on the ramparts of the castle Elsinore.

Ghost says, my brother Claudius murdered me, stole my throne and my wife Gertrude. Revenge me! Hamlet is tormented. He becomes cruel to his sweetheart Ophelia, he's disgusted with his mother, and everyone thinks he's gone mad. In fact, he's pretending to be mad. Claudius is suspicious and sends Rosencrantz and Guildenstern to spy on him. Some actors arrive, and Hamlet instructs them to do a play about a king murdered by his brother. After the play, Hamlet shouts at his mother Gertrude and accidentally kills Ophelia's father Polonius, thinking it's Claudius. Ophelia goes mad, drowns herself. Hamlet kills Ophelia's brother Laertes in a duel, then finally kills Claudius – who also kills Gertrude by mistake. Hamlet, poisoned by Laertes' sword, dies in the arms of his friend Horatio. At the end, Prince Fortinbras invades Denmark. Okay? Ready, everyone? Let's begin. Act One, Scene One.'

As she read the stage directions – 'The castle of Elsinore. In one of the towers. Darkness' – my nerves spiked. How fortunate, I thought, that Gertrude has hardly any lines in this play.

'Man hunak?' Ibrahim began, too energetically – *Who's there?*

'Bal anta ajib,' said George. 'Qif wakshif 'an nafsika!'

''Asha-l-malik' *Long live the King!*

'Barnardo?'

The English words of Act One, Scene One echoed perfectly in my mind alongside the Arabic. *'Tis bitter cold and I am sick at heart.*

At Mariam's *Enter Ghost*, Majed, unspeaking, struck a martial pose upright in his chair, and soon Horatio was describing the battle between Old Hamlet and Old Fortinbras. Amin recited this first long speech of Horatio's with a conviction and understatement that made everyone look up and watch. He was barely reading his script. I did not have long to dwell on this, however, because Scene Two was about to start, and my first dialogue with Wael was coming up. My focus on the pronunciation of my lines became so total I had no attention to spare for the way Wael delivered his. I was depending almost entirely on the sounds of the words and relinquishing control over the meanings, modulating my tone according to some non-verbal intuition, like the dynamics in a piece of music, though more random. I hesitated over a vowel or two. I drew breath. *It seems to you, Madam?* said Wael beside me. Across the circle, Mariam caught my eye and smiled.

By the time we finished the read-through, an army of children accompanied by two grown women and an elastic-looking young man named Sami had entered the theatre. They were a circus school, said Sami, and had booked the theatre from 4 p.m.; it was now ten past. Mariam sighed, unapologetic, and marshalled everyone out into the overcast afternoon, first to eat shawarma on a street corner, then to sit in an upstairs café. We took a window booth and ordered coffees, rolling smokes and laying out our scripts, already dog-eared and slashed with photocopied biro across entire scenes and through the names of characters who'd been cut, their lines redistributed. The read-through had exhausted everyone and we sat for a few minutes in silence. A television above the bar showed a pale man in a suit gesticulating at a parliamentary podium before the Israeli flag, followed by a shot of Salim Mansour getting into a car. *SALIM MANSOUR* ran the headline. *TEMPORARILY SUSPENDED BY THE KNESSET ETHICS COMMITTEE. EXCLUSIVE INTERVIEW WITH HIS COLLEAGUE, MK SLAIMAN JAFFAR.*

(In a mixture of Arabic and English.)

MARIAM   Don't look at the screen. *(Pause.)* So. What do we think
         the play is about?

Silence. SONIA *watches* MARIAM.

AMIN   *(Tentatively.)* War.
MARIAM   Good.

Pause.

MARIAM   What else?
MAJED   Families, family drama.

| IBRAHIM | Free will. |
| MARIAM | *Very* good. |

Pause.

AMIN	Revenge.
MARIAM	Yes, that's a big one.
AMIN	Important.
MARIAM	Very. (*Pause.*) Can we think of anything else, even small things you picked up, that stick with you when you think now about this play?
AMIN	Death?
MARIAM	Yes. There is a lot of death.
IBRAHIM	Martyrdom. Hamlet is a martyr.
MARIAM	That's great. Martyrdom. (*Pause.*) Anything else?
WAEL	(*Speaking for the first time.*) National liberation.

Everyone looks at WAEL.

| MARIAM | In what way, national liberation? |

Pause.

WAEL	If Hamlet is a martyr . . . (*Leaves off.*)
MARIAM	You mean Hamlet is a martyr like a Palestinian martyr.
WAEL	(*Shrugging.*) Yeah.
MARIAM	Okay. Let's discuss that a bit.
WAEL	I'm just saying that because Ibrahim—
MARIAM	Nothing you said was wrong, I think it's actually very interesting.
IBRAHIM	It's not a very optimistic vision of national liberation, if everyone dies in the end.
AMIN	True.
MAJED	This might be a stupid question
MARIAM	Nothing is stupid.
MAJED	but which nation is Hamlet liberating?

Pause.

GEORGE	Denmark. No?
MAJED	But are you sure killing Claudius liberates Denmark? Doesn't killing Claudius give Denmark to Fortinbras?
MARIAM	Well—
MAJED	And then is Denmark supposed to be Palestine? Or is Denmark Israel? This time out of joint thing, something rotten in the state – the state of Israel? I'm not being sarcastic by the way these are genuine questions.
MARIAM	I don't think we need to be so literal—
AMIN	Yeah.
MARIAM	there can be a suggestion—
GEORGE	What then about the Queen, Gertrude?
MARIAM	What about the Queen?
GEORGE	I think she *does* symbolise Palestine.

Pause.

MARIAM	And why do you think that?
GEORGE	Because Gertrude ... Gertrude is raped by Claudius.
SONIA	What? Gertrude doesn't get raped.
MARIAM	Let him finish.
GEORGE	Thank you.
SONIA	But that's ridiculous.
GEORGE	Gertrude is, you know, the land who gets *manhoobi*.
MARIAM	Looted.
GEORGE	Like Palestine does, and like Palestine part of her accepts this, part of her betrays the old king, forgets what it used to be like, forgets her loyalty. Like those traitors on the inside, and those people who sold land to the Jews and, you know, these kinds of people, this betrayal is also the story of Palestine. It's not just we have been oppressed, it's also we have betrayed ourselves, our brothers.
SONIA	This is a very particular reading of the play.

82

MARIAM	Did anyone else make that interpretation? That Gertrude stands for Palestine?
SONIA	Gertrude stands for Gertrude. She's a character.
GEORGE	She is raped, though.
SONIA	When is she raped, exactly? I think I must have missed that scene.
MARIAM	Well hold on, maybe rape is too far. But remember *ight-isab* means rape but it also means *usurping*. Like, *yaghtasib al-ard*. So in that way—
AMIN	You know I had this feeling, actually you know . . . well, I read this at school, this play, in English actually, and so I felt like I knew *Hamlet*, like I knew – I mean I had this very particular idea of what happens in *Hamlet* and then reading it just now it was very surprising.
MARIAM	In what way surprising?
AMIN	*Bima'na innu* I thought *Hamlet* was a more general play, more generally about a people, struggling, that this *to be or not to be* is a kind of general idea. But this time it sounded to me more like just a young man having a hard time . . .
MARIAM	That's good, that's good.

AMIN *shrugs, self-conscious.*

MARIAM	So let's go back to that speech then for a second. It's on page 107. Everyone ready? Wael, will you read?
WAEL	(*Clears his throat.*) Ah – akun am la akun? Thalika huwa as-su'al.

    (*Shall I be or not be? That is the question.*)

A-min al-anbali lin-nafsi an yasbira-l-mar'u 'ala maqaali'i ad-dahr al-la'eem wa sihaamihi

    (*Whether it is nobler of the soul that a man should suffer the slings of outrageous fortune and her arrows*)

Am yush-hira as-silaah 'ala bahr min al-humum

    (*Or to draw weapons against a sea of troubles*)

Wa-bisaddiha yunheeha? Namuut . . . nanam . . .

    (*And by opposing them end them. We die . . . we sleep*)

MARIAM   Stop, stop there. Great, thank you, Wael.

MAJED   (*To Sonia.*) Interesting that he says *we* die.

SONIA   Right. Of course, in the original—

MARIAM   So what do you think of the fact that the two options Hamlet sees are to die or to live? What do you think of that?

Silence.

AMIN   He's suicidal.

MARIAM   Mm. Is he?

Silence.

MARIAM   Let me put it this way. Later in the speech he says: That unknown region from behind whose borders . . . *La ya'ud musafir.* A traveller does not return.

SONIA   Ah. His father.

MARIAM   Exactly.

IBRAHIM   Exactly what?

SONIA   The Ghost. Someone did return. He's saying, it's a choice between life and death. But really, what Mariam is pointing out is – there's a third way. You can be a ghost.

Silence. Above the bar, footage is playing of a 2013 interview with Salim Mansour about John Kerry's peace deal. The coiffured newsreader reappears and the previous footage of Salim getting into a car plays on the wall behind her.

AMIN   Do you think he's forgotten the ghost by that point? Is that why he says that?

IBRAHIM   It's very Western, this idea of ghosts.

MARIAM   It could be a jinni.

IBRAHIM   It doesn't say jinni, it says *Tayf.*

MARIAM   Faris, what do you think?

FARIS   About what?

MARIAM   About anything, the Ghost, or anything else in the play.

FARIS	(*Speaking slowly.*) I thought it was very, very good.
MARIAM	Okay.
IBRAHIM	(*Elbows on the table.*) Basically, right, Hamlet is a guy who thinks too much and talks too much and can't get it together.

MARIAM *laughs and glances at her phone.*

MARIAM	Okay. Everyone, let's take a break? Ten minutes, then we'll get back to talk about tomorrow.

IBRAHIM *sighs performatively.*

IBRAHIM	(*To Sonia.*) You want to come outside?
SONIA	Sure.

SONIA *follows* IBRAHIM *down the stairs and outside. He lights a cigarette. Moments later,* GEORGE, AMIN, MAJED *and* WAEL *appear behind them. Their voices slightly precede their entrance onto the street.*

GEORGE	And then there was this guy, you would not believe.
AMIN	*Terrible* actor. So, so bad.
MAJED	Where was this again?
GEORGE	Amman. We had a discussion after the show for the foreigners, and there were kids from schools nearby. We went around talking about the countries we came from, and I said something about occupation blah blah and Amin said something about Gaza and then it came to this guy and like, oh my God.
AMIN	It was unbelievable.
GEORGE	He goes, Thank you, Kuwait is a very peaceful place, we have no problems at all, we are brothers and we live in peace.
AMIN	I said, Oh you are from Switzerland? How is Switzerland, is it nice? Is it comfortable?

GEORGE   And he goes, Yes Kuwait is very peaceful, very comfortable.

          MAJED, AMIN *and* IBRAHIM *laugh.* WAEL *approaches* SONIA *and leads her a little away from the others.*

WAEL   I guess we should, like, talk about stuff. Like, our characters.
SONIA   (*Encouraging.*) Okay. You want to talk about Hamlet? I'm not actually playing Gertrude, obviously, but I'm happy to discuss.

          Long pause. WAEL *looks pensively into the middle distance.*

WAEL   Do you know when I realised I wanted to be an actor?
SONIA   When?

          Pause.

SONIA   Don't be shy.
WAEL   I'm not shy.
SONIA   Okay.
WAEL   (*Speaking slowly.*) I knew it was my . . . destiny . . . when I realised I was behaving like other people. Do you understand? I was doing the movements of other people, the talk of other people, their . . . how do you say? (*Gesturing.*)
SONIA   Mannerisms?
WAEL   Yes. All my *manner-isms* are from someone else.

          WAEL *touches his hairline with both hands, as though making sure the gel has held.*

WAEL   I don't know who I am underneath.
SONIA   That's okay.
WAEL   I know it's okay.

SONIA	(*Laughs, falls silent.*) I don't know what I am underneath either.
WAEL	(*Letting out a gust of air.*) This is getting a bit heavy, Mama.
SONIA	You said it first, dear.
WAEL	I heard you had a great career. So far, y'ani.

SONIA *laughs again.*

WAEL	Why do you keep laughing? Mariam saw you in London. You were brilliant, she said.
SONIA	Really?
WAEL	I like this word 'brilliant'.
SONIA	Do you know what she saw? What the play was?
WAEL	I can't remember.
SONIA	You don't know how long ago?
WAEL	No, sorry.
SONIA	(*Pause.*) Was it *The Seagull*?
WAEL	Could be, I have no idea.
SONIA	It doesn't matter really.
VOICE	Wael Hejazi!
SONIA	Who was that?
WAEL	I don't know. I can't see anybody. Oh. Hi.

Enter GIRL.

| GIRL | Ya Allah, it's you! Ya Allah! |
| SONIA | I'll leave you. |

SONIA *looks towards the rest of the group, clustered around the doorway to the café building.*

WAEL	No no no, you can stay. Please stay.
GIRL	I love your music so much.
SONIA	Oh, I see.
WAEL	Thank you, God bless you.
GIRL	Would you sign something?

WAEL	Of course.
GIRL	I don't have anything except my notebook.
WAEL	That's fine, I'll sign your notebook.
GIRL	(*To Sonia.*) Hi.
SONIA	Hi there.
GIRL	Thank you so much, Wael, thank you.
WAEL	It's my pleasure.

Exit GIRL.

GEORGE *whistles.*

MAJED	Mister Famous over here, Mister Rock Star.
WAEL	What can I say.
GEORGE	She was cute.
IBRAHIM	Are we going back inside? Where did Mariam go? I thought she was [*inaudible*]

GEORGE, AMIN, MAJED *and* IBRAHIM *exit into the café building.*

WAEL	(*To Sonia.*) Did you know, you remind me a bit of Fairuz.
SONIA	(*Laughing.*) Thanks.
WAEL	I'm being serious. But only from this angle. When I move – it's gone. From here, though, there's something.
SONIA	Thank you, Wael, that's kind.
WAEL	Not kind, just being honest, Mama.
SONIA	Please stop calling me Mama.
WAEL	(*Laughing.*) You *could* be my mother, you know.
SONIA	How old are you?
WAEL	Twenty-four.
SONIA	I would have been fifteen.
WAEL	Here she is.

SONIA *looks up to see* MARIAM *has come downstairs. Gradually, the rest of the cast appear behind her again.*

MARIAM	We need to go.
SONIA	Really?
MARIAM	My brother—
SONIA	Oh?
MARIAM	My younger brother, Anwar. He's been babysitting but he has to leave now.
SONIA	Right. We should go, then.
WAEL	It was great talking to you.
SONIA	And you, Wael.
WAEL	I'd love to talk more, talk business, you know.
MARIAM	Business? What do you mean business?
WAEL	I meant, like, acting.
MARIAM	Ibrahim, you ready? Everyone, quickly, we'll have a chat and then I'll let you go. We're meeting tomorrow at ten.
MAJED	Shit.
MARIAM	Why?
MAJED	Nothing.
MARIAM	Homework for tonight is to memorise the first three scenes.
GEORGE	Are you joking?
MARIAM	As best you can. Why are you worried? You don't have that many lines at the beginning, George.
FARIS	Whereas Polonius, he has many lines in Scene Three.
MARIAM	So I'll see you all tomorrow. Ten o'clock. Ready, you two?
IBRAHIM	Yes.
SONIA	Yes.
MARIAM	Ibrahim will be on the sofa, sorry Ibrahim.
IBRAHIM	I'll sleep anywhere.
MARIAM	Do you still need a lift, George?
GEORGE	Yes please.
MARIAM	My car's on the other side. Come on, guys.
SONIA	Uh, Mariam—
MARIAM	Yes?
SONIA	Can I talk to you for a second?
MARIAM	What's up?

SONIA   Am I coming in tomorrow? I mean, I know I'm staying
            at yours—
MARIAM   It's completely up to you. You're free not to come, and
            you're free to come. I would obviously be very grateful
            if you came, since I still don't have a Gertrude.
SONIA   (*Hesitating.*) Okay.
MARIAM   Have a think. Maybe it's fun. It's not the end of the world
            if I have to do it but, yes, it would be a big favour if I
            could concentrate on directing instead of reading.

Ramallah looked deserted at first. But as Mariam drove, with me
and Ibrahim on the dark back seat – George jumped out in a neighbourhood called Ein Misbah, after which Mariam glanced back at
us and said, Now I'm just your chauffeur, am I? – pockets of life
presented themselves on the roadsides, illuminated bars swiftly visible on dark and otherwise residential streets.

I tried to make sense of what was happening. Whether, by coming along to the read-through, I had already agreed to play Gertrude
in a production in the West Bank. The choice, it seemed, was mine.
Was it? I knew how it was when things started going wrong, especially at the beginning of rehearsals. Even the most seasoned
director in Mariam's situation would be panicking. If the dynamic
of a cast couldn't set because new elements were still anticipated,
morale could be threatened and those men might begin to doubt
their woman leader. I looked at her ringed fingers resting on the
steering wheel: all silver, none gold, and she liked gemstones, a
green one on her thumb and a red on her right forefinger, a garnet –
and then I realised in a kind of mental non sequitur that I actually
wanted to be in her play, and I wasn't sure why.

'Do you look more like your mother or your father?' said Ibrahim.
His smooth head was silhouetted by the window.

'My aunt.'

'I remember your aunt quite well,' said Mariam over her
shoulder.

'Rima.'

'What an amazing people we are, so varied.'

'And what an arrogant people,' said Ibrahim. 'So proud of ourselves.'

Mariam laughed. Ibrahim's hand rubbed his scalp, then landed on the empty seat between us. It was a nice hand, attached to a bony wrist.

'And how's your father?' said Mariam.

'He's good. He's in London. He just retired, actually. I think it's taking a little while for him to adjust.'

'Retired in London. You know Sonia's father was a big, active guy in Jordan in the fifties and sixties.'

'Serious?' said Ibrahim. 'That's cool.'

'Lebanon,' I said. 'He was in Beirut.'

'I thought it was Jordan.'

'What's the news on your brother?' said Ibrahim.

'I don't know,' said Mariam. 'He called me that first day but I haven't heard anything since. You saw the TV. Look, look, you see that street, Sonia?'

She was pointing to our right. In the microsecond of passage I saw an alleyway curving behind a hardware store.

'During the intifada, the second one, my husband and I were stuck there while the Israelis were bombing us under curfew. Actually, first we were stuck in the theatre. It was just us and two others, and we were there all night nearly, drinking coffee in the second row. It was miserable. We told each other stories. We laughed, you know.'

I glanced at her hands again, although Haneen had already confirmed that Mariam was separated from her husband. On her fourth finger, a pink painted rose on a silver ring.

'When we finally managed to get out, at like three in the morning, we were basically the only ones driving on the street.'

From hand to hand: I looked down at Ibrahim's, planted on the seat between us. Slyly I examined the position of his shadowed body and made out that it was an unnatural posture.

'Then we were driving through that alley towards the main road. And suddenly, we saw these other cars in front of us. And they were going up this road and starting to reverse, like crazy, zigzagging.

Then you see these cars are riddled with bullet holes. And we look up, and we see settlers shooting down at us.'

'Fuck,' said Ibrahim. 'That's so crazy.'

'Crazy is right. God, I'm glad that's over now.'

'Sonia, were you here in the intifada?' said Ibrahim.

'For the first one.'

'Wow,' said Ibrahim.

From his tone, I knew he wanted to ask how old I was.

'I was a kid,' I said. 'In Haifa for the summer holidays.'

'Ah. Like me.' He gave a crooked shrug.

'Where did you grow up?'

'Umm el-Fahem.'

'You're from the inside.'

'Can't you tell?'

I looked at him. 'No.'

We were in a totally residential area now, gliding down sloped streets. Two little girls picked their way along the cracked tarmac, ducking under the branches of a tree.

'How do you feel about being in a play in the West Bank?' he asked.

The question made me wonder how he felt about it.

'I'm not in the play,' I said.

I also wondered whether the other actors were mostly West Bankers, or '48ers like him, like us, helicoptering in.

'Right,' he said.

As I turned to look a smile broke on his face. Either he'd drawn closer to me or the light outside had changed, because he was more visible than before, and I could see he was mocking me. A pleasant charge ran down my spine.

'Sometimes it's good to do things that are unexpected.' Mariam addressed the wing mirror loudly. 'Sometimes it's good to take a risk. It doesn't always have to be about your career, you know.'

'I only came for the free ride,' I said, joking and not joking, wanting to check Mariam's presumption. 'I'm visiting my aunt and uncle. I haven't been back in so long. This whole thing is like a trip down memory lane.' I cringed at my use of the phrase. 'Anyway, I don't mind helping out until you find someone.'

'Some two,' said Mariam. 'We need an Ophelia as well.'

On the backs of my eyelids, Harold stared at me with a familiar mixture of desire and disdain.

'I was in a TV show in London, once,' said Ibrahim. 'Though we did most of the filming in Amman.'

'I thought I recognised you. What was it called?'

'*Harnessed.*'

'Yes, *Harnessed.* You did a great job in that.'

Ibrahim looked pleased. I was lying; I had not heard of the show. I made a mental note to google it when I had Wi-Fi. Mariam parked on the roadside and Ibrahim jumped out to push a pair of gates open with a familiarity that caused me to wonder how often he came to Mariam's house. He jogged after the car as we scrolled up the short driveway. Beside a ruined little garden stood a one-storey building with diamond-point embossed bricks. Cracked flowerpots lined the path to the door, and on the unmown lawn a wooden bench reclined, weather-beaten. Someone had left a coffee cup tilting in the grass. A cold rush of air met us from behind, and Ibrahim said in English with an American accent, 'Open the gaddamn door, Mariaam,' and I saw, above the house, the moon skating brightly between banks of cloud, as if caught on a current.

'Beautiful.'

'It was built in the fifties,' said Mariam, turning on the hall light and removing her coat and shoes. 'Hello!' she shouted into the house, then carried on: 'It belonged to my aunt. She didn't have any kids, so.'

Three pictures hung above the doorway to the kitchen: a watercolour landscape, verdant, somewhere in Europe – I imagined Mariam buying it while on holiday, or picking it up at a market stall in Jaffa – and on the right a framed child's drawing of a house, rhombus-shaped and stretching to the side, as though to take off into the air, the chimney pulsing smoke. In the middle, a tinted antique family portrait, at least a century old: two sons in sailor suits, father in tarbush, mother in lace.

'Hi, Mama!'

A child with a dark velvety head rushed from a doorway on the other side of the kitchen and grabbed the corners of Mariam's cardigan. His features were smudged from weeping.

Mariam asked, 'What happened?' and I noticed a man in a blue hoodie, arms crossed, leaning against the fridge. 'Just the usual stuff?'

'Yeah, I think so. He's okay. Hi, I'm Anwar. Mariam's brother.'

'Anwar's doing our set design,' said Mariam. 'He's a painter.'

Anwar shook my hand, his slender cheeks and dimpled chin appearing under the light, then, after shaking Ibrahim's – *hey, bro* – he kissed the boy and slouched to the door.

'I'll call you tomorrow,' said Mariam. She heaved her son up with her thin arms. 'This is my friend Sonia. Say hi to Sonia.'

The child shot an eye at me, then rubbed his face on his mother's chest.

'Hello,' I said. 'What's your name, then?'

'What's your name?' echoed Mariam. The boy would not reveal his face. 'Why are we shy? My-name-is-Emil.'

Emil started crying again. He was tired. I leaned against the counter. Where was Ibrahim? I ran the tap to fill a glass of water, and Mariam said: 'Take a bottle from the fridge.'

I did not, however, take a bottle from the fridge. I watched Mariam holding her son and, to my confusion, felt an urge to weep myself. I twisted my hands on the counter behind me. Mariam circled the coffee table, Emil whimpered. I longed for Ibrahim to reappear so I'd have something else to fix my attention on.

'Time for bed,' said Mariam. 'I'll be back in a moment, Sonny.'

Only Haneen called me 'Sonny'. Alone, aimless, I opened the cupboard. Wire-fastened jars held grains and nuts and dried apricots. I stared at them. Cheap, IKEA-type jars, full of ordinary foodstuffs. And yet they seemed to me to be the jars of someone who cooked and ate good, wholesome food, who bought dried fruit in bulk, who stored things and didn't eat them all at once, who fed others, who had a beautiful grubby house that smelled faintly of incense, and disordered unalphabetised shelves of books in Arabic and English guarded by an array of trinkets, wooden things with patterns on them, photographs and drawings, a loud metallic clock dangling a steel cockerel. I closed the cupboard. One day I might be intimate with this house the way Ibrahim was. I looked across the homely mess of the sitting area, already storing up the pain of leaving it. A toilet flushed, a tap ran, and Ibrahim appeared from a door, rubbing his hands on his jeans. He was smiling.

'Shall we get something to drink?' he said.

'Sure. Actually, no, I'm fine.'

He opened the fridge, leaning on the frame. On the back of his neck two long wrinkles intersected like waves. He poured orange juice into a glass then stared into the room, drinking, and his gaze fell, his eyelashes long and dark. His jaw flexed with some internal machination and I knew he was thinking about me. Like a switch, his interest had sparked my interest.

'You have everything you need?' said Mariam, emerging.

She picked a length of red fabric off the floor and began folding it, her arms extended, Christ-like, before kicking a green dinosaur under the window.

'Anyone hungry? Sonia this one is your room, and Ibrahim you're going to have to sleep here, I'll get some sheets and a proper pillow.'

'Like I say, I sleep anywhere.'

Mariam flopped onto the sofa and flung her head back dramatically. She stared up at the ceiling. A part of me still recoiled at her straightforwardness. She seemed to know exactly what she was doing and why – she had an uncomplicated sense of destiny. It was years since I'd felt that way. I pitied her for her future disappointments. I also envied her for their futurity.

'Tired?' said Ibrahim.

'My worry, you know,' Mariam swivelled her ankle while placing her hands behind her head, 'is that people will *only* come to see Wael. I think that would be a shame.'

'I thought you said that was the reason you cast him,' I said.

She looked startled.

'Part of the reason, I mean.'

'I think Wael has star quality,' she said defensively. 'There are

other benefits . . . you know, high profile, this that. But the play –
the play—'

'There's no shame in it, they do that in the West End all the time.'

'By the way, have you decided?' she said, cutting me off. 'If you'll
come to rehearsal tomorrow? If you do I'm going to double you as
Ophelia, I hope you don't mind.'

I shrugged.

'Great,' said Mariam, sounding both satisfied and unsurprised.

Just like that, I'd consented. And not by an act of will but almost
by accident, by a shrug. Maybe the guilt of my mistake, outing
before Ibrahim what Mariam had apparently told me in confidence,
had lowered my defences. I hadn't known it would embarrass her. I
felt I had tripped. Ibrahim pulled out his script and started pacing
back and forth before the cooker, mouthing.

'Wait,' I said. 'Actually.'

'Actually?' said Mariam.

'I don't think I can do it. I'm sorry. I have to see my relatives.'

'You have to see them immediately? Can it wait a couple of days?'

'Er.'

'Just say yes,' said Ibrahim, irritated.

'But.' I released a little air from my throat. 'Ophelia?'

I pictured Wael wagging his finger at me, saying: Get thee to a
nunnery.

'We have Majed playing Claudius,' said Mariam. 'He isn't exactly
old. I don't care so much for realism.'

'Oh my God,' said Ibrahim, flicking through the pages. 'You said
the first three scenes, right? What's the time?'

'I'm not expecting you to learn them all,' said Mariam, waving
her hand. 'Just do your best.'

Ibrahim lifted an eyebrow. I extracted my own script from my
handbag and felt around for my yellow highlighter pen, sat on one
of the dining-room chairs and began glancing through for Gertrude. 'The Queen,' was her label. After that, I looked for Ophelia,
which I outlined in biro to distinguish them. There were two scenes
in which I would have to read both characters, sometimes in

dialogue with each other. It struck me as funny, or poetic, that as Gertrude I would be reporting my own death as Ophelia.

'I'll leave you guys to it,' said Mariam. 'I need to go to bed.'

I let out a laugh that turned into a sigh. Ibrahim joined me at the table and we read our scripts under our breath. After a while, he said, 'Can I run through this long speech with you? It's Laertes, about to go away, warning Ophelia.'

'Sure.'

Ophelia had a couple of short lines in between Laertes' speeches. I mispronounced two case endings and tried not to be self-conscious when he corrected me.

'Perhaps now he loves you.' His gaze hooked onto mine, and though I knew he was completely involved in the exercise of his memory and it had nothing to do with me, I returned the look with matched intensity. 'And now no blotch nor lie pollutes the virtue of his will. But you must fear, once his rank raised, his will shall escape his grasp.' I did not remember this scene from the read-through, but it came immediately after my first scene with Wael so I may have been too flustered to concentrate. Now Ibrahim was saying, 'Fear it, my dear sister.' He straightened up and sighed. 'Do you smoke? That's as far as I've got.'

'You have it nailed pretty well. I'm impressed.'

'We've had the scripts for a while. That was actually part of my audition speech.'

'Still. Pretty good.'

'Cigarette?'

'No, thank you.'

I smiled. Ibrahim stayed where he was, standing above me. His mouth stirred, an almost-pursing of those pillowy lips. He was so close I could see his heartbeat slightly agitating the lapel of his shirt. A laugh was trapped inside me. If I opened my mouth it would fly out, like a bird.

'Okay, I'll be back in a second,' he said, slipping on his shoes and leaving through the front door.

I stood for a moment in the empty room, hearing the faint

mosquito call of the filaments in the light bulbs, then put on my own shoes and followed him.

'Hi,' he said, looking up.

I'd planned to say, 'I needed some air,' but ended up saying nothing. I leaned against the doorframe. The garden was black. Occasionally a car sounded, passing on the road. Ibrahim reached for a terracotta pot full of dead cigarettes and stubbed his own out on the rim.

'So you gonna let me in then or what?' He smiled. He had white regular teeth and slightly receding gums.

'Oh, sorry.'

I stood straight to let him pass, and then with an unthinking confidence I stepped forward and brushed my body against his. Before I could lift my head, he jumped away and ran a hand over the back of his skull.

The word 'sorry' was again on my tongue but I held it, caught between apologising and pretending nothing had happened. My insides flushed. I turned so that he couldn't read my eyes and had a vision of myself falling and smacking my head on the wall, my skull cracking back, blood everywhere, throbbing in thick red streams down my face. I shrugged.

'I think I should go to bed. Otherwise I might fall over.' Then, ignoring his silence, I tottered indoors as though drunk on tiredness, falling this way and that.

The spare bedroom was clearly used as an office, with two wooden desks covered in books and paper. A single mattress lay on the floor, beside another pile of books. Novels, mostly, and some big coffee-table art books, several in French. Mariam had given me two blankets, both floral.

When I lay down and shut my eyes, the same bearded face loomed, unconnected to anything, a habit of mind. I pushed him away. As I drifted off, I thought not of Harold, nor even of Ibrahim, but of Mariam. Of Mariam's house, and of Mariam's child, and of Mariam's straightforward, repugnant, magnetic light.

6

MAJED, *Claudius* and *the Ghost*. Forty years old, a Jerusalemite. Chronically silly, tall, with a malleable face, sculptural beard and coloured glasses. He alternates between two pairs, blue and yellow. Majed is sensitive and kind, and beyond a shadow of a doubt the worst performer in the cast, which leads me to wonder why he has been given the parts of the Ghost and Claudius, and not Rosencrantz, for example. But he has a resonant voice and stage presence, and, very occasionally, transcends hamminess to reach a sudden, shocking magnificence, which leaves the others pulling awed faces and clutching their chests. Majed is married to an Israeli of Yemeni origin named Nina and has two young kids. He is a wonderful tenor and sometimes after breaking extravagantly into song will apologise to Wael with his hand on his heart as if he has committed a grave offence.

AMIN, *Horatio*. Twenty-five years old, from Balata refugee camp in Nablus. His family fled Jaffa in 1948. He is short and athletic and still looks like a teenager. Blue eyes, cappuccino-brown skin, lovely curls. Speaks English with a twang that suggests a childhood diet of American TV. Both his parents died in a car accident when he was five, leaving him to be raised in the camp, nominally by his aunt and uncle but really by his older brother who sounds like a bit of a thug and has the slightly unimaginative nickname 'The Rifle'. Amin is sincere, idealistic and given to lofty talk of theatre and freedom. The great Palestinian theatre directors of the past are his idols, and they are all men. His casting as Horatio is perfect. He is the most resistant to Mariam's authority, and often sulks when she gives him notes, although his sulks are usually overridden by his desire to prove himself.

GEORGE, *Rosencrantz, Francisco, Fortinbras*. Ramallah-born and raised, son of an engineer and a literature professor. Mariam affectionately addresses him as 'Gigi', to which George pouts and sticks out his hip. I take a while to twig that this is a reference to the Palestinian supermodel Gigi Hadid. George has no issue, seemingly, with appearing in Israeli movies and serials, and yet is extremely proficient at articulating all sorts of ideological positions ad hominem with great clarity and force. His actual politics remain uncertain. When pressed he is known to say, In the end, I like people for people. Little fazes him. Like Majed, he has a comic bone, but where Majed is soft George is hard. He is an intuitive actor and never writes anything down. He can be taciturn and broody. His moustache and wide jaw vaguely recall Burt Reynolds. He stands with his feet flat and slightly askew, like a ballet dancer.

IBRAHIM, *Laertes*. (And *Guildenstern*, and *Barnardo*.) Thirty-six and a '48er. He lives in Haifa in an apartment co-owned by his ex-wife who now lives in Corsica. He has strong political opinions and does not like being challenged. Practises yoga every morning, is forgivably vain, all of his limbs are shapely and slightly stretched-looking, and he says things like, Well, I'm glad *someone* is at least *trying* to throw rockets at Tel Aviv. Ibrahim spent four years in Germany doing an undergraduate degree in Psychology and performing in experimental theatre, including a couple of absurdist adaptations of Ibsen and a great deal of Brecht. When he laughs, one of his eyes always convulses shut, and it's hard not to smile when you see it.

FARIS, *Polonius, Gravedigger*. The eldest of the cast by some twenty years, possibly more. Untidy grey hair, porous skin, stout build. He's the head of a small local community theatre in Bethlehem, which, in his absence, is being jointly run by his nephew and some young Spanish volunteers. Faris has neither spouse nor children. When I gently enquire about this – putting the question first to Ibrahim, then to Mariam – I catch traces of a half-remembered story, about a love that Faris lost when he was young, after which he never recovered. Like mine, his face lacks symmetry and looks completely different from different angles.

WAEL HEJAZI, *Hamlet*. Musician. Twenty-four years old. Wael's grandparents were refugees from al-Lydd and he grew up in a camp near Ramallah. Since winning a popular televised singing competition he has been granted diplomatic privileges by the Palestinian Authority, which, although they don't mean much in real terms besides the granting of certain travel documents, have stirred up resentment among West Bankers who might be in sticky situations documents-wise, although the resentment is directed more at the PA than at Wael. Wael inspires a mania in teenaged girls. He is closest in age to Amin and I detect some rivalry there.

> *Day Three of Rehearsals. Enter* SONIA, MARIAM *and* IBRAHIM. AMIN *is tossing a skull up and down in the air. The eye and nose cavities are revolving.* FARIS *is eating a sandwich.* GEORGE *and* WAEL *are on their phones.*

WAEL	Mama! Good morning.
SONIA	Hi, everyone.
FARIS	Good morning.
SONIA	(*To Amin.*) Is that real?

> AMIN *pretends to throw the skull at* SONIA. SONIA *screams, transforms the scream into a laugh, and runs her hands through her hair.*

MARIAM	Where's Majed?
AMIN	Not here yet. (*To Wael.*) What are you wearing, man?

> WAEL *looks down at himself. He is wearing a collared shirt made of stiff-looking shiny blue-grey fabric. His shoes are very white.*

WAEL	What's wrong with it?
AMIN	(*Laughing.*) Are you about to go onstage and perform?

MARIAM	Yes, he is. Hamlet the Shiny Dane. Okay, where the hell is Majed? We need to discuss some things before we start.
AMIN	I can call him if you like.
IBRAHIM	(*To Sonia.*) Have you been in a play by Shakespeare before?
SONIA	Yeah, I've done some Shakespeare. You?

IBRAHIM *shakes his head.*

MARIAM	(*Addressing everyone.*) You shouldn't be afraid of Shakespeare. That's what I want to get into your heads, eventually.
AMIN	Why would we be afraid?
MARIAM	Just . . . just with that sense that he's *Shakespeare.* You know. But you can fuck about with this text as much as you would any other play. Understood?
AMIN	Understood. Fuck Shakespeare.
WAEL	Yeah, Shakespeare's an asshole.
MARIAM	All right, all right. Now the thing about *Hamlet* specifically is that anyone who plays Hamlet in London, Sonia can back me up here, any Hamlet in London is haunted by all the ghosts of the Old Hamlets, I mean of all the famous actors in the tradition. That's not meant to pressure you, Wael; in fact, the opposite. Because Wael here is haunted by other things, by things he can't even express yet, maybe. We are all of us haunted by a mixture of traditions, events, memories. So I don't want you to bow down to some grand idea of a far-off English Shakespeare, no, as Amin says, Fuck Shakespeare. We're free to play. I'm going to call Majed.
AMIN	(*To Sonia.*) Did you know, there's a version of *Hamlet* in Arabic that has a happy ending?
SONIA	How does it end?
AMIN	The Ghost comes back again and gives the throne to Hamlet. Hamlet becomes king.
SONIA	Huh. What about the suicide part? They cut it out?

AMIN	I don't know, I haven't read it yet. But I have a question. About catharsis.
SONIA	Okay.
AMIN	Does it still count, if it's happy?

SONIA *is surprised to see* AMIN *looking at her sincerely.*

SONIA	I guess if a happy ending releases you, then—
AMIN	Pity and fear, though. There's no pity and fear.
SONIA	Right. To be honest, it's been quite a long time since I read that stuff, Aristotle.
AMIN	Did you also know catharsis is a medical metaphor?
SONIA	I did not.
AMIN	Yeah. (*Suddenly awkward.*) So when the Arabs translated Aristotle they skipped that part, about catharsis. They said the purpose of tragedy was happiness.

IBRAHIM *makes the triangle yoga pose, right arm in the air, left around his left ankle.*

IBRAHIM	That's why we don't have a tradition of theatre here.
AMIN	We have a tradition. It's comedy. Satire – satire?
SONIA	Yes, satire.

IBRAHIM *sinks into warrior pose, breathing deeply.*

IBRAHIM	Even though our history is all tragedy.
FARIS	Excuse me, don't forget, in the twelfth century—
IBRAHIM	Oh, spare us the Salaheddin speech.
SONIA	Faris, how about you?
FARIS	I work in the community mostly.
SONIA	In Bethlehem?
FARIS	Yes. We work with the children in the camps, we put on plays, we do after-school activities. It's good to get them off their computers, talking to each other. Also it is a good therapy.

> IBRAHIM, *upside down, makes a face that only* SONIA *sees.*

SONIA	What?
IBRAHIM	(*Standing up.*) Nothing.
AMIN	What is it?
IBRAHIM	Nothing nothing. It's just the art as therapy thing is . . .
FARIS	I don't mean therapy like you come into the theatre with a problem you're having at home and then we perform it. Although sometimes we do that, it's good for improvisation. But I mean in general, it makes you feel good. That's why we all do it. All of us. You don't agree? It makes us feel good.
IBRAHIM	I don't believe in theatre as therapy.
FARIS	What do you believe in, then? Theatre as freedom fighting? (*Laughs.*) Like our friend who got killed? The freedom-fighter womaniser soldier?
AMIN	Woah, woah.
SONIA	Who?
IBRAHIM	(*Rolling his eyes.*) No one.

> *Enter* MAJED *and* MARIAM.

GEORGE	Here he is.
MAJED	There was traffic by the checkpoint.
GEORGE	That's what they all say.
SONIA	Good morning.
MAJED	(*Looking at Sonia.*) Aaaah, she's back. Look at her, my charming, faithful wife.
MARIAM	Okay, everyone, are we ready?
MAJED	Lend me a serious listening ear to what I shall disclose!
GEORGE	What?
AMIN	He's quoting the play.

We started with one prolonged on-the-ground breathing exercise and three rounds of Grandmother's Footsteps, in which Majed struck increasingly ludicrous poses when the grandmother turned, making the real challenge not to remain still but to contain our laughter. There was something about Majed's height that made this particularly difficult, and the way his cheeks wobbled as he slid across the floor. Then the electricity in the theatre cut out in the middle of Act One, Scene One. With a faint dying whoosh, the room turned completely black. Even the Emergency Exit signs did not appear to be working.

'What the fuck?' said Ibrahim in English.

'What happened?' said Mariam in Arabic.

'Electricity,' said someone else, dully – probably George.

'Okay, everyone,' came Mariam's voice from further off, 'wait here while I go and find—Shit.' A metal clang of chair legs, followed by a blast of light as she opened the swing door, silhouetting Amin, George and Majed in medias res on the depressed stage before it banged shut again.

'I'm not staying here,' said Ibrahim.

'Nor me,' said Wael. 'Sorry, sorry.'

'No apology necessary,' said Faris. 'This is very unusual.'

I extended my arms to feel the empty space I might walk into. At that moment, I sensed someone close behind me and turned to see who it was. The wings were even darker than the stage. I would have said, Who's there? but the likelihood that it was Ibrahim stopped my tongue as well as my breath. I was ready to be outraged if he kissed me. I imagined his pillowy lips. He may have murmured something but there was too much commotion out on the stage to discern tone or word or even height, although I could, surprisingly, smell him, a deodorant odour close to cologne, heady and clean.

As I turned back, someone in the stalls switched on a phone torch and the blackness of the wings lifted to a dark grey. I checked behind me: no one there. I followed the others into the foyer and saw that Ibrahim was already exiting into the car park. I wondered how he could have snuck backstage so quickly and so secretly, and cast my eye over the rest of them. Faris sat on a lone plastic chair while the others sprinkled tobacco into cigarette papers and leaned against the wall like a fresco of men in some Italian town square, wearing sweatpants. It seemed unlikely to have been one of them. The thought that some other person, some unknown man, had come up close like that in the dark, shivered through me. Amin pointed at the buildings across the road and said: 'Looks like it's just us.' A café light was on.

Mariam appeared, looking annoyed. She had finally found Dawud. There was a dispute with the Palestinian Authority over the payment of utilities, and although she'd failed to make sense of the details, the essence was that the Israelis said they were owed money, so the electricity was cutting out every few hours. 'We'll rehearse in my garden,' she said without hesitation.

We drove in convoy to the Masyoon neighbourhood. At the house, we dragged out an old carpet from a cupboard and, using a few kitchen chairs, forced some geometry onto Mariam's wonky lawn. Three days in and the only people who actually knew some lines were Amin and George. With both female parts I still hardly had anything to say, but I needed to follow the vowel marks in the script to get the grammar right. At one point I mispronounced a very simple word, li-amalina, 'for our hopes', as li-almaniya, 'for Germany', and we all cracked up. But even George and Ibrahim, whose formal Arabic was very strong, needed correcting sometimes.

Shade was spare and the family-sized bottles of Coke and Diet Sprite that Mariam brought out of the fridge warmed fast on the grass and lost their fizz. She banned sunglasses because we needed to see each other's eyes. Wearing a baseball cap, and reading as Ophelia, I squinted at Ibrahim across the bright grass while he delivered his warnings about Hamlet flatly from memory, stripped of any of the first night's charge. A loud flying insect kept landing on my skin, and as I rebuked Laertes I shook my limbs, trying to make this look like a gesture of irritation.

Mariam was not giving any stage directions; she wanted us to try the scenes organically before working on character and blocking. Wael seemed very nervous. I compensated for having two parts by making my Ophelia girlish, then dropped this mid-scene for a forthrightness that felt more genuinely naïve. Facing away from Ibrahim and putting my hands on a chair, my thoughts slipped into a parallel stream. Over the last couple of days he'd greeted me normally without any prolonged looks. I wondered if my fumbling that first night had stamped out his interest. I recalled the heat of that presence in the dark backstage, and the memory roughened my blood, and my brain diverted to Harold, vivid and hateful but still the first port of call for thoughts of longing. Faris entered from the bushes as Polonius and flamboyantly ushered us through the remainder of the action, and then it was time for lunch.

'It's hard on Wael,' said Ibrahim, sitting on the kitchen counter. 'It's a lot of lines for him. A lot of pressure.'

Amin dropped like a dead body over the arm of the sofa and landed on the cushions with his mouth open, pretending to snore. A gigantic moth revolved against the ceiling, then landed on a picture frame.

'It is a bit tiring doing this rehearsal in the sun,' said Faris in English.

'Let her not walk i'th'sun,' I said.

'The sun breeds worms in dead dogs,' said Ibrahim, misquoting.

'You're from Denmark, right?' said Amin, opening his eyes.

'Holland.'

'Ah, okay.' He shifted onto his side and faced the bookcase. 'Would have been cool if you were actually a Dane. Gertrude the Dane.'

Haneen used to say, I never feel more Dutch than when I am in Palestine. Neither of us spoke Dutch and our mother had lived in England since she was seven.

'Woah. Mariam is fucking sexy.' George was holding a framed photograph. The image was too far to make out but I could see she was standing on a beach.

'Mariam is what?' said Mariam, walking in.

George innocently replaced the photograph on the bookshelf, slipping the stand back open with his fingers. Then he said, 'Fucking sexy,' and gave a big grin.

Amin laughed. I felt a pang, not of jealousy but of defensiveness. I remembered a remark Harold once made about my appearance. It is a shame to waste you, he had said, with his finger on my lip, as though I was something he had made. He said it so tenderly, and it sounded so confusingly like a compliment that my indignation was slow to rise. And when it finally rose – since what did he mean *to waste me*, was he detecting signs of decay? Was I supposed to be procreating? Starring in blockbusters, preserving my face on celluloid? And how dare he? – by then I was alone in the bed. Mariam closed her eyes for a quick deep breath and flicked them open.

'Let's take twenty minutes and we'll get started again,' she said.

After the break, she put us through a laborious physical warm-up that seemed designed specifically to relax Wael by exhausting him, and which exhausted the rest of us in the process. I began to wonder if what Mariam called Wael's star quality was simply a question of being famous and handsome, although occasionally a charisma revealed itself between the crossfire of his nerves. I felt for him. Some of my younger students were like that, blocked from naturalness by the presence of their peers and the fear of being judged. The waistband of his jeans, revealing a section of underwear when his shirt blew up on the air, required constant adjustment and was receiving at least as much attention as the script in his hand. In the scene with the Ghost, he touched his quiffed hair and half-shouted many of the lines. When Mariam suggested he move around more, his hands and legs trembled mid-motion as if his very body parts lacked conviction about the directions they were travelling in. Mariam paced, clutching a small red notebook and running her fingers up the ridges of a biro. At the end of the scene, finally, she sent everyone except for Wael and Majed indoors.

My own first real experience of acting was at university. I had spent a large portion of my childhood and adolescence wearing a leotard and making shapes before a mirror, but while I'd been in a few school plays I'd never had a main part or taken drama particularly seriously. During my first term at uni I appraised the dance offerings with disappointment: a few groups here and there seemed poorly organised and uninspiring. By the third week I'd basically given up when I came across an advert in the college paper. 'Dancer/actor wanted. Willing to experiment. Training involved.'

The play was Paul Margueritte's *Pierrot Assassin*, and I auditioned for the title role. Pierrot has already tickled his wife Columbine to death when the play starts, and over the course of the action he re-enacts the murder, playing both parts. The script had no words, but instead of directives for how the actors should move, it was composed of lines of speech to prompt physical interpretations. The two directors, Shay and Veronica, were second-years: Shay was a muscular young woman with a smoker's rasp and a Russian fur hat, Veronica officious and fluent in the jargon of the biz with a curtain of wavy blonde hair. She'd done a foundation course at Lecoq in Paris. I guessed the audition went well because of the look in Veronica's eyes, which stayed very open. Instructed to interpret a single word – wind – I danced as though trying to move forward against a gale, losing control every now and then, pressing into the wind with my side, then giving up, spreading my arms, closing my eyes, bending backwards slightly and shuddering with each of the harder gusts. At the end, they both applauded.

The rehearsals for *Pierrot* were gruelling, physically and emotionally. There was one moment in the play that I struggled to master, and only really cracked once they brought Michael on board as movement director. It was the point when, having acted out his crime, jumping on and off the bed to play both himself as murderer and Columbine his victim, laughing and dropping his laughter, Pierrot abandons the corpse role and stands up straight, wringing his hands. Then, he bows over with sorrow and remorse. I was a dancer, I knew how to move – in many ways, this play was a perfect gateway between dance and theatre – but I didn't yet have the skill to express emotion onstage in a way that was convincing.

After his remorse, Pierrot begins to wriggle. An external, invisible force appears to be acting upon his body. He no longer plays the other, the part of Columbine, his opponent. He is only, horribly, himself, he is laughing, uncontrollably, and now he is falling upon the bed to meet his own death by laughter, his arms outstretched as if for a crucifixion. At the climax he jerks, and lies still. Spotlight on Columbine's portrait. Laughter.

Even before the run started, we developed a reputation across the university theatre scene. The six of us – me, Shay and Veronica, Michael, Sarah who played Columbine's portrait, and Aidan who played the undertaker – became known as a mysterious gang who experimented with method acting. We drew looks in the pub as though we were in some kind of cult. Under Michael's influence we had started practising techniques of emotional recall, and through a series of occult games played late at night on the badminton court we summoned dark private feelings from our pasts to share with each other, which we re-experienced in the act by exposure. After each story the teller named the emotions it provoked. This naming was especially supposed to help me. With the exception of Sarah, who was steely, everyone wept. To ritualise it, in between the stories we clapped a complicated rhythm, which ended with the teller clapping three times on their own.

Years later I could still remember the most dramatic divulgences. Shay's mother was violent and took laxatives to lose weight; under pressure to be thin Shay had copied her, and although she'd recovered from the laxative abuse, she and her mother were estranged. Shay's whole personality also seemed different in the light of this information, grown in complication and humanity. Michael described the time he lost his mind from anxiety about what he would do with his life; this confession involved jumping into a crouch and groping the ground. Why Veronica hated her father was not clear; she wept before she could finish explaining. Sarah described her fear of flying, her discovery that she had a sister – offspring of an affair of her dad's – and her first love. I can't remember what Aidan shared, but remember feeling close to him afterwards, sitting beside him on the ground, wanting to hold his hand but refraining.

Like the others, I cried during my own stories, and also, to my surprise, made Michael cry. I told them about my parents' divorce, then my adolescent struggles with my sister, then I spoke of Haifa and the fighting. Finally I came to Rashid, the hunger striker in Bethlehem. How I felt bonded to him, although I couldn't explain why. How my sister and I had been brought in to see him, and he had seen us right back. 'He is what we have become,' his mother had said. I described how I'd thought about those words afterwards, failing to work out how Rashid's starvation was symbolic other than as a general motif of prolonged suffering. I named my emotions: guilt, sadness, discomfort, fear, longing.

There was another emotion that I didn't name. While I was doing it, I felt sick at myself for telling this story. A small and shameful part of me wanted the others to be impressed. I was the centre of this event, the centre of the play; being the centre was addictive. Someone else's suffering; my own ends. I started crying, and then the clapping rhythm began. I clapped three times and freed my hands to catch the tears on my face. Suddenly I understood that this feeling sick, this sense of exposure and shame, was part of the story's strength. It arrived in my mind all at once: how useful this was for Pierrot's remorse.

My performance notably improved after this exercise. Everyone said so and I felt the difference. Telling the story of Rashid left a sharp, singed feeling, as though the thinnest layer of skin had been removed from my body, making every sensation more intense and flushed with an undercurrent of risk.

Onstage, Sonia Nasir was gone. What remained were a set of emotions and a body to express them. Empty space teemed around me. I dredged up my invented memory of a murder, constructed of the clay of real feelings, which suggested my body along certain directions that I enlarged, exacerbated, made legible to the punters in the gallery. I, white and tragic phantom with a putty face, skidded across the stage. I reached for and touched that sharp edge of inner darkness, and pulled it out under the spotlight to commit my wicked act. After the death struggle, the remorse. Remorse burst inside me and tears ran down my face. Every night I began anew, immaculate, not predicting. My mind led my body and my body was no obstacle. Every night, Michael held my arms after the curtain call, delirious with pride, and kissed me unerotically on the lips by the stage door. For opening night my mother flew all the way over from France. Haneen, who had recently started her PhD in London, drove up with my father for the final show on the Saturday.

It might not have been my best performance – we'd been doing it for a week, matinées and evenings, and I hadn't yet learned how to conserve my energy during a run – but Saturday night was infused with a special intensity for everyone. Our adventure together was coming to an end. In the second half of the play, I turned to look up at the painting of Columbine and caught sight of Haneen in the audience. A fleeting vision of my sister's face, and, beside her, our father. I instantly saw my body from the outside, as though I were sitting with them in the stalls. I became a marionette: using my body in exactly the manner Michael had trained me out of, pulling the strings on remembered movements, relying on my muscles to make certain shapes rather than my mind. I was sure my cheeks were reddening under my white make-up. As I bent over with repentance, I became aware, for the first time, of the dissonance between performing pain and hearing laughter. I completed the final sequence in a state of terror. When we took the curtain call I nearly wept, certain we were bowing to cover disaster.

After washing my face, I exited the stage door and saw my father and Haneen standing ready with a bouquet of flowers. The whole thing was great, and so bizarre, said Haneen, and Shay and Veronica cuddled me extravagantly and called me their genius before introducing themselves to my father and sister. Not even Michael seemed to have noticed that onstage slip of self-consciousness. He took my watery eyes for sadness that the run was finally over, and called me a silly ninny. He looked rather sad himself. We said goodbye to Baba and Han by the car and set off for the cast party, where the whole night would soon be lost from memory in a swill of alcohol and mourning. As we walked to the producer's house, I found myself beside Aidan, the undertaker, who was holding a beer and kept whooping. I reached for his free hand.

7

I rang Uncle Jad from Mariam's phone. Go to the roundabout, he said. Rima will meet you there and bring you to the house.

The taxi pushed towards the outskirts of town, and, as we descended, the buildings thinned on one side and submitted to a string of sudden valleys. I heard thumping music and looked for the source, and lighted on a white car full of young men, two sitting on the boot, winding with farcical slowness up the rocky path towards a hilltop.

At the roundabout Aunty Rima came into view, standing in the shade outside a minimarket. Her hair was henna-red, and her back was lightly humped. I extricated myself from the taxi, my bag strap catching briefly on the lower blade of the door, and we kissed each other.

'Welcome,' she said. 'You look exactly the same. I'm glad you came, finally.'

I drew on an ancient habit and searched for an older version of myself in my aunt's face. 'Rima is what Sonia will look like when she's older' was once a family refrain. Eleven years had passed since I last saw her, and she was smaller and the edges of her full lips were creased from smoking. Time had brought out features we didn't share, like the nose, hers rounded where mine flared. Speaking in gestures, she conducted me around the corner and down an alley, under a bower and over a terrace to the front steps of a modern villa. On the top step, she studied three keys across her palm. Light shifted in the frosted window. The door opened.

'Uncle,' I said.

What remained of Uncle Jad's hair was white and fluffy, and the weight he'd gained gave his face a feminine shapeliness. One arm leaned on a walking stick.

'Sonia, Sonia, Sonia.'

I stepped up for three bristly kisses.

'You have made my day. You have made – my – day!'

He lurched into the salon. Bright naïve paintings of Palestinian villages adorned the wall. The windows looked onto another building.

'We used to have a view,' he said, observing me. He heaved into an easy chair made of plasticky cotton with loose threads at the seams. The rest of the furnishings had a show-room quality; a few objects looked fit for a stage-set, as though you might turn them over and discover they were plaster moulds in imitation of real things. A lace doily, diagonal across the coffee table, was kept in place by a painted urn.

'It's a lovely house,' I said.

'It has two levels! Rima will show you later.'

I looked round and saw she hadn't followed us.

'How are the boys?'

'Tareq is in Germany now. He is a chemist.'

'I remember.'

'Married a German. Tony is in America.'

'Married?'

'Yes, yes.'

His affirmation was almost dismissive, which made me think the question had called to his mind, as it had to mine, Aunty Rima's age-old ferocity towards my mother, whom she was known to dub 'my brother's foreign wife'. And there: her sons abroad. Actual foreign wives. Rima entered with two glasses of orange juice on a tray.

'You're not sitting with us, Aunty?'

'I am cooking. I will sit in a while.'

Her shoes clopped away across the tiles. Once she was gone, Jad said: 'I heard that you're married now, Sonia?'

'No. I was married.'

'Ah, I'm sorry.'

I hadn't planned to share that. I wondered if I should pretend I was a widow. Marco was alive, as far as I knew, in East London with his girlfriend and their kids. A choice lie could smooth out a rough surface, especially in this family, and in this case Jad could feel sorry for me and I would keep my pride. I pictured the contexts in which

I would be exposed and sampled the embarrassment. *How long has Sonia been in mourning? Sonia seems quite happy – considering the circumstances.*

'How often do you speak to my father?'

'Not very often. Every now and then.'

'I didn't even know you were in touch until he told me last week.'

'Well, Sonia, last year, I don't know if you know this but, I had a health scare.'

'I didn't know. I'm sorry.'

'Thank God I am fine. In any case, I don't like this . . . dividing.' He cleared his throat.

I listened for Aunty Rima in the kitchen. Too cowardly to confront me herself, she was making Uncle Jad her proxy. I wondered if that was the reason behind this whole rekindled relationship-on-the-phone with Baba, to build a bridge between the siblings. In that case, what was I? A proxy for my father?

Maybe the slip about my marriage emboldened me, or maybe it was just a feeling that time was short and pretence was pointless, but I found myself saying outright: 'I saw the house. In Haifa.'

My uncle's breath became heavy. He looked down.

'The outside of it,' I said, already losing heart. 'We didn't go in. And it was at night, in the rain.'

Our eyes met and he inhaled. 'It is a beautiful house. We don't go back to Haifa much these days.'

'You don't mind living here, in the West Bank?'

'To be honest, it's nice to be with only Arabs. We came for my work initially but now I'm retired. Naturally, I miss the sea. Rima goes for the mail and errands, her friends, but for me it's not very comfortable. In the car, you know. I have some problems walking. That's funny to you?'

'No, oh no, I was just thinking. It's funny that the West Bank should be a place people from Haifa move to.'

'The boys say the same thing.'

'They visit often?'

'Tareq doesn't like it here. Tony comes but it is far, he's in California – those are his daughters.'

He pointed at a photograph of two young women with their arms around each other. Pans clashed in the kitchen.

'We will eat in half an hour.'

Thus commenced the old game of insisting yes and insisting no, which only bolstered my desire to get away. Jad gave up on insisting that I stay rather faster than I anticipated, however, which gave me a feeling of missing the bottom step, expecting resistance and losing my balance when there was none. Already I was describing this visit to Haneen and rolling my eyes, saying, Classic behaviour. I still don't get why you even bothered, she replied acidly in my head.

I had bothered because Baba wanted me to. I pictured him alone in London, watching television and doing nothing, and the grief I lacked at the sight of the Nasir house hit me suddenly, in my uncle's new house in the West Bank, a dirty grief like wind-blown sand, abrupt and painful. I hated feeling pity for my father. It caused me pain.

'Did my father tell you whether he's planning to come back?'

'You'll have to ask him yourself,' said Uncle Jad, with evasive cheer. 'Did you know that *we* lived outside for a while? I worked as a surgeon in Munich. Good money. Plastic surgery. That's how we renovated the house. But, finally, I don't like doing breasts and faces for this, I didn't like it in the end.'

'Do you two talk about the past much?'

'Oh, Sonia.' Frustration bubbled over his face. 'We put that behind us.' Finally, unintentionally, I had punctured the surface. 'We are old men, what is the point of grudges?'

'I didn't mean *that* past. I meant further back. I meant, before the 'sixty-seven war.'

'Well, that's ancient history. So, are we going to eat or are we going to eat?'

'I'll head out and leave you to it.'

He sighed. 'Rima? Sonia is leaving. Please come back again, my dear. You made my day. I am so happy to see you.'

'Me too.'

'Rima!' He struggled to his feet.

'You don't need to, Uncle, honestly.'

He flapped his hand at me and then Aunty Rima arrived, using an apron to dry her arms.

'Where are you going?' she said. 'You can't leave, I'm making lunch.'

She looked appalled. I faltered. 'Oh, okay,' I said. 'I didn't realise you were cooking for me.'

Uncle Jad laughed diplomatically. 'She didn't realise!' he said.

'If you're sure,' I said, weakly. 'I missed your cooking.'

We followed my aunt into the kitchen. The table was already set, plates arranged around a saucepan of rice and another of stuffed courgettes in yoghurt. I recognised the cutlery. I turned over one of the forks, with a white ceramic handle, as we trotted out the small talk. A little of politics, a little of cooking, variations on a certain recipe, we make it differently in the north, in Ramallah they cut it finely, a little of the neighbourhood, the new high rises. Once I'd assimilated their changed appearances, my aunt and uncle became once more those figures who had dominated my childhood, and whose tensions with my parents had seemed a natural part of the family's fabric rather than something that would cause it to rip. At different points in the conversation, I caught each of them examining my face, and I wondered how they recalled me, the shy second daughter, and how differently I must strike them. I started babbling about what it was like to come back after so long. I faked ease, occasionally I repeated myself. I spoke at length about Haneen.

'She's so brilliant,' I said. 'I really miss her when I'm in London.'

'That's nice,' said Jad. 'I wish Tareq and Tony were still good friends. That's the reality with siblings, you never know as they grow whether they'll stay close.'

A silence commenced. I bulldozed through it. 'It's challenging for her,' I said, waving the fork around. 'Teaching in Tel Aviv. You know? She could have taught in the UK but she chose to come here. She's committed like that.'

Rima nodded vaguely. I wondered why I was talking so much about Haneen. Perhaps I was deflecting attention from myself, but I was also thinking about my father, and his new desire to patch things up. An entire world that had once seemed natural and immutable had disintegrated; it was sad. Even the house where we used to gather was gone.

'Haneen takes after your father,' said Aunty Rima.

'He is really a *noble* man, your father,' said Uncle Jad.

I glanced up at him.

'*Nabil* – his character follows his name,' he said. 'I always admired him.'

'Did you really?'

'We heard the stories about Beirut and Jordan,' he said.

'What stories?'

He smiled. 'They leave the youngest out, sometimes, don't they?'

'I think people tell Haneen things and assume she tells me.' I laughed, embarrassed.

Jad said I should ask my father directly and I responded that my father didn't tell many stories any more, not that he ever really did.

'Well, he was active, you know, it was the sixties,' said Uncle Jad. 'He joined the PLO. I think he was doing translation work. I mean, probably a few different things, you know it was an all-hands-on-deck situation. But the point is that he was somebody who said: I don't care I am from the inside, I don't care I have an Israeli passport, it doesn't matter to me. You know he wasn't afraid. But, also, he never showed off. He never said: Look, I did all these great things. That's why I mean he was noble. And maybe that's why he didn't tell you.'

I hunted for subtext but couldn't see any. I looked at my aunt, wondering if these were thoughts that she shared.

'No children, Sonia?' said Aunty Rima.

I hesitated. 'No,' I said. 'No children.'

Rima said nothing, cutting a stuffed courgette with her knife. I felt a small burst of anger, which I controlled by keeping still. This moment did not need to be difficult, especially since I'd already revealed my divorce to Jad. But I was annoyed to be forced around this sudden and totally irrelevant corner when what I wanted was to keep going, to hear more about my father. I didn't need to care what Jad and Rima thought of me. All the same, an elementary and irrational longing for my ex-husband was being revived. The longing gave him a form and there he sort of was, sitting quietly in the next chair, protecting me with his presence.

Haneen used to call Marco The Silent Man, although he wasn't particularly silent. He was quite reserved, but I'd found this quality comforting. He threw me into relief; I was expressive and passionate when I was young, especially when we first met, I was always narrating myself aloud, charting the passage of my emotions. Marco was my audience, steadying me. He never narrated his own in return, though, which forced me to glean meanings from his behaviour, and from what he didn't say, and sometimes I was wrong.

I said the food was delicious. My aunt thanked me and passed her husband the salad bowl, arranging the servers at the right angle for him. Their very gestures showed how they had grown to fit each other, like the stiff braiding of a vine.

The fact of my divorce being unknown to these two painted the divisions in my life in strong colours. It wasn't like Marco was uninterested in Palestine. He had always asked Haneen about her life here. When she stayed with us in London during the holidays or for a conference, I'd drift on the edge of their conversations while she explained the blockade on Gaza to him, or the Oslo Accords, or described the nightlife and the landscape, and he said things like, Fascinating, why don't we go, Sonia, we could do it next year, and I'd pour more wine and say, Yeah, definitely, it's been so long. Excuses were easy to come up with. It's stressful, it's violent. In the end, the only place Marco and I ever went to in the Middle East was Morocco, where we spent a week in Fez and another in Marrakesh, and I struggled with the dialect, which meant that even though I was the Arab it was Marco who spoke for us, communicating with everyone we met in French.

As we cleared the dishes I told my aunt and uncle about the play. I wasn't going to be in it but the director was great and they should attend, I'd text them the dates.

'I don't understand,' said Uncle Jad. 'You're in the play or you're not in the play?'

'I'm just helping out until they fill the roles.'

'But why not?' he said. 'You're a wonderful actress.'

'I didn't know you'd seen me in anything.'

'Of course, your father sent us, more than once! I loved the one with the police. I could hardly believe it was you.'

'Thank you,' I said. 'That was a while ago. Anyway, I meant to take a break from working, coming here. I don't know if I want to play those parts.'

This wasn't true. I did want the parts. I'd spent several weeks preparing for Harold's Gertrude audition, rereading the play closely and devising an interpretation of the character, taking my lead from night-time conversations with Harold, who was trying out his ideas with me, often implying that my being in the show was a done deal. I'd realised that Gertrude and Arkadina had a lot in common: both were mothers with troubled sons, both were coping with the approach of middle age, both had active sex lives, and experienced power and powerlessness in different contexts. Gertrude just had less to say.

'Who's the director?' said Aunty Rima, using the masculine form of the noun.

'Mariam Mansour. From Haifa. Salim Mansour's sister.'

'The Mansour family!' said Uncle Jad. 'Our old neighbours.'

'And Wael Hejazi is playing Hamlet,' I said.

'*Wael Hejazi is playing Hamlet?*' said my aunt. 'Well, we must definitely see this, Jad.'

'You know him?' I said.

'Of course,' said my uncle. 'I love his song "My Heart is from Palestine".'

I laughed. 'He's very talented.'

Rima lit a cigarette. I finished my coffee. I thanked them, I should get going. At the door we saw the afternoon had passed and darkness was already freshening the air.

'Send your father my best,' said my aunt, kissing me. She smelled old. 'And that I am sorry about everything.'

She stepped back and considered me. This time I felt she was not looking at me but through me, as though I were an emissary, a medium for a ghost, not understanding what I channelled.

'Bye Aunty, bye Uncle.'

Jad looked down at me from the ledge as through a clearing fog.

'Ya Sonia,' he boomed, sending me back twenty years. The white hair was nothing; the buffoon beneath was the same. Emotion was bringing out a vulnerable look on his face. 'You always had a lovely energy. I had this feeling you would do great things.'

I watched him, mortified. Then I realised that he was regarding me not with the sadness of disappointment, but with the sadness of memory.

'You were so independent,' he said. 'You went off and did whatever you wanted, always.' .

This certainly didn't correspond with my memories of our summers in Haifa, memories of boredom, of being shuffled this way and that. Nor did it square with Jad's famous insistence in those days that I 'speak up'.

'Did I?' I said.

He had a damp smile on his face. 'Yes.' He gave a long wistful blink. 'Goodbye, little dancer.'

The first time I fell pregnant I was nineteen. It happened right after I played Pierrot. I had spent most of the cast party in the garden with Aidan, the undertaker, soused with adrenalin and vodka, and each time we hung out in the weeks that followed we were progressively less drunk, which I took as a sign our tryst might have some legs. Aidan was skinny, pale, Dublin-raised, studying History and Politics; could be laddish, occasionally passive, conspicuously good-hearted. I'd say to people, with an emphasis that implied quotation marks: Aidan is a 'good' person. Maybe I fancied myself bad in comparison, although I'm not sure on what grounds.

I didn't tell him when I found out. Primarily I felt embarrassed, as though my body was misbehaving. I could have gone to the clinic near student housing but I didn't, I chose one on the other side of town, half an hour away by bus. I took the first pill with the nurse and the second later, in my room, and spent the weekend bleeding it out. I didn't tell anybody. Not Haneen, not my mother. Maybe I was punishing myself; maybe I was in too much shock to ask for help. Either way it was one of the more lonely episodes of my life.

I was supposed to meet Aidan that Sunday at the pub, but I didn't turn up and I didn't give an explanation. Immediately after the abortion, my embarrassment turned into resentment. I didn't respond to the two notes he left in my mailbox. The first asked if I was angry, and that if I was then would I please tell him why. The second said he didn't think it was fair to leave him in the dark like this, and if I had just gone off him it was only polite to tell him to his face, and that if I wouldn't it meant I was a coward, which meant he had made a mistake about my character, and he was sorry about that. This accusation cut me. It felt scarily adult to call me out on my silence, rather then to let it slide, which was what I would have done. At dinner in hall I became electrically conscious of him and positioned myself at a meticulous distance. Then I grasped onto this distance like it was a solid thing, something I could rely on, or at least focus on. Our mutual friend Denise said he kept asking about me, and what the hell was the matter with me anyway, I was being very weird. A week later, in a spirit of vengeance, but also because frankly I wanted Aidan to stop informing everybody and his mother that there was something wrong with me, I told him. In public, in the college bar, in one of the booths. He stared at me while I was speaking, and then he mumbled that he was very sorry that I had to go through all that, that he wished he had known, and his eyes looked wet, and then the noise of the student bar overwhelmed us as if someone had turned up the volume and I looked down at my glass flushed with shame and surprise at my own cruelty.

My second pregnancy happened ten years later. I was twenty-nine and had been married to Marco for a year.

His sister, Lessie, had been in my year at drama school, and I first caught sight of Marco across the kitchen at her birthday party, stooping in the thundery light from the window, glass in hand, looking for a place to sit. Someone said, Oh there's Marco, Sonia that's Lessie's brother, and I watched Marco's long and slightly awkward shape move away from us and then turn, a crest of black hair standing up off his high forehead, and though there was no way he could have heard his name his gaze locked onto mine. His eyes were dark, close-set, impenetrable.

Their parents came from Milan but he and his sister were born in London. The parents were wealthy and helped us buy the flat. Marco reviewed plays and films for a living but wanted to write novels. When I think of him now I see him reading on our white sofa, freakishly still. I liked looking at him more than he liked to look at me, I think. There was something animal and instinctual about his interest in me, it made me feel my presence and voice were more important to him than my appearance. I liked that. We were among the first of our friends to get married.

Our life was rundown and makeshift, which seemed romantic at the time. A wisteria gripped the balcony of our dinky place in Clapham, flowering unpredictably, and in the sitting room by the fireplace a stack of boxes stood unpacked for three years, full of lampshades and old shampoo bottles. Everything seemed provisional, everything was a proposition; life was exciting because we were approaching it, we were in a constant state of arrival. We discussed having children in passing and mostly outside the flat, on train platforms, in restaurants, half-performing for passers-by, or for each other, playacting our future lives. Or maybe that was just me; maybe Marco was sincere and only I was false. Or does hindsight make me harsh, was it possible I did not feel any contradiction then between the notion of future children and the hopes I had for my career, from which a pregnancy would have derailed me? Unlike many of my friends I was not sincerely plotting my life in advance, projecting the ideal ages for ideal salaries, neighbourhoods, colour schemes. Nor did Marco have any interest in anything he called bourgeois, a term he applied haphazardly to the calculated suburban dreams of the people we mixed with. Outside the working day, he read and wrote his ideas down in a blue notebook with a chaotic handwriting that, fortunately perhaps, I couldn't decipher, or composed stories in the tiny room beside the bedroom that we called the cupboard-study, which just about fit a desk and a bookshelf, and looked down onto a garden that we couldn't access.

The year it happened, Haneen was back in Haifa after giving up a lecturing position in London. She was doing research for a new book on the political economy of something or other, something to do with Palestinian farmers, and spent her days interviewing people and conducting seminars. From a young age she'd had a string of boyfriends, and no doubt she still had lovers, but by this point if anyone was the career woman it was her. No family members bothered any longer to nag her about marriage, but I may have also provided a buffer, my decisions being a foil to hers as hers were to mine. My father liked to tell me, Don't leave it too late! but my mother never raised the question of children. Actually she was suspicious of Marco, she'd always said don't marry a Mediterranean man if you can help it, although I explained that Marco was not like that. At which she had said well don't marry too quickly, although I had done that anyway.

We conceived by accident. First I was terrified, then we were delighted. The news cracked the future open. We discovered that, after all, life was well under way; we had arrived there long ago. We didn't feel ready, but no one does, we said. Cautiously, jokily, we referred to the incipient life as *it*, and waited until the fourth month to tell Marco's parents, and then we told my mother. I was playing Solange in *The Maids*, with another play, a piece of new writing called *We Are Never Alone*, lined up for after that, but I estimated that both runs would be over before I started showing.

I arranged a lunch to tell my father. It was a Sunday, he and I met at an Italian restaurant. We had barely glanced at the menus when I began to experience a terrible ache, deep, abdominal, and it sharpened when I twisted, I was trying to soothe it by twisting the same way I soothed period pain. I said I needed to go to the hospital and he said, Are you sure it's not just trapped wind? I said I was pregnant, and then the pain turned the angle of its knife slightly and I gasped and grabbed the edges of the table, and my father said, Ya Rab. I closed my eyes, trying to focus, but as far as I could tell there was nothing coming out from between my legs.

At the hospital they gave me something strong for the pain, tested my blood pressure, and did an ultrasound. Then the doctor said we needed to do a hysteroscopy. I evidently looked stricken because he said very quickly, It just means we use a camera. I changed behind a curtain into a hospital gown and he offered me a sedative, which I accepted, and then I lay down for my examination. Implement in one hand, he stared at a screen. Then he finished and waited for me to close my legs and sit up. I had something called a uterine septum: my womb was divided into two chambers, separated by a wall. They hadn't detected it on the ultrasound because of something to do with 2D imaging. We were lucky to have caught it when we did. Once it was taken care of, there should be no problem with fertility, although I should rest before trying for another pregnancy. Do you want me to go out and tell them? I nodded, noting the plural. I followed him after a few minutes and found my father and Marco in the doctor's office, gawping, speechless. I really wished there was a woman with me. I was going to need surgery. First they would have to induce a miscarriage.

I hate the word miscarriage. I hate the suggestion of responsibility, of carrying wrongly, like a miscarriage of justice. But the doctor was only using it as a euphemism so he wouldn't have to say the other word, which I also hate. Lo and behold, not giving it a human pronoun had not stopped it becoming human in our minds. The shadow of a third, lightly imagined, now vanishing. Marco sat beside me while my father marched up and down the hallway, his bald head bobbing through the blurry glass window. It's still only a little bean, I said, holding Marco's hand. It's just a thing, it's just a bit of genetic crap, but I was already weeping and he had a horrible look on his face. It's early, I told him, I'll do the operation and then we'll try again.

Sitting there in my backless gown, I wondered whether, if I mourned this loss, it meant that on some ethical plane I ought to have mourned the other one too. Marco released my hand and wrapped his arms around his body in an unfamiliar, self-protective gesture and bowed his head. I felt more worried about my father, marching up and down the hall. He hadn't even known I was pregnant, and now I was both pregnant and about to be not pregnant within the space of a few hours.

They gave me a local anaesthetic for the procedure, but I would have to come back the following week for the surgery, so that I could fast properly for the general, and so my body could recover from the abortion. Can I have a woman doctor?, I asked the nurse who took my blood pressure, and I noticed as she spoke that she cringed slightly: if I wanted to do it today he was the one on duty. But that's so unfair, I said, like a child.

The procedure took fifteen or twenty minutes. Afterwards, Marco and my father came and sat beside my bed. Those minutes have been almost totally wiped from my memory. A feeling of exasperation comes to me, and a desire to leave my body, to be unconscious. A craving for my sister, or my mother, or really any woman, any woman would have been better than those two terrified-looking men. My father drove us home, and when I undid my seat belt outside the house he took hold of my head and pulled it down towards him to kiss me on the forehead.

Marco made a frittata and then we went to bed. I skimmed sleep for what felt like a few minutes at a time. The bed became an object on which I was pointlessly lying, I may as well have been lying on the kitchen floor. The bleeding was persistent and uncomfortable. At some point he rolled over to me and whispered, Can I get you something? I said, No, thank you, and he fell back asleep. After that I couldn't even skim, I just closed my eyes and opened them periodically to stare into the darkness. I watched the curtains grow light, then my blood woke and thumped around my body, and I sprang out of bed as though something inside me was uncoiling. I made too much noise in the kitchen, dropping crockery in the sink, and Marco was soon rumbling around in his pyjamas while I narrated my morning tasks in a variety of accents, Now I'm going to take a shower, whoops-a-daisy, I said I'd put the kettle on, didn't I, Marco will you check if there's bread, and though I could tell he found this both irritating and disturbing I couldn't stop myself. I was due onstage for a matinee that afternoon; I had no understudy. Marco left for work and I dawdled in the flat until midday, tidying superficially, arranging objects on surfaces. I drank a lot of coffee and then ate three bananas in quick succession, which I promptly vomited onto the kitchen floor. The look of the yellow lumps in their brown liquid sobered me. The bleeding had not stopped, I was exhausted, and I acted badly.

At the weekend, I called Haneen. She didn't offer me any guidance, she just listened patiently to me sobbing, which seemed easier like this, on the phone, without the embarrassment of her body nearby; I threw my whole self into the sound, it came tearing out of me like an artery had been punctured, and I clutched the plastic handset at my ear, getting as close as possible to my sister's voice, which was saying nothing in particular, stroking me with maternal noises. Feeling calmer, I called my mother, who was very upset by the news. That conversation didn't last long. On Monday I had the surgery. This time Marco did not gawp, but touched the back of my neck, seeming to know what he was doing. When I woke in the hospital bed, groggy and disabled with morphine, he was already holding my hand.

It became clear over the week that followed that something had changed. The flat felt vacant. Marco spent more and more time in the cupboard-study, and even those nights I was not onstage I barely saw him before I slept. I had no energy to point out how unkind this was; my agony was taking too much from me, as were my performances as Solange, which I wrung out of my body like water from a cloth, crying, *Madame is dead! Laid out on the linoleum, strangled by dish gloves*. The pressure of those performances was draining but they were also a lifeline. Being required at the theatre at a certain time each day stopped me falling off a cliff, and there was something else, too, a feeling that would come over me onstage, mid-scene, in silence, a something very pure and close to dying, to standing on a kind of precipice of life. It involved being looked at, but it was not vanity. It was a sensation of being useful, and then used up, which freed me from myself. In one performance I lost control of my voice, but for the most part I managed fine. The reviews were generally positive, although we didn't get any major coverage.

There was a two-week break before rehearsals started for the next play. I lounged around the flat trying to rest, pacing our bedroom, the living room, the squashed kitchen, and still somehow I barely saw my husband. My moods rose and fell like tides and I spent my energetic moments going over the script, inventing another version of myself, an optimistic young wife, my life ahead of me, reaching back into my memory for those feelings. *An innocent woman* was the phrase Michel the director would use during the read-through, opening his hand like a flower, which irked me. It was a fine, unmemorable play, almost a two-hander, following a young couple whose flat is burgled. An Egyptian-British guy named Adam was playing my husband, and the burglar who appeared at the end was played by someone called Ralph.

One morning in that first week, I woke to silence and a strange glow coming from the curtains. Marco's side of the bed was empty. I listened. Padding footsteps; a door closing. The bedroom curtains, drawn, revealed a white street: every car and dustbin and post box and treetop wore a pelt of snow. I drank my coffee slowly by the living-room windows, the muffled brightness affecting me like the placid aftermath of crying. Occasionally Marco would cough in his study. I managed to be an hour late for rehearsal. I ran for the bus through the sludge, then from the bus to the theatre. It's okay, it's okay, Michel called softly as I stormed up the stairs. Adam smiled, mouthed hello, then pointed at my feet. Sonia, what's that?

Blood on the floor, watery with snow, had taken the jigsaw shape of my rubber sole. My pulse began to hammer. My first thought was that it was coming from my underwear. The stage manager pointed out a gash on my ankle, which was visible through my tights. Oh fuck, I said, lifting my leg. How could you not feel that? said Adam. Interestingly, looking at the wound brought the pain to life, and suddenly I couldn't stand up it hurt so badly. Maybe it was the snow, I said, maybe it numbed me. Adam located a first-aid kit while I unrolled my tights and left them snaked on the wet floor, trying not to gasp when he dressed my wound in iodine. It's not deep, he told me, it's a lot of blood but that's just gravity, you've been walking. I asked where he had learned all this, and he winked and said, Many lives. I did the whole rehearsal seated like that with my leg on a stool.

At some point during the next few weeks, my attraction to Marco shut off like a tap. I didn't like his smell, and when he touched me, which was rare, I felt a cat's repulsion. Judging by the hours he spent voluntarily out of my company, he may have felt the same way. The difficulty ebbed and flowed, and sometimes we dressed the stale evening air with light chat, the same way Haneen and I used to play cards as kids to make boredom tolerable. Sometimes we'd finish a bottle of wine and a velvet silence would arise, and at the end of the silence we'd have sex. I couldn't remember what it was like to feel satisfied.

I called Haneen on the landline at the weekends while Marco was playing tennis. She was the only person whom I told I wasn't fine. I confessed to feeling attracted to Adam. The script involved a lot of kissing. Out of scene, something in the way he looked at me played loud chords upon me, although he may only have been looking at me with concern. Undoubtedly he could see I was struggling. We spoke in Arabic, ostensibly to make jokes at Michel's expense, really for the sake of sharing a secret. Haneen diagnosed this less as a sign that I was genuinely interested in Adam and more as a symptom of something wrong, or missing, in my marriage. A week after the play ended Adam left a message on the answering machine, saying he wanted to see me. It was mixed in with a batch of other voice-mails that Marco played while I was unpacking, finally, a box of our books. I bent down to hide my reaction. Who was that? he said. My cousin, I said smoothly. I did not return the call.

The passing of time amazes me. The pretences you can keep up day-to-day, clinging to roles that don't fit any more, guided by notions of duty that you take too long to realise don't make much sense and no one is holding over you. Maybe, having watched my own parents' marriage fail, I was particularly reluctant to admit my own was failing. Or maybe it was just fear that kept my head down, because to discover life anew was terrifying, an act of abandon that struck me, when I eventually did it, as similar to that common nightmare of walking onstage without your costume, forgetting your lines. Marco had become opaque to me. For months at a time it might feel we were back to normal, but then something would happen to remind us we could no longer reach each other. Silences emerged miles high that I had no hope of scaling. Yet we continued to pay our mortgage, the signature of our self-deception, and two and a half more years went by like this, even though our fantasy of a child had long since died and the morning came and went when we both woke and heard in each other's voices that it was over, and one of us got up anyway to make the coffee, and the other put a coat over their pyjamas because we'd run out of milk.

8

After leaving Jad and Rima's, I did not take a taxi straight to Mariam's, but alighted instead near the Manara roundabout. At a store selling nuts and coffee, I asked for a handful of raw almonds. The shopkeeper scooped the equivalent of four handfuls into a paper bag and I paid and walked downhill towards the marketplace. The street was fluid with taxis and cars and shoppers and passers-by, coming in and out of cafés and shops, hopping over the pavement bars, manhandling the traffic. A tent across the square housed a group of men sitting with placards, protesting in support of a hunger strike. Above them, Palestine flag bunting hung between the buildings, and the lamp posts were covered with stickers advertising the boycott movement. Haneen once compared Palestine to an exposed part of an electronic network, where someone has cut the rubber coating with a knife to show the wires and currents underneath. She probably didn't say that exactly, but that was the image she had brought into my mind. That this place revealed something about the whole world. I looked in through the window of a bakery where three guys were dropping hot rounds of bread onto a conveyer belt.

It was almost the end of market day and many of the vegetable stalls were empty or being wrapped in tarpaulins. A man loudly offered me tomatoes. I replied to vendors, smiling, no thank you, no thank you, and after one tour of the market departed into the street. I turned a corner and stumbled, squashing something with my foot. A voice cried out, and I slipped and grabbed the wall, my paper bag flying, scattering almonds over the ground as my knee hit the brick. An old man sat behind a wreckage of dislodged fruits and plastic punnets. He looked up at me with a disgusted expression. One extremely ripe guava had split its wet seeds over my shoe. I extended my hands.

'I'm sorry! I didn't see you, I'm very sorry, please, let me give you some money.'

I unzipped my wallet, shaking.

'Are you all right, madam?'

A man was beside me.

'Thank you, yes, I'll be fine in a moment, I fell by accident. Please take it?' I addressed the fruit seller.

'Are you sure you're all right?' asked the man beside me. He had slicked hair and a wide, bony face.

'Yes, yes.'

'Your hand is bleeding,' he pointed out.

'Oh yes.' Both my grazed palms were spotting with bright little globules of blood. The sight awoke a pain in my knee. I left the fifty-shekel note on the ground and walked away. Rain started to fall as I gained the wider street, it was turning the greens of the trees greener, the pavement a living grey. I lifted my hands to let the sky wash them, which it did poorly and very slowly.

Mariam stood as I entered. 'Could I ask you to watch Emil for a few hours?'

She was wearing a denim jacket and holding her car keys. Salim had been taken in for questioning and was just released: she was driving to Jerusalem to see him. Emil was asleep in the bedroom; I could call if I needed anything.

I took it as a sure sign of Mariam's distraction that she, from whose eyes I expected nothing to escape, did not remark on my grazed hands. I said of course that was fine and, once she had left, washed my hands in the sink, and then in the bathroom pulled down my jeans to examine my knee. It was only lightly bleeding, the skin jagged but easily cleaned and dressed with a plaster. I carried myself to the sofa and listened, exhausted, to the silence. I had so looked forward to the day ending and yet it kept dragging on. I closed my eyes and lay back, just to rest a moment, just to restore myself. The springs squealed as they compressed. I felt a tickle of anxiety and took a moment to locate the source, to remember – Oh yes, the man I fell on. Oh yes, Jad's pronouncement when we said goodbye, Little dancer. Located, they stopped bothering me so much, and then my legs turned to stone.

I opened my eyes. My head had fallen to one side and the first thing I saw was Emil standing in the doorway. He might have been there for some time. He wore blue dinosaur pyjamas and held his hands behind his back, his pupils fixed on me from under the tilted dome of his forehead. Our eyes were on a level. His hair was disordered and his lips, small and pronounced, hung apart. Seeing me wake, he began to approach, but stopped behind an armchair as I sat upright.

'Hi, Emil.'

He riveted his eyes to the ground, absolutely still, as if he thought that if he didn't hold me in his sight I wouldn't be able to see him either. I was more at ease with children without their parents. Mothers always reminded me of my exclusion from a certain kind of knowledge, that the only childhood I could refer to was my own. But alone with Emil I could meet him evenly, and take notice, for example, of the lesson he'd yet to learn about the limits of perception, that the world does not close off when you are sleeping, and that in order to hide it's not enough to put your head against the wall and shut out the light with your fingers. I sympathised.

He sprang to life and made for the coffee table to retrieve a large thin hard-backed book, which he ferried over to me. The title was in English. *Greek Myths*.

'You want me to read this to you?'

I hadn't heard him speak any English yet, but he'd lived for some time in America so I assumed he could. And possibly could read it, too – I couldn't remember the age at which children learned to read. The moment I opened the book he dropped all caution and pushed his way into the loop made by my arms, aiming for the pages, which he stroked forcefully aside until he arrived at the birth of Athena. An illustration showed an armed woman surging out of a bearded man's head.

'Metis was pregnant with Zeus' child,' I read. 'An oracle told Zeus that if Metis had a son, he would grow up to usurp him. You know what that means? It means Zeus would no longer be the king of the gods, his son would be the king instead. And Zeus didn't want that, so what did he do?' I scanned ahead. 'He decided to eat her. He ate her! Cripes.' Reading again: 'And Metis was very wise, and she gave Zeus advice from inside his brain. Charming.' I noted that Emil was watching my face instead of following the characters on the page, and therefore perhaps could not read, after all, but was only listening. I started to improvise. 'And so, locked up inside Zeus' brain, Metis began to sew and sew and sew, and she sewed a whole suit of armour for her unborn child, and meanwhile her belly got bigger and bigger and bigger. And sometimes, just to annoy Zeus, she would bang her sewing machine and he would get a little twitch behind his eye.'

Emil giggled.

'One day, Zeus started to have a terrible headache. This time it was worse even than when Metis banged her sewing machine. It was pounding, pounding, pounding, like someone trying to get out. The headache became so bad that eventually Zeus asked his friend Ares to open his head with an axe. Can you imagine? A headache so bad that the best thing you can think of to get rid of it is to use an axe?'

He gazed at me. I was not sure he had understood.

'I can't imagine that,' I said.

'I can,' said Emil.

'Oh, can you!' I said, pleased. We were comrades. 'And so Ares lifted the axe, aimed at Zeus' head, and THWACK! The head split open, and out sprung Athena, dressed up in armour and ready for battle.'

'Ah,' said Mariam. 'He's making you read the myths.'

The fan had masked the sound of her entry. She padded barefoot to the armchair and sat with one leg tucked beneath her.

'Sorry about that,' she said.

'I was enjoying it.'

Emil was still locked in the circle of my arms. I lifted one to free him but he stayed there, looking over at his mother.

'How is Salim?'

'A bit shaken but okay. He's angry.'

'Did he explain what this is all about?'

Mariam shook her head. 'They never even questioned him. They just held him in a room for a few hours.'

'Are you serious?'

'You're not very maternal,' she said, watching her son. 'But he seems to like you.'

And they were back, those guileless bad manners. I chuckled half-heartedly and closed the *Greek Myths*, and a little hand trapped itself between the pages before withdrawing in defeat.

'Ouchy,' I said, and kissed the fingers. 'I think children like performers. It doesn't have much to do with mothering.'

'I'm sorry I said that. It's been a long day.' She picked up the book and looked at the cover. 'You know how all the statues of goddesses in ancient Greece kind of look like men? I learned this recently. It's because all the artists' models were male, that's why they're so muscular and have big hands, and their breasts look so weird, like round fruits they just stuck on. Because they did just stick them on.'

'I guess I thought that was how women looked in ancient Greece.'

'Nope. They looked like us.'

She rose and turned the lights on in the kitchen area, filling a pan with water and setting it to boil.

'Have you ever been directed by a woman before?' she asked.

'A few times. I've directed a bit myself. Also I teach so I suppose I direct my students.'

'Haneen didn't tell me you taught.'

'Not sure it's much of an accolade. Actors who teach are actors who aren't acting.'

'Teaching takes skill. Emil, sweetie, put that down.'

Very slowly, Emil laid a large silver salad server back on the table. Mariam took a baklawa tin from one of the cupboards and, gasping operatically, removed the lid, releasing a must of pencil sharpenings. The tin was full of paper and crayons. He protested. He wanted to watch television. Next followed the business of finding a cartoon and sitting him on the sofa. Mariam returned to the kitchen area to put the box away, brushing away my offer to help prepare the meal.

'Where's his father?'

'Hebron.'

'Oh. Is he around? I mean, does he . . . ?'

'He takes him once a month.'

'Once a *month*?'

'That's the deal. Do you eat peppers? When we were married he'd get a permit every two months to come to '48 for a week or so. Now I try to spend half my time in the West Bank so he can visit more frequently,' she said, colourlessly, in a way that suggested frequency had not been attained. 'In any case, it's good to have a place to land when I'm working here, and so on. When he starts school next year I guess it will be less, though. I want him to go to school in Haifa.'

'Once every two months is not very much.'

'We divorced a year ago.'

'I'm sorry.'

'Don't be. He's not a good guy.'

'What happened?'

She spent some time dicing an onion with a large knife.

'I'm also divorced, you know,' I offered.

'I know,' she said with impatience, as though the point was not relevant.

'Okay.'

'The problem was,' she said, 'he couldn't even fake it.' She ignited a burner and poured oil into a frying pan. 'Optimism, I don't know, some sense of, something in the future.' Her hand pranced beside her.

'About the situation.'

'The future. He had no dream.'

'Bit hard to fake a dream, no?'

She met my eye. 'You *have* to fake it.' Her gaze flicked to Emil, as to a wing mirror or a blind spot. A green cartoon fish was shaking on the screen with high-pitched laughter.

'Even when the situation is this shit? Sorry.'

'He can't hear us. What I mean is don't bring it home, that's all I'm saying. Smile, pretend. How else can you raise a child?'

'You mean pretend the future is brighter than it is.'

'But it is bright, Sonia! It can be, that's the point, for him at least even if not for us, even if you don't feel it, or I don't feel it. If you don't feel it, lie! There can be possibilities, maybe not here, maybe not . . . Though, I want him to stay here. I don't want him to be one of those kids who leave because they can. But I'm not bringing him up hopeless, either.' Even in her dismay she was exultant. She was so clearly outlined, polished by the weight of the world against which she was pushing.

'He has Israeli citizenship.'

'Yeah. His ticket to heaven.'

'When you say dream, though, what do you mean, a dream of what?'

'When was the last time you came to the West Bank?'

'God, I don't know,' I said. 'The nineties.'

'What for?'

'We came to Bethlehem, I seem to remember.'

'To the church? Post-Oslo or before?'

Vagueness did not fly with Mariam. I surrendered. 'It was the end of the first intifada. My uncle Jad brought us.'

'Rima's husband, the Muslim.'

'Funny you remember. Yeah. He had much more reverence for the Jesus hole than his two Christian nieces.'

'You didn't like it?' She sounded oddly offended.

'Of course we did. But you know, we were teenagers.'

'Oh wait, I'm remembering this story. Haneen told me. There was a kid in the camp who was hunger striking, and he died.'

'I don't think he died.'

'Haneen said he died. A few weeks later. I'm certain of it, actually, because it's part of her narrative of why she became an academic.'

'What?' I said.

The kitchen hummed. Mariam started wiping the table. He died a few weeks later? My memory was in spasm. I was seeing Rashid on the mattress. Didn't they force-feed him, wasn't that the whole point? I'd always assumed they had saved him. I had even asked Haneen later on about it – I was sure I had.

'When did she tell you that?' I asked.

'A long time ago.'

My body went cold. She laid out the plates and I could feel my throat closing up. I put my hand to my face, ready to hide tears if they started. I was remembering an expression of Haneen's the year after we saw him, a wide-eyed look the whole family would comment on, rabbit-in-the-headlights we called it. I'd become pre-occupied with my parents' separation, which after a period of explosive arguments had spread a depressed mood over the house, and I resented Haneen for not being there with me. She developed a reputation as a study-a-holic, reading relentlessly and leaving the library only to see her activist friends, and at dinners during the holidays at our mother's new flat articulating everything she experienced in a moral fever of black and white. The course of her life had seemed to be clarifying at the same rate as she receded from mine. She wanted to distance herself from whatever was sordidly boring and middle class and British about our family. I assumed that was just her reaction to the divorce. Something else was snapping into focus: the meaning of Rashid in this. He'd died a few weeks later. Why had she not told me?

Of course I'd wondered about him. I wondered what happened to him afterwards, and whether he left the camp – mainly, I wondered how that experience had marked him later on, and I'd occasionally wondered if he remembered me. For some reason, I never thought much further than that. Our trip to meet him in Bethlehem in the summer of 1994 remained a significant memory for me, pregnant with meaning and revelation, largely because it was my first contact with a very particular range of emotion – and now I hated myself for treating experience like this, like a colour palette. The vanished possibility of Rashid's life was appalling. It shoved me violently from the centre of my world to its edges. What I thought had happened was totally wrong, it was clashing against the reality, which had carried on without me, without my aware-ness. Or, rather, had not carried on at all. There was I, taking it for granted that his life had kept on going, when in fact I'd met him at the end of it. There had been no thereafter.

The smell of food returned me to the present. Mariam portioned out the stir-fry, light and shadow jostling over the table as she filled the kitchen with movement. She set her son at the head and cut his chicken into small chunks.

'So. Tell me about *Hamlet*.'

'Tell you?' I said.

I saw she was trying to distract me.

'I don't want grand metaphors,' she said. She chewed, swallowed. 'But I have this feeling I'm going to be tiptoeing around them.'

'You'll be fine as long as you don't make Majed wear a kuffiyeh and sunglasses, and speak with a stutter.'

She shrieked, and I glanced up. She was covering her mouth. Laughing. 'Oh God!' She slapped her forehead and banged her elbow onto the table. 'I'm just so bored by it all. The *symbols*. The keys, the kuffiyehs – I mean, is this all we have? Olive trees? Is this really all we have?'

This reaction seemed so over the top that I was about to ask if she was all right, but instead I found myself saying: 'Oh, come on, you can't say that. It's our heritage.'

'Heritage smeritage. I'm telling you. This is part of the problem.'

'You're being extreme.'

She wiped her eyes. I tried to eat serenely.

'You're in the play, aren't you?' she said.

The answer was obvious. 'Yes,' I said, unable to stop it sounding like a confession.

She gave me a solemn nod, and smiled in a strange remote way. The silence became intolerably dramatic.

'Why don't we just make Ophelia a suicide bomber,' I said, 'and call it a day?'

But Mariam's hilarity was spent, and she responded in full seriousness: 'We can't. Someone already did a version like that quite recently.'

9

Act Two, Mariam's garden. During the break, Ibrahim rotated the straw of a juice carton towards his mouth and said to me: 'You've stopped hesitating.'

'Hesitating how?' I asked.

We had just completed the scene in which Majed and I, as King and Queen, set various people to spy on Hamlet, who was acting mad. I didn't think I'd been hesitating.

The straw at his lips went orange. 'You're with us,' he said, exhaling. 'In the play.'

'Oh. Yes.'

'Just as I thought.'

'What does that mean?'

'It means I knew you'd join us.' He poked my shoulder, then said, 'I'm glad.' I smiled – he added: 'I mean it was obvious. You've got nothing else to do.'

I made a noise of outrage and then Mariam appeared, flustered, saying goodbye into her phone. 'Ready?' she said to me.

We began the afternoon with the Creature Game. I was the right flank, my body was the creature's leg. I whooshed with my mouth. Wael was an awkward tail. I positioned myself closer to him, encouraging him with my whooshing. Amin was the creature's jaws, snapping as he led us across the lawn. Then we paused, drinking water, while Mariam fielded phone calls from both her brothers and paced beneath the lemon tree.

I had started to contemplate, with envy, the way the Mansour siblings worked together as a team. By contrast, my family seemed so disconnected. And of course we were, geographically. That evening, Mariam remarked, You're quite different, you and Haneen, and I wondered if the same comparison had crossed her mind. Later, I called my sister from my room. I wanted to ask about Rashid, about what had happened, and why she hadn't told me, working myself up to face both my anger and my shame. I'd have gone on a walk for privacy but I needed the Wi-Fi in the house, so I just opened the bedroom windows, hoping that would disperse some of the sound. I could hear the television was on in the living room.

Instead of jumping into it, I began with my encounter with Jad and Rima, how strained it felt. 'What was the deal with them,' I said, 'with Uncle Jad and Baba? Jad said he really admired him.'

'Did Dad ever tell you about Maher?'

'Who?'

'A friend of his in Lebanon.'

'No. He didn't tell me.'

Maher, she said, was a refugee from Haifa who ended up in Beirut, where he lived with his mother in Shatila refugee camp. His relatives back in Haifa kept his commitment to the cause alive, although they never spoke directly on the phone. Instead his mother would call them periodically, acting as the medium for their relationship with her son, to whom she conveyed the conversations afterwards. The reason for this arrangement was that Maher was involved in the struggle, and one had to assume the Israelis knew this, and if they knew that he was also in touch with his family in Haifa, that family would be at risk of reprisals. They might lose their house, for example. Palestinian citizens of Israel were often punished for treason in those days if they were caught communicating with Palestinians outside who were in the movement, even if they were relatives. It was called consorting with the enemy.

'Isn't that what they're accusing Salim of?' I asked.

'We don't know officially, but yeah it's probably something along those lines.'

Maher and our father first met outside the cinema one night. Baba was a student at the American University of Beirut and himself very active, albeit not in the way Maher was.

'In what way was Baba active,' I said quickly, 'will you tell me?'

'I mean, you know, he was active. In the university.'

'But what does that even *mean*, "active"? What was he doing? What were his activities? How did he *act*?'

'I don't get the impression he picked up a gun, if that's your question. Let me finish the story.'

A year before our father left for Paris, Maher was shot by a Lebanese militiaman outside the camp. When Haneen said this, something sparked in my memory. I *had* known my father had a friend who was shot in Lebanon. But I'd absorbed the information sideways. I'd obviously heard the name 'Shatila', and assumed the friend was killed in the massacre of Sabra and Shatila in 1982, which was long after our father had left Lebanon. Yes, it was Shatila, but thirteen years before the massacre. Baba was twenty-two.

'He was standing next to Maher when they killed him,' said Haneen.

'No,' I said.

1969. Gamal Abdel Nasser's pan-Arab dream had shattered, Israel was occupying the West Bank and Gaza, our father Nabil was studying for a physics exam, and it was summer. Maher made his way across the border to Haifa with a team of commandos to light the oil pipeline leading from the refinery to the port. More than a thousand tons of blazing oil spilled out into the sea. The fire raged for five hours. Maher escaped the round-up and returned to Beirut, where he hid inside the camp for several weeks. One evening, he came out to meet our father on the street. He was shot almost immediately by a sniper. Baba carried the warm body back to Maher's mother, and, from that night onward, said Haneen, he would sleep in Maher's bed. Maher's mother cooked for him, washed his clothes, sewed the holes in his jackets. When he moved to Paris the following year, Maher's mother came in the taxi with him to the airport, and kissed him goodbye.

'He told you that? That Maher's mother kissed him goodbye?'

'Yeah,' she said, uncertainly.

The story was making me ache. For both young men, the living and the dead. For Maher's mother. I imagined my father sleeping in the camp, in Maher's place, as though it might stop the loss from striking his mother too suddenly. It hurt me that I was hearing this from my sister and not from my father directly – and, more, that I'd probably already heard it once and hadn't been listening properly, or had forgotten it, or was too young to understand. I tried to picture my father as a young man full of convictions, which had dissipated later, blunted by time and suffering.

'Does Mama know these stories too?'

'I assume so,' said Haneen.

'What does this have to do with him and Uncle Jad?'

Paper rustled on the line, and the timbre of her voice altered as she moved between rooms.

'I guess my point was that Jad only really became politicised when he was like fifty, or something.'

After we hung up I realised I hadn't even got round to asking her about Rashid.

We had five weeks until opening night. The solace and the sadness of a play with a limited run is this, that you can trace the arc of progress in advance. Like entering a love affair you know will end, we recklessly enjoyed the highs while they lasted, and valiantly endured the things that were difficult, for they too would pass. There'd be two weeks of performances in Bethlehem and then I'd fly back to London, where classes above the pub would resume in September, and auditions would trickle in, hopefully.

I texted Haneen photographs of Mariam extending her biro like an orchestral baton, and some others of the cast in-scene. My sister replied with coloured heart emojis. I missed her phone calls and she didn't answer mine. One night my father asked me how she was, and I had to say I didn't know.

The theatre settled its debts with both the Palestinian Authority and the Israelis and the electricity was working again, but we didn't rehearse there every day. Since our performances would be open-air we continued to use Mariam's garden on days when it wasn't too hot. Ibrahim found a flat to rent with Faris for two months while I slept in Mariam's spare room, which meant I could enter the backstage area of the tree shadows on the garden rehearsal days with a coffee in hand, while not in a literal nightgown yet with the feeling of coming straight from bed, a Gertrude-cum-Lady-Macbeth, while *the boys*, as Mariam and I took to calling them, were warming up on the lawn.

Our solutions to the problem of Gertrude and Ophelia included cutting some parts of Act Three, and filming Ophelia's dialogue in Act Four so that I, as Gertrude, would address myself as Ophelia on a screen; the drowning would also be projected, a larger-than-life body floating on a stretched canvas above the stage. We played character development games with the script, improvising scenes that weren't there. We recited Hamlet's soliloquies as an ensemble and then we recited the Ghost's lines together, until we were all ghosts all booming at Wael, and then we passed the lines between us like a ball, repeating them in a circle with Wael as the eye, every voice distinct, and for the particular actor whose speeches we had commandeered these exercises showcased a range of possible intonations and meanings, and as a group they rallied our animal sensitivities to one another. They also had a visible effect on Wael, who looked, I must say, increasingly haunted.

The suspension of Salim Mansour remained in the local news, alongside the Israeli attempts to demolish a Palestinian village in the Jordan Valley, where a group of foreign activists had stationed themselves. It became public that the accusations levelled at Salim, as Mariam had conjectured, concerned his involvement in arts funding in the Palestinian territories. Some sources claimed that his coordinating with the Palestinian Authority, not only to fund his sister's production but to improve facilities for the arts more generally, counted as cooperation with people who desired the destruction of the Israeli state and was therefore treasonous. That this flew hard in the face of the fact that the Israeli state itself had long been coordinating 'security' with this same 'terrorist organisation' none of the major outlets remarked upon, but many on Twitter loudly pointed out, although given that most of the comments I read on these posts appeared to come from trolls or other activists, or occasional bystanders keen to share their opinions on the topics of peace, terrorism and brotherly love, this seemed to me largely a case of preaching to the deaf and to the choir.

At least it's good publicity, we said. More than half the articles on the subject used a photograph of Wael smiling with microphone in hand, sometimes a picture of Wael beside a picture of Salim, sometimes pointing out that they were cousins, and sometimes they also used images of peripheral PLO members in their youth as fighters, dressed in military garb with Kalashnikovs and long sideburns. Some articles even named the dates of the principal performances in Bethlehem, and I thought it was only a shame that they didn't also share a link to the production website.

Nothing is more flattering to an artist than the illusion that he is a secret revolutionary. These public developments created a feeling among the cast that we were, in fact, preparing ourselves on a training base for an operation with a transcendental goal, that in combing our translated lines for subtext we were fighting the odds in the name of Palestinian freedom. Amin's air of melancholy conviction became more pronounced, and during our smoke breaks I watched him glancing at the ground or distant buildings or the sky. I noticed it in Ibrahim, too, whom I couldn't help paying close attention to, and in George, both of them becoming more ardent, more alert, on those mornings when a new mention popped up on their Facebook feeds.

The pressure affected Wael negatively. Many of Mariam's exercises were devoted to helping him access something new in his character, or to calming him down. Sometimes I felt like taking him aside and saying, You know what, Wael, it actually doesn't matter how convincing you are as Hamlet. The more important thing is that you are in the play, and everyone loves you and will come to see you, and once they have seen you they will continue to love you, or will love you even more. But the truth was I wasn't sure everyone did love him. The atmosphere of competition that I'd sensed at the start of rehearsals, for which I held Amin initially responsible, had been taken up by George and even, disappointingly, Ibrahim, and tainted with scorn. Whether Mariam detected it was unclear – the symptoms were so mild, you needed to be watching to catch them in the grain of their everyday interactions, warm-ups, transitions, breaks, mealtimes, goodbyes: a reluctance to include Wael, an avoidance of eye contact, a note of exasperation. I wondered if this didn't represent a microcosm of Wael's larger presence in the Palestinian imaginary, which, I was beginning to grasp, also had its darkness.

The heat that first week was intense and I drank litres of water on the days we spent in the garden. At one point Ibrahim reached out a hand towards me to wipe a blob of suncream from my nose and I giggled, batting him away. We worked through the entire play and from start to finish Wael played up Hamlet's angst with a teenageryness that was a familiar if not particularly profound interpretation of the character. Mariam was not pleased. She wanted something harder and darker. Eventually, and influenced perhaps by the media-fuelled revolutionary mood, she instructed him explicitly to pretend he was a fida'i. This was pitching for some of the deepest waters of Wael's psyche: we all knew one of his uncles had died in the War of the Camps, and another fought in Jordan before Black September. As with the other exercises, we did it together first: a round of physical training, jumping over flaming logs (rolled-up yoga mats) with loaded guns in hand (mimed), a game of limbo that transformed into crawling under low-lying barbed wire, then an off-duty scene in our camp, smoking cigarettes and scarfing rations. Amin wanted to smoke for real; Mariam said no, you did a gun without a real gun, you can do a cigarette. Then we ran through Act Four. Hamlet has killed Polonius, hidden the body, and now thwarts Claudius's attempt to have him executed.

We sat on the floor with our backs against the walls, legs crossed or splayed, sipping from water bottles, in a mood of anticipation. A window was opened to let in some fresh air, as well as the noise of rapid gunfire, probably from a wedding celebration. We rose to our feet as the scenes required, thinking less of our own lines than of Wael's, watching his fida'i-infused Hamlet for new, convincing signs of the psychic mutilation of someone who has just committed murder and is speaking in riddles.

I knew it would not be an easy fix. Still, I was hoping for progress. But Wael's fida'i had no darkness at all. He was a blank, sincere warrior, pure of intention, unburdened by mortality. *The body is with the King, but the King is not with the body*, he said without irony or ambiguity, as though repeating orders from a higher in command. He was not a living fida'i facing death, but rather like one already dead, a fida'i of the imagination, idealised, glorified, untouched by mortal fear because he had already been immortalised into a sym-bol. His antic disposition came over as mild frustration, manifesting as ordinary, adolescent sarcasm.

In a manner quite different to her usual directing style, Mariam called everything to a stop mid-scene.

'Wael,' she said, 'I need you to be more mad.'

'*Mad*,' said Wael. 'Mad.' He massaged his temples like a stage magician. Then he said simply: 'I think I'm worn out for the day.'

Ibrahim met my eyes, thrusting his hands into his pockets and pulling them outward so that his tracksuit bottoms looked like clown trousers. Wael poured water from the drinks table into a cup and avoided looking at anyone. I felt sorry for him.

That evening, after collecting Emil from nursery and setting him before the TV, Mariam said: 'I wonder if I've made a mistake. Per-haps I should have given the part to Amin. I can't turn my rehearsal room into a one-man drama school.'

'It's not going to come all at once,' I said, in what I thought was a reassuring tone, which was really my teaching voice.

That night I called Haneen. She answered with a long exhalation as though she'd been holding her breath.

'Sorry we keep missing each other,' I said.

I faced my reflection in the window, clear in the light of the desk lamp: my wet hair pulled into a bun, my white pyjama shirt under-lining my tan.

'I think you're a workaholic,' said Haneen.

'You can also pick up the phone.'

'When am I going to see you? I was getting used to having you around.'

'Shall I come stay this weekend? I need some more clothes.'

'This weekend would be great,' said Haneen. I heard the clash and spatter of crockery under a running tap. 'Sonny, you're not angry with me, are you?'

'Why would I be angry?'

'Just because, I mean I assumed you were busy. Anyway, I wanted to say, I know I was uneasy about you going there at first, but that was only because I'm tense.'

'You're being very formal.'

'I'm really glad you're doing it. I think it's great that you're playing an Arab finally.'

'What are you talking about? I'm Gertrude and Ophelia. They're Danish.'

'But in Arabic.'

'I mean, I guess.'

'By the way, I saw the student again, Yunes, the homeless guy. I was out jogging and I passed him on the street. He waved, so I stopped to say hi. He looked good, he was wearing smart clothes – I guess that means he took the job. Anyway, it was brief but he was friendly.'

'There you go. I told you he was only horrible to you because of his situation. Humiliation makes men nasty.'

The next day was Thursday. In the morning after the warm-up, Mariam announced, with a performance of composure as though it were all part of a larger design: Today, Wael, you are going to be an Israeli soldier. When was the last time you were at a checkpoint and some soldier was a real asshole to you?

There were a few laughs. Wael dropped a bright white grin. Ibrahim cracked his knuckles, Amin looked trepidatious, George gleeful, presumably all of them summoning the primordial image of the Israeli as he existed in the occupied Palestinian mind: young, insolent, cruel, bored, armed. But Mariam stopped our imaginations in their tracks by saying no, only Wael is doing it this time. This was the game: Wael is the soldier, and we are passing through his checkpoint. She instructed Wael to choose a Jewish name and to keep it to himself. Then he left the room and we shuffled into a line, getting ready to go to work, or to visit our relatives, fiddling with our IDs and permits. Mariam gave the signal, and Wael as the soldier entered.

The atmosphere in the room shifted. I felt it in my chest at once – a falling. Wael walked to his sentry post, which was a chair balanced on a wood block. We began to play at our humiliation, the routine turning through the stiles of the checkpoint, waiting for the light to go green, stuck when it turned red, which Wael choreographed by jabbing his finger on an invisible button. He awaited us with a bored face. Ibrahim went first. He became a sullen, resentful youth, some version of his young self, I imagined, passing his bag and his shoes through the X-ray machine, shaking off his watch. The soldier stared at him. And then, once Wael had let Ibrahim pass, he called him back again, addressing him in Hebrew-accented Arabic. He took another look at Ibrahim's document, typed something into his computer, made an inaudible phone call. He dismissed him and jabbed the button. My turn. I faced Wael in his booth and marvelled at his blankness. This was far more sinister than the boredom of the off-duty fida'i. He looked relaxed, perfectly still, watching me. The effect was unnerving, and I played upon feeling unnerved; and at the same time with the double vision of the performing artist I could sense the waves of triumph radiating out from the corner of the room where Mariam was standing.

'Thank God!' she said as we walked home. 'I knew he had it in him. I knew it was there. I'm like Michelangelo, with a big lump of rock.'

Mariam's arrogance was becoming endearing to me, because it was coupled with her straightforwardness. I would have said she seemed unscathed were it not that the longer I stayed in her house, the more I understood how much she'd suffered. It was rather as though, through all the twists and turns, she had clung on to some innocence. As a director she was a chameleon: a hard leader who turned abruptly maternal, became innocently questioning, a confidante, a therapist, a manipulator, a sibyl. She spoke with her hands, plucking ideas from the air. The boys revered and rolled their eyes at her in equal measure, impersonating the way she said *Pause*, with her hand slightly bent, held out before her and gently lowered as though knighting someone.

For me, working with her felt like being a student again. There was something am-dram about the whole affair, with our seriousness always at risk of being punctured, and our primary rehearsal space being our director's front garden, hidden from the road by trees but surely audible to passers-by. Also Mariam believed more sincerely than most London theatre practitioners I know in a real conduit between art and politics. At the same time, she freely applied her cynical tongue to the cultural life of Ramallah, 'which does not,' she emphasised, 'represent the West Bank,' although to Palestinians visiting from Haifa and Jaffa, in which I included myself, it seemed wild enough, with its mixture of rubble and construction, patrolled by mangy cats. The audiences here were mostly bourgeois and Christian, she said disparagingly, even though this was arguably a description of both our backgrounds. One night she extemporised upon the broader risk that art might deaden resistance, by softening suffering's blows through representing it. I said this was an easy statement to make when you were a citizen of a nation that granted you some of a taxpayer's privileges even if not all of them. In any case, I wasn't sure it was true. Let people enjoy their art. What was the harm?

'And let them eat cake!' said Mariam. 'Listen, you need to understand,' and as she said this she was trimming her hair over the bathroom sink, wetting it with her fingers and then combing with her left hand to extend the curls and *snip*, a black curl fell and separated on the white porcelain, and addressing me in the mirror she went on to explain her theory, which she presented as truth, that when you read a novel about the occupation and feel understood, or watch a film and feel seen, your anger, which is like a wound, is dressed for a brief time and you can go on enduring, a bit more easily, and so time goes on running like an open faucet and each film at the cultural centre ends and we applaud as the credits roll with the list of crests of institutional donors like great European aristocratic families of old, and while there are moments in these concerts and poetry readings and lectures and plays when you might feel connected to the other people in the room, to the people behind the screen, you might feel a kind of flowering in the chest at this sight of your community's resistance embalmed in art, some beauty created out of despair, all of this means that in the end you, or at least the middle classes, are less likely to fight the fight because despair has been relieved, momentarily, and perhaps our *Hamlet* would be just another version of this narcotic and what, if anything, could we do about that?

I laughed. 'Fatigue stops people fighting. Not theatre.'

'Did you know that in the old days,' she went on, 'when Mustafa al-Kurd used to perform, the audience would leave the auditorium and immediately go out into the streets and demonstrate? Did you know that? That would never happen nowadays.'

Mariam was battling herself, I could see that. She didn't really think art was bad for resistance: she wanted me to supply the counter-argument, because the counter-argument was what she wanted to believe. She ran her finger around the sink to collect the black threads, washed them away, then reached robotically for the broom, with no emotion on her face as she swept the floor. Fundamentally this woman lacked frivolity: she was weighed down, she was too needed by her work, by politics, by motherhood. My lightness felt grotesque in comparison. I was even, by now, starting to detect in her a maternal sensitivity to me. That, for example, she knew and appreciated I had abandoned some pride by joining her play – which might mean that her reverence for my working life in the UK was, if not a performance, at least exaggerated to soothe my ego. It saddened me that she might think I required soothing. But perhaps I did require it.

Over the course of the week, we traded intimacies. I told her a little about my marriage – just the outline: how we'd met, what he did for a living, how long it lasted. And then she told me about hers.

Her ex-husband's name was Hazem. They met in America while he was visiting relatives in Michigan, and she was doing her MFA at SUNY Buffalo, in upstate New York. Her school friends had predicted that she would go away and stay away, but she was determined to prove them wrong, to bring what she learned back home with her and make art 'that meant something', rolling her eyes at herself when she said this, her irony a poor cover for her sincerity. Hazem visited an old friend of his in Buffalo and came to see a play she was in, by chance, he didn't usually like plays; every part of their meeting seemed balanced on chance, like the wind had blown everything a certain way, which, later, it would just as casually dismantle. Or so it sounded when she described it; I'm sure it didn't feel so wind-blown at the time. Hazem fell in love with her while she was on the stage playing the main part. Of course she was the main part, I thought; no one falls in love with a minor character. While she insisted that she came back to Palestine because of her convictions, it was easy to see the other narrative, which was that she returned for the sake of Hazem. Then the problems began.

She was the one with the freedoms. She was not earning much but still she came from a comfortable liberal family, and had grown up with the privileges of an Israeli passport among the Jewish majority in the north – citizenship rights, ease of movement, protection from certain kinds of violence – while Hazem, progressive as he claimed to be, educated as he was, enlightened as he was, had been raised and lived almost the entirety of his life in Hebron, the most besieged city of the West Bank, albeit, granted, outside the old city and out of range of the piss and trash the Israeli settlers threw down at the streets.

'The instability there is really something else,' she told me. 'It's not a place to raise a child. I mean, of course they raise children but if you have a choice – it's horrible. It's a constant battle, constant vigilance.'

She narrated the fallout of the marriage with long ellipses. 'I saw signs that first year in Hebron, I guess I chose to ignore . . . The truth is, once you're a certain way in, if you look behind you it seems too far to go back. So you ignore and hope you are mistaken. You keep swimming, you try not to think about drowning.'

On Friday we were supposed to leave Ramallah at 8 a.m. We left at half past with a bag of bread and a punnet of washed figs. Mariam was going to drop me at Haneen's. She had a funding meeting in Haifa to which she was bringing Wael and Ibrahim as representatives of the play. You're using me, said Ibrahim with the shadow of a smile. The morning was fresh, and as we curved round the highest points of the suburb I could see a bank of mist in the distance, a thick line of darker blue on the horizon, which resembled the sea. Mariam played Nancy Ajram quietly from her iPhone via Bluetooth; I, in the front passenger seat, ate a fig squashed inside a piece of bread, and Wael dozed in the seat behind me.

'Oh,' said Ibrahim. 'Shit.'

'What?' said Mariam.

Ibrahim was looking at his phone. 'Two Israeli guards were killed outside Al-Aqsa Mosque. An hour ago.'

'Oh my God,' said Mariam.

'Who did it?' I asked.

'Three Palestinians from inside. The Israelis are closing al-Haram al-Sharif.'

'Ay-ay-ay,' said Mariam. 'Be prepared for a long drive.'

One foreign national with an Arab name, two Palestinian citizens of Israel and one West Bank resident with a temporary permit sit in a car with yellow Israeli plates approaching a checkpoint. The line is sluggish: the soldiers are investigating every vehicle, regardless of the number-plate colour. Near the windowless tower, a shabby Israeli flag roils on the wind, looking not at all like those forlorn fraying Palestinian flags that, once illegal but now par for the course, adorn electricity pylons across Ramallah, but rather somehow eternal and careless, a mark of the ragged outposts of empire. Part of the checkpoint itself is surrounded by scaffolding, and the red plastic webbing around the base has broken down, the stick supports in the corners pointing at odd angles. A tap on the driver's window: a slender soldier bends over wearing a very large green helmet like an upside-down basket. He has blond eyelashes. A typical rigmarole of identification cards and passports ensues, conducted in Hebrew with the driver. Then the soldier points at the youngest of the men, the West Bank resident, sitting in the back. Hebrew switches to Arabic. The soldier tells him to get out of the car.

'I have a permit,' says the young man.

'He has a permit,' repeats the woman driving.

Another soldier appears on the other side of the car. He opens the rear door and orders the young man out; the threat has materialised so quickly, unspoken, that if he does not comply they will force him out. Wael gets out. The soldiers escort him into the building at the checkpoint.

As they are passing through the doorway, the blond soldier taps him on the back of the head, and Wael's shoulders flinch into an automatic hunch. It is as though the scene is playing on a roll of film, which from this frame onward has been bleached.

I was hardly aware of my body as I thrust my door open. I only knew my vision filled with white. And now I was outside, and the morning air was cool on my face and hands. Propelled by an alien force I marched over the uneven, untended terrain that preceded the checkpoint, the rubble and trash and random horizontal blocks of concrete, towards another soldier now standing to attention with his gun ready. Dimly conscious that Mariam and Ibrahim were shouting at me from the car windows, *Come back, Sonia, come back*, the crucial thought swooped through my mind that the soldier might suspect I had a knife, a suspicion I knew was grounds for shooting to kill, and although my ability to pass as a foreigner might offer me some protection I nevertheless dropped my pace and lifted my arms to make clear that my hands were empty. Rage was making me vibrate. Strangely, as I neared him, the soldier turned to one side, as if to ignore me, except that his hands were on his weapon and he looked ready to use it. He was young, probably eighteen or nineteen. Perhaps he didn't know how to respond to this situation, the approach of a possibly raving woman in white linen trousers and Converse sneakers. He spoke rapidly into his walkie-talkie. Oh God, what am I doing? I thought, and then I said loudly in English: 'Where have you taken my son?' My voice came from somewhere other than my mouth, somewhere further away.

The soldier gave me a confused, human look, while the walkie-talkie, which he was holding by his face, emitted a stream of Hebrew.

'Your son?'

'Where have you taken him?'

'Get back in your car.' In those five words it became clear to me that he had a British accent.

'Where are you from?' I asked.

'What?'

'You're English.'

'Show me your passport.'

'I left it in the car.'

'Go and get it.'

'Are you from Manchester?'

'Get me your passport, Madam.'

'What the hell are you doing here?'

'What am *I* doing here?'

Our exchange was splashing quite far outside the normal waterways of this scenario: soldier, civilian, military checkpoint.

'I can't believe you're from Manchester.'

'I'm not from Manchester, I'm from Leeds!' said the soldier. 'And I'm here defending my people. Now get back in the car.'

'*Defending.*' Disdain and outrage made me spit the word, compounded, I suppose, by the fact that he was about half my age.

'I'm being serious.' His voice was becoming gruffer but I could see he was warning me, that this being British had drawn an uncomfortable cord between us, to which he had already made an accidental concession by addressing me as though I were a human being. Backing down from that must have been a challenge; possibly it required a certain level of training. 'If you don't cooperate,' he said, 'they're going to be really tough on you.'

Now the blond soldier, the one who hit Wael on the back of his head, appeared from the booth. My exchange with the soldier from Leeds had affected me, too: my rage was losing its purity as the reality of the scene impressed itself upon me, the jostling of the guns on their belts and their ready fingers, jangling in my awareness, leaching me of courage. I am not sure it even deserves the name of courage; it was more like a temporary lunacy from which I was starting to sober, the fog lifting. I wobbled over the trash back to the car, still trembling but no longer from anger. The blond soldier followed a few paces behind.

'This is ridiculous,' I said, very Englishly, avoiding Mariam's eye as she scrolled down the window. I watched my hand shaking, extended before me. 'Passport,' I said. I was frightened of what would happen when they saw I was Arab. The soldier took it directly from Mariam's hand, bypassing mine.

'Get in the car,' he said.

I got in the car. We watched them lumber away in their bulky greens, walkie-talkies crackling.

'I'm sorry,' I said.

'What the *fuck* was that?' said Ibrahim.

I didn't respond. A terrible fast lightness had taken over my body, like the wheeling of the wind around an empty fireplace. We waited about an hour. Cars passed us, were checked, went through.

'Here he comes,' said Mariam.

And there was Wael, and a soldier holding my passport and his ID. Once Wael was in the car, we drove off.

I turned round in my seat.

'Are you all right? Did they do anything to you in there?'

Something cracked in my chest. Everything in Wael's face was slightly creased and he was unable to look at me directly. At the same time, he seemed not to know where else to put his gaze, so his eyes shifted back and forth, up and down, like a dog's. I knew this look. I had seen it on the face of a defendant when I was doing jury service for a robbery case, the young man standing in the booth in white shirt and blue tie, hair combed and parted, listening to the verdict before an audience of strangers, lawyers and jurors. It was an expression of defeat, and of shame. I have never seen this expression on a woman's face.

We sat in silence the rest of the way. I tried not to think about Ibrahim, and instead compared, in a detached way, my personal terror at being punished as a foreign national with Wael's very real position of risk. To soothe myself, I replayed the scene three or four times in my head, altering the ending each time until I had achieved a perfect fantasy, in which Wael demonstrated to the soldiers who he was by standing there at the checkpoint, raising his arms, and breaking into song.

10

Two hours later, we entered the outskirts of Haifa, in the industrial quiet of a Friday noontime, a little while before the start of Shabbat. The concrete buildings here, however tall, always appeared squat, topped with the round grey petals of rooftop satellites, stroked by shaggy palms, and the granary rose before the water like a gigantic windowless castle, replete with turrets, constructed with irrational proportions as if from a child's drawing. As we wound our way towards Mount Carmel, everyone in the car long having retreated into his or her own thoughts, I watched the city's vistas appear and vanish with an alert melancholy that reminded me of the day I arrived, more than three weeks ago. I thanked Mariam as she pulled up outside the car park, noticed that she looked pale and thoughtful, and then I waved at the others, who both waved back. I straightened up and crossed the tarmac.

'What's wrong? You look like you've seen a ghost.'

Haneen opened the door in a silk shirt with a multicoloured pattern of stripes and dots.

'It was a bad journey,' I said, dropping my bag off my shoulder like a child returning from school. 'I hate Israel.'

'Welcome home.'

I kept it vague. Haneen would be angry about my outburst so I only said they detained Wael for a while, and then segued into general dismay at the shutting of the mosque compound, the first time it had been shut since the second intifada, meanwhile suggesting we have wine with lunch. She agreed to the wine with enthusiasm and then, while we were eating, recited the names of three young men from Birzeit who were arrested last week 'as a preventative measure' on suspicion of planning to organise demonstrations against the killing of the young man named Nidal in Jerusalem. The soldiers came and took them from the university campus.

'Suspicion of planning to organise,' I repeated, tearing a piece of bread. 'How did they know? From Facebook?'

'Or there might be a collaborator at the university.'

We'd heard nothing of this in Ramallah, which seemed strange, since Birzeit was only a twenty-minute drive away. Haneen made a passing reference to 'The Ramallah Bubble'.

'We're all in our bubbles.'

'Sure, though that's not really what they mean by it.'

'Who is *they*?'

She hesitated. 'People, I guess.'

After lunch I ran a bath. I lay facing the toilet, my knees bent, the rubber anti-slip webbing beneath my feet. The steam heightened my wooziness from the wine and heavy food. Since we started rehearsals I'd been eating half-heartedly, alienated from my hunger. I didn't want to lose weight, though; whenever I did my nose got bigger and I quickly looked older. With the toes of my right foot I worked the hot tap for a few seconds, felt the flood of heat at my ankles, then played row-your-boat to spread it evenly around the bath.

I thought about Rashid, and wondered whether, refusing food, he had kept track of the hours, the days. Did the days and nights eventually blur, the movement of the sun blocked by the abat-jours? He had seemed ageless in the dim light of that small room, young and old at once. I thought of anorexic girls whose puberty has stalled, leaving them crossed between elderly ladies and overburdened children with false smiles, apparently perfect, teeth unstained, until their organs began to fail. A blue glow on the wall tiles: my phone screen was flaring. I wiped my hands on the bath towel and tapped it open.

Ibrahim

Today 15:05

hey

you ok?

A bit worn out but all right

How is Wael?

me too

he seems fine

Did you have your meeting?

not yet

tomorrow

want to get a drink later

Sure. Where shall we meet?

masada st 8pm

i can pick you up

Cool. I'll walk. See you there

'Sonia, are you still in there?'

'Yes.' I dropped the phone onto the bath mat and sank my hands back into the water with a sigh of pleasure. 'I think I'm taking the first bath this bathroom has ever seen.'

'Can you tell me if there's anything in the laundry basket?'

The basket stood in the opposite corner, beside the basin.

'Now?'

'Can you just be helpful please?'

'I'm in the bath.'

Nevertheless I stood and padded, dripping and cooling, across the mat.

'Yeah, there's some stuff. Some socks, some black stuff.'

'Okay.' Pause. 'I'll wait then.'

I inserted one leg and then my whole body back into the heat.

'Han?'

'Yes.' Her voice was close: she was still standing on the other side of the door.

'Why did you never tell me that Rashid died?'

'Who is Rashid?'

'Come on. The boy we came to see with Jad when we were teenagers. The hunger striker.'

I heard the door open, and sat up so I could turn round. She was lit from behind by the sofa lamp and leaning on one hip, chewing the inside of her cheek. For a full second her eyes bored into mine. Haneen had this way of staring straight at you without any self-consciousness, which I think some people mistook for intense engagement, but I, knowing her well, knew she was not really looking at me. I predicted she would deny knowledge of the death, or knowledge of my not-knowing. Then she said: 'I called Uncle Jad and asked him. I don't know why I didn't tell you.'

'Right. But you told Mariam.'

She continued to stare. Again I imagined she would make an excuse, and argue that, for example, she had only told Mariam many years later, and that she hadn't intended to exclude me.

'I'm sorry,' she said.

And with that we had drawn into the room the long frail story of our sisterhood, and all the petty crimes committed, the crosshatching of intention and advantage and betrayal.

'I didn't think—' She dropped the thought. 'I don't know.'

She had been about to say: *I didn't think you would care.* My anger glowed softly; I drew warmth from it.

'We can talk about it if you want,' she said.

'Tomorrow,' I said, twisting back round. 'I'm going out tonight.' I sank my body down the length of the bath and dipped the back of my head. As I slid back up I heard her say, over the crashing water: 'Oh. Okay.'

She was injured. But I would not invite her for the drink. I wanted to be cruel, and I also wanted to be alone with Ibrahim. Haneen shut the door and I returned, comfortably indignant, to my reverie, and closed my eyes, and my thoughts leaked and merged. I avoided thinking of Rashid, and thought instead of people who had died in baths. Saint Cecilia. Jean-Paul Marat. Agamemnon. I remembered a newspaper story about a man who fell asleep and drowned and was discovered by his child who broke down the bathroom door with a chair. My mother used to warn us not to fall asleep in the bath, which made me afraid, but more of the embarrassment of being discovered without my clothes on than of actually dying. The bath-water cooled and my fingertips wrinkled, turning white.

Ibrahim brought two beers to our table outside a bar on a small winding street that I'd frequented during my first week in Haifa, and which, Ibrahim explained, was a centre of Arab nightlife in the city, hosting a handful of café-cum-bars in which everyone seemed to know each other, and many of the men had dreadlocks, and Ibrahim and I were at least ten years older than everyone else. There was even an article about it in the *New York Times*, he was saying as I watched a tattered kitten investigating the wheels of a car on the other side of the street.

'So, yeah, anyway, I did some pretty crazy shit,' he whispered.

He had started telling me almost apropos of nothing about his involvement in the second intifada. We were now speaking in English, which he had initiated. I wondered if that was because of the subject matter and the risk of being overheard.

He was sitting beside me, his bald head golden in the half-light. He leaned closer over his beer, and hunched, looking up at me.

'I'm not like that any more, though. It was really dangerous, with my passport. They made this policy that if you're a citizen you'll get much longer in jail than if you're from the West Bank.'

'But at least you'd be in a civilian jail.'

'Well, yeah.' He looked as though he hadn't thought of that. 'I suppose that's true.'

'What kind of things did you do?'

'The usual shit. Preparing for operations. Carrying them out.'

I nodded, alert to the violence this implied. I looked at his bony wrists, one of them dangling a silver chain, and wondered if he'd ever killed anyone. 'And they never found out?'

'Of course not. If they had I wouldn't be here.'

In that case, he was running a large risk in telling me. I felt sure he was exaggerating his involvement. I'd assumed that he asked me for a drink primarily to make up for getting shirty with me earlier in the car. As he continued talking this idea was displaced by a sense that he'd been impressed by my anger at the checkpoint, and wanted to impress me in return.

'This stuff at Al-Aqsa, though,' he went on. 'It's not the way. The time for fighting with guns is over.'

'Right. It's the time for acting.'

'Acting, yes,' he said. 'In English it is a nice play on words.' A belated smile burst forth, full of teeth. 'Sometimes a play is like an operation from the old days.' He continued to grin, now I was the one being teased; he gulped some beer and set the glass down clumsily so that the table rocked on the uneven paving stones. 'You plan it, there's a script, but you never totally know how it's going to go. It's there, it's gone. It's like a firework.'

'It's like a play until it's not like a play,' I said.

He wiggled his eyebrows.

'Until someone gets hurt,' I said.

'Perhaps you don't know this, my dear, but theatre can be very dangerous.'

A group of young women on a pair of conjoined tables next to us erupted into laughter. Ibrahim switched to Arabic.

'Tell me about yourself. Why you became an actress.'

'We haven't finished with you yet.' I did not feel like talking about myself. More importantly, this was the first time since the read-through that we'd been alone, and only now that it was being satisfied did I realise how strong my curiosity about him had grown. 'When was your personal *awakening*?' I asked, emphasising this slightly formal word.

'Politically?'

'Yes.'

He stretched his arms behind his head and leaned away.

'My grandfather on my mother's side. He was in the resistance in nineteen forty-eight. We're from a village near Nazareth, originally.'

'It goes way back.'

'Yeah. And then I did my Masters in the West Bank, actually. So that was probably where I . . . where I woke up. Although the mid-nineties, or late-nineties, I guess, it was an optimistic time in some ways, you might remember. But I was pretty awake already, when I think about it. It's hard to know really, looking back, because most other kids my age didn't have parents like mine, maybe they didn't know or didn't think about or talk about all this at home. Remember there's also a fear of collaborators inside. There were a lot when I was young. You're not free to talk, you have to be cautious.'

'I don't think we knew much about collaborators,' I said.

I thought of my father, the cagey drop in his voice, the way he slouched out of rooms mid-conversation. When we were kids he would insist on spending summers here, yet while here he became even quieter than he was in London. I had always thought it was an effect of the family's force field, to make him shy and avoidant. But I supposed there may have been other, larger reasons.

'Usually you can tell who they are,' said Ibrahim. 'Someone gets a promotion he didn't deserve, or suddenly has a lot of money and a new house. They say all the informants from the West Bank get retired to Jaffa. It's shameful.' He was speaking English again but with some smaller words of Arabic mixed in, mostly the sentence ligaments and exclamations, *shame, usually, they say, someone*. 'There used to be whole families who informed for the Israelis, like a family business. I don't know if they use them very much any more, the Israelis, they probably don't need to, their control is so total, everything is electronic. Our backs have been broken. You know that, right? You know they've won.'

'If they'd won they wouldn't need to keep bludgeoning the Palestinians. We haven't won but it doesn't exactly look like they've won either.'

I was pleased with the coherence of this statement. Ibrahim seemed annoyed that I'd interrupted his monologue.

'And then,' he looked right at me, 'there was this other thing that happened, when I was in my twenties. A protest in the north. They killed thirteen of us. Palestinian citizens of Israel.'

'I remember that.' I did: the year 2000, the beginning of the second intifada. Footage of a twelve-year-old boy killed in the cross-fire in Gaza was playing again and again on the television, the Israeli army were killing Palestinian protestors in Jerusalem, and when villagers in the Muthalath demonstrated in solidarity they were put down as violently by the police as if they were occupied West Bankers and not citizens of the Israeli state. It was a reminder that Palestinians 'inside' were far from untouchable.

'Three from Nazareth. One guy I knew really well. He was my friend. We went to the same school. He went out on the first day and a sniper killed him.'

The girls at the next table started to sing 'Happy Birthday'. Ibrahim rolled a cigarette, stuffing it so full of tobacco that threads protruded from the end. He held his lighter under the tuft until the flame reached the paper. I thought of hay bales burning in fields. Neither of us had mentioned the incident at the checkpoint but it lay beneath everything we said.

'For me and Haneen it was the first intifada,' I told him. 'That was what woke us up. More her than me, though.'

'You seem awake.'

'I think I'm pretty sleepy in comparison with my sister.'

He smiled. I could see he found me cute. The barman, a slight man with a copious beard, started wiping a vacated table, and Ibrahim waved his arm for attention and ordered two more beers. I would have preferred a shorter drink but I didn't want to correct him. The alcohol was clinging delicately to the inside of my head, trimming my awareness of myself and my surroundings.

'I was a ballet dancer first,' I said. 'When I was a child.'

'Is that right?'

'Then I started acting.'

'You miss dancing?'

'Sometimes. You have to be very disciplined to dance. It can be negative when you're young.'

'Really?'

'You're a human being trying to be a straight line. At least with the kind I was doing. It's good training, I'm glad I did it, but I think acting is better. You don't have to subjugate the body so much.'

As I was speaking, the beers arrived. Ibrahim gave the barman a masculine nod and then, returning his attention to me, widened his eyes. 'Wow,' he said. I wondered, too late, if the word *subjugate* was a bit extreme. 'That's intense.'

We finished our drinks; it was almost midnight. He would drive me home. On the way to his car, I glanced at the line of bars on our right, where people were smoking and settling up. The road dipped and abruptly we saw the sea ahead of us, black and silky.

'This country is really tiny,' I said.

'Yes.'

'How long to drive from top to bottom, do you think? Golan to the Naqab.'

'I mean—'

'Without checkpoints. In a perfect world.'

'I don't know. Six hours, maybe.'

And yet this tiny place occupied such varied terrain – desert, sea, mountains – and such a large space in the global mind. As we walked I thought about Amin, who enumerated his family members imprisoned or detained so frequently I sometimes wondered if he was jealous of them, and at the same time I sensed that his arrogance was undercut by a fear of being forgotten, of languishing in jail without the world's attention, when one of the only things that might make it all worthwhile in the absence of actual liberation was the possibility of impressing someone later, a journalist or a weaker man or an attractive woman. Meanwhile, the world, so far as one tended to call mainstream western media 'the world', remained at least more concerned with the Palestinian cause and Israeli exceptionalism than, for instance, Yemen, which no one seemed to want to talk about, and here we were in the centre of Haifa's nightlife and it was an alleyway, a lane, with four bars-slash-cafés, and this was worthy of a write-up in the *New York Times* about the cultural renaissance of the city among the Palestinian middle classes. Palestinians in search of an audience had become comparatively good at finding one.

The lock on the passenger door was broken on the outside so he had to push it open from the driver's seat. When he did not start the engine immediately, I knew he wanted to kiss me. His seat creaked. I tipped my head to encourage him. At a comic delay he met my eyes. And then his breath was on my face, and although I'd noted his lips were large and smooth I hadn't expected them to be quite so soft. He didn't open his mouth at first, and then he did but only slightly before drawing away and starting the car. Neither of us spoke. I watched the dim buildings under the street lights. We stopped outside an apartment block on a boulevard near the Baha'i Garden.

'I didn't even ask you if you wanted to come,' he said.

'That's okay,' I said. 'I wanted to come.'

He led me by the hand as we climbed the stairs, which began outside and then without any transitioning threshold became indoor stairs. My thighs ached. Finally he stopped and unlocked a door. It was a small apartment, the sofa was in the kitchen, a window above it showed a fat crescent moon, stark in the darkness. There were two posters on the walls, an illustrated Abdel Halim Hafez with white teeth and a copy of the ubiquitous VISIT PALESTINE poster from the thirties, in which a silhouetted olive tree frames a view of Jerusalem. Both struck me as evidence of a touchingly clichéd taste, as though I had glimpsed some childish part of him. I asked about the lights, and he whispered: 'Wael,' shaking his head and leading me to the sofa. He reached up and held my face in both palms, and then we were bending our knees and sinking. In place, he jerked away.

'Do you think Mariam will be able to tell?'

I was surprised how much this question stung me. 'Tell what? That we kissed?' I asked, with haughty comedy. The warmth in my chest was turning cold. I wondered if this was, in fact, a terrible idea. I let him kiss me again and then said: 'I should go.' And stood up.

'Really?' Disbelief forced his voice out of a whisper into a speaking tone.

'Yeah, my sister. Wael. You know. Thank you, though.'

I approached the front door, trying to be casual. The beers were ruining my act, it was hitting me at a lag that it didn't make any sense to say I wanted to come to his house and then announce my departure within five minutes. My tiredness was hurting.

'Please stay,' he said. 'It's one in the morning.' The moon stared in. His body looked lonely on the sofa. 'I'll drive you if you want, but it's better if you stay. We can just sleep. I'll sleep out here, you take the bedroom. I'd offer my spare room but unfortunately I have a celebrity guest.'

Within minutes we were both in his bedroom. He did not turn on the lights in there either. It was easier not to think in the dark.

None of the stages of undressing, touching, being touched particularly thrilled me, although my body was responding normally. I'm sure the alcohol was to blame. Once he was inside me I returned to myself, and soon I was saying Oh repeatedly, until he put his fingers in my mouth.

I slept quickly and when I woke it was still dark. Ibrahim's breathing told me he was awake. I turned over.

'What?' he murmured, so close to my ear that I shivered from the warmth.

I knew he meant, What are you thinking. I didn't respond.

'I want your skin so much,' he said.

'That's not creepy.'

'Your freckles. Don't make me laugh.'

'I don't have many freckles.'

'There's one here.'

'Stop it. I'm chilly.'

His smell was all over me. Dark varnished wood, red berries. I plunged my hands under the duvet and laughed when he yelped at my cold fingers. Then I put them under my armpits to warm them up, and he wrapped a leg over me to do the same with the rest of my body. I liked the pretence of wrapping ourselves around each other for this purely practical reason. I nestled against his chest. He had sparse silky hair on the top part only and there was a dip before his belly.

'That first day,' I whispered. 'When we were in the theatre.'

'Yes.' He lifted himself on an elbow and looked into my eyes, as though he had been waiting for me to bring this up. 'I'm sorry about that.'

'You don't have to be sorry.'

'I think I was just embarrassed.'

'Why?'

'I don't know . . .' He rubbed his head. 'It was all quite fast.'

'Anyway, I knew it was you.'

'What do you mean?'

I changed to English. 'In the dark, in the wings.'

'The wings?'

'You came up behind me.'

'Oh, no, I was talking about being cool with you that day.'

'Oh. Well, there was someone in the theatre who came very close to me during the blackout. I thought it was . . .'

We both fell silent. I dozed, absorbing the information. After a few minutes, his body became too warm. I stuck a leg out of the cover for the cold air.

'You seem restless.'

'I think there's a lump in the mattress.'

'I mean in general.'

'To be honest, I'm slightly disturbed about the guy in the theatre now. Who do you think it was?'

'One of the staff? Maybe it was Amin, or one of the others.'

He dismantled this concern so easily I was forced to face what was actually bothering me.

'I'm not sure I understand why you needed to be cool with me,' I said offhandedly.

A laugh came from his chest. 'But you didn't even notice!' he said, picking up my hand.

He began to tickle my palm. The very concept of this gesture irritated me. I struggled with the temptation to pull my hand away and wipe it on the cover, struck once more that I may have made an awful mistake. The remaining weeks of rehearsals and performances unrolled before me like a carpet, upon which I would have to tread cautiously, keeping my distance from him. Everyone would guess what had happened anyway. With a thrill of panic I wondered what Mariam was going to say.

'Are you subletting your place in London?' he said.

'I own it,' I said with force, to convey how irrelevant the question was. 'It's the one sensible thing I've ever done.' The sensible thing, actually, was getting possession of the flat after my divorce, but it was better to sound as though I'd bought it myself. 'I don't really like the idea of someone else in my space. Anyway, I should get going.' Finally I pulled my hand away.

'You're actually getting up?'

'Why is it so cold in here?' I said, standing, lifting the bottom edge of the duvet in search of my underwear.

'Sonia, calm down, honey, it's okay. You're really restless.'

'Can you stop saying that? It's very objectifying.'

'What!' His left eye convulsed shut. He laughed ecstatically. 'You are ban*anas*.' He sighed and sat up against the headboard, arms folded. 'At least put some clothes on.'

'What do you think I'm trying to do?'

I bit the insides of my cheeks. I didn't feel like laughing. The room brightened: he'd switched on the lamp. My shirt and a sock were on the floor but not my knickers. I stood straight and faced him, one hand sarcastically on my hip, the other on the back of his desk chair. I knew exactly what he saw when he looked at me: my childless waist, my low-hanging breasts, my clear ribs, curved belly, sturdy thighs.

'Are you worried?' he asked in Arabic, and a sombre note entered his voice.

'I don't really know what I'm doing.' I dropped my hand as my body went slack. It was a relief to speak honestly.

'I'm not an idiot,' he said. 'If that's what's worrying you.'

When I lay down again, he put his fingers in my hair and wrapped me in the duvet. Within a few breaths I had warmed up, and then I was asleep. I opened my eyes to the sunrise and a sweaty but not unpleasant smell from Ibrahim's armpit. I waited for the sky to turn blue before slipping out of the bed. My clothes were easy to find in the daylight. I dressed in the hall and left before either Ibrahim or Wael was awake.

II

Sunday. Balcony at Mariam's apartment in Haifa. SONIA is standing by the railing with a view of the sea. The day is overcast. Hearing footsteps, she looks up to see WAEL coming out to join her.

SONIA   (*In Arabic.*) How are you doing?

WAEL   I'm okay.

SONIA   The funding meeting was all right?

WAEL   Inshallah.

     Pause.

SONIA   (*In English.*) That was really shit. What happened at the checkpoint the other day. I'm sorry.

     WAEL shrugs and screws up his face into a dismissive expression that says: It's fine. The shrug and the expression somehow cancel each other out. Sound of shouting in the street below.

SONIA   Nice to see the sea, uh?

WAEL   Yeah. If only we had this in the West Bank.

SONIA   Could do with some more space over there.

WAEL   You know what, I think you're right. Yalla, let's talk with the Israelis. We'll do a deal. Sort something out.

     SONIA laughs.

WAEL   Do you remember that story? About that guy in the West Bank who couldn't swim?

SONIA   No, I don't know it.

WAEL   There was this guy who couldn't get a permit, his parents were refugees from Jaffa, or Haifa, or I can't remember where. He kept applying for a permit and they wouldn't give it to him. And he wanted so badly to see the sea, probably his ancestors were sailors or fishermen or something. Then finally he married a girl from his camp, and the moment he got married the permit came from the Israelis almost straightaway, and then he went to Jaffa and swam in the sea, finally. And the first time he swam in the sea he drowned, because he never learned how to swim.

SONIA   That's awful. What an awful story.

WAEL   Yeah, it is.

SONIA   Who was he?

WAEL   I can't remember, actually.

SONIA   You just heard it from someone.

WAEL   Yeah. Or maybe I saw it in a movie, I can't remember.

WAEL *turns to lean back against the railing, facing the house.*

WAEL   I guess every family has a Nakba story.

SONIA   Right.

WAEL   I mean, you must do.

SONIA   I'm not sure.

IBRAHIM *appears in the balcony doorway, carrying a kitchen chair. He places it by the wall facing the view. MARIAM and HANEEN appear one after the other, also carrying chairs, which they arrange in a row. MARIAM returns with a fourth chair for SONIA and WAEL, in case they need it.*

MARIAM   I know it's bright out here, but imagine it's dark, the closet is dark.

WAEL *goes inside, stands at the threshold of the balcony door.*

MARIAM   (*Arabic.*) Are we ready? Take a breath. In. (*Pause.*) And out. (*Pause.*) I hear him coming.

Enter WAEL.

WAEL	How, Mother, what's the matter?
SONIA	Hamlet, you have your father much offended.
WAEL	Mother, you have my father much offended.
SONIA	You answer with a tongue of idleness and nonsense.
WAEL	You question with a tongue of idleness and nonsense.
SONIA	What's the matter with you, Hamlet?
WAEL	Oh, what's the problem now?
SONIA	Have you forgotten me?
WAEL	No by the cross I did not forget you. You are the Queen, your husband's brother's wife, would that you were not. You are my mother.
SONIA	Then it is best if I put to you someone who can speak.
WAEL	Calm yourself and sit down, do not budge. You will not go until I set up a mirror for you where you may see the deepest depth of yourself.
SONIA	What is it you wish to do? Will you kill me?
MARIAM	Okay and that's when Faris comes in. I like what you did just then with your face, Sonia. Keep going.
SONIA	Help, help!

WAEL *wields an imaginary sword and, deciding quickly, plunges it into* IBRAHIM's *side.*

IBRAHIM	(*From where he sits beside Haneen, doubling over.*) Ah! Help, help!
WAEL	What is this, a rat? Dead, dead, by a dirham.
IBRAHIM	Yes, I'm dead.
MARIAM	(*Whispering, prompting.*) He's killed me.
IBRAHIM	Yes, he's killed me.
SONIA	Oh woe is this, what have you done?
WAEL	I don't know. Is it the King?
SONIA	Oh what a rash and bloody deed!
MARIAM	Mm.

WAEL	A bloody deed – almost as bad, good Mother, as kill a king and marry with his brother.
SONIA	(*Brief pause. In a low voice.*) Kill a king?
WAEL	Indeed, lady, that is my word. You wretched, rash . . . uh.
MARIAM	Wretched rash intruding fool.
WAEL	Wretched rash intruding fool, farewell.
MARIAM	Take a breath. Let's stop it there. We'll run it from the top. This time, okay, I want you to feel less bound by the words. Try to think *through* the words. I want to see your intentions hitting each other

(*Making hand gestures, searching for her metaphor.*)

like arrows, I want you to aim, Wael. What are you doing with those words? Think. I want to tell you that Hamlet, for me, is one of the cruellest characters in Shakespeare, or ever really. Because of him, his girlfriend commits suicide. Think about it. You kill her father, and then she kills herself. You have something really vicious inside you. Something nasty. And what it really is, I think, is your hatred towards yourself turned outwards. All the bad feelings, all the venom, are spat outwards at the women. Gertrude calls your words daggers because that's what they are, they are knives, they are punches in the face. You are punching your mother in the face. How much poison must a man have inside him to punch a woman in the face like that?

WAEL *looks upset.*

IBRAHIM	You're not giving him much space for his own interpretation.
MARIAM	Ibrahim.
IBRAHIM	Sorry.

Closet Scene, again. This time with more movement and more emotion. SONIA uses the chair to protect herself from WAEL. WAEL repeatedly, aggressively, moves it aside.

SONIA	Kill a king?
WAEL	Yes, lady, that was my word. Wretched, rash, intruding, fool – farewell.

Pause. SONIA and WAEL turn to MARIAM to see the effect.

MARIAM	Good.
HANEEN	That was *excellent*, guys. Really excellent.
MARIAM	Okay. I want to try something else.
IBRAHIM	Are you saying that as Sonia's sister or as an objective observer?
SONIA	Please, Haneen has never flattered me.
MARIAM	Haneen is a truth teller,
SONIA	Some of the time.
MARIAM	that's why we're friends. Okay so we're going to do the next part of the scene just after Hamlet kills Polonius but missing out Wael's side of the dialogue, so Wael you just stand there and don't speak. Don't act or do anything with your face either. Sonia, you know them well enough now, go through his speeches in your head and leave as much time as you think they need. It's important not to rush. It won't be exact but do your best. The point is: respond to what you are hearing.
SONIA	Right. (*Pause.*) Okay. Shall I start?
MARIAM	We need Ibrahim to finish his cigarette, it's distracting me.
IBRAHIM	(*Stubbing his cigarette out in an ashtray.*) I'm finished.
MARIAM	Great. Ready, Sonia? We'll stop at Enter Ghost.
SONIA	Ready.

Everyone watches SONIA. At first she is tense, standing silently before WAEL. Sounds: birdsong, traffic, the sea, music from a passing car. Gradually, she relaxes. Fear appears on her face.

SONIA   What

SONIA   What have I done

SONIA   What have I done that you can dare to fire your tongue
          against me with this insolence?

SONIA   Oh—

SONIA   Oh, what act is this that roars so loud and thunders in
          the index?

SONIA   By God that's enough, Hamlet,
                you are turning my eyes into the depths of my soul
                and I see spots there so deep and black
                their colour will not dissolve

SONIA   Enough – enough – your words are stabbing my ears like
                daggers – no more, my sweet, Hamlet, please

SONIA   No more, no more

| MARIAM | Enter Ghost. |

Silence.

WAEL	Wow.
HANEEN	Very good.
IBRAHIM	That was excellent.
MARIAM	Sonia, you okay?
SONIA	Yeah, I'm fine.
MARIAM	How did that feel?
SONIA	Good.
MARIAM	Here's a tissue.
SONIA	Thanks.
IBRAHIM	That was something, really.
MARIAM	Do you guys mind going inside for a moment, so we can talk in private?
IBRAHIM	Sure, yeah, no problem.
HANEEN	That's fine.
MARIAM	You as well, Wael, inside.

HANEEN, IBRAHIM *and* WAEL *step inside the house, leaving* MARIAM *and* SONIA *alone on the balcony.*

MARIAM	Sonia.
SONIA	Yes.
MARIAM	Whatever you were thinking about just then. I'm not going to ask what it was. But I want you to think about it every time we do that scene.
SONIA	Right.
MARIAM	It's okay if I ask you that?
SONIA	Yeah, of course.
MARIAM	Sure?
SONIA	Sure.

We did the scene once more, putting Wael's lines back in. My emotion was still rolling inside me but I reduced my shaking to a tremor.

I wept properly and continued to hear, instead of Wael's actual spoken lines, the ghosts of the lines that had come to life in my head. Mariam was right: the attention I'd been paying to his performance had been interfering with my own. Once she cancelled him out and left me to converse with his silence I could feel the contrast. My first words, *What have I done?*, spoken in that vacuum, under the bright sun, with the sea behind me and my sister and a man who might become my lover before me, unleashed a fear that reared up inside me like a flame, protected from rage by the thinnest of membranes.

Mariam was wrong, however, to assume I was imagining something in particular. I was skilled enough by now to access feelings when I needed them, to manipulate without emotional cost the material of my self. She instructed Wael to recall the dark stillness he'd achieved in Ramallah – she didn't say, Think of the soldiers, but they must have been on his mind. His voice remained stuck in the same high register, alternating between a few repeated tones, but Mariam's face at the end declared we'd done well, and her terminating words, *Enter Ghost*, were uttered with a triumphant smile at Haneen, and as everyone fell from their positions into the ratty chatter of intermission, she disappeared inside to make coffee. Returning with cups on a tiled tray she announced: Take the afternoon to yourselves before the drive back. She said this to everyone, but we knew it was for Wael, for whom, as a West Bank ID holder, even a famous one, a few hours 'inside' was not an occasion to be taken lightly.

I had lied to Wael. Of course there is a Nakba story in my family. I didn't hear it from my father, though; I first heard it from my aunts when I was eleven or twelve. Aunty Nadia did most of the narrating, Aunty Rima chipped in every so often or parroted her sister's words. We were on the veranda eating, or drinking tea, maybe. I remember it was a chilly evening and I was wrapped in a blanket.

On 22 April 1948, Teta Aida stands at an upstairs window, looking down at the street. She is holding my infant father and watching the crowd of people fleeing below, pushing in a sluggish panic down the alleyways towards the sea.

Unlike most of their neighbours, who left hours if not days ago, my grandparents have decided to stay in the house. They have had a rare premonition that if they leave they will not be able to come back. The militias have already taken the centre of the city. Haganah trucks are visible in the squares, driving Arabs by armed force down to the port. The Nasir house has not yet been commandeered by the Zionists. It will take years for this to become a source of pride, that despite everything that is about to happen they cling on, despite how frequently, repeatedly, their resolve will almost be broken. A miracle, they will say, kept it whole under the butts of the Zionists' guns. For four days my grandfather has been keeping vigil by the door, holding an old pistol. He is shivering with exhaustion.

Aida's eye lands on a couple in the crowd. The man carries a little girl; the woman, in a green dress and black headscarf, carries a bundled-up baby. Beyond the city, beside the oil refinery, boats jostle around the dock, loading with people and crawling away across the water.

The woman in green, who, like her, holds a baby, appears to Aida as another version of herself, a version that has decided to flee. This means that by watching the woman, waiting for her to disappear into the crowd, Aida is also waiting for the possibility to disappear that *she*, Aida, might flee, taking baby Nabil with her. Once the woman in the green dress has gone, it will be certain they are staying.

The woman in green stops walking. She is like a stone in a river, the crowd flows around her. In a single swift movement, she opens her arms and drops the baby onto the ground. Aida screams. She steps closer to the window. Her husband, my grandfather, runs to her side, expecting troops at the gate, seeing none. Down on the street, the man beside the woman in green snatches up the bundle as his wife collapses on the ground. He unravels it. In the second before the revelation, Aida understands what has happened. The man lets the blankets fall, lifting something white. It is not a baby. It is a pillow. He opens his mouth and pushes the pillow into his face as though he might devour it. His back is shaking.

'Did they go back for the baby?' we asked.

'She tried,' said Nadia. 'The crowd was too strong. Then the Haganah arrived and we don't know what happened.'

'We know what happened,' said Rima.

'You know what I mean,' said Nadia.

More than once after hearing this story as a child, I had climbed over the sofa and stood at the window where Teta stood, and even then I found it puzzling that the woman could really have mistaken her baby for a pillow. And also that Teta could have had so clear a view of the couple from that height and angle, such that she could see the precise goings-on of what they were and were not carrying, in the midst of hundreds of panicking refugees. But in the Nasir family, the story of the Nakba is the story of the woman in the green dress. And if the story was true, then was the child left behind killed? Or did the child live, as the child lived in the Kanafani story, adopted by a Jewish family and raised as a Jewish Israeli? And was the child a boy or a girl? And what shade was the child's skin, and how did that affect his or her life? And, in the event that the story was not true after all, then why had it come into being? Was it a parable Teta invented to prove to her children she'd made the right choice, staying with her baby and husband in their house? I'd had the sense that there were times, during the years under military rule, when they wondered whether it was a mistake to have stayed. Whether they should have left with the others and found another life, in exile, and let their house keys, carried with them, lose their function and turn into symbols. In the end, of course, they were glad. They did not have their country but at least they still had their home.

I had no particular reason to conceal this from Wael. Except I suppose there's a time and a place for every story, and maybe I just didn't feel like telling this one then.

Ibrahim gave me a pointed but indecipherable look as he followed Wael through the front door. They were going to drive up to Stella

Maris for a meal before heading to Ramallah in Ibrahim's car. Mariam, Haneen and I made a salad with what was left in Mariam's fridge, and carried the table onto the balcony. The apartment was small, with none of the character of her Ramallah house, although the arms of the sofa were worn and the shelves had books on them. When her brothers were in town they also stayed here, she said. Their parents lived nearby so it was ideal for when Emil came along. Of course, she said, they live right by your grandparents, their old house. We sat round the table and trapped the napkins under our plates.

'I have trouble looking at the sea, for some reason,' I announced.

'Nice at this time of day, though,' said my sister. She opened her mouth as she forked an oily wad of leaves and added, once her mouth was full, 'Not too bright,' wiping her lips.

'I think there's something about the blankness I find hard to look at. It's too big or something, it repels my eyes. When I go to the beach I'm always staring at the shore, looking for pebbles and shells and things. It's like my eyes can't handle how large it is.'

Mariam smiled in a way that made me feel ludicrous. 'I love the sea,' she said. 'Maybe that's because I grew up here.'

I wasn't sure if she intended this as a put-down. Haneen asked about the funding meeting.

'It went well, sort of. They liked us, they were impressed by Wael and Ibrahim, and by the idea of a global tour.'

'Global tour?' I said.

'They were all Europeans?' said Haneen.

'The problem with these European funders is they don't want to give directly to a group, it has to go through an institution, and we're not an institution. And even then there are conditions and criteria, you have to address particular themes, like, I don't know, women's issues or something, and you have to do x number of shows in x number of weeks. You lose your freedoms and it becomes very annoying.'

'What's that about a global tour?'

'NGOisation of the art world, basically,' said Haneen.

'Exactly, very patronising, signing things we don't want to sign. Don't worry,' she added, addressing me. 'It's hypothetical. Makes us seem more impressive to the funders. Oh no, don't do that,' she said as Haneen reached for our plates.

Haneen ignored her and carried them inside. As Mariam rose to follow, I put my hand on her hand.

'Can I ask a favour?'

'Of course.'

'I want to see my grandparents' house one more time before we leave.'

I did nothing beyond lower my voice but she understood. This suggested to me that our bond had overpowered her bond with my sister, even if only for the short term, for the duration of our play. We went inside to wash up and Mariam told Haneen we should get going back to Ramallah sooner rather than later, did she need a lift home? My sister seemed neither offended nor suspicious. On the way to the car, I looked at my phone.

Ibrahim
Today 17:43

hey

hope everything's ok

18:04

hope you're not angry

I slowed on the pavement to respond before I lost the Wi-Fi.

Of course not

Why would I be angry?

i don't know

i feel a bit stress

Everything's fine

We arrived at my sister's building within a couple of minutes. I stepped out of the car to hug her goodbye, struck by the softness of her small body, her narrow back under my arms. I promised to call more often, to return to Haifa on another weekend, or maybe she could visit us in Ramallah. Neither of us had brought up the death of Rashid since Friday. I sat in the front and Mariam indicated left uphill. At the end of an ordinary residential road, beside a large rubbish skip, two enormous wild boars stood side by side, chewing. I twisted round.

'Were those boars?'

'Probably,' said Mariam.

On its way down, the sun paused behind a cloud, and I started running through potential names and cover stories for whoever answered the door. *Hi, I'm so sorry to interrupt you, but my name is Anita. I thought your house was really beautiful so I just wanted to knock on the door and say hi. Hi, my name's Anita Waksman, I'm a journalist from something newspaper doing a piece about the old houses in this street, I wondered if I could ask you a few quick questions. From the* Guardian. *From the* Telegraph. *Hi, I'm Anita from* Haaretz. We pulled up, my feet hit the pavement, my stomach jumped. The car lock bleeped. By the intercom at the gate was a porcelain nameplate.

'You read Hebrew.'

'Albert Klein,' Mariam read aloud. 'Sounds like a doctor from the nineteen seventies.'

I squared down the intercom.

'You want me to ring?' she said, interpreting. 'They might get aggressive. Well, I guess it's not like you lost it in 'forty-eight, at least they don't have that to deal with.'

It wasn't dark yet but a light came on in the kitchen, startling us. We were enacting a Palestinian cliché: coming to see the house the family had lost. Although, as Mariam pointed out, my case did not quite fit that mould. I looked up at the building: I wanted to see it clearly, without any received sadness. I was no longer ashamed of having felt none when we drove past on my second night: my responses were genuine, they occurred independently of our national drama; I saw virtue in being true to myself, and to my shapeless inner turmoil. Or was that just another narrative I was spinning to comfort myself, in the face of what I lacked? In my sister's heyday as an angry grad student she was always accusing people of Western individualism at the expense of proper commitment to their community. She probably thought that about me, as someone whose bond to this community had been thinned out by distance and the disconnection of someone moderately traumatised as a child. That was probably why she never told me about Rashid. The window above the kitchen flooded with light, and then another next to that; Mariam and I stared up at the glowing honeycomb, and my eyes were drawn to the middle window where, as with X-ray vision, I observed the spot where the sofa had been, and conceivably still was, and where Teta had stood before she was Teta with my father in her arms, and I with my arms empty below was the woman in the green dress.

'Mariam,' said a man's voice behind us.

Mariam turned. 'Salim?'

A man stood behind us on the street. He was taller than he looked on TV.

'Oh my God! I didn't know you were in Haifa.'

'I didn't know you were here either,' said Salim, kissing his sister. 'I only came for the day. I'm going back to Jerusalem later.' He flashed me a smile and mouthed, *Hi*. His clean-shaven jowls and flattish nose gave him a soft bear-like look, which just saved him from being extremely handsome.

'Hello,' I said.

'Did you come by the flat?' said Mariam.

'No, I parked up by the beach and walked down to the house.' He pointed his thumb over his shoulder at the road behind him, where the Mansour family lived.

'I haven't had time to see them,' said Mariam. 'Are they okay? We came for a funding meeting, and then we had to rehearse.'

'They're fine. The meeting went well?'

'No,' she said. 'We're fucked.'

This was obviously quite different from the sentiment she'd been conveying to us back at the flat. I peered at her, then turned back to Salim.

'I'm Sonia.'

'Salim.' He shook my hand with his very large warm one. 'You're the sister. You don't look like her at all.'

'I am the sister,' I repeated. 'I'm so sorry about everything that's been happening to you.'

He shrugged, and made a 'What can you do?' expression. 'I remember when you were small.' He smiled again. 'Were you in the meeting?'

'Oh no. I'm just a freeloader.'

'The house,' said Mariam, pointing. 'It's the Nasir house.'

'Ah.' He looked up at the building. 'Ah, yes, of course. Albert Klein,' he added, reading the nameplate. 'You're going to tell them who you are?'

'I haven't decided.'

'It would be interesting to see who *they* are, at least,' said Mariam.

Salim looked down at me with a pitying expression. 'Your relatives did sell it, you know. So it's not really like—'

'I know, I know, it's not like—'

'Is there any news?' said Mariam.

'Oh, always. Life as normal.' Despite the jeans and sandals, he had the full and serious bearing of a politician, and his speech and gestures, even in his sister's presence, were a little too controlled to seem natural. 'We're working on a new campaign for the election. And now there's been this shooting.'

'We heard.'

'They're going to jump on this, the Israelis. They're going to use it to control the compound.'

'Disaster,' said Mariam.

'But it's so quiet here,' I said. I tried to think what not being quiet would consist of – bomb sirens, perhaps. Fighter planes, soldiers in the streets.

Salim looked like he was going to qualify this, but then he just said, 'Yes,' and shrugged. 'Listen, Mariam, don't worry about the money. We'll sort something. Whatever happens this won't affect the play, I promise.'

'At this point,' she said, jabbing her finger at him, 'if *you* do anything to help, they're going to fuck us all over.'

'Over my dead body,' said Salim in English.

'Ugh,' said Mariam, shutting her eyes. 'Please never say that.'

The front door opened. A man stepped out wearing a white T-shirt and long denim shorts. We fell into a creaturely silence, and I looked into Salim's eyes and he looked into mine as the man opened the gate, then closed it behind him. I waited for him to walk past so I could get a good look. He didn't walk past. I turned round.

The man was middle-aged, with round cheeks and pale irises. He began to address Salim in Hebrew. Nothing about his face gave any clues to what he was saying, and Salim's response was similarly enigmatic. The man's response to Salim's response involved a slightly raised voice and raised eyebrows.

'Okay, we're leaving,' said Mariam in English to me. 'We have to go.'

'Take your friends,' said the man, waving at me with an eerie smile, also in English. 'This is not a bar.'

'I know it's not,' I said. 'It's my house.'

'It's what?'

'This is my family's house. My dad grew up here.'

'Okay.' His expression was blank.

'I just . . .' I began, conscious that Salim, an important politician who repeatedly featured in the news, was standing right behind me. 'I just felt nostalgic. That's all.'

'Well, that's very nice. But you can keep your nostalgia quiet. Thank you.'

We watched him re-enter his house, and shut the door. I thought I heard him turn the key in the lock, but I may have imagined that. Mariam insisted on giving Salim a lift and as we walked to the car, something enormous scuffled in the bushes beside us.

'Haifa really has a problem with wild boar,' I said.

'Yes,' said Salim. 'It's chronic.'

Mariam started the engine. 'Keep your nostalgia quiet. I mean really fuck you.'

'I don't think I handled it particularly well.'

'You handled it fine,' said Salim.

'What was he saying?' I asked.

'He was just being an ass, telling us to get away from his property,' said Mariam. She took a right-hand turn onto a boulevard.

'If it was anywhere else, any other country,' I said, 'it just wouldn't be such a big deal. Would it?'

Neither of them responded. In the car park above the beach, Salim kissed his sister and touched my shoulder, said he was looking forward to the play. Mariam waited for his headlights to come on and glare down the cliff before reversing back onto the road.

'Is he close with Haneen?' I asked.

'Oh, yeah, very. She didn't tell you?'

'Yeah yeah,' I lied. 'She mentioned something.'

12

On the way back down to Ramallah, the Arabic radio said the Israeli army had again attempted to demolish the village in the Jordan Valley, where the activists had formed a ring around the generator, holding hands and singing. And not only the compound of Al-Aqsa but the entire Old City of Jerusalem had now been closed for two days. This was the first time in sixteen years that Muslims were barred from the mosque, and the Israelis were installing metal detectors at the entrance, a move that was already drawing ire across the Muslim world. The news broadcaster speculated that the attack on the guards that precipitated this came in response to Israeli settlers trying to take over the compound.

'Is that true?' I asked Mariam.

'Yes,' she said. 'Settlers went in there last month with the chief of police.'

A Jordanian girl, trying to enter the West Bank for a wedding, had been arrested at the Allenby Bridge and was being detained without trial.

'They keep calling her Jordanian,' said Mariam. 'It's like it's the only way to get international attention. They do something to one of us who has a foreign passport, suddenly that person's a foreigner. Guy comes over from the States to see his family, gets killed, immediately he's American not Palestinian. Killing a Palestinian is normal. Kill an American? God forbid.'

She switched on the Bluetooth with a jab of her thumb. The first song was an acoustic Bob Dylan. She raised the volume.

'I've made a decision about Gertrude,' I said.

'Oh?'

'I think she's not guilty. I mean, she doesn't know about the murder. She's still mourning her dead husband. But she's confused, trying to replace one man with another.'

'Right.'

'But then also I want a part of her to *suspect* Claudius. So she's sort of half-complicit. If that makes sense.'

'Yes, that makes sense. I like it.'

We listened to the music, and my mind wandered, and like a piece of mental flotsam that angry line in Wael's voice drifted across my thoughts, *I must like a whore unpack my heart with words*, and I considered what it meant, exactly, and whether it really had anything to do with being a whore. Mariam reduced the volume slightly.

'Sonia, I want to ask you a personal question.'

'Oh dear.'

'I've been trying to decide whether or not to ask you.'

Dylan was singing about an Italian poet.

'Ask.'

'Your part is very important to me.'

'Which part?'

'Gertrude.'

'Okay.' I waited. 'Is there something wrong with the way I'm playing her?'

'You're doing great. You're a talented actress.'

Nothing like an assertive compliment to let you know a criticism is on the way.

'The end of Act Four is still a bit stiff,' she said. 'I'm wondering if it has to do with the language.'

'Right.'

We had grown up with both languages. My first words were English, Haneen's were Arabic, but we also started lessons in formal Arabic when we were young because my father wanted to be sure we could read, not only talk. Unlike Haneen at a certain point I stopped making an effort to read things in Arabic, since nothing in my life required it, and then even the dialect became a language I only spoke regularly with my family. In English my thoughts were clearer and more complex, I knew the plays and the books. I was sure I dreamt in English, although Marco used to say I spoke in Arabic in my sleep.

'My mother's half Dutch,' I said, as if that explained anything.

'I know,' said Mariam. 'I was wondering about practising the willow tree speech in English to see if we can make it flow differently. What do you think?'

'Sure.' I couldn't pretend I wasn't put out by this. 'What exactly isn't working about it?'

'I guess,' she said, thinking, 'it feels distant. A bit, sort of, refined.'

'I suppose it's quite a complicated speech.'

'Have you ever wanted children?'

'Excuse me?'

'I'm sorry. I didn't mean to blurt that out.' She looked away from the road, at me. 'Motherhood is important in the play. I think it's a key element.'

I took a moment to assimilate the question. Actually, I'd predicted she would ask me about children at some point. I felt we'd come close to the topic several times. We streamed down the highway. The darkness lay over me like a blanket.

'You don't have to answer.'

'Oh no, I'm not sensitive about it.' And saying that I felt it was true, and that I didn't mind telling her. On some level I even wanted to. 'I'm just thinking.' I folded my arms and leaned back against the headrest. After a while, I began, and let instinct dictate what I should give her and what I should withhold.

When I reached the story of my second pregnancy, I noticed she'd lowered the volume of the music to a single bar above silence. I hesitated, thinking about playing Solange. I could hear the holes in my account while I was telling it, passages of silence and explanation and blame. She didn't press me for details and for a moment I wondered if she'd stopped listening. Or if I'd led her off into thoughts of her own separation from Hazem. We had passed the checkpoint and were entering Ramallah now, familiar streets rose around us, familiar pavements and buildings. I had a feeling of homecoming.

Even though I had wanted to tell her, by the time we reached the house, I felt raw, and not in a good way: there was no badminton court clapping ritual to catch me this time. Just Mariam's unexpected silence. It was pretty much the opposite of catharsis. Then, at the door, she faced me with a decisive movement and wrapped her arms around me, pulling my chest towards her chest, my face into her hair. But her delay had cut me off like a blade and I didn't receive the hug as I might have if she'd embraced me in the car. She pulled back and looked me in the eyes, but I had already let the curtain fall.

'Was this a method acting exercise?' I asked. My sarcasm was thicker than I intended.

'No.' She was standing so close I could feel the breath in her words. 'I would never do that.'

'Okay.'

'But I feel like I know you a bit better now.'

I wanted her arms around me again. She put her key in the lock.

'If you really want to,' she said, 'it's not too late. You know that, right?'

'Yeah yeah. I guess the whole thing, I don't know.' I followed her inside. 'Marco has kids.'

'Does he?' She sucked her teeth. 'Of course, you don't want to be waiting around for someone.'

'Hey, sister,' came Anwar's voice in the hall, followed by Anwar himself, swinging Emil from the armpits before catching him on his hip. Emil looked ecstatic. I noticed a silver hoop in one of Anwar's ears.

'Hi! Hi, Mama's darling,' said Mariam, reaching out. 'Did you miss me? How was everything?' she added, looking up at her brother.

'Fine, fine,' said Anwar. 'We drew pictures, we played games. He slept well.'

The child clambered onto his mother and Anwar zipped up his hoodie, saying he'd left some beer in the fridge, and slouched out. Mariam wafted into the kitchen with Emil in her arms, commenting enthusiastically on a narration already too quiet for me to hear – Oh how nice, ooh! Did you really? – and knocking the kitchen chairs into order. The lamps were on in the living room. The colouring tin lay open on the coffee table amid a chaos of drawings on printer paper.

I said goodnight and slipped away to my office-bedroom even

though it was barely nine o'clock. I wanted to be alone. I undressed, washed my face, slid under the covers. I wanted to feel at ease with having told Mariam so much. I said to myself that most people, good people, respond well to vulnerability, and anyway she'd asked me a question and I'd answered it.

One of the things I hadn't told her about was the physical pain. I assumed it was some kind of infection, maybe a consequence of the operation, but for a while I was too depressed to ask a doctor. When I finally visited my GP he said there was nothing wrong and that it must be stress. He replaced the modesty blanket as I released my legs from the stirrups, snapping off his horrible blue gloves while wearing a sympathetic but doctorly frown. I could visit a physical therapist in Harley Street, he told me, and he typed out a referral while I pulled on my jeans. Outside I bummed a cigarette off a nurse and wept dramatically, my hair sticking to my face.

The physiotherapist was called Shoshana. She wore a Hebrew name-necklace. On the first appointment I made a mental note to tell Haneen, to make her laugh, before remembering that it would entail telling her about the pain. Shoshana instantly supplied the womanly, practical atmosphere I'd yearned for at the hospital. She was unemotional, kind, capable. Her cropped brown hair had a sharp grey parting, which expanded during the period I saw her, and she always wore matte lipstick and the same pair of earrings, big silver discs secured at the base with green beads. Her office was purple, with oversized wind chimes pinned nonsensically to the walls; a framed poster of a red swirly painting hung above her desk. The first time she touched me I tried to close my legs from the pain. It burned. Shoshana, unfazed, gripped my legs open, instructing me to breathe. Before long this became routine, and not even embarrassing, for me to open my legs on the bed and for her to pull on her surgical gloves and lubricate her fingers and push them inside me, pressing at the edges until the pain dulled.

One day she asked, 'Have you ever been the victim of sexual violence?'

Hands washed, at her computer. I was on the edge of the bed, feeling sore. 'No,' I said.

'Okay.'

She nodded, eyeing the screen. I regarded the swirly red poster.

'Does it still hurt when your husband touches you?'

I returned my eyes to her. I had told her about the womb septum, and the operation. We had never discussed my sex life.

'I don't have a husband,' I said coldly.

'Okay,' said Shoshana. Her eye fell to my hand, which wore no wedding ring. A long opaque silence ensued. Every silence has a climax, and when this one arrived I stood as though lifted on strings and thanked her, which may have been what she was waiting for. Then I floated into the hall, where I told the receptionist to cancel me for next week, and that I didn't need any further appointments.

I was sensitive and volatile throughout that period. I felt like a scrap of newspaper dancing on the draught above a fire, constantly about to burn and vanish. But what upset me just then was not the question of whether or not my husband touched me, which by that point of course he didn't really, but the question of whether or not I had a husband at all. I'd registered at the clinic as Sonia Nasir, there was no Ms or Mrs or Miss, there was no way Shoshana could have known I was married. The weird unfathomable silence she'd allowed into her purple room enraged me, partly because it implied a completely inappropriate judgement, and as I charged towards Baker Street tube station I thought that if I ever saw her again I would scream at her, because how dare she introduce any awkwardness at all, I was her patient, there was a script for these things, she had just told me to relax and put her fingers inside me and asked me an extremely intimate question.

Considering this episode as I lay on the mattress in Mariam's spare room, it occurred to me for the first time that I might have got it wrong. Shoshana may just have been curious about my name. She may have recognised it was Arab and wondered if it was mine by birth or by marriage. If that was so, then her awkwardness was not about my marital status but about my ethnicity. I wasn't sure this was preferable to my first theory; it might in fact have been worse. In any case, her exercises worked and the pain eventually disappeared.

When bad things happened I used to think: Now I can play a

woman whose friend has died, really convincingly. Now I can play a woman whose family collapsed, really convincingly. Now I can play a woman whose marriage has failed really convincingly. Now I can play a woman who has lost a child really convincingly. The problem was there weren't that many of those parts around. And in the end, onstage, most pain reads the same. You sort of only need one bad thing to happen to you and you're set for life.

I do think I would have benefited at the time from some representation of a similar experience, though, whether in a book or a film, or even something small like a poem. Something for the company, just so I could feel I was walking down a path already trodden by other women, that I was not the first to cut my way through that wilderness. Possibly I didn't search hard enough. Or maybe the subject doesn't make for good narratives, given that it revolves around absence, it is an event about nothing, it was an event I did not, lying there on the hospital bed, even get to witness, I had no idea what it looked like, I felt only the awful scraping of my cervix, which resounded in my head the way building work on a street outside can resound inside your body. Thinking back on it I have nothing, I have only the pain and my sweating hands.

That night at Mariam's, Marco skulked across the scenery of my mind. The last time I had seen him was at a production of *Wide Sargasso Sea*: I had just sat down, alone, and suddenly there he was, down near the stage in his long coat, examining his ticket stub. The shape of him was so recognisable it was like accidentally catching my own reflection. He was with a woman, Piya. I'd never seen her in real life. She was petite. I felt exposed, alone in my row, but he didn't look up in my direction. They took their seats in the front, and she raised her arm to point, and he leaned in to listen.

I turned over and, feeling a draught, pulled the cover further up my back. Then I drifted off and dreamt of my mother, or at least she was the last thing I saw before I woke. From a distance, at the top of a staircase in a white nightgown, like an icon, and I was inhaling her damp hot smell while I hugged her, my face in her belly, her arms on my back, which meant I was a child. Then I emerged into morning, my mouth was dry, I looked up at the grey ceiling, and drew my cold left foot back into the warmth of the bedclothes. I wondered if mothers existed forever in their children's minds as jumbles of features, colours, smell, touch; and recalled the shock of clutching at a woman in the park or at pick-up after school who resembled mine in some basic aspects – fair hair, large breasts, rounded shoulders, the kind of cardigan she liked – and who, looking down at me, was not my mother. I was fully awake now. I reached for my phone and switched it on. It was quarter past eight.

Hi mum how are you?

Pouncing dots appeared.

I'm good darling!! Painting again feeling energised!! How is everything?? Xxxx

The force of my dream dissipated. And with it, my mother as an assemblage of features also fell away, replaced by a human being with a personality.

Good

Did han tell you I'm in a play here?

Yes! Please be careful

When can we chat?

Now?

Frank is sleeping

I can call you tonight

No probs

Love you xx

Xxx

Mariam was growling over her breakfast as she watched the news. The Israelis were demolishing the village. Noise of concrete falling, car wheels turning, voices yelling. Last night they arrested three of the activists who had encircled the generator, and who turned out to be American Jewish college students. Dust fell from the jagged lips of the bulldozer as it mauled the side of a building. A father wept during his interview. Where will we go now? he said. He opened his hands, showing how empty they were. The reporter switched to the situation around Al-Aqsa. Prevented from entering the mosque compound, Muslims were praying in the streets outside. Even those over the age of fifty, whom the Israelis were allowing to pass through the metal detectors, were refusing in protest. 'Look at that,' said Mariam, staring at the screen. Wide shot of people chanting on Salaheddin Street, near the old city walls. Hundreds praying in the middle of the road, right beside the soldiers. My eyes were puffy and I had a light headache. Mariam prepared bread and cheese for Emil then disappeared to her room. Emil said the word 'breakfast' quietly to himself, as if testing it out. Mariam reappeared with a few large pieces of cardboard under her arm and told me, Yalla, we're going to be late.

We had only a few minutes alone in the car between dropping Emil off and parking outside the theatre, and we spent them in silence. In the foyer, Dawud jumped to his feet to help Mariam with the cardboard.

'Don't worry, they aren't heavy,' said Mariam, resisting.

He dashed to open the door. 'Do you need anything, can I get you anything? Coffee?'

Mariam said, Thank you, we are fine, and as the door swung to behind us, she murmured, *Does he want to audition or something?* George was lying on his back onstage, hands on his stomach; Majed paced the stalls, wearing red glasses and a woolly jumper, reciting his lines; Ibrahim, Faris and Wael were absorbed in their phones. The atmosphere of a grumpy Monday. Mariam arranged three chairs facing the audience, and when, at twenty minutes past the hour, there was still no sign of Amin, she announced we were start- ing, and would we all take a seat please. She positioned her three boards on the three chairs and flipped them over. They were three large elaborate drawings of a set, tinted with watercolour.

'God,' said George, 'did you do those?'

'My brother Anwar. He has class today so he couldn't join us.'

'I knew it,' said George, raising a silly finger. 'This is a Mansour family operation through and through. Something is rotten in the—'

'Zip it,' said Mariam.

I moved closer to see better. The drawings were elegantly cartoonish, like sketches by fashion designers, depicting the stage at different moments in the play, beneath a dark blue sky with white moon and stars. Anwar had also drawn the environs, and apparently the set was going to compete in height with the separation wall itself, beside which it stood, and which featured a black-windowed military lookout tower and some pale indecipherable graffiti. In the third iteration of the design, one of the windows in the tower housed a pale grey face. The stage was greater in height even than in width; a huge swerving staircase joined the floor with a gallery, drawing the eye upwards to an enormous chandelier, which was painted a faint yellow but labelled in pencil: *Gold*. The chandelier hung from a structure behind the stage. Above the staircase, a tall skinny window on the backdrop showed a view of fields and hills, labelled: *Like the Galilee*. I felt I was finally grasping the issue of funding. It was an issue of scale. Mariam wanted to make a real spectacle. Even her choice of play made more sense to me now.

GEORGE   They're never going to let you build it as high as the wall.

   MARIAM *smiles*.

MAJED   And that's the size of us? (*Points at a human figure in Drawing 2.*) We are very small.

IBRAHIM   (*Coming to sit beside Sonia, whispering.*) How did you sleep?

MARIAM   We're going for excess. That's the . . . main idea.

SONIA   (*Whispering, laughing.*) Fine. Thank you.

GEORGE   (*Hopeful.*) Our costumes, too? Will they be Eastern style?

MARIAM	The costumes will be very simple. And you'll all be barefoot.
GEORGE	(*With dismay.*) Barefoot? Are you serious?
MARIAM	I want you to look vulnerable. To contrast with the set.
MAJED	Like Ophelia, all tears.
FARIS	Wait. That chandelier is *very* large. How are you going to hang it?
MARIAM	A crane.
FARIS	You don't think it would be better to make this all a bit more sha'abi? More popular? It looks intimidating.
MARIAM	That's my intention, that's the effect we want. Grand.
IBRAHIM	'We' want.

FARIS *stands up, trudges over to the boards, and demonstrates with his fingers.*

FARIS	How about this? If you made this part smaller, and you take down the stairs – which will be expensive to build, by the way—
MARIAM	No, Faris. This is the set design. We've already started making it.
FARIS	(*Taken aback. Pause.*) With what money?
MARIAM	We have money.
FARIS	From where?
IBRAHIM	Why do you need to know, Uncle? She's the director.
FARIS	(*Hands on hips, looking between them.*) In my experience, you can run into big problems. Is it international, from these people you met in Haifa? Europeans are very demanding.
MARIAM	(*Irritated.*) It's not European.
FARIS	Then where is it coming from? We need to know.
MARIAM	(*Disbelieving.*) Faris!

FARIS *eyeballs* MARIAM.

MARIAM	My brother is sorting it out.

FARIS	Salim? He's still helping? Oh, no. Oh no no. You need to be careful. I really hope this is not known in public.
MARIAM	We are being careful. He's helping us in an unofficial capacity.
GEORGE	That also makes me nervous, to be honest.
MAJED	(*To George.*) It really is a Mansour family business, eh?
MARIAM	(*Emphatically.*) Listen. It's going to be fine. But that information about my brother doesn't leave this room. Understood?

IBRAHIM *exchanges a look with* SONIA.

SONIA	(*Whispering.*) Did *you* sleep okay?
IBRAHIM	(*Whispering.*) Honestly? No. (*Hesitates. Pulls out his phone.*)
MARIAM	(*Looking at Ibrahim.*) We started barely ten minutes ago, I'd appreciate if you could pay attention.
IBRAHIM	I'm just texting Amin.
MARIAM	Fine. (*Sighs.*) So, this area, this rectangle near the front, is going to drop below the level of the stage for Ophelia's grave. In the third act, the staircase is going to be dismantled, like . . . this. And the Ghost, we're going to do the Ghost using shadow.

IBRAHIM *passes his phone to* SONIA. *He has written:*

> They are calling for a day of rage for alaqsa
> because of the electronic gates
> Im worried about amin

SONIA	(*Whispering.*) Why don't you text him?
MAJED	When you say shadow, what do you mean by that?
IBRAHIM	(*Whispering.*) I already did.
MARIAM	We have a very powerful stage light, and Majed you'll stand in front of it, and we'll cover you in black so we can't see your face. And the light will be at an angle, like

	this, so the shadow will be very large, and it will appear here, beside the staircase.
MAJED	Like a Shadow Theatre.
MARIAM	Exactly. But bigger.
SONIA	(*Whispering.*) That's why you didn't sleep?
MAJED	And my voice?
MARIAM	We're going to record you whispering, and play it very loudly.
IBRAHIM	(*Whispering.*) No. I'm feeling angry. This shit in Jerusalem got to me yesterday.
MAJED	Mm, that's good. Very good.

SONIA *nods, unsure what to say.*

MARIAM	Tomorrow we're doing a cast trip to Bethlehem, to have a look at the progress.
IBRAHIM	But Jerusalem will be crazy.
MARIAM	We're not going through Jerusalem. We'll go by Wadi an-Nar.

GEORGE *groans theatrically.*

| SONIA | What? |
| GEORGE | I get carsick. It's very . . . like this. |

GEORGE *makes snaking movement with his arm.*

| MARIAM | Where's your solidarity with Amin and Faris? They have West Bank IDs. |

Enter AMIN.

MARIAM	Finally. Thank God for your safety.
AMIN	Hi.
IBRAHIM	You okay, brother?

| AMIN | Checkpoint. (*Drops rucksack.*) Fuckers. |
| WAEL | I'm sorry about that. |

AMIN *scowls.*

SONIA	What happened?
AMIN	They made me stand in the sun for like an hour.
MARIAM	Ouff.
FARIS	There *is* something in the air today. Sometimes you smell it, something wrong. (*To Sonia.*) You don't feel this in England, right?
SONIA	When something really big happens, which affects everyone. But no, I guess that doesn't happen very often.

Mariam embarked now on a monologue, describing new blocking patterns and props, glancing at me repeatedly. In Act Three she wanted to introduce concrete and trash from the surrounding area onto the stage, as Elsinore decayed towards the play's conclusion. Parts of the set would be constructed of a special fast-drying polymer ceramic, which could shatter and be reconstructed quickly for the next performance. Before long she was announcing the warm-up, and by the time we were on our feet she had ceased looking at me. Ibrahim had started to follow me with his eyes instead. Taking my place in the circle, windmilling my arms, I wondered if Faris was right, and there was something in the air. Throughout the physical the others seemed on edge, focusing on their hamstrings in silence, with none of their usual playfulness. Maybe the street ambience had seeped under the theatre doors, maybe Amin had infected us with his anger at the soldiers. We did a quick vocal warm-up too but skipped the ensemble game since we were running behind. We began with the Gravedigger scene. Faris kneeled ready before the grave. Ibrahim and I, sitting near each other in the stalls, watched Amin take his position in the wings, ready to enter with Wael. At the crucial moment, Amin stuck out his leg. Wael flew forwards, arms out, and skidded a metre across the stage.

'What the fuck?' shouted Ibrahim, and while I jumped over to help Wael, Ibrahim ran up the stage stairs and smacked Amin on the shoulder. 'What do you think you're doing?'

Wael was already on his feet. He bounced, shaking his hands. 'It's cool, it's cool.'

'Are you sure?' I said, touching his arm. 'You're not hurt?'

'Yeah, yeah, no I'm fine.'

Faris, still kneeling, bellowed over his shoulder: 'STOP MESSING ABOUT,' and I released Wael in surprise. I'd never heard Faris raise his voice. His shoulders were hunched and I glimpsed a red face before he turned away again. I expected Mariam to take the reins, contain Faris, rebuke Amin. She didn't move. She glanced between her notes and our tableau, before finally calling out: 'You all right, Wael?'

'Fine.'

Faris sighed through his lips like a horse. Amin thrust past Ibrahim, leapt off the stage and pushed out through the doors. Ibrahim watched him go, hands on the back of his head. George and Majed swapped looks. For the first time, I feared a mutiny.

'Ibrahim, can you stand in for Amin please?' said Mariam, leafing through her script.

Majed and I were the first to go outside during the break. Amin was smoking in the car park, trying to keep his balance on an unstable rock, his legs trembling, one foot jerking to the ground and back. The moment he noticed us he jumped off entirely. His face darkened, he flung his spent cigarette away and lit another. It was easy to blame 'the situation' for bad behaviour, but to me it was obvious that Amin was jealous of Wael because Wael was playing Hamlet, and because he was famous without being a good actor. Ibrahim, having followed us with Mariam and George in tow, asked Amin for a word behind the cars. The way he deepened his voice and nodded prevented the exchange from humiliating Amin, who returned the nod and followed. I accepted a cigarette from Majed, puffed once, then held it between my fingers until it went out. The others discussed Al-Aqsa. George pointed out a sleek black BMW and said to me: 'That's Wael's.'

Ibrahim and Amin's forms appeared dimly through the windows of another car. Now they were moving; they were coming back.

Amin's gait was springy, but that was deceptive – his expression was just as sullen as before. I searched Ibrahim's face for clues. To my alarm, he fixed me with an intense look of desire. I sent a glare in return, trying to push him off, to signal – Please stop being so obvious – but he seemed to think I was communicating something which he must decipher, and increased his keenness, twitching his head curiously. I had predicted it might be hard to conceal what had happened between us. I hadn't imagined he would make quite so little effort. I switched my attention to Mariam, who, with her way now paved, addressed Amin in a tone of gentle authority. We must respect our colleagues, she was telling him. She had full sympathy for whatever had occurred that morning; nevertheless, we must make productive use of our anger if we are going to function as a company and as a team. We must not turn that anger on each other. Having transformed 'you' into 'we', she now expanded the point into a lesson for us all, explaining that later in the week we would do some exercises as an ensemble on this theme, dealing with our anger. Faris, the main proponent of the therapeutic model of theatre among us, rolled his eyes, while Ibrahim, who I would have expected to take the most umbrage, was apparently too preoccupied by staring at me to pay any attention to what Mariam was saying. What I really craved was for Mariam to look at me. But her gaze passed over me lightly, as though I were just another of her children.

We traipsed back inside, littering the ground with our butts. Why had I confided in her about my pregnancies, and in such detail? Because she'd asked, that was why. But I'd also done so immediately after hearing she was disappointed by my acting. It seemed plausible to me that I'd been trying to win back some advantage by impressing her with a tale of suffering. This thought made me weary. I watched her giving notes privately to Ibrahim, who, hands on hips, nodded at the ground, listening. I wondered if anything had ever happened between them. An irrational jealousy spiked in my chest, until Ibrahim, sensing me, met my eye with that same irritating intensity, and my jealousy evaporated.

I wasn't needed after lunch so I walked back to Mariam's alone. At least Ibrahim had pretty much wiped Harold from my mind. When I woke in the mornings he was no longer there. I hadn't even noticed, I'd been so distracted. The street leading to the market was crowded as usual, but after three men in quick succession catcalled me I made a turning uphill and chose a quieter route to the house, twisting my hair into a rope and then a knot at my neck. Inside a corner shop, a group of men sat in a circle drinking coffee. I returned their greetings and thanked them for letting me through to the fridge, where I extracted a can of Diet Sprite.

'I'm fifty years old,' I heard one say, 'and this is the first time I ever saw it closed.'

An older man pointed out to the shopkeeper that I was ready to pay.

'Two shekels,' said the shopkeeper, jumping to life. 'Thank you.'

'The situation is not good, right?' I said.

'Hundreds have come from all over the world to pray, they can't pray, they pray in the streets. On the asphalt. And it's hot! Look how hot it is out there!'

I held the cold can all the way back between my palms. Even the emptier streets felt ominous, agitated. I entered a fruit and vegetable shop near the house, selected lemons, a couple of shrunken avocados, and when the shopkeeper smiled and said: That's it?, I said, Yes, and added:

'It's miserable what's happening, isn't it?'

He punched numbers into his calculator, swapping items on the scale. Then he, too, gestured at the street behind me. 'The weather doesn't help. This humidity.'

Outside the house, my phone, connecting to the Wi-Fi, vibrated and brightened.

Mariam Mansour

Today 15:51

Could we have a chat this evening? I'll be back around 6.30.

The message was innocuous enough. So why did anxiety muscle through me as I unlocked the door? I slid off my shoes, put the food and my Sprite in the fridge, and drank a glass of water, cooling my wrists under the tap.

a) *I have noticed something is going on with you and Ibrahim.*
b) *You are acting badly.*

I sank into the sofa and looked up at the bookcase, at the novels, the classics in Arabic and English, the myriad plays, a few Hebrew paperbacks. *Heart of Darkness*. James Baldwin. A large quantity of Jung.

c) *We are going to try your lines in English tomorrow. Here's a copy of the play.*

There was a shelf of poetry collections at the bottom. Samih al-Qasim. Baudelaire. A critical anthology of the Symbolists.
Or, maybe:

d) *I need your help with Wael and Amin.*

I looked at the message again, then checked the *Guardian* website, scanned headlines about British electoral politics. I rang my father.
'Hiii,' he said. 'Where did you disappear to?'
'What?'
'You haven't called me.'
'I'm calling you now. Sorry, we're rehearsing a lot.'
'How is the play?'
'It's okay. What are you eating?'
'Lunch.'
'Sahha. We're going to Bethlehem tomorrow actually, to see the set.'
'Be careful. I'm watching the news. May God destroy their house. I hope there is a video. Of the play, not of this shit. I'm very proud of you, Sonia, do you know that? Especially that you are doing it in Arabic.'
'What's for lunch, then?'

'Sandwich. How is Haneen?'

I looked through the window at the garden. 'Baba?'

'Yes?'

'I'm feeling quite sad at the moment.'

'Don't be sad.'

'It's hard here. The atmosphere is, it's heavy.'

He chewed, slurped. 'It's complicated.'

'It's not complicated.'

'Okay,' he said, like he was admitting defeat. It was the same tone he used when I was a child if I ever challenged him. He closed down the discussion immediately by pretending he was letting me win.

'Can I ask you?'

'What.'

'What you did in the seventies.'

He gave a sigh that approached a groan.

'Does Haneen—'

'Not on the phone.'

'Okay. Well, will you tell me . . . something else, will you tell me about your childhood?'

'Sonia.' Then, relenting: 'What do you want to know?'

Laundry swayed on the line. A bird stepped on the lawn and took flight, aiming at a tree.

'Will you tell me when you realised what was happening?'

He was moving around: I pictured him getting out of his chair, walking across the room. Lowering himself onto the couch. 'Listen.' He paused. 'It wasn't until I left Palestine that I really knew Palestine.'

'What does that mean?'

'Just wait for me to finish. Listen.'

Silence. I waited.

'I was born into it,' he said finally. 'Okay? I was born a few months before the Nakba. You know this. You know what it means? It means it was already my reality. I didn't know what it was before. Teta and Jiddo didn't talk about it. And I didn't ask.'

'Did they talk to you about collaborators?'

'What? What has collaboration to do with it? We didn't talk

about any of it, like I told you. There are no collaborators in my family.'

'I wasn't suggesting.'

'We are a good family. My great-uncle fought with Qawuqji.'

'I know that.'

'We are good stock, we weren't these elite, y'ani . . . Okay?'

'Baba, I know, that's not what I was saying.'

'Okay. So, as you know, I went to boarding school in Nazareth when I was nine years old.'

I wasn't sure I had known that, but I didn't want to interrupt him.

'I remember, we have to get a permit to move to Nazareth from the military governor. I couldn't believe that. I said I am going to school. Why the permit? And slowly, slowly, I started grasping it.'

'When you were nine years old?'

'Maybe, no, not nine years old. Maybe a little older. But I grasped it. And I didn't like it. Later, you know, they changed our residence to Nazareth, in the school. And the school started, at the end of every month, getting permits to allow us to come to see our parents. So, slowly, slowly, I started to feel the Israeli persecution and mistreatment of us, of the Arabs.' He cleared his throat. 'And then, slowly, slowly, I started grasping the reality. You see? Workers can't go to their work without a permit. People can't develop their lives without a permit. And later, by the time I went to Beirut, I was already completely politicised. In a sense. I graduated from the high school as a young, politicised, conscious student. So, when military rule ended I was nineteen. Right? I was a . . . a . . . I joined the party when I was sixteen.'

'Right.'

'In nineteen sixty-seven I stayed. Okay? Then, after the census, an Anglican priest smuggled me across the Naqoura border to Lebanon, and I spent four years in Beirut.'

'What? Did you just say a priest smuggled you?'

'What I'm telling you is, in Lebanon I really understood. Because it began then, the movement, properly. The movement outside. And I saw the refugees. I didn't see refugees before, you know? Not like this. And I saw the people, active. Before nineteen sixty-seven there was no . . . Up to nineteen sixty-seven the name even vanished from the UN.'

'You can say Palestine.'

'Mm.'

'You said it a few minutes ago.'

'Did I? Well.' He was silent again, searching for his thread. 'The West Bank was annexed to Jordan, okay? Gaza was under the Egyptians. And we, the Arabs here, I mean there, we were meant to be like Israeli citizens. There was no . . . no . . . at all.'

'Were you sad to leave for Lebanon?'

'No, like I told you. It began for me then, even. In a sense. I understood properly. Because the grievance of the Arabs in Israel . . . Okay, it's oppression, but it's not the biggest grievance.'

'Huh.'

'I need to drink something now.'

'Wait, Baba. A bit longer. Please.'

'What do you want from me?' he said plaintively.

'I want,' I said. 'I want.' I sighed.

'Forget about it, my love. Palestine is gone. We lost her a long time ago.'

Outside, a weak breeze revealed itself, touching the leaves of the vine, of the trees. I waited for him to repeat that it was time to go. He didn't.

'How did you feel when the first uprising started?' I asked.

'Hm.' He grunted. 'Well. You know, Sonia, it gave me a strong feeling.'

'Did it really?'

'Yes. Something I had not felt for a long time. I didn't want to be too hopeful. But I felt happy.'

'You never said that to me before.'

'Mm.'

'And were you disappointed by what happened afterwards?'

'Stupid question.'

'Sorry.'

'It's okay.'

'You know, I went to Haifa again at the weekend.'

'Oh, yes?'

'I went to the house. I went to see who was living there.' I paused for his response, but he said nothing. 'It was a Jewish guy, with his family. He didn't like that we were there, outside.'

'You told him who you were?'

'Of course.'

'Good.' He sucked his teeth and breathed a laugh. 'He was scared of you. You're like a ghost to him.'

'Me?'

'We haunt them. They want to kill us but we will not die. Even now we've lost nearly everything.' His laugh deepened. 'Zombie apocalypse.'

More questions were occurring to me but I knew he was too worried about phone tapping to answer them now. I wanted to ask about his friend Maher, for example. It would have to wait until I was back in England, although I wondered if I could ask Haneen, who obviously knew more than I did. I said goodbye and waited for him to hang up, then stayed where I was on the sofa. I felt calmer, thinking of him. Regardless of what he intended, he had fortified me. The key rattled in the lock.

'So,' came Mariam's voice, followed by rustling, the clink of a chain, and then she entered, shoeless, lifting her handbag and jacket onto the table. She was wearing freshly applied mascara and bronzer, and as she sat, sighing, I noticed her eyelids were slightly swollen.

'You look exhausted,' I blurted out. 'Where's Emil?'

'Anwar's.' She ran a hand through her hair, and looked at her fingernails. 'How are you?'

'I'm sorry about this Amin business. I hope Wael's okay.'

'Oh, they're fine, it happens like that sometimes. It's hard to keep things outside the rehearsal room here. It's not a normal place to make theatre.'

'I'm sure.'

'So I have some news.'

'Oh?' I shifted my body to face her. My voice was unconvincingly light.

Her eyes narrowed beneath her lashes. 'I have found an actress to play Ophelia.'

In the effort to suppress my surprise, all I managed was another: 'Oh?'

'Her name is Jenan. She auditioned in the spring but her family weren't happy about it. They've changed their minds. Are you okay?'

'Yes. I'm fine.'

'Okay. Good. Why are you laughing?'

'I don't know – I guess I was expecting. I don't know what I was expecting. So, wait, am I still Gertrude?'

'Yeah yeah yeah, you're still Gertrude. No don't worry about that. You're a great Gertrude.'

'Right.'

'You're definitely fine with this?'

'Of course. Jenan. That's great. I was a stand-in anyway, no? I would have been the most matronly Ophelia ever to grace a stage. Me and Wael – it was all getting a bit Oedipal.' I was talking too fast. 'When do we meet her?'

'Tomorrow. Phew. I'm glad you feel this way.'

'I'm not that much of a narcissist.'

'I don't think you're a narcissist at all.'

'Really?'

She cackled and stared at me, like she was seeing something I couldn't see.

13

Dear Sonia,

I've been thinking about you a lot. Rehearsals are going well, I'm
pleased with our set designer and the previews have sold out. We're
exploring some ideas we discussed in the Seagull, chaos &
fatedness, the 'yes, and yet', excess / proliferation etc. The whole
cast has a great energy and I'm happy with Polly Atkins as Ophelia,
she's very agile & has gravity and I think a real future ahead of her.
This is her stage debut and she's made the transfer well. Of course
I miss you and wish you were with us. Last week we got talking
about explosions from splitting something very small, like an atom. I
thought of you, I thought you would have had some things to say
about that !

Listen Sonia I know you're angry. You have every right. I behaved
terribly. I was glad to read about you playing Gertrude. I know its
funny to say but I didn't know you were Palestinian. For some
reason I thought you were Lebanese. Anyway it sounds exhilarating.
Wishing you best of luck with the performance.

Harold
--
Sent from my iPhone

I reread the email, not moving from where I stood.

'What's happened?' said Mariam, aiming her fob at the car.

'Has there been something about us in the news?' I opened Safari
and typed: wael hejazi hamlet palestine. 'Oh my God.'

Something Rotten in the State of Israel: Palestinian production of *Hamlet* causes international stir

Arab-Israeli sibling collaboration on West Bank production provokes Israeli outrage

They had used a photograph of me and Wael in the garden. I was wearing black tracksuit bottoms and a white T-shirt, looking sad, hands clasped. Wael stood in profile to the camera, his quiff in silhouette.

'You're looking at the article?' said Mariam.

'They called you Arab-Israeli,' I said, opening the passenger door. The metal was already hot.

Mariam drove out into the road as I scanned the article, illegal fundraising, Arab-Israeli Member of the Knesset, local pop star. 'Does this mean there's been a leak,' I asked, 'about Salim, that he's still helping us? Or is this just old news?' Sources close to the government, dubious, contravention, new information come to light, terrorist organisation. They cited two previous censorship cases in Palestinian theatre, the one Mariam had told me about from a few years ago, when the Israeli Minister of Culture cut funding to a theatre in Haifa which caused it to close down, and an incident during the first intifada when a text that didn't pass the military censor was performed anyway, and soldiers raided the stage mid-scene. I checked the article's byline. Not an Arab.

'Could be either,' said Mariam. 'We should check the Hebrew press.'

'So how exactly is Salim helping us?'

She pointed at my phone. 'Do you mind?'

I pressed the power button until the screen went black.

'So, some of the funds are coming from the usual diaspora networks. And now Salim's using connections in Kuwait and Qatar to get more, to build on a bigger scale. Israel's list of enemies is long so it's possible in one of the meetings in Jordan there was someone with links . . . But anyway you have to understand that this is the pretext, not the reason. Our production demonstrates what we're capable of. We have some institutions already but they're basically West Bank only, you know? We want to build things that are country-wide, for all Palestinians, everywhere. They've stopped us having political unity but we can put money into building cultural unity, of a kind. There's obviously also a PR aspect to this. It's been a PR war since nineteen forty-eight.' She paused. 'One of the first projects would be in Jerusalem.'

'They won't like that.'

'And another in Haifa. The connections between them are under wraps, they look like individual projects but actually they're pooling resources. I've barely talked about this to anyone, although of course we should assume they have access to everything. If they don't know yet, they will at some point. It's about timing and tactics.'

'I guess this means you're not pleased. About the write-up.'

'I wanted it to stay secret for longer.' She sighed. 'We should feel sorry for them, really. I would if they weren't such assholes.'

'Don't take this the wrong way, but I'm kind of amazed you thought you'd get away with it. Salim's a politician. I mean,' I caught myself, 'it's brave of you.'

'They get away with so much. We at least have to try. We might fail. Lots of people have failed before us. Basically everybody failed, actually.'

'Where did they get the photo?'

'Our Facebook page. I took it.'

Wael lived in at-Tireh. Entering the neighbourhood, I surveyed the pavements for the shapes of Uncle Jad and Aunty Rima. We drove into an area with villas set back from the roads and electric gates, and parked outside a comparatively modest house half-hidden by vines on an arbour.

My thoughts lingered on Harold. I brushed aside the vague pleasure of his attention, my embarrassment about playing Gertrude – he thought I was *Lebanese*? I put his name into Google and the first hit was a photograph of him appended to a write-up in *The Stage*. He was ogling the camera, leaning his cheek on one hand, looking slightly overweight and very pretentious. Then Wael's front door opened and a middle-aged woman in a hijab, long dress and slippers waved at us. Mariam rolled down her window.

'Hi, Aunty!' she shouted. 'I've missed you!'

'Come inside!' the woman shouted back. 'I'll open the garage!'

'We can't.' Mariam gestured randomly at the dashboard. 'There's going to be traffic. Everything is fine? Say hello to everyone from me!'

Wael appeared beside the woman, a leather jacket over his arm, and kissed her on each cheek before jogging down the path towards us. From the back seat he reached for our shoulders.

'Hey.' He squeezed mine. 'Looking good in that picture, Mama.'

'I'm not your mother. It's going to be very hot today, I don't think you need that jacket.'

'It's part of my costume.'

Mariam shook her head, rolling her eyes. I smiled. Wael's verve reassured me; it meant that Amin's malice yesterday hadn't really affected him.

We needed to pick up George and then we could set off for Bethlehem. Mariam was right about the traffic. The current of air from the windows petered out as we crawled forward in the still heat. A little boy carrying a tower of tissue boxes forced one box through the passenger window and waited for Mariam to pay him, which she did. A hilltop emerged on the left, bearing a perfectly symmetrical Israeli settlement: identikit houses with porches and solar panels, fanning out along the summit, revolving slowly past us.

George's village lay just beyond Ramallah, and his apartment block stood haphazardly at the end of a dirt track overlooking a valley of trash and small trees. Wael jumped out to press the buzzer, and George came out wearing a purple T-shirt with the slogan 'End the Siege' in Arabic. He had trimmed his beard into a goatee.

'Nice shave,' said Mariam, as he got in the car.

'You saw there's been a leak?' said George. He rolled down his window completely and leaned his elbow out. 'At least we'll have a real press night. All the journalists in their bulletproof vests. Those lovely helmets.'

Wael and Mariam both gave a strangely emotional laugh, taut like stringed instruments. Over my shoulder I saw George's face was deadpan. I fixed Wael in my wing mirror, and felt a pang at the sight of his curated outfit, his hair-sides trimmed, the top gelled and combed, his eyes flicking over the view. Why, I wondered, did I feel more protective of this wealthy pop-star than, for example, of Amin, who was objectively the more vulnerable one, and who, unlike Wael, had been unable to move out of the refugee camp where he lived, where he'd been raised as an orphan? Human relationships are not social services, and love has nothing to do with deserving, but it still didn't sit well with me that I should find it harder to love the hardened child. I reminded myself that neither Amin nor Wael was a child, and swinging my head in the other direction again was startled to meet a glare from George that seemed to say, *I see you.* I snapped my eyes back to the road. I could not explain why my neck was burning.

We decelerated as the road dropped and the earth rose on either side. The stream of cars honked senselessly. Truck wheels skidded in the loops of the valley, winding up the gradient ahead.

'At least it's too slow to make us carsick,' said George as we curved down into the wadi.

'I'm dying from the heat,' said Wael.

'Oh, be a man,' said George.

'Yes,' said Mariam, 'everyone knows men don't feel the heat.'

'I said you wouldn't need that jacket,' I said.

We slugged our way down and then up again, and I asked Mariam why the traffic was so bad if the day of rage wasn't until tomorrow, and she replied that it was rush hour. After some thought she added that the Israelis were probably slowing passage through the checkpoints, doing more body searches. And West Bankers with permits would be hurrying to Jerusalem to be ready for the morning's protest, which meant that even those who'd normally take the shorter route to Bethlehem via Jerusalem, having the Israeli or foreign passports or Jerusalem IDs or temporary permits that afforded them that privilege, would probably take the West Bank way through Wadi an-Nar to skip the traffic.

'A big side effect of the occupation,' said Mariam, 'is traffic jams.'

When we arrived in Bethlehem it was almost noon and I was so hungry that my legs wobbled as I climbed out of the car. Opposite two hotels with stars and crosses on their welcome signs, a double-decker coach spilled pilgrims onto the pavement, a crowd of baseball caps and lanyards, as a guide waving a purple feather on an upright wire shouted in a language that sounded Scandinavian. We followed Mariam through their midst towards the separation wall, which, blackened from bygone flames, cut off one end of the street. As we drew nearer, the graffiti became visible: a half-obliterated depiction of Leila Khaled, another of Malcolm X, something about Guernica and a cartoon Christmas tree. A corner to our right, imperceptible until we reached it, revealed an alley of shops in the shade of the wall. The shop owners watched us but none tried to advertise their wares. I glanced as we passed and saw the customary tourist trinkets lying in cheap wicker baskets, icons and images carved from olive wood, bracelets of saints' faces, bundles of thin beeswax candles, earrings made from old Ottoman coins. A few coloured kuffiyehs, some Banksy key rings.

'Yo,' said Ibrahim.

He and Amin were smoking by the wall. Faris sat on a concrete block drinking a can of Coke from a straw. They looked as pale and weary as I felt. Ibrahim, I noted, did not meet my eye, but fell into line behind me, and in a few seconds the alley opened into a street that led away from the separation wall, and where, at a small corner restaurant with dusty plastic chairs, a man was tonging falafels into a basin of hot oil. Mariam asked him for eight sandwiches, and I added that I'd also like a coffee, no sugar, and when my sandwich appeared between my hands I ate it too fast, swallowing big lumps of bread and licking tahini from my fingers. Ibrahim had switched positions and was now up ahead with Mariam and Faris. Faris, the only Bethlehemite in the cast, was striding along with a tour-guide air, visibly pleased to have us on his turf. As I watched the back of his grey head, his fury from yesterday when Amin tripped Wael returned to me, and I wondered whether, being the boss of his own theatre here, he found it difficult to be directed by someone so much younger than him, who was also a woman. Theatre might be collaborative but every production is also a matrix of shifting unspoken hierarchies, determined by factors like the number of lines an actor has and their relative fame and experience, and as I watched Mariam and Faris walking beside each other I saw these overlapping hierarchies briefly conflict with the terms of the world, from which our play was usually a shelter. To complicate matters Mariam was also from the inside, which gave her those particular advantages. She was nodding along to Faris's narration, following his hand when he pointed, and as he gesticulated enthusiastically to punctuate whatever he was saying I felt a flash of a familiar, uncomfortable pity. I drained a small water bottle, crumpling the feeble plastic in my grip. We stopped outside a vast, keyhole-shaped wooden archway, on top of which a gigantic iron key rested on its side.

'Aida refugee camp,' announced Faris. 'They took this thing,' gesturing up at the key, 'to the Biennale in Berlin.'

To the left of the arch, a ramshackle building, seemingly deserted, was marked by a blue UN sign and flag. On the right, a black painted wall, covered in white writing. Names, hundreds of them, under the title: WHEN OUR CHILDREN ARE KILLED ... JULY 2014. I peered through the arch down a road that also ran alongside the wall, which gave me the odd feeling that I'd lost my bearings, since how could the wall be back there and also here, ahead of us? I saw houses, a lookout tower, an electricity pylon, a fluffy eucalyptus tree. Yalla, said Mariam, and we moved off, and within minutes the buildings and shopfronts had also melted away, and we faced a random assortment of edifices and landscapes: a disused factory, a corridor of wire walls, a neglected-looking house with a large top-floor window in which a shadow was moving, and behind that what might have been the remnant of a quarry, a tract of empty land, trash-strewn. A couple of wild blond dogs loped around the bend. The scene was both rural and industrial, and although it wasn't the same it reminded me of those unplanned in-between spaces you sometimes come across in London, when unaesthetic municipal structures produce concrete leftovers, functionless plots, deserted underpasses, places that weren't intended to be places but might, if they are large and lucky enough, be converted into playgrounds or skate parks or communal gardens, with flowers painted onto the asphalt. Public space hewn from the rubble of public spaces. We clambered on over the dirt, past a garage where two guys were hosing down a car, until finally, ahead of us, we saw the set.

The first thing I thought of was a church. The peaked roof was so tall it was like a spire reaching heavenward, and though unfinished it was cleanly and beautifully painted, creamy white with gold and blue details. It struck an even stronger contrast with its surroundings than I'd anticipated. They hadn't, after all, built it higher than the wall but they were giving it a run for its money. The clearing for the audience, bordered by a couple of residential buildings, a dejected-looking supermarket and a store selling antique embroidery, currently contained a couple of parked cars and a few chairs, upon which the tech team were sitting, drinking from little paper cups and directing the labourers. There wasn't much shade and everyone seemed slow, sweaty, thirsty. And there, on a black tarpaulin on the ground, lay the gigantic chandelier. A wooden body painted gold carried what looked like hundreds of cut-glass teardrops of graded sizes. Anwar stood beside it while a wiry man with dreadlocks crouched and gestured at the light-bulb sockets, lifting a huge glass droplet between his fingers. On Anwar's other side a young woman with cropped hair took notes on a clipboard. Her T-shirt revealed defined biceps. '*Amazing*,' said George, marching towards them, hands on his hips. 'Look at that thing!'

'Jenan!' Mariam called.

Another figure, on the far side of the stage, raised a hand. A shadow swung over my heart as she came towards us.

'Ahlan wa sahlan,' said Jenan, placing a hand on the apron of the stage for balance, stepping over the rubble. She wore a collared patterned shirt, slightly flared jeans and a black hijab with a purple trim. I looked into her eyes, which were large and brown and earnest, and thought, Oh dear, she's perfect. She kissed Mariam, and when she reached a hand forward to shake mine, one side of her mouth rising more than the other, and said, Hey, the impression I had just formed turned slightly on its axis. Her voice was low and metallic. The boys waved at her and said their names.

Mariam asked: 'Was it hard to get here?'

'I knew it would be crazy so I left early.' Jenan shrugged. 'I've been here a couple of hours, but it's no problem.' Her voice was so low, in fact, that I wondered if she was a smoker.

'Oh, I'm sorry about that,' said George, in an unusually gallant tone. I checked his face, which was still deadpan.

'And yet Majed is not here,' said Mariam.

'Majed's always late,' George explained to Jenan.

'Majed is not always late!' said Wael. 'People say that whenever he is late but, actually, more often, he isn't late. In fact, because people are always saying he's late, Majed worries more than most people about the time.'

Jenan smiled genially in a way I suspected she would not have were he not Wael Hejazi. No one else responded to Wael's outburst. Ibrahim was walking up the side stairs onto the stage, and we followed him in single file and formed our usual circle, everyone shaking their arms and legs, bouncing on the balls of their feet. A glistening, freshly painted area at the back was marked off by tape. I, on the further edge, was in the sun. My neck was starting to sweat. The eyes of my shaded castmates fixed behind me and I turned, twirling my wrists and rolling my shoulders, to see we had acquired a small audience of tech crew, some of the workers, and a few passers-by. Some were already sitting on the ground, several had started filming on their phones, presumably zooming in on Wael. Four or five little boys jostled each other near the supermarket; you could tell, maybe from the way they walked, tiny and wild but with the postures and gestures of grown men, that they were children from the camp. The crowd grew, noisy with interest. Mariam led us in one of our chants and a stamping dance, obviously to entertain them with the purpose of advertising the show, and then she instructed us to explore the set. I heard one of the kids run up and ask in a loud voice, What's going on?, and Mariam and Anwar explaining that we were rehearsing for a play, and that yes, that is

Wael Hejazi, and he is going to be the main character. I stood at the bottom of the half-finished stairs, holding the banister as if to climb them, and Ibrahim materialised beside me. He wore a baseball cap but with his head tilted up the sun shone on his features. His smile was hidden and his brow was heavy. My animal self responded to his smell and I leaned closer, adopting our conspiratorial tone from yesterday.

'Everything's okay with Amin?'

His eyes fell on me as if by accident.

'What do you mean?' he said tonelessly.

'That thing with Wael.'

'Amin is fine.'

He shifted his eyes back to the staircase, pulling at the banister slightly as though testing its strength, then skipped down to the stage floor and moved off, cracking his knuckles. So be it, I thought. I had wanted him to play it cool. Now he had cooled.

Jenan and Wael sat dangling their feet over the edge, facing Mariam. The crowd drew closer to watch. Jenan was holding a script, and I tuned in just as Wael was telling her he had never loved her. He was already noticeably less wooden. Jenan followed the script with her eyes but fused this into a performance of absorbed listening. Then she started speaking, and I saw she was rough around the edges but also that there was something nice about this, the untrained movements, occasional breathiness, a harshness that veered her away from the usual Ophelia clichés. Physically she was about the same size as Wael, so there wasn't anything frail about her. She spoke the classical language with the smoothness of someone who had undergone Quranic training, and the contrasts between her inflections and mine rang out to me; inevitably, our interpretations of the character were different, and my reading of Ophelia was striking me as more obviously to type. If 'playing to type' is something you can say about a part, as if Ophelia was the one inhabiting me; but maybe she was, Ophelia the cultural icon, trailing significations and pop references like flower petals, and perhaps this was the core of it, that I had a cultural hangover and Jenan did not, Jenan might not have even seen let alone been haunted by that drowning Pre-Raphaelite Ophelia with her hands cupped above her submerged body like water lilies. Watching the pair of them, I indulged a mental tic I'd developed of translating words and phrases back into English, comparing meanings and sounds. The original was so well-worn inside me it was practically a patchwork of quotations, tinny with centuries of repetition, impossible to prevent them shadowing the attic of my memory, *Rich gifts wax poor when givers prove unkind, We are arrant knaves, believe none of us.* Wael was telling Jenan for the third time that she ought to go to a nunnery, *ith-habi ila deer rahibat*, when a voice shouted: 'Sorry I'm late!'

Everyone turned at once. The lanky figure of Majed was running towards us, wearing an Adidas tracksuit and yellow-framed spectacles, lifting dust with his sneakers.

'I got an interrogation order.' He was out of breath, wiping his lenses on his T-shirt. 'My wife made me go back for it. She freaked out, police in the house. Hi, everyone,' he added as he put his glasses back on, and did a double-take. 'Who are all these people?'

'Open rehearsal.' Mariam hesitated before switching to English and lowering her voice. 'What's it for, did they say?'

Majed handed her a folded page. The circle of people around us watched, the camp boys jostling each other, conferring, *jaysh, jaysh*. I had an odd thought that Mariam could have spoken in Hebrew, since this was a tourist town and everyone understood English – but of course the sound of Hebrew would not be well received this side of the wall. Mariam read the interrogation order, which was itself, I now saw, entirely in Hebrew, met my eye, and then met Ibrahim's.

'Do you think they know your brother's still involved?' said Ibrahim.

Mariam blew her cheeks out.

'How?' said Wael.

'Talk about it later,' said Mariam. 'Finish the scene first, guys.'

Jenan and Wael returned to their positions to complete the dialogue. Both looked rattled, particularly Jenan, which was understandable: she'd just joined us, she was feeling out our dynamic, and now not only was a new dynamic hatching but a threat had materialised, of interrogation, of danger. Of dissolution, even. As far as I was concerned, if the Israelis really made an effort to stop us it would not be worth the fight. We were mere human beings, there was only so much we could do. The only person who didn't look unnerved was Mariam, who stared at her actors as though with the force of her gaze she could make them more sturdy. I had a feeling I sometimes get when I drink too much coffee, which was that while standing still, watching Jenan and Wael, another more agitated Sonia was wriggling inside my skin, trying to get out. I was thirsty as well and I needed the loo, and in this state of physical discomfort something strange happened. My viewpoint switched, and as though I were in a dream and my perspective had been breached I moved like a surveillance drone and saw our project from above, situated fragilely in time and place, this summer, this side of the wall. Accompanying this vision was a fear, almost a premonition, that it was all foretold anyway, everything had been decided in advance, we were only acting parts that had been given to us, and now some inexorable machinery was being set in motion that would sooner or later throw our efforts out into the audience, dismantle our illusions, and leave us cowering before the faceless gods of Fate and State.

I walked a few paces over to the angled shade cast by the set and its scaffolding. Moving there heartened me. I looked up at our tall wooden stage, which had been drawn on paper and brought to life. It was strong, it would withstand the rain, it was a monument, a 'work', like the giant key at the refugee camp, which had probably been praised by some critic at some tent at the Biennale. It was terrible to take heart in the thought that a monument was less likely to be bulldozed than an ordinary person's home, but no sooner had I thought this than I doubted it was true. I doubted the power of what Mariam called 'PR', whether being photographed many times, appearing in a newspaper, could ever really protect a building or a human life when it came down to it. Valiantly Wael and Jenan were carrying on, and then Jenan was completing her final speech, saying of Wael: *I see now that refined and noble intellect ringing as sweet bells jangle discordantly, detestably,* and after the silence that signified the end of scene came the sudden fracturing of applause, and our crowd became restless, homing in on Wael, calling his name. Mariam announced a ten-minute break – 'And then we'll run the fencing scene, and then we're going home' – and I watched her sit beside Jenan, making wheel-like hand gestures, taking the script from her and licking her fingers to flick it back a few pages.

'I dreamt about you last night,' said a voice. It was Amin, beside me, rolling a smoke.

'Really? What was I doing?' I couldn't keep the edge out of my tone. His friendliness unnerved me.

'Trying to remember.' He ran the sticky margin of his paper over his tongue. 'It wasn't about you, the dream. Don't be scared.'

'I just made an appearance.'

'Exactly.'

'Minor character.'

'Right.'

On the stage steps, Wael held his jacket rakishly over one shoulder while strangers crowded around him. He leaned in for each selfie; his white smile flashed and shut, flashed and shut. He looked much more comfortable being famous than being Hamlet. The other cast members were engrossed in their phones. I left Amin and walked over to Anwar, who was mixing a small tub of something pink with a thick brush.

'Congratulations,' I said. 'It's looking incredible.'

'Thanks, thanks.'

Up close, Anwar appeared older than his low-slung jeans and hey-dude manner implied. He was grey at the temples and had some softness around the chin.

'How's your brother?' I asked.

'Salim? He's okay. I'm not sure . . . yeah, I don't know.'

George's voice reached me then. 'Why would he do it to himself? There's no logic.'

I turned round. George and Ibrahim were standing beside a closed-up shopfront about six metres away. Ibrahim was squinting with thought, or the sun. I listened but couldn't hear anything else, and then Jenan approached me, fanning herself with her script, to ask if I'd come with her to find a toilet. As we crossed back towards the shops, she asked me where I was from.

'Here.'

'Bethlehem?'

'Palestine.'

'I know, I meant where.'

'She's a Danish spy,' George shouted.

I jumped. He was grinning, still a couple of metres from us. Typical of George to swim up and slice through a conversation like that, as if just to let you know he'd been circling your legs in silence. Then again, I too had been trying to eavesdrop, on him.

'Excited to be in the play?' I asked Jenan, switching tack.

'It's great,' she said. 'I'm happy I could do it after all. There's a café up here somewhere.'

We took a road out of the open space of the stage area that immediately steepened. I clung to the shade. Jenan seemed unbothered by the exercise.

'So who do you think it was?' she said. 'That let slip about the funding?'

'Maybe no one. Maybe they're running on old news.'

'But Majed's going to be interrogated.'

'True. Excuse me, sir, could we use your bathroom?'

The café owner rubbed his hands together. 'I'm sorry.' He shook his head. 'It's not . . . not good for ladies.'

Jenan thanked him and led me round a cobbled corner directly to a hipster café with air conditioning. A couple of bearded guys looked up from their laptops as we entered. Behind the bar, a woman in an apron worked a gleaming espresso machine. We took turns to use the toilet and I bought two bottles of water.

'Are you actually Danish?' said Jenan as we stepped back into the heat.

'No. Dutch, kind of.'

'And the Palestinian part?'

'Haifa.'

'Ah. Are you . . . ?'

She was hesitating. What is the best way to ask someone if they are the offspring of refugees?

'My grandparents,' I said. 'I used to stay with them every summer. In Haifa.'

'Lucky you,' she replied with such swiftness that I faltered. I couldn't tell if she was blasé or offended, and I could only see half her face because we were walking beside each other. 'I'm from Nablus,' she said. 'I've never been to Haifa.'

We turned the corner. I thought about saying, *But my other grandfather was a refugee from Tiberias*. Even in my head it sounded defensive. I said: 'I'm happy you're with us.'

'Me too.'

'It would have been funny if Mariam was Ophelia,' said Jenan. 'Don't you think? She's so much older than Wael.'

'Well, if it wasn't you, I think I would have played Ophelia.'

Jenan jerked her head. 'You?'

'I mean . . .' I trailed off. The stage came into view. From a distance the fragmented stairs looked beautiful and deliberate against the backdrop of the separation wall, like a Piranesi staircase, leading nowhere. Mariam waved us over.

'Look at us all on our phones,' she was saying. 'Is that everyone?'

She started a headcount. The tops of her cheeks were pink from the sun. I probed my discomfort at this Ophelia issue. Why was I embarrassed? More to the point, why would Mariam conceal from Jenan that I had been playing Ophelia before her? And why, when she delivered the news about Jenan, had Mariam been so nervous about my reaction? I'd had my own qualms about playing Wael Hejazi's love interest. I looked uneasily at the two women, who were smiling at each other.

'A person looks at their phone,' said Mariam, 'and a bubble appears around them, separating them from everyone else.' She put a hand on her hip in a manner that normally would not have irritated me. I glared at her hand, the ringed bendy fingers. I'd not previously felt anxious about my position in the cast hierarchy. Maybe I considered myself exempt from the rules, since I was from outside. Actually my position was dependent on Mariam. I was living in her house, so we arrived at and left rehearsals together; I was her ear, her friend, and until today we'd been the only two women. She had obviously anticipated the threat that Jenan would pose. I wasn't aware that she was testing me, but perhaps she was, and I had failed.

'This shit is the antithesis of theatre,' said Mariam, gesturing at their devices. 'Get off your asses, guys, and do the fencing scene.'

'Get off your ass, Wael,' said George.

'Don't be rude,' said Ibrahim.

George smiled, put a finger in his mouth and popped his cheek. Wael and Ibrahim began stretching their hamstrings. I hadn't seen them rehearse the fencing scene yet but I knew they were training with a movement coach from a dance school in Ramallah, who also specialised in dabke and capoeira, which seemed fitting, one being our native folk dance, the other a hybrid martial art developed by African slaves in Brazil. I took a spare chair.

'I used to do capoeira when I was younger,' said Wael, reaching a hand towards my bottle with familial insolence. I gave it over and he tipped his head back to pour, water falling down his cheeks.

'Wallah,' I said.

'Once, I even snuck into '48 to do it.' He wiped his mouth, screwing on the lid. 'We were with a bunch of German girls, and a Mexican guy called Pablo.'

'Before you were famous?'

'Long before. Thanks, Mama.'

I caught the bottle in both hands as he ran at the stage and leapt up the stairs to face Ibrahim. They wielded bamboo sticks, bouncing with bent knees. Suddenly Wael growled, charged and jumped into Ibrahim's arms. Ibrahim yelped, dropping his stick to grab Wael under the buttocks, then whirled him around before letting him slide down, cracking a one-eyed smile. I laughed, and Mariam called, Are we actors or are we monkeys?, but I saw on her face what I was feeling, an affection and nonsensical pride, as though we had anything to do with how lovely they were.

They resumed positions.

'Okay, Majed, are you ready?' said Mariam. 'Come, Hamlet, come and take this hand from me. Whenever you're ready.'

'Come, Hamlet,' said Majed, stepping forth as King Claudius.

Something exploded on the street behind us. I flew to my feet. An arm of white tear gas looped up over the buildings.

Mariam groaned. 'Just what we need.'

'Fuckers,' said Ibrahim.

Majed looked frightened behind his glasses, holding his arms out as though he might fall. Like me, he checked everyone else's faces to gauge how scared he ought to be. No one seemed terrified but they all sprang into action, and Ibrahim and Wael jumped offstage while the tech crew scrambled for their things like a storm was coming.

'Come on guys, come on guys.' Anwar waved his arm at his team. 'Yalla walk, walk.'

Shouting reached us from the next street over, and then screaming. We saw children running, heard more cracks of tear gas, saw several more thin loops of white, reaching higher this time. A voice speaking Hebrew, warped by a megaphone. Gunfire. I followed the others in a crouching run round a corner. Within a couple of streets, there was practically no noise at all. We straightened up but without dropping our pace; Faris ushered us behind a building and I thought to myself how fortunate that we were actors, that we stretched and exercised every morning, so that someone like Faris could run just as fast as little Amin.

We arrived at the main street. The pilgrim buses were gone. With Jenan right behind me, I opened the back door of Mariam's car and saw Ibrahim's baseball cap coming in through the other side. We squashed in, me in the middle, and through the windscreen I saw two soldiers strolling into the road. One, curiously, held a camera, which he pointed in our direction before scanning the rest of the street up to the wall. George shut the front passenger door and Mariam went into reverse, facing me, and as if she had read my mind, said: 'Don't worry, Sonia.'

George said, 'They took a dancer last year, no one knows why, and he's still in administrative detention. He was from Germany.'

The blood rushed to my face.

'George, please,' said Mariam.

'Why did we think this was a good idea to come today again?' said George.

'We needed to stick to the schedule,' said Mariam.

'And now they're going to shut us down anyway,' said George. 'What's the point in doing a play when there are massive protests going on? What the fuck is the point?'

'This is not helpful,' Ibrahim boomed.

'If you don't let me concentrate,' said Mariam, 'we'll have an accident.'

Exploding tear-gas canisters thrummed louder as we edged down another street. Three little boys stood clumped by the corner of a building. I was sure they had been among our spectators earlier. They had masked their faces with kuffiyehs. One of them played with a pair of rocks, tossing them in the air like dice.

'Be careful,' said Ibrahim, pointing at the boys. 'Go back, go back.'

Sure enough, as we reversed, the corner where the boys stood erupted with gas, and the boys ran back alongside our car. Four soldiers appeared in the mist, lumbering in their knee-guards. Behind them, a truck. The cloudy scene receded as the truck halted, swivelled, and began to spray something onto one of the buildings. A shopfront had already pulled down its metal shutters, and above it I saw an arm frantically closing a window.

'What's that?' I said.

'Skunk water,' said Jenan.

A putrid smell was already reaching us. Mariam swerved down another side street, which became a dirt track. Soon we could see the hills, and we opened the windows, breathing heavily. Everything looked normal. A farm, a restaurant, a military checkpoint.

'Sorry,' said George.

'You know what?' Mariam said. 'Oh.'

'What?'

'Are Amin and Wael in the other car?' she asked. 'I didn't mean to leave them together.'

'Amin seems to be in a better mood today,' I said.

'Brahim, will you text them?' said Mariam.

I looked straight ahead as we entered Wadi an-Nar. The valley was a different story from the back seat. My nausea overwhelmed me as I gripped the edges of the two front seats, stiffening myself as best as I could against Ibrahim, although it would have been more natural to lean on him. I would have liked to lean on him. By the time we reached Ramallah my lower back was aching and I was ready to go home, but Mariam insisted on buying us dinner and drove to a café-bar in a residential neighbourhood.

The night was balmy and quiet. An old neon sign hung above the door; some Arabic hip-hop was playing faintly inside. We took two tables surrounded by fairy lights, with a motley selection of wooden benches and metal chairs. Ibrahim brought out a round of beers and paper menus. I waited for him to look at me, but he did not. On the adjacent table sat three foreign women, their foreignness announced not only by their complexions and tense expressions but also by the harem pants and sandals and scarves they wore, as though Ramallah was a desert and they were sleeping in tents. On the other side of the road a derelict villa gaped at us, and up the hill a hotel flashed its lights. There was no one else in the street. I ordered a chicken salad, which arrived after everyone else's meals, and consisted mainly of bread.

'Is this my salad?' I asked the waiter.

The waiter looked at my plate. 'Yes.'

'Could I bother you for some bread on the side?'

The waiter hesitated, then laughed, falling out of character.

'The food went downhill here,' said Ibrahim.

'Here, no one knows,' said Jenan.

I thought at first that she was referring to the food, but she'd put her fork down and was watching a group of young people chatting and drinking inside the bar.

'Or they do,' she said, 'but, khalas, they don't care what's happening.'

'The Ramallah bubble,' I said.

A man in the window, probably in his sixties, wearing a tarbush and a velvet waistcoat, sat alone before a neglected backgammon game. He was also watching the group of young people.

'Hey, hey,' said Mariam, as two figures on the road drew into the light. Anwar and Majed.

'Hi, guys,' said Anwar, one hand in his back pocket, the other fingering the buttons on his shirt. Majed stood slightly behind, glasses up on his head.

'Where are the others?' said Mariam.

'Faris stayed in Bethlehem,' said Anwar. 'He couldn't face the journey. Wael and Amin went home.' He looked at his sister. 'You need to call Wael.'

'What happened?'

'He says he's quitting the play.'

'He's what?'

'What happened?' I echoed.

'He argued with Amin. It escalated. It was a bit ugly.'

None of us could believe that Wael would really have quit. But the dejection on Anwar and Majed's faces was not fading and Wael wasn't responding to Mariam's calls. She walked away over the dark road and we could hear her saying, Let's talk about it in the morning, there's no need to be hasty, and when her tone hardened I exchanged looks with Ibrahim; she was obviously speaking to Amin, trying to keep a lid on her anger, one long stream of speech ending with: Please call me back as soon as possible.

'What did they fight about?' I asked Majed.

'At first it was about the article, the funding thing. Amin said he wouldn't be surprised if Wael had snitched, and then he said Wael was a terrible actor. He said some pretty mean stuff.'

'Oh, Amin, why?' I said. I took out my own phone. 'What's the Wi-Fi password?'

Anwar craned his head to look through the window. 'Hope2017. Lower case.'

Wael Hejazi
Today 19:09

Love are you okay?

I followed up with:

> I'm here if you want to talk.

Then:

> Call me when you have a
> chance

Mariam had disappeared behind the cars parked on the other side of the road.

'I doubt the Israelis even *need* a snitch,' I said. 'They're probably following Mariam's emails. I knew he was jealous of Wael.'

'See that guy in there?' Ibrahim pointed at the man in the tarbush who was not playing backgammon. 'Spy.'

'Really?'

'It's well known.' Ibrahim was addressing me finally, his pupils catching little half-moons of light. 'Not for *them*, though. For our guys.'

'They're not my guys,' said Jenan.

'You know what I mean,' said Ibrahim. 'The leadership.'

Jenan lifted an eyebrow.

'Obviously they're not my guys either,' said Ibrahim, opening his hands.

The man in the tarbush stayed impassively in profile, watching the bar scene. An elephant was embroidered on the back of his waistcoat. He looked far too conspicuous to be a spy. It sounded like a made-up story.

'Try not to worry,' Ibrahim called out into the road.

Mariam was striding back towards us. She sat and put her head in her hands, the curls hanging between her fingers. 'Someone roll me a cigarette,' she muttered.

'Give it until tomorrow.' Ibrahim unwound his tobacco. 'He won't really have quit, I promise you.'

Anwar shut his eyes, clenching his teeth.

'Try not to worry about it now,' I said.

'You don't look very well,' said Jenan.

'Yeah, are you okay?' I said to Anwar.

'I was actually talking to you,' said Jenan.

'Me?' I said.

'You look pale.'

Now that she said it, I did feel a bit off. I murmured, 'Too much sun, probably.'

Mariam held her cigarette very far up her fingers, almost between her knuckles. 'I shouldn't have let them go together.'

I chewed on a piece of bread, and thought of the puzzle about the cabbage and the goat and the wolf: how to cross over a bridge one at a time without one of them eating another one. But what if the bridge is being fired at by Israeli soldiers? You can't take your goat and leave your wolf when the bridge might suddenly collapse.

'They're not your children,' said Anwar. 'They're grown men.'

'Now the question is,' said Majed, '*did* they find out about Salim and the funding, and if so, how?'

'Is that really the question?' said Mariam. 'They have the best surveillance technology in the world.'

'They're going to interrogate me. I'm allowed to ask.'

Mariam blew her cheeks out. 'I'm sorry, Majed.'

'When is it happening?' said Ibrahim.

'Two days.'

The texture of our silence changed. I felt a chill and realised George was looking at me. I flipped up my empty palm.

'What?'

He shook his head as if he didn't understand.

'Have I done something?' I asked.

'I don't know.'

'We're starting late tomorrow,' said Mariam. 'Half past eleven. Take some of the morning off. I think we might need more drinks.'

'I'll help you,' said Anwar.

The Mansour siblings stood and went inside the bar, deserting me. I reached for my teacher's voice.

'It's been a difficult day,' I said, addressing everyone and no one, specifically avoiding George. 'Let's be kind to each other.'

I couldn't shake a feeling of invasion. I glanced at the others, all inscrutable to me. Jenan leaned back in her chair, hands in her lap, watching Majed, her brow furrowed; Ibrahim kept shooting his eyes at her; Majed was obviously angry with Mariam but inhibited by his mild manners, and only shifted in his seat, touching his glasses. And beside me I sensed George's presence in infrared, glowing with an aura of hidden motives. He never let anyone know what he really thought except in jest. He was hard and slippery, he was like a stone you catch beneath your swimming feet where you think there is only sand. And he didn't like me. That, at least, was obvious.

14

'Why don't you have a fucking phone that works?'

'Haneen, calm down.'

'And Mariam's not picking up either! You're both unbelievable. Rubber bullets kill people. Sometimes they fire live rounds.'

'Everyone is fine. It's been a bit stressful, though, so can I call you in the morning?'

'Whatever,' said my sister faintly, and then she hung up.

I caught my first glimpse of Mariam's ex that night. He parked in a blue Renault outside the house, and I waited in the doorway while Mariam walked over and pulled Emil from the back seat by the armpits. The driver's face was masked by the reflections on the windscreen but I saw gelled curls and something of his bodily movements, one big hand combing the air. Mariam straightened, and the Renault lurched rudely into gear and drove off.

Inside, Mariam dropped into a kitchen chair and stared at the fruit bowl. Emil and I stood watching. I wanted to comfort her but I stopped myself, and instead I turned and put water on to boil, placing teabags into two cups lined with tannin residue, snapping a twig of sage in half, drawing the cloak up over my panic. My sympathy was laced with fear, specifically a fear of loss, that what had been steady beneath me was shaking. I hadn't realised quite how much the play meant to me. I was no different from Amin and the others, I was relying on its structure to hold me. And when I say the play, I think what I mean is Mariam. Emil was also visibly disturbed by his mother's mood, hovering by the fridge. He walked over to the sofa, humming, and after a moment began to scamper back and forth. I sat down at the table. He pounced on me to ask what I'd like for lunch, even though it was nearly bedtime.

'Stop it!' Mariam erupted.

He cowered, murmured, '*Mama*,' while his mother's voice stayed high, caught on a wire: 'I've had it! Play in your room!'

The child froze, looking at his small hands. He began to cry. I looked on in horror. I wanted to rush forward and hug his little body, but once more I controlled myself, and then Mariam reached for him herself, cringing with remorse. Emil wailed more loudly.

'Oh, I'm sorry, sweetheart,' she said, 'I'm sorry. I didn't mean it. Mama's a bit stressed. Come on, my love, let's put you in bed.'

I stayed at the table as she carried him, sobbing, into his room. Eventually his crying ceased, and then Mariam appeared in the doorway, and I readied myself for the torrent.

'I'm exhausted,' she said in a strangled voice.

'I know you are,' I said, and stood. My armour fell off as she came towards me for a hug. I was moved to be the one to catch her. Her weight made me feel solid, it made me more than I was.

In my room, I tried Wael again. To my amazement he picked up.

'I've quit,' he said thickly.

'So I've heard.'

'I can't do it any more.'

'What did he say to you, exactly?'

'It doesn't matter. It's too much pressure, I can't take it.'

'What if – what if Mariam fired Amin and found a replacement? Would you come back?'

'I can't tolerate it and my parents can't tolerate it either. It's not just Amin, it's everything.'

'Please, don't rush this decision. Mariam's worked so hard.'

'I can't be Hamlet, Sonia. I'm sorry. I know it's a big honour but I'm exhausted, more than I ever am from singing, I'm exhausted in my soul, and we haven't even started the show! I know my limits. I come home at night and my mother says, What are they doing to you, you look like you've been fighting in a war. I have bruises on my legs.'

'What did Amin say?'

'He insulted me. He called me a normaliser. And he said I'm a weak actor.'

'A normaliser?'

'I have some Israeli fans.'

'Look,' I said, 'Amin has his own issues, sometimes it's hard—'

He interrupted: 'Amin is a jerk, I get it. My point is, it's hard enough without the people you're working with making you feel . . .' He gave a long, loud sigh. 'You know, I'm kind of famous here. I'm not being snobby.' He said this last word in English.

'I know, sweetie.'

'Mariam should give the part to Amin.'

'You're going to give him what he wants?'

'He's a much better actor than me.'

'It's not a competition.'

'The only reason Mariam wants me is because I'm Wael Hejazi.' His voice was musical with sadness.

'Listen,' I told him, 'I'm a teacher. I teach acting. And I can see you have something. Something special, you have – star quality.'

I hated myself for using this phrase. Plainly Wael hated it too because he groaned.

'I'm a singer,' he said.

'You're a performer. You already know the part. You'll get there. You've come so far.'

He was silent.

'Please,' I said. 'Think about it.'

'I've already thought about it.' He jumped from Arabic into American English. 'It's been cool to know you, sister. Don't be a stranger, okay?'

I switched on the ancient dusty white fan in the corner, lay on my mattress, and played some videos of Wael on YouTube on my phone. He tacked back and forth over a black stage, cheekbones glossy, and I noticed how big his lips were, how flexible and elastic, so that his grin was a movie-star grin, slow to stretch across his face, reflecting the adoration of the crowd, his ears going back as though he were bashful, which he evidently was not.

Sleep eluded me. A wedding party started up down the road with amplified electronic music and shouting and car horns so loud I'd have believed it if someone told me the guests were dancing in the garden by my window. I didn't hear a peep from Mariam or Emil, although I did have a pillow over my head most of the night. No sooner was I finally asleep, it seemed, than I was woken again by the call to prayer. My skin was flaming. I drank a whole litre bottle of water from the fridge and sat on the dark couch waiting for the sun to rise, which it did abruptly, hardening and colouring the room's interior, the tables, the pictures on the wall, in a matter of seconds. I checked my bank statements and the news on my laptop, and then Mariam materialised at the entrance to the bedrooms in a flannel dressing gown.

'It's a disaster.'

I closed the computer. 'It's not a disaster.'

'The whole thing has failed.'

'He might change his mind. They had a bust-up. They're just boys.'

'No.' Her eyeline was drifting. 'No. We just spoke. He was very calm and definite. What an idiot I – I worked so hard on him.'

She rubbed her eye. It was true that, despite having no acting experience, after only a few weeks Wael was able to shift between the different characters and moods of one of the most demanding roles in the history of theatre with pretty remarkable competence. Besotted tormented teenager, rampant angry bereaved son, unwilling leader, unwilling hero, heaven's scourge and minister. He may not have been the strongest in the cast but Mariam had at least made him into an actor.

'The thing is,' she said, 'I don't want to generalise about men, but.'

'But what?'

'This wouldn't have happened if they were girls.'

'I really don't think that's true. Women can be just as selfish, and just as cruel.'

'Men are destructive, they're idiotic, when they want to they can control their feelings but then they go and blow everything up because they haven't processed any of their shit properly. I know I should have been prepared for conflict between them but you know what?' And she met my eye, defensive. 'I *was* prepared, after what happened at Monday's rehearsal, and I didn't want them to ride together, I wanted them separate.'

'You can't control everything.'

'I've been working so hard to pull this off and Amin, I'm going to kill him, but also Wael, they just stamped on it. They don't give a flying. To them it's just, I don't know, it's not very important. It's just playing to them.'

'It's the day of rage today,' I said, by way of distraction.

'It certainly is.'

She stopped and looked through the window. I watched her, her slept-on hair standing up at the back. I took my phone outside.

The sky was a stinging blue. Beneath it the garden looked like it had shrunk in the heat. Or maybe I was so used to seeing it full of the cast that it felt smaller without them, the way rooms shrink when you remove the furniture. The waking day had not yet ripped the moisture from the air, which felt damp and cool on my skin.

'Haneen, there's been a fuck-up.'

Whizz of a passing train. 'There's been a what?' my sister shouted.

'A *fuck-up*.'

I explained about Wael, about Mariam, about Majed's interrogation.

'Listen, I want to come down and help, but my car is in the garage and it's chaos out there. Have you seen?'

'Day of rage?'

'Fifty people wounded outside the mosque after the street prayers last night. Even the sheikh's in hospital. You know, they were all praying in the streets, because of the metal detectors.'

'Yes, yes, I'm aware.'

'I don't know how big the response will be, you know it's ridiculous actually the way the—'

'It's not a great week really, is it?'

'Are you kidding? It's *beautiful*. Watch the footage. I was thinking we should try and go down there and join them.'

'You're not worried about getting shot?'

'Listen Sonia I've just arrived at the post office, can I call you later? If she rages don't go cold on her. Give her a hug. She'll freeze up if you go cold on her. Love you.'

'Why would I go cold?' I asked, but she'd already hung up.

Mariam had disappeared. I tried Wael again, he didn't answer, and then I showered and dressed and found myself jammed in a mental dialogue, playing all the different parts, hamster in a wheel, what I would say to Amin, what would I say to Mariam about Wael, what would she say back. I boiled water for coffee. An hour elapsed. When at eleven Mariam hadn't reappeared it occurred to me, with dismay, that she might have taken Emil to day-care without letting me know. But her car was still in the drive, dusty in the sun. I waited a little longer and then knocked on her bedroom door and asked her name. A throat cleared.

'Come in.'

I'd never been inside Mariam's bedroom, even though we'd been living together for weeks. Compared to the rest of the house it was surprisingly bare. A single strip of embroidered fabric nailed over her window functioned imperfectly as a curtain, leaking light either side; another embroidered strip lay across the duvet. An old-fashioned bureau beside the bed held a mirror and an army of tiny essential oil bottles, opposite a frail chair with a pile of books on its lap. And Mariam and Emil, like a pair of lovers silent after an argument, lay in the bed, she with an arm draped around his middle, he looking down his nose at me, motionless, one small foot poking out from under the duvet.

'You can come in,' she croaked, 'don't be shy.'

It felt strange to stand while they were lying down so I sat on the end of the mattress, which sagged beneath me. Mariam yawned.

'You look a bit ill,' she said. 'You should drink water and have some salty things.' She bashed a pillow behind her to sit upright, controlling a sigh. Emil squirmed, objecting, and flipped over, nuzzling against her waist.

'Can I ask.' I leaned closer. 'How much were you paying Wael?'

Her eyes scoured my face.

'Was he a big expense?'

'One of the biggest.'

'So, without him, funding is less of a . . . ? Right?'

'Right.'

'That's what I thought.'

Our phones sang at the same moment, mine in my pocket, hers lighting up on the dresser. She reached over her son.

'Haneen is here,' she said, eyes on the screen. 'Did you call her or something?'

'Yes. Yeah, hang on, I'll get the door.'

'The boys will be arriving soon,' I heard her say after I'd left the room.

Haneen was sweating on the doorstep in a grey trouser suit, her hair stuck to her forehead.

'How did you get here so fast?'

'I found a Palestinian taxi driver in Tel Aviv. It's like an hour without traffic. Is she here?'

'Wait. Haneen.'

She'd already walked past me and was opening the fridge. 'What?' She lifted out a bottle of water.

'You mustn't let her cancel the show. Without Wael the budget goes down – we can still do it. We just need someone to play Hamlet.'

She eyed me as she drank, then stopped to say, breathlessly: 'Can one of the others play Hamlet?'

'Amin is very good. Although I would hate to give it to him, he's the one who bullied Wael. But even if we use Amin, that leaves us without a Horatio. There might be time to audition but then there'll be a delay. There are a *lot* of lines. Although knowing Amin I bet he's already memorised them.'

She gazed through me. Almost in slow motion, she shrugged and turned out her lip. 'I'll discuss it with her.' She walked straight to Mariam's bedroom. She didn't need to be told where it was.

I faced the array of dirty dishes in the sink, our half-finished cups of tea from last night, a grimy sponge floating in a bowl, and when I glanced at the window there was a dark figure hunched cross-legged on the garden bench, struck by the shade of the lemon tree. Ibrahim. His arm was going up and down, to and from his mouth, a wisp of smoke travelling out into the sunlight. He hadn't seen me. I crouched to look for a new sponge under the sink and, not finding one, stood to see Majed had joined Ibrahim on the lawn. Then Faris opened the gate.

'Sonia!' Faris waved, his voice thinned by the walls and window. Majed and Ibrahim also looked up, conferring inaudibly. Faris gave me a full-body shrug and headshake, asking for an explanation. He was wearing a short-sleeved shirt of pressed checked cotton. I went out through the front door, pulling my cardigan tight.

'Hi, guys. Mariam's got a bad headache. She's still in bed. How do you feel about giving her today off? Can someone call Dawud at the theatre? We should rehearse there, if we can.'

I ignored the glance that passed between them, and went inside to tell Mariam the plan.

We waited by the public entrance to the theatre for Dawud to come and unlock the doors. There was a demonstration a few blocks away and we could hear shouts and chanting. Otherwise the street seemed normal, with pedestrians passing in and out of shops, paying for sandwiches, hurtling to work. Jenan said she'd crossed the demo on her way up and it looked small, relatively speaking. Apparently it was the same the West Bank over: the call for a day of rage had met with weak responses, even though the scenes in Jerusalem remained tremendous, hundreds praying in the streets, in the heat. 'Even priests are doing the Muslim prayers,' said Ibrahim.

'Ahlayn!'

Dawud was running on his long legs towards us, hair flopping, fiddling with the keys.

'I'm so sorry I kept you waiting!' He stooped to unlock the doors.

'Not at all,' I said. 'I'm sorry it was last minute.'

'How is your family?' said Faris.

Dawud straightened. 'They are fine, thank you.' He clutched his side, panting. Even so, I thought he looked troubled by the question, and I wondered if he was from East Jerusalem, or had relatives there.

I led the warm-up in the cool auditorium. Everyone was serious, and Amin and Majed seemed particularly sour. When I asked Majed how he was feeling, meaning about the interrogation tomorrow, he grunted and mumbled something I didn't catch. I directed Act One, Scene Three with Polonius, Laertes and Ophelia, giving Jenan the same blocking Mariam had given me, and I took notes, focusing on Jenan's delivery. When we broke for coffee I stepped out onto the dirty curved step before the building. The shouting from the demo was quieter; probably people had gone home for lunch. Across the way, a woman was undressing a headless aqua-blue mannequin in a shop window, tilting and hugging it from behind to reach the buttons of its long coat. One of the theatre doors beside me opened with a big cough.

'Oh hello,' I said.

Faris smiled, and the bags under his eyes lifted and deepened. His nostrils were packed with grey hairs and a tissue poked out from his chest pocket.

'Would you like to direct the next scene?' I said. 'I'm trying to think of all the scenes in *Hamlet* that don't have Hamlet in them.'

'I would be happy to,' he replied, warm and condescending, and I bowed, as though we were two old men making a wager.

'Thank you.'

He folded his arms by grabbing his elbows, cradling himself, and nudged his head at the building behind us. 'Theatre in Palestine is not what it was, you know.'

I looked back at the foyer. The theatre entrance had an air of faded extravagance, vaguely imitative of a London playhouse. Balding synthetic velvet ropes, framed sepia photographs of bygone shows. A marble floor, gathering dust. I peered through the dirty glass, peopling it with crowds from days of yore, the pre-show loitering, the aisles clogging after the curtain fell.

'When was the golden age, would you say?'

'Seventies, probably. Seventies to the early eighties.'

'And you were involved?'

'In a small way. I was on the fringe of the big guys. You know,' and he took a deep sigh, planting his hands on his hips, 'the whole concept of an independent Palestinian theatre started to emerge in the seventies. Before that, I think, it was very Egyptian.' He paused, then revised: 'I don't know, actually, I was young. I actually don't

244

remember any theatre outside of schools and churches and this. There wasn't much and it wasn't in dialect. It was in classical. Then when things *really* started, everything was in dialect, and it was basically all experimental.'

'Then it's unusual what we're doing, a play in classical Arabic?'

'You could say unusual. In Palestine. I don't know, maybe because we feel our art and things should be really *Palestinian*, not just generally Arab. The idea, back then, when it started properly, was: look, you can do resistance without going full-on political. You know? You could be subtle, have a subtle social and political commentary, without preaching, without slogans, and so on. One of the strongest plays I saw was this one that was so powerful and so good, so well made, that the *New York Times* wrote about it, *Le Monde* wrote about it –'

'Wow.'

'– *Washington Post* wrote about it, the whole Israeli press wrote about it. The Arabic media was interested in it. The play was called *al-Atmeh*, Darkness. It didn't talk about the occupation, it didn't talk about the military, it didn't talk about resistance. It just exposed the situation through – it starts with a play. A play within a play. It starts with somebody going onstage, someone who's fed up with life, who wants to commit suicide. And then,' his eyes widened, 'the lights go out.'

I laughed.

'Yes, just like the other day in the theatre here,' he said. 'So the director comes out with a flashlight, and he says, Please excuse us, we just need some time and we'll fix the lighting, and then we'll go on with the play. And the whole play is the audience waiting for the lights to come back on, and the director trying to find someone in the audience to fix the electricity. And in the beginning the audience thinks this is a real power cut. The actors are spread out, and they start acting from their different positions. One says, Give us back our money, we paid for this. A woman stands up and introduces herself and her fiancé, and there's a scene where this fiancé has the woman inside a plastic bag, pointing at her, describing how beautiful she is, and they're going on a honeymoon to Europe, and she's inside the plastic bag, suffocating, trying to get out. So they had women's issues, they had the Israelis,' he counted off on his fingers, 'they had the sheikh come in and say all this darkness is because you are disobeying our blah blah blah. You had the exploitative business people – you know, the whole cross-section of society appeared there in the play. The intellectuals just talking talking talking, as intellectuals do.' He chuckled. 'Everyone gets on the stage to show that he or she is trying to fix the thing, but they don't do anything, they just want to show off. And there were many scenes that didn't have any dialogue, which were like interpretive dance, physical body movements. Beautiful stuff. To cut a long story short, in the end, the lights come back on. Because a worker, a carpenter, he's the only one who goes onstage and works silently, without talking. And he fixes the electricity. But he also gets electrocuted and dies. And the question becomes, whose responsibility is that?'

One large eyebrow rose on his forehead. I grinned like a child at a hakawati.

'One of the scenes, I remember, was beautiful. They came around the audience giving candles to everybody. Very beautiful. It stayed in my mind, for ever, this scene.'

'You remember it well.'

'I went to every performance.'

'How many were there?'

'Four, I think.'

'And what about the rest of the audience, how did they respond?'

'Fantastic,' he said, shaking his head. 'Fantastic audiences.' He paused. 'In some Israeli newspapers they pointed out this play as a security issue. And they said, you know, these people are calling for a revolution.'

'There were Israelis in the audience?'

'Yes, yes. Journalists, and others who were Palestinians in '48. *These days,* everything is about money. Have you noticed? It's all about fundraising. This whole drama is about fundraising. This is the problem. Money. No one did any fundraising back then. Why does Wael need so much money? That's the real question. Why does Mariam think money is the answer? I think it's really sad because, well, I can understand the need to have a living, for theatre people to make a living off theatre, I mean, *I* need to make a living, but I think this . . . Who needs to produce a play with two hundred thousand dollars? Why? Why do you need this? Salaries of four thousand dollars a month. Why? You know? The spirit is not there. Something else replaced that spirit of giving that we used to have. Of volunteering, of passion. That you want to do something.'

He raised a fist at the street. Two tall young women in hijabs passed by, clutching schoolbooks to their chests.

'And when did you get involved?'

'After that show. It inspired me. I wanted to join the group, but I was working in a bank and I had to support my family in Bethlehem.'

'How old are you, Faris? If you don't mind me asking.'

'Seventy-two.' He looked at the ground, as if processing this. 'How old are you?'

'Thirty-eight.'

His eyes narrowed. 'So you are young, and, at the same time, you are not young.' He gave a thick bark of laughter. 'I remember being thirty-eight,' he added.

We ended rehearsal at six. Before we left, we each either gave Majed a hug or put a hand on his shoulder, wishing him a sombre good luck. As far as I knew, no one had raised the subject of Wael – bar Faris's complaint outside about fundraising and money. Faris gave me a lift back to Mariam's in his old brown car, which bleeped with increasing frequency when he didn't put his seat belt on.

'I hate being policed,' he said, drawing the belt like a sword from his hip. A moment later, he remarked: 'I hope they don't ruin it for us. We have a good play on our hands.'

I made an agreeing noise. There wasn't much else to say.

My sister was leaning against the wall outside Mariam's house. Her jacket hung from the crook of her arm.

'Hey,' I said. 'How is she?'

'You okay to go for a walk?'

'Ominous response.'

'She's much better. Let's drive somewhere.'

Mariam's keyring, a faded embroidered blue square, was dangling from her hand.

'Did you talk about it with her?' I said.

'She's thinking it over. She said maybe you could all play Hamlet. Take it in turns.'

'Not sure about that,' I said, getting in the passenger seat. 'Sounds experimental, in a bad way.' I imagined us swapping costumes, passing a Hamlet Hat around the stage before a baffled audience.

She drove us directly to Wael's neighbourhood, and at first I thought we were going to talk to him. Then we missed the turning that led to his house, and the city petered out around us as we emerged into the valley of Ayn Qiniya. An enormous hospital grasped the opposite hillside, near to a children's playground. We descended into an olive grove dense with young fruit, and I waited for my sister to speak. She was always the one holding the reins.

'I think the show has to go on,' she said finally, with a straightforward use of the cliché that demonstrated how little experience she had of theatre. 'Without Wael it's not going to draw the crowds the way she wanted to, but that's okay. She's brilliant, Mariam, but as you've probably noticed she can be naïve. She has a utopian side.'

'I don't think she's naïve,' I said.

She drove uphill again and parked on a dirt track. We stepped out and walked for a while. The sun was getting wispy, wrapping itself in white. I've never been a nostalgic person but standing there with my sister, looking down the slope and inhaling an air vigorous with green smells, I was seized by a strong wave of emotion. I don't know if the emotion was negative or positive per se, it was more just a powerful internal movement, a kind of seasickness. Maybe it was the strain of the last few days building up inside of me and breaking. A greyish-green Israeli army truck hobbled over one of the roads below us.

'What the fuck are they doing here?' I said.

'Day of rage, day of rage,' said my sister. She sighed, walking ahead.

'Tell me about Mariam. How you guys became friends.'

She dropped her pace to be on a level with me and, as she began to speak, I sensed something finally coming loose between us. I think that, sometimes, when calamity strikes and puts normal life under strain, feelings that have been stifled by everyday evasion can break free and make it easy to talk where before it felt impossible. Clouds, parted, dissolve. I wondered if this was always happening in Palestine, where calamity was always so close. Or whether it was different for those who, living here, endured it without respite, for whom constant calamity was itself the condition of normal life.

Haneen said she'd met Mariam, thinking they were strangers, while standing in line for coffee in the middle of Tel Aviv. Ariel Sharon gazed mournfully out at them from the newspaper of the guy in front, beside the words 'The Last Battle', and the two women fell into a muttered conversation about the prime minister's stroke. Mariam seemed eager to talk. She'd recently returned from America and was friendless, trying to find her feet, alienated in the West Bank with her husband, alienated when she returned to Haifa, neither here nor there, burdened wherever she went by the feeling that she was foreign.

'She told me once that theatre is always a home for outsiders. That people in theatre are misfits. Would you agree? I thought that was an interesting idea.'

'Maybe.'

I wasn't concentrating on her question because I was wondering why Haneen needed to excuse Mariam's openness that day, oh she must have been lonely, she must have been desperate for friends. She remembered exactly what Mariam was wearing: brown knee-high boots and a white skirt. I told her that I also remembered exactly what Mariam was wearing when I met her in Haifa a month ago at Haneen's flat: a sleeveless blue dress and ankle boots.

'You're wrong,' said Haneen. 'She was wearing jeans.'

'No, she was wearing a dress.'

'I remember because I asked her if she wasn't hot when we got into the theatre.'

'I remember the dress pretty distinctly.'

'You're mixing it with another memory.'

'I don't think so.'

'Well, I was also there.'

'We don't need to argue about this.'

A wind was up, her hair was blowing around. I was moved by how age had changed her. Nature was dishevelling her, drawing out a severe, skullish beauty I didn't often see. Her powerful frown and unadorned eyes looked almost genderless. She did a funny thing with her jaw, as though she was chewing the air, and then carried on.

She and Mariam drank their coffees together at a little table, and, rambling down a few paths of their biographies, discovered where they intersected: in childhood, in the summer, in Haifa. Joy of recognition; friendship accelerated. This was before Salim Mansour's political career took off, she added, which would have made Mariam identifiable in a different way.

'And when did you have a relationship with Salim?'

She looked at me, amazed.

'Oh, come on.'

'What?'

'We ran into him in Haifa the other day,' I said. 'It seemed obvious.'

'Really?' She grimaced and grabbed the trunk of a young tree to steady herself, stepping over a pile of rocks. 'I met him through her, not long after that. At a dinner.'

She skipped the details about the relationship and cut straight to how it ended. Salim was still entangled with his ex-girlfriend, an Israeli dentist named Suzanne, although he denied it and claimed they had what he called a 'mature friendship'. Suzanne was single, and he spent a lot of time with her, and often called her for advice, even in Haneen's company.

'What kind of advice?'

'Stuff to do with work, with family – logistical things. Or if something mechanical broke, like his dishwasher.' A smile entered her voice. 'She was very good at fixing things.'

'Weird.'

'I was going through my own phase, though, too, you know. I

was trying out some sort of Buddhist thing. Being free, letting others be free. I didn't know what I was talking about. As you know, freedom can be quite a vague word.'

But it was easy to blame herself for being too permissive when really the fault lay with Salim, who ought to have finished things properly with Suzanne before embarking on something with her. Ought to ought to ought to. They were both pretty young at the time, both clueless; there were no hard feelings. Salim just wasn't available in the way that he thought he was. They became good friends.

'You make it sound simple,' I said. 'Did they get back together afterwards?'

'No. He stopped calling her when his appliances broke, and he ended up marrying an Australian woman. She's nice. Phoebe.'

'That doesn't make you feel terrible? That you fixed him and sent him off to another woman?'

'I've let it go. I love him as a friend.'

'I'm sorry if I – sorry if that was insensitive.'

'That's okay. You are quite insensitive sometimes,' she said benevolently.

'Am I really?'

'I gave you a sanitised version, don't worry, the reality was a lot messier.'

'It's not so different from what I've just been through, actually.'

'The director?'

'Yeah.' I flushed. Of course she knew about it. 'Except he was actually married. Is married.'

'I didn't like him when I saw him after the show.'

'Oh yeah?' I looked at her with appetite, for confirmation, affirmation. Tell me the bad things, tell me he's not worthy of me.

'He seemed like a bit of an ass.'

'I wish you'd told me that earlier.'

'I don't think you'd have listened. You had to let it play out.'

I didn't contradict her. This analysis felt patronising even if it was accurate. We kept walking. The sun would set soon. In my mind's eye I saw Jerusalem; I saw streets of prayer, bodies bowing.

'Was there a reason you didn't tell me about Salim?' I asked. 'Where was I at the time?'

'Sometimes – has this ever occurred to you?' She bent to pick up a smooth stone by her foot, and began rubbing off the soil, letting the silence run for so long that I wondered whether she was doubting what she'd started to say. An accusation, perhaps, that I had not been a good sister. Finally, she said: 'Sometimes we're too sentimental. Like, as though the best thing in the world would be to end up with a Palestinian man, or a Palestinian woman. You could say it's because, oh, I don't know, you want to share Palestine with the person closest to you. But even that sounds a bit like ethnic nationalism. Don't you think? None of us is pure, you and I aren't, no one is, it's nonsense, it's ideological. We're meant to be better than that. Better than them. Or maybe – maybe I'm being unfair. But also, you know, the men here suffer so much. I know women do too. In many ways women suffer more. I guess I feel there's something about being a man, when a situation is set up to humiliate you. Didn't you say that, the other day? Humiliation makes men nasty.' She paused. 'Not that I'd say that about Salim, necessarily.'

'But you would about Mariam's husband.'

'Did you meet him yet?'

'No.'

'Honestly, Hazem was an education for Mariam. She was a sheltered person. We're all sheltered, you and I have been sheltered, it's not a criticism. But, you know, to take a look at what's going on, to go to the camps, to see the suffering of your people. He politicised her. But at a cost.' She threw the stone, which tripped down the slope between the trees. 'Maybe all's fair in love and war. Only it's not, is it? Not since the Geneva Convention.'

'That's a terrible joke,' I said.

She laughed and then was silent. Hazem's elder brother, she said, had been tortured and killed during the final phase of the first intifada. His younger brother was still in jail for stone-throwing. They grew up in Hebron without a father – their father had also been killed, although she couldn't remember when or where. The mother, Um Naji, was particularly fierce.

'Have you visited Hebron yet?'

'No,' I said, wiping the back of my neck.

'The kids there. You really have to be tough.'

So Hazem was Mariam's awakening, I thought, as Rashid had been Haneen's. My sister agreed that Mariam returned to Palestine for Hazem's sake, despite her claims of intending to come back anyway. He became an engineer but struggled to find work. They moved from Hebron to Ramallah, where he took a job at an architecture firm. The pay was spotty. He was depressed. They had a child.

'Sometimes, I think, love and politics . . .' said Haneen, and trailed off again. I could hear someone singing in the distance.

Only once in my life had I dated a Palestinian. His name was Johnny, and he wasn't political at all, he was a spoiled hedonist with a good heart who worked in the private sector. His humour was dry and he smelled lovely. He had been overweight as a child – I'd seen photographs of him tubby in a onesie, and at fifteen with a beard and paunch that could easily have persuaded a bouncer he was in his mid-thirties. After crash dieting at twenty he became vain about his looks, and he ate a single meal a day, usually a bowl of cereal. His skin was very smooth. I ended the relationship after a few months, fed up with being an appendage, and with him constantly checking his reflection in mirrors and shop windows. I was also in my first year of drama school and anyone who was not an actor could only hold my interest for so long.

Johnny's family were refugees from Akka who managed off the back of their Christianity to secure Lebanese passports in the fifties. Extracting that he was actually Palestinian and not Lebanese wasn't straightforward. The primary identity he laid claim to was Beiruti; he went on and on about the parties in Beirut. I couldn't work out what exactly about these parties was so amazing but I inferred eventually that being close to danger and political cataclysm was like a party drug, even though Johnny himself didn't seem much concerned with the particularities of the cataclysms. I imagined later that this was a blind continuation of his family's attitude: they'd denied their Palestinian identity during the civil war. They even changed their accents.

The last time I saw Johnny, I hugged him throughout our good-bye. This was more from cowardice than kindness: the distress in his eyes was unbearable to look at. He laid his head on my shoulder and I heard him swallowing loudly, repeatedly. How fragile he felt in my arms, like a little boy. In the light of Haneen's comment I wondered if there had been any of that homing instinct in him, buried deep, and that was why he wanted me.

Haneen stopped by a fat olive tree and sat down, the seat of her trousers instantly covered in dust. The straps and lace of her bra were visible through her shirt.

'Do you think that's why Mum married Dad?' I asked.

'I don't know.' She faced me. 'I'm sorry, Sonny. I know you came here to see me. And I wasn't very available. I felt a bit overwhelmed.' Her lips twisted to one side. 'I can see why you wanted to spend time here with Mariam instead.'

I was taken aback. 'Oh, Han,' I said, and sat beside her. 'I didn't join the play to avoid you. I'm really sorry if it felt that way.' My own apology sounded limp. I knew she needed me to say something else but I didn't know what. I put my arm around her shoulders. 'If you need to talk,' I said. And then: 'I'm glad you came down, it's good to see you.'

The call to prayer reverberated from several mosques, the words chasing each other in different voices. She got to her feet, brushing off her legs.

'We should get back.'

Mariam was holding a pair of kitchen scissors. Half her hair appeared to be on the floor around her feet, thick wet black curls twisted like seaweed.

'Oh my God,' I said.

'What the hell?' said Haneen.

Mariam smiled at us, bashful. 'I just decided . . .' she began; she wobbled. 'If I'm going to play Hamlet I want to look—'

'You're going to play Hamlet?' I said.

'I'm the only one who knows the lines. I've thought about it. Everything is ready for the show, we can't delay. I'm the only option.'

She put down the scissors. She looked insane with her hair like that, short at the front, enormous at the back.

'Why not, I say,' I said loudly, stepping forward. I wasn't sure which one of them I was performing for. 'That makes a lot of sense. I'll help you. And you're going to look great with short hair. You've got that lovely neck.'

'Oh, thank you.'

'Shall I do the rest?'

We turned it into a deliberate operation; I set up a chair, a mirror, fashioned a gown out of two small towels, fastening the corners at her shoulders with elastic bands; Haneen put on music and prepared a snack of bread and za'atar, which she ate most of, very quickly. Mariam watched herself in the mirror. I imitated the gestures of hairdressers, pulling the hair out between fingers, snapping the scissors along at an angle, running my hands over her head, shaking out the curls. At least the curls would conceal my mistakes.

'So I think, after this,' I said, brushing through the back, pulling at a knot, 'we should run a few scenes.'

Mariam's reflection nodded at me. I snipped around her silhouette, trying to match the length at the front, stepping backwards and forwards to gauge the effect, closing in on her nape to even out the line. I'd removed at least six inches. Done, I announced, and she thanked me with a head-bow like a grande dame and rose to sweep the reams of black hair into a pile, which gave me and my sister the chance, at last, to meet each other's eyes. Haneen looked troubled. I gave her a long blink that said, Don't worry, it's under control.

We sprayed our ankles and I lit a giant citronella candle, which I put by the bench outside while Mariam washed her face. As we took our positions in the garden, Anwar appeared at the gate with Emil, who was dressed as Superman.

'Wow, your hair,' said Anwar.

He stayed to watch and I held the boy on my lap. There were enough of us to form a kind of circle around Mariam, in the candle's intimate light, which created a ritual feeling. My nerves clanged as she shook herself off, shorn like a lamb. Haneen was ready with the cues but Mariam needed no prompting, she knew the monologues by heart. I expected her to start with *To be or not to be* but she went straight for Hecuba. First, though, she spent a moment with her eyes closed, her hands planted on her chest. I felt the pre-emptive embarrassment of a child watching an adult play at a children's game. But I was not a child. I was going to take mental notes and direct her as needed.

Her head rose on her neck to reveal a face like breaking glass, glowing red.

'What a rogue I am,' she said quietly, and then, dropping her voice almost to a whisper, spat: 'What a peasant slave.'

On my lap Emil breathed deep and slow, thumb in his mouth, bewitched but not frightened. Accustomed to his theatrical mother, he knew to keep very still.

'Is it not disgraceful,' said Mariam, 'that this actor,' her eyes were already watering, 'in an account from the imagination, in a dream of passion, compels his soul to wear his delusion so that it *blazes*? His visage blanches from it entirely. Tears in his eyes, frenzy in his features, his voice breaks and trembles. All function of his body embroiled in his delusion – all of that, for nothing? For Hecuba! What is Hecuba to him, or he to Hecuba, that he should weep like this for her?'

I wished the candle was bigger, the better to illuminate her. I couldn't believe how fantastic she was. It was obvious why Hazem fell in love with her while she was onstage. Her short hair made her look vulnerable and youthful. She pronounced the Arabic delicately, with a careful knowledge of the cadence and grammar. As the monologue went on I glimpsed, like apertures of light through a fog, certain things she'd been trying and failing to extract from Wael – in particular Hamlet's mortal sense, that he's already a dead man when the play begins. Perhaps it was a common director's fantasy to play the lead, to be the thing itself, to enjoy both the power and the glory. Sometimes in her words I heard a shrill of loneliness, something very Mariam, and beneath it a glint of ruthlessness. Her mission was visible in this speech, and so was her frustration, and so were her ghosts. Simultaneously I was thinking about how to choreograph her movements, since she was keeping fairly static, just raising an arm here and there, and she'd also need to work on her projection for a big stage, a big audience, especially without a microphone. But when she said the words, *Am I a coward?* she looked at me, and I felt the weird irrational joy of someone observing a mystery in a place of worship. And I realised, in a short ecstatic rush that pinned me into the present moment, that this low voice of hers, intentional or not, instinctive or contrived, was perfect for this context, for this staging, this audience, here in the garden. She came to the end of the speech and I understood that this was not a rehearsal, exactly. It was a performance, and it would never be repeated. We gave her a standing ovation. Emil ran out and grabbed her legs.

'Well *done*,' said Haneen. 'I don't know why I doubted it.'

'You doubted it?' said Mariam. Her arrogance was earned and she knew it.

Haneen would stay the night. While Mariam took Emil indoors, my sister and I walked to the butcher, selected a chicken in the bluish light of the counter, paid and crossed over to a vegetable store, and while we were bagging lemons, carrots, onions, tomatoes, she suggested passing by a sweet shop for dessert, so we finished up and set off in the direction of the town centre.

'I have a different question,' she said, rearranging her grip on the vegetable bags.

'What's that?'

'Do you resent Mum for leaving?'

She was really seizing her chance to clear all the air. 'No,' I said. 'I think he'd already abandoned her, in a way.' Once upon a time, this would have become an argument. 'Baba's a difficult man, and she provided everything for everyone.'

'Not any more.'

'We're not kids any more.'

'Do you know where we are? Have I got us lost?'

We stopped beside a shop selling gas canisters. Everything looked different in the dark. I peered around a corner and recognised one of the houses.

'This way,' I said.

'Yunes?'

A tall man stood on the street ahead, one foot on the barrier between the pavement and the road. He glanced up at the sound of Haneen's voice. It was Dawud, the theatre manager.

'Oh hey,' I said, and as we came closer I saw his hand was at his ear. 'He's on the phone. That's Dawud. He works at the theatre.'

'I have to go,' Dawud told his phone. 'Hi, Professor,' he said to Haneen.

'What are you doing here?' she answered.

Dawud's eyes lifted and tunnelled into mine. My stomach plunged.

'I'm visiting,' he said.

'This is my sister, Sonia,' said Haneen.

Dawud's chest was going up and down. 'I know.'

'This,' said my sister, 'is Yunes. He's a student at my university.'

'Do you have two names?' I asked him.

15

'Your homeless student,' I said, as Dawud, or Yunes, hurried away from us on his long legs. At the end of the street, he broke into a run.

'Yes,' said Haneen.

We stood side by side unspeaking. Then I looked at her gazing after him, and said, 'That's weird.'

'You said he works at the theatre?'

'Yes. Dawud.'

'How long for?'

'Don't know. We should ask Mariam.'

She looked at me. 'I feel ill.'

'Does this mean he's been watching us?' I asked.

Haneen was quiet for a long moment. 'There might be another explanation.'

We rushed home in silence. The smile on Mariam's face vanished as the words tumbled from my mouth. She swivelled, listening, her shoulders tensing up.

'Oh my God,' she said. 'He's an informant.'

'We don't know for sure,' I said. 'But it was pretty unnerving. He started like a – like a guilty—'

'No, there's no other reason. It's obvious,' said Mariam. 'He's how the news got out about Salim.'

'Let's not jump to conclusions,' I said.

The other two shook their heads at each other. They were several steps ahead of me.

'And I felt so sorry for him,' said Haneen.

'You should still feel sorry,' I said.

'No,' my sister replied with force. 'He's a little fucker.'

'But why all this effort for a play?' I said. 'They must have more important things.'

'They leave no stone unturned,' said Haneen. 'I'm angry with myself, I should have guessed . . . those new clothes.'

'We have to tell the others,' said Mariam. 'It might convince Wael to come back.'

'I don't see how,' I said.

'Amin's going to apologise to him.' She paused. 'Shit,' she added after a moment.

'I mean, you could try,' I said, loading my voice with caution. I was thinking of my last conversation with Wael, which had not inspired much hope.

The next day, minus Hamlet the elder and Hamlet the younger, we congregated for a garden rehearsal. Mariam was breaking her own rule and keeping her phone on loud and in her pocket: Nina, Majed's wife, would update her by text about the interrogation. Today, focusing was going to be difficult. Besides Majed's interrogation by the Shin Bet, it was also Thursday, the start of the weekend, plus the streets of East Jerusalem still looked like a gigantic outdoor mosque in response to the Israeli security measures around Al-Aqsa. Everyone congratulated Mariam on her haircut, which looked starker in the daylight. I couldn't tell what they really thought but I found it hard to believe they didn't see it as evidence of her emotion run riot.

I took charge of breaking the news about Dawud. I didn't say anything about his living in the department building at my sister's university, I just said he'd been a student she recognised and that his real name was Yunes. While speaking I happened to glance at Ibrahim, and like a gong the memory of our first rehearsal hit me, the unidentified presence backstage during the blackout, the odour of deodorant. Ibrahim's lips fell apart and his cheeks gained colour, which I took to mean he was thinking the same thing, and a shadow of our intimacy inserted itself into the gaze, which he broke free of, looking down, while I felt an alarming rush in the lower part of my body. I crossed my legs, appalled, and yanked my attention to George. George wore an iron frown. Beside him, Amin kept rubbing his hands over his face, which crumpled and opened repeatedly at Mariam. This sign of his remorse was satisfying, although my anger at him had still not cooled.

IBRAHIM	Is this going to change anything with Wael?
AMIN	(*Sadly.*) No.
SONIA	(*Surprised.*) You spoke to him?

AMIN *nods gravely.*

| MARIAM | We leave it for now. Wael needs a break. For now – (*facing the rest of the cast*) – I'll stand in as Hamlet. (*Looking at each cast member, daring them.*) |

Silence.

JENAN	I think that's great. Very modern.
MARIAM	Thanks.
JENAN	Hamlet as a woman.
MARIAM	Now the order of play today is Act Two, Scene One, Polonius and Ophelia. We're skipping Claudius and Gertrude, going straight to the Hamlet–Polonius dialogue in Act Two, Scene Two, on through Rosencrantz and Guildenstern, then Polonius and the players. The transitions need work. Sonia will be my extra brain and take notes when I'm onstage. On your feet.

The morning finished itself quickly. The news about Dawud had chilled everyone, and where there had been suspicion there was now shame, and a compensatory warmth and politeness. Faris complimented Mariam on her Hamlet, while proposing she stand more *like this*, setting his feet wide in the grass. It's not realism, she replied. Just a suggestion, he said, lifting his hands. Mariam reconsidered, and said, Okay let me try. While she practised striding back and forth over the lawn, Amin ordered lunch over the phone. I followed Mariam inside to fetch extra napkins.

'Did you tell Majed what to say?' I asked.

She flicked a switch on and off, looking at the ceiling. A bulb had blown.

'Nothing we are doing is illegal, even by their laws. They're trying to intimidate us. That's all. They haven't made a single arrest.'

We were approaching that stage of rehearsal when, now that we knew the set and could pass between scenes with fluency, the play was clicking into place. Transitions are like glue, invisible but crucial, and we were about to run the entrance of the players – George, Amin and Ibrahim – for the fifth time when Mariam looked at her phone and said that Majed was home. Everyone dropped their poses to crowd round. Amin said, What did they ask him? Mariam texted the question. Response: *The play, the funding, any links he had with terrorist organisations.* I pictured Majed in the interrogation room in his cardigan and coloured glasses.

'We're good, guys,' said Mariam, looking up with relief and some triumph. 'We just keep going. They put more obstacles, we climb over them. Thank God. Thank God. Okay, from the top one more time, and then it's time for the weekend. And you all have Sunday off, we've got a tech meeting. What a fucking week.'

Haneen, who was staying another night, was making curry for dinner. Entering through the hall, I paused by the kitchen doorway, and my eye alighted on the framed child's drawing of a house, with its sloped roof and smoking chimney. Was this a universal child's idea of a house, regardless of the native architecture of the country where the child lived? Who in the Middle East had a chimney like that? Where did kids learn this stuff from – kindergarten scenes in American movies? Mariam emerged in leggings and a hairband as though about to do an aerobics class.

'By the way,' she said, seeing me standing there, 'Ibrahim is straight. Just so you know.'

'I know,' I said.

Her warning tone bewildered me. She walked past me into the kitchen and told Haneen how great it smelled. I ran my mind back over the day but failed to identify what might have inspired this remark.

I wondered about it again over dinner, watching Mariam eating and laughing. Ibrahim's divorce was common knowledge. Maybe she'd noticed that he liked me and wanted to imply that I shouldn't encourage him. I supposed that this meant she had no suspicions about what happened in Haifa, which was a relief, at least. I thought back, puzzled, to Ibrahim's coldness in Bethlehem. When I returned to my room, I saw he had texted me.

Ibrahim

Today 21:43

are you asleep?

No

Why

just wondering

Wondering what

wondering if you were
asleep

'Sonia, can I talk to you?' said Haneen, cracking my door.

'Of course.' I put the phone face down on the mattress. 'Han, what's happened?'

She looked distraught, a vein swelling in her temple. 'I don't even know any more.'

'What happened?'

'I've been thinking about the boy.'

'Which boy, Dawud?'

'Yunes. Yes.'

'You know that's not your fault – come, sit down.'

She sat in my chair, her knees pointing inward, and touched the edge of the dictionary on my desk. Beside it, a stapler, a small pile of books, an eye-mask, a chewed pen. She put her elbows on the wooden surface and her face in her hands. She was still wearing her work clothes.

'Do you want to borrow a T-shirt?' I asked.

I had no cupboard, so I'd been keeping my clothes folded in piles on top of my suitcase. Haneen was actually the first person to enter the room while I was in it and her presence accentuated how cramped it was. I bent up the folded ends of my shirts, flipping through them.

'I can't stop thinking about it,' she said. 'You know, why *did* I take this job? Why *do* I work with them?'

'You're not serious. You're quoting the guy who's spying for them.'

'Sonia, I work at an Israeli university.'

I was trying to find a specific yellow V-neck. 'If you're not happy there, leave.'

'You don't know anything about my life.'

I dropped the shirts. 'Haneen! You have to stop turning on me whenever you get upset. It's not a very nice habit.'

'What is my discipline?'

'What?'

'What is my discipline, what do I teach?'

I hesitated. 'Political . . . histor—'

'*Sociology*. I'm a sociologist.'

'I know you have this idea that I'm an incredibly self-centred actress,' I said.

'We used to be a family.'

'We *are* a family.'

'Look at us,' said Haneen. 'I'm the only Nasir left in Haifa. Everyone is dead or gone, or doesn't want to talk to me. Do you know why Uncle Jad and Baba hate each other?'

'No. Why?'

'Nor do I!' Her hands flew up in the air either side of her head. 'No one knows! It's a total mystery!'

'Okay, Haneen. Calm down.'

'And now, *after* Jad sells our family house, an actual old Palestinian house in Haifa, they start talking again. I mean, what is *wrong* with these people? Maybe I'm a fantasist. Maybe I'm too attached to some old-fashioned idea of what a family should be.'

'I'm sorry to say this,' I felt my temper rising, 'but I think you probably are. I don't know a single family, Western or Arab—'

She shook her head, looking at the ceiling. Then her eyes, glossy, rested on me. She wasn't accusing me; she was imploring me. In that moment, however, the fact that she had come into my room to ask me for comfort filled me with dark outrage.

'You know what? It goes both ways, Haneen,' I said.

'What?'

'I may not be a perfect sister, you know, but at least I try to communicate. Yet somehow I always seem to be living in a fucking castle of silence. Everywhere I turn there's a huge wall. Sometimes you remind me so much of Marco that honestly it's uncanny. I don't even want to know what that says about me.'

Her mouth fell open and her forehead seized up. 'I wasn't even saying about you, Sonny, I was talking generally!' She opened her hand, gesturing at the room. 'Our family fell apart, I mean . . . Why do you have to take everything so personally? Not everything is about *you*, specifically.'

'Oh my God,' I said. 'What do you want from me, exactly? I don't think everything is about me, saying that is a very typical, it's a very convenient way to get out of responsibility. Angelic Haneen, perfect politics, perfect daughter, totally selfless, looking after everyone. And yet you don't! You don't look after everyone!'

My lips were trembling. I was hijacking her moment of pain, I knew that, that this was her scene, but the injustice was too sharp, it struck me the way a child feels injustice, that she should complain to me about family when all along she had made me feel like this, when she had robbed me of knowledge, when she never even tried to think about how it might affect me. I, too, had been there.

'Since when have I ever thought I was angelic?' said Haneen. 'I'm trying to tell you . . . I'm trying to tell you that I think I fucked up! I've made the wrong decisions. What are you even . . . I don't even understand what you're talking about.'

'You hurt me,' I said. 'You left me out of it. Why? Why didn't you tell me?'

'Tell you what?'

'Anything, everything. No one tells me anything! Baba won't even tell me.'

'Sonny.'

'I'm sad, I'm sad, I'm sad,' I said. I wasn't acting, I was being honest. My cheeks were wet. I couldn't see anything. 'I didn't even ask about him. And he was dead. And he's been dead all this time.'

Haneen fell quiet, registering who I was talking about. When finally she said my name, I noticed her eyes had filled with tears.

'Hey,' she said, softly, wobbling. 'I think that – I think I thought,' she struggled, her mouth working, 'that I was protecting you. But, maybe, yeah. Maybe, you're right. On some level, I did want to keep him for myself.'

On the backs of my eyelids, an after-image of him lying on his mattress. It was an old memory now, it had come to represent so many different things. I guess that happens to the dead. I opened my eyes. My sister was still gazing at me. A powerful beam of emotion directed, not through me, but very much at me. Woodwork creaked in the hall and I wondered if Mariam was listening to us. I took a deep breath. I sat on the floor, near Haneen's legs, and held on to one of her ankles. I believe whole minutes passed. My sister may not be good at talking but physical contact calms her, like a cat.

'You're lonely,' I observed.

'Do you think that's why I live in Haifa?' she said, looking down at me.

'Do I think what's why?'

'I mean, do you think that's why I chose this, because I have a fantasy about family? Like, I came back, as though I have ties.'

'I don't think you came back for family,' I said. 'And you do have ties.'

'But if I'm here for Palestine, then why am I *there*? Why am I not here?' She gestured at the room. She meant the West Bank.

'Because, well, because Haifa is part of it,' I said. 'You teach, you're an example, you teach about the history—'

'Three summers ago, you know,' she blinked hard, looking down at the tiles, 'I went on a protest for Gaza. And there was a counter protest outside the university. They were screaming at us, horrible things. I saw people from my department there, people I work with, and a bunch of my students. I know they all saw me. Imagine if it hadn't been the summer holiday. If I had to go in on the Monday and teach them.'

I let the silence in, thinking. Haneen started to unbutton her shirt.

'You can take the yellow one,' I said. 'Actually, you can take anything.'

'Thanks.' She stood up. 'I should shower first.'

'Haneen.'

She stopped in the doorway.

'Why don't we go to the demonstration in Jerusalem tomorrow?' I said.

She hesitated. 'Yes, why don't we go? It's a good idea. I'd like that. Me and you, in the morning. You're sure?'

'Of course.'

'We should leave early. The traffic will be bad.'

Ibrahim

Today 22:59

Are you asleep

yes

Haha

having a fucking weird
dream

What about

well

theres this woman from haifa
whos also from england and
i'm doing a play with her

and i'm worried she's going
to leave

Hmm

I wonder what that means

We're going to Jslm

now?

> In the morning
>
> Come if you like

who is we

> Me and my sister
>
> We decided

not mariam

?

> She has Emil this weekend

you should be careful

> We'll leave before evening
> prayer

it still might be dangerous

> You don't have to come

let me dream about it

ill let u know

> We're leaving at 5 am

hmm

> So I should get some sleep

yalla

we talk tomorrow

Ibrahim didn't join us in the morning, which was probably for the best. I woke when the azan needled into my ear, stopping, starting again, and then I felt a hand on my face and opened my eyes to see

Haneen crouching beside me, fully dressed, whispering, Wakey wakey. We were borrowing Mariam's car because it had yellow Israeli plates. Haneen wanted to risk a shortcut through a settlement checkpoint. I dozed in the front seat until we approached the soldiers, at which point we put on the Israeli radio and pretended to be relaxed. Don't smile, look bored, Haneen whispered, before saying something in Hebrew. They let us through. As we entered Jerusalem, however, soldiers began knocking on our windows, extending their hands for our IDs, and even once we were out of the car they repeatedly interrupted our route to the old city. We hadn't put on our jilbabs yet. Twice, someone with a gun said we weren't allowed any further. Maybe I give in too easily but both times I was ready to admit defeat, return to Ramallah and sleep, but Haneen, displaying a grasp of the language that astonished me, talked back unafraid, emphatic, her tone flipping between outrage and righteous surprise, while I stood dumbly pretending to understand, until the resolve of the soldier who was trying to stop us flickered into bewilderment, and then into exasperation, at which point he or she let us pass with a dismissive hand.

We bought coffees in paper cups from a kiosk and drank them at the bus station. A distant rumble contracted gradually into the clamour of voices, and soldiers appeared, and then a demonstration came surging down Nablus Road, waving Palestinian flags. Four boys near the front carried a painted cardboard model of the mosque. We kept tight to the bus station. Two loud *tuck-tucks* followed one after the other and the tear gas started to bloom. We ran for shelter in the restaurant of the Jerusalem Hotel. The crowd was already dispersing and when I looked back through the window I couldn't see anyone injured or on the ground. Of course the gas was fairly opaque. The restaurant manager greeted Haneen familiarly and invited us to take a seat.

He opened a large bottle of water and poured out two glasses. Yesterday, he told us, it was pretty calm until the sunset prayer, when a round of chanting erupted into commotion. Rubber bullets, real bullets, gas: the works. Two people shot – or so he'd heard. Didn't bode well for today. He looked out through the window, frowning, and plunged his shoulders up and down, as if loosening a knot.

Yet here we were. My nerves were already racked. The manager left us to drink our water in the sunlight. Han and I didn't say anything to each other. We covered our hair.

By noon we were standing in the women's section near the old city wall. The Israeli police had set up blue metal barriers to fence us in, or fence us out, and lurked behind them, dressed in body armour and electronic devices connecting them to their state. Several also wore nineties wraparound sunglasses. The army wore emerald berets, or pale green baseball caps. We wore hijabs, jilbabs, long dresses, skirts. Some women carried prayer rugs over their arms. You could roughly tell who here was a member of the faithful and who was here in solidarity, although it didn't feel like it mattered much. My sister stood to my right, and to my left was a young woman named Reem, who lived nearby in Shu'afat; she was doing a literature degree in Abu Dis. She said there were solidarity protests in Malaysia and Istanbul, and showed me a brief clip on her phone of a moving crowd. Plastic bags of supplies, water, food, sagged around our feet. We had more space than the men, who, far outnumbering us, occupied almost all of Salaheddin Street. I watched them assembling into rows, ready to pray. All told, the crowd was probably a few tens of thousands strong.

I looked at my sister's cheek, half hidden by fabric. A month ago she had tried to dissuade me from even visiting the West Bank, claiming I would be in danger. She wanted to protect me, but at the same time she wanted me to witness. I watched her watching the men, watching the soldiers, with blank determination. A grey-haired man in a bulletproof vest approached. He had a weathered journalist's face, and was carrying a camera and, more disconcertingly, a gas mask. He pointed his camera at us and looked through the viewfinder, squeezing shut his exposed eye. My sister turned away. I overrode a weird impulse to smile at him.

A kind of civic infrastructure had arisen around us. Blue and white Portaloos stood along the old city walls either side of Bab al-Zahira. A Red Crescent tent was erected between the men's and the women's sections, I guessed to treat the wounded if, or when, the clashes recommenced. One group handed out food, sandwiches, falafels, bananas; a young man delivered a bagful to our area, which two women took charge of dispensing. Another group passed around bottles of water. A hajjeh offered me a paper bag of pumpkin seeds, I took a few, Haneen said no thank you, touching her chest. We had brought our own sandwiches in clingfilm, which were probably failing in the heat. We had been in the sun for hours, I was wearing high-waisted trousers under my jilbab. No matter how much water I drank I couldn't seem to quench my thirst. One woman held an umbrella for shade; others stood against the cold stone of the wall.

Though we had missed Salat al-Fajr, we were here for the midday prayer. I'd never performed a Muslim prayer before but Haneen knew how and I was going to copy her. The general mood was one of anticipation and camaraderie. We laughed, we pointed discreetly at the soldiers, we asked each other where we'd travelled from today. At the same time, anger ran through us like a wire, holding us together. The sky was pale. A woman handed me another bottle of water, calling me *khalti*, and I thanked her. My nerves crackled with the electricity of opening night. I dread chaos. But this did not look like chaos. Here was order, ritual, routine, care. The streets were no longer streets. The streets were a place of worship. The streets were a stage.

A young woman soldier put her boot up on a barricade. Her colleagues rumbled into their walkie-talkies, fingered their batons and guns. I was curious about what they were thinking. Did they believe they were guarding against a group of Muslim fanatics? We, the backward natives. Did they genuinely believe they were waging a war against Islam, or Islamists, as they liked to paint it in the media sometimes, when they claimed solidarity with victims of terror attacks in Western capitals, saying, *We know how it feels, it's just like what we have to go through*? Or did some of them know what they were really doing? Or was that something they avoided thinking about? Not my fear but my pride was pulsating through me now. Let them think we were fanatical. I did not care. I discovered I was proud that they might think it of me.

The call to prayer started just after one o'clock. A man at the head of the men's congregation was reciting, wrapping his hands around his mouth to project his voice, hurling his body into the sound. He wore a striped T-shirt. We, like the men, organised ourselves into rows, I found my sister's hand and squeezed. We did not have prayer mats. Someone offered us a spare, though we protested; finally my sister passed it to me and I laid it down – electric blue, synthetically soft, with a red scalloped mihrab. The melody of the call faltered, the man's voice strained – someone stepped between the rows to hold a megaphone to his mouth, and his call expanded, reaching us clearly.

The sheikh in conical hat and sunglasses took over for the khutba. Some of the congregation lifted their phones to film him. We stand on the earth under the blue dome, he said, pointing at the sky. The crowd bowed, revealing a line of journalists shouldering video cameras, lifting boom mics. Shutters snapped on the cameras. *Ameen*, said the crowd. *Ameen*, said the crowd. *Ameen*.

There is now, and there is afterwards. There comes a feeling of life opening. We lift our hands, we say God is great. We fold our hands, we say God is great. We bow, there is the grand rustling of bodies moving. We rise, and I began to feel a strange elation, one of thousands, moving at the same time, bowing at the same time, rising at the same time. It did not matter who or what I was. I was present, chanting God is great. We kneel with our foreheads to the ground, my hands in the soft pile of my borrowed mat. We stand and repeat, and we kneel and sit on our heels and turn our heads from side to side, assalamu alaykum wa rahmatullah, assalamu alaykum wa rahmatullah. We rise to our feet for the final time, and my sister touches my arm and kisses my cheek.

Within half an hour, the Israelis were firing tear gas again. At the first crack, the lines splintered. I ran to the wall amid the cushion and fabric of other women's bodies. We hurried, bullets thundered, I broke into a run, pulling the jilbab from over my head. My heartbeat choked me – or was that the gas, acrid in my throat? My eyes were stinging, my nose streamed. I covered my face with the cloth and reached for the wall for balance as we slowed into a bottleneck, mingling with the men, who held prayer mats over their heads for protection, blanketing their ears against the bangs. I glimpsed two or three Red Crescent employees rushing, someone being hauled onto a gurney. As soon as I could run again, I ran. Behind us, the streets were smoking. A fire had started on Salaheddin.

My sister reached my side and led me on a long route past shuttered shops. We weren't alone, either; ten, twenty, fifty other people were taking the same route, and we all slowed to a walk and moved together in a strange silence. My cough wouldn't leave my chest and my hands were sore. Haneen looked dreadful and her eyes were red. I assumed I looked the same.

The restaurant of the Jerusalem Hotel was empty, the music turned low. A man cleaned cups behind the bar. Haneen uncovered her hair and immediately discovered on her phone that a young man had been killed near Damascus Gate. His name was Mohammad Mahmoud al-Sharf. She turned the screen to me, and I saw a bloodied corpse on Facebook before she snatched it back. The restaurant manager set glasses of milk and cloths on the table. I looked through the window. Outside, men were running for shelter. I copied Haneen and bathed my face and hands in the milk, which was soothing and cooling, although as it dried my skin began to hurt again. My eyes watered. Life pounded through me, uselessly, and my sister looked at me with concern, her face briefly clown-white with milk before her skin showed through. I knew she felt responsible, even though this had been my idea. I didn't know how to reassure her. I also couldn't stop myself from shaking. She suggested washing off the milk and I followed her downstairs to the toilets.

'Water is better than milk but I didn't want to offend him,' she said once the tap was running.

I bent over the sink and splashed my face several times.

'Who orchestrated the protests?' I asked.

'The Islamic Waqf were the first to call for boycotting the security gates. After that, no one, I think.'

'But someone told the people where to stand.'

'I don't think so.'

'Then how did they know what to do?'

She shrugged. I dabbed at my wet sore face then followed her back upstairs and ordered coffee. Across the street, a cameraman was trailing another foreign journalist. The pair of them looked superimposed, calmly dictating into their devices, narrating over a background of smoke and fear. Why did I hate them? Was it because they spectated, and seemed, in watching, to do nothing? But it wasn't nothing. We needed the cameras. Half the power was in the recording, that the event was already being doubled and broadcast. Because of them, we were not only in Jerusalem, we were everywhere.

We paid and walked to Mariam's car, lights flashing unlocked. Beyond the buildings, black smoke drifted over the sky. In the passenger seat, I apologised for being a mess. Don't be sorry! said my sister, checking her blind spot. Don't ever apologise. After nudging through traffic we were soon speeding cleanly along the freeway towards Haifa. Green fields folded past, and I had a horrible, useless revelation, which was that in some way the meaning of our *Hamlet* depended on this suffering. The context gave our *Hamlet* its force. I knew Mariam had already had this revelation. Our play needed the protests, but the protests did not need our play. My face was burning. I wanted to rip it off.

As she drove, I thought about being Pierrot. The day Michael, the movement director, joined rehearsals, he had examined my body like a tailor, told the directors to leave the room, and proceeded to lecture me about the importance of motivation.

'Every person,' he had said, looking away, absorbed by his words, 'every *body* moves differently from the next person's body when their mind goes through something. When you're sad, you,' he pointed, 'are going to move differently from the way *I* move when *I'm* sad. I can still read your movements, but they're not going to be the same as mine. But if you make a *straight line* from emotion to movement – *your* emotion, *your* movement – then the audience will not only read you, they will *feel* you.'

'Yeah. Got it.'

'You haven't got it. But that's okay. Take it from the moment you have that thought: *Okay, I'll have a drink.*'

He watched me, not sitting this time. He folded his arms and moved along with me like a walking mirror.

'Why are you looking at me?' he said.

'I'm not looking at you.'

'You're aware of me. You're imitating an idea you have of someone drinking whisky. Drink the whisky. Trust the glass. Don't look at me.'

I tried again. It was hard. He was right, I was too aware of him – aware, apart from anything else, that he was about to criticise whatever I did, which undermined every movement in advance. Sure enough, the moment I set down my invisible whisky glass he opened his mouth and inhaled ceremoniously.

'Your body's got to react to two kinds of invisible forces.' Two fingers of his left hand came up, to make this clear.

'Okay.'

He began to pace the width of the badminton court.

'One of these is a mental force, like I want to open the door. I want to kiss you. I want to stand up. I want to sit down. Et cetera. This is your intention. Or, you have a strong feeling that causes your body to react, without an intention.' He flung his arm out in front of him, and bowed, drawing his hand to clasp his forehead. 'This is an emotion,' he said, returning upright. 'The other invisible force is external. Something we cannot see is acting on your body. And your body reacts. Okay? If you're a mime on a street corner you have an invisible wall, right? Or like this.'

He stopped walking abruptly. He crossed one leg over the other, tilted to one side, his arm stiff as a board, his wrist a hinge, his hand flat out. With a little lurch a table materialised beside him, and he was leaning on it. I started laughing. It was perfect: I could see a table there. At my laughter, he softened. He regained his balance from the invisible table and dusted off his hands, as if he had really been touching something.

'Most of the time, you're reacting to one or more invisible forces at the same time. I'm angry, and I'm trying to avoid a bus. I'm tired and I need to open the door. Et cetera.'

'Right.'

'It sounds complicated, I know,' said Michael, looking satisfied with his own ability to grasp, or to invent, complicated concepts. 'But once you've got the forces really clear in your mind, your body does the work for you. You don't need to make the shapes: you need to focus on the force.'

'May the force be with you.'

Michael replied with sincerity: 'More like, trust the force. I trust the table, and I trust my body to fall on it. If there's a clear line from the force, the body follows, and does the counterbalancing. Don't imagine what the audience sees. Focus on the thing that makes you move, makes you stop, makes you change direction. After that we'll do the fine-tuning.'

Michael had made me believe it was possible to draw a pure line between motivation and effect. Between conviction and action. It was a question of control. As when a painter makes a line on a canvas, but instead of paint and colour, it was my body and voice and my emotional history and my reaction times and everything that was part of my self. The prospect, this challenge, exhilarated me. To eighteen-year-old Sonia, perfecting that line had seemed a worthy thing to do with my life.

We paused in traffic; my sister looked ahead with a prim unconscious hand at her lips. I saw a parallel between that and this, and wondered if she was really so different from me. I opened my window as we began to move again, and felt the wind on my face. My sister switched on the radio. The difference was that this was real.

I fell hard asleep that night as though I had a virus, and slept thoroughly for several hours before surfacing in the dark. The moon was a silver blur in the black sky above the harbour. As intensely as I'd slept I was now awake, and I wondered what had woken me. Memories of the day returned piecemeal, the sounds of prayer and gunfire. My sore muscles shifted in the hot bed, my lungs still tight from the gas. I realised I was desperate for air. I'd forgotten to put on the fan. I reached to open the window, and as I turned the handle, I was visited by an eerily strong conviction that there was a stranger in the flat. I almost vibrated with the knowledge. It was as though I'd heard a footstep or an unfamiliar voice outside my door, though I had not. Other noises entered my ears through the now-opened window; jackals moaning on the hillside, the sea whispering, the watery rush of night-time cars. I brushed these off, holding still as an insect, confining my attention to the apartment beyond my bedroom, trying to catch sounds. My heart was going wild, I felt full of blood. The awake part of my brain knew this was probably nonsense. Nevertheless, I needed to dispel the ghost. I got out of bed and walked into the hall.

There, in the hallway, someone was standing by the door. I gasped. A thin blue light, very faint, lay on the skin of his forehead. One arm hung rigid by his side, like something made of wood. That was all I could see. I can't say how long I stood there. I was frozen with shock – shock, in part, that my intuition had been accurate. My faceless adversary stared back.

'Why don't you leave?' I said.

Even though he was right by the door, he didn't move or make a sound. Why? He must be frightened. Another explanation came fast on the tails of this one, which was that he was not frightened. No, on the contrary: his continued presence by the door was a threat. He was here for a reason. He was here for me. This produced in me a flash of unthinking anger and I stepped forward to defend myself, and at that exact moment so did he, and then I saw he was a woman. And before I had even seen the frame of the mirror I knew it was there. The revelation fell on me like cold water, and I breathed, I'd been holding my breath. I walked slowly up to the mirror and looked into it, at myself. The mirror had not been there before. Haneen must have hung it in my absence. I supposed I had walked straight past it last night.

I can't explain why this was, but even though I now knew the intruder was my own reflection, my relief was only fleeting. Probably I was still half-asleep and stripped of rational defences, but my reflection looked strange to me, with the dark apartment in the background, the meagre moonlight. Where my face felt tight with distress, a pair of knowing eyes looked back. The mouth almost smiled. I heard, or thought I heard, a tiny breath on its lips, and I hurried childishly back into my bedroom. Once I'd shut the door I could laugh a little, climbing into bed. I immediately heard the wail of a mosquito, and practically with relief at the excuse this gave me, put my head under the covers for protection.

'I bought it at the market ages ago,' said my sister in the morning. 'It's been sitting in my office.'

In the daylight I could see the mirror's frame: narrow, gilt, topped with a wooden bow. Besides a few age spots along the bottom edge of the glass it was in good nick, but it didn't really go with the rest of her furniture. From where I sat, it reflected Haneen drinking coffee at the counter, with a section of the window behind her; an ornate frame for a mundane scene.

I didn't tell her what had happened during the night. In the intervening hours the episode had retained its sinister tinge, and felt private the way a disturbing dream feels private, as though it might reveal things about you. I touched the thick bumpy lip of an unfamiliar bowl on the counter, glazed brown-green.

'Is this also from the market?'

'No. I started a pottery class.' Haneen rubbed her neck with her bony fingers. I pictured them gripping clay. 'What's funny?'

'You are.'

We were gentle with each other that weekend. We didn't talk much, but sat often on the sofa together reading; she one of her scholarly books with their unappealing spines, me a novel, or *Hamlet*, which I opened like a religious text, at random, meditating on my lines and visualising the Day of Judgement, by the wall in Bethlehem, beneath that looming chandelier. Haneen was a slower reader than I remembered, but not distractable, turning pages at a steady pace. I took baths, we took walks on the beach, and watched episodes of American sitcoms with soundtracks of canned laughter. On Saturday we stopped for a mezze lunch in a restaurant garden, and she read the news aloud from links posted on the Twitter accounts of young local journalists. Four Palestinians had been killed by Israeli fire on Friday, one in the West Bank and three during the Jerusalem protest; one of the corpses was smuggled out of the hospital so the Israelis couldn't hold it hostage for bartering;

three Israeli settlers were killed in a West Bank settlement later that night; afterwards, the Israeli army demolished the assailant's home in a nearby Palestinian village; that morning, on Saturday, at the Israeli Embassy in Amman, a security guard shot dead two Jordanian workers; details of this incident were unclear, with rumours of a gagging order from the Israeli government, who refused to let the guard be questioned, claiming diplomatic immunity; and during the demonstrations in Gaza on Friday, numerous more had been injured by Israeli fire – and I noted, listening to her read, how often English-language sources leaned on passive verbs for Arab fatalities, as though fearful of pointing the finger. My main impression of this mode of reporting, death by death, was one of distortion, and this made me think about whether stories of a few were always more compelling than the story of the many, and whether that was why Teta's Nakba story was about a woman in a green dress, and not one about thousands of refugees, thousands dead. Then I looked up at the sea stretched beneath the sky and wondered if the problem was mine, if only I struggled to look at big expanses, so that this horizon pushed my gaze away with a kind of reverse magnetism, and my eyes were drawn to the pebbles and shells near my feet, close, vivid, clearly defined. Maybe I was the one who needed stories of women in green dresses. Mariam wasn't like that. Nor was Haneen.

The stories continued on Sunday. The Palestinian Authority froze security coordination with the Israelis, who added cameras to the metal detectors around Al-Aqsa, against the recommendations of intelligence organisations, for whom, I assumed, frozen security coordination was a pretty major impediment to controlling the occupied population over the coming days – and after following all of this in a state of exhausted tension, first on Haneen's little phone screen and then on the TV news, we opened a bottle of wine and set out the ingredients to make fattet batinjan. Han toasted rounds of bread while I cubed the white flesh of an aubergine. Sheikh Imam sang from her portable speaker.

'You remember,' she said over the music, 'how Marco was sort of jealous of your career?'

'Excuse me?' I stopped my knife.

She was sitting just beyond the circle thrown by the overhead lamp, with the window and the dying light of the sky behind her. I couldn't see her face properly but her posture told me she was floundering. I twisted down the volume dial.

'What are you talking about?'

'I don't know. I guess Baba could have been wrong.'

'What did he tell you?'

'Wasn't Marco trying to write a novel?'

'So?'

'He was a struggling writer. You were a successful actress.'

I laughed, relieved, returning to my aubergine. My imagination had already started concocting evidence, words slipped, an unlikely confession from Marco, that familiar stranger who still squatted in a neglected outhouse of my mind. 'I don't think so, dear,' I said.

'You were in several shows in the West End, and you were always rehearsing for something. Most actors spend long periods not working. Whereas, you. Not that I know anything.' She lifted a hand in fake humility. 'I always felt,' she said, and halted.

'Felt what?' I asked. 'Don't say nothing.'

'I was going to say, sometimes, I felt he wasn't very generous with you. Marco had a hungry – he seemed hungry, sort of. Does that upset you?'

'It's weird talking with your silhouette, can you come into the light?'

She shifted along the counter and entered a purple glow from the lamp's glass. Her expression was wary. I'd often felt we remembered the past differently, but mostly when it came to our childhoods; certainly not to my own marriage.

'I was so worried,' she went on. 'I felt so far away. I had nothing to offer, it was terrible.'

'Han.'

'And then one day on the phone you said, Thank you this was really helpful, in a very kind of proper voice.' Her glasses had slipped to the end of her nose. 'I remember being surprised because I felt useless.'

'Just listening, you helped me.'

'Thanks for saying that.'

'Oh, come on,' I cajoled, trying to let the air out.

Haneen made a face and, rising, switched on the oven. The silence resolved into a family silence, without awkwardness. I finished dicing and said: 'You know, Marco did write a novel.'

'What was it about?'

'Guess.'

Her eyes widened. 'No.'

'What better subject?'

I threw up my arms. Her eyes darted to the knife I was holding.

'Oh my God,' she said quickly, possibly more at the knife than at what I was saying. 'Was it good?'

'You think I read it?'

I didn't tell her I'd read the online reviews. And that this was how I'd learned that Marco's protagonist was a writer whose wife couldn't get pregnant. Or that, in light of this, those afternoons after the abortion when Marco had disappeared into the cupboard-study took on a different meaning. That while I was out there, suffering, he was in there writing about it. Betrayal was not the word, it had too many syllables. My rage became so strong that there were times when I felt like my head would split open. I had gathered from the reader-reviews that his style was skeletal, probably after the French Existentialists he worshipped. The only substantial criticism was that the chapters written from the woman's perspective were sometimes unconvincing. Sometimes unconvincing! No one expressed strong feelings about the book, which came out quietly from a trade publisher, there were some warm reviews but nothing major, and it had remained his first and only attempt to date.

'What was the title?'

'Please don't read it.'

'I was just curious,' she said, but she turned to arrange cutlery on the table, moving her handmade bowl out of the way.

The idea of Marco's envy played upon me throughout the meal. That the frail roots of his resentment, which had been so painful and baffling at the time, could have been detected by my father of all people. I scanned my memories. No particular events or signs occurred to me. But I did think of absences – of warmth, maybe, of encouragement. And his sharp impenetrable gaze, onto which I used to project such benevolent passions. To call it jealousy still seemed like a leap.

'You know,' I said, as Haneen offered me second helpings, emptying a serving spoon onto my plate, 'I always felt I was less than you.'

My sister frowned, looked down. I myself wasn't sure where that had come from. I hadn't meant to reproach her. Maybe on some level I thought that such a fissure of straight-talking had now opened between us that I could displace years and years of complicated sediment, much of which existed out of sight, out of consciousness, just like that, in a word, an accusation disguised as a statement of fact: sister, this is how you made me feel. She was toying with a cut triangle of cucumber. My real agony was not about Marco but about her. That she'd thought well of me, after all. She hadn't only thought I was someone foolish who played games for a living. This was the revelation that surprised me onto the verge of crying, childish before my blurring plate of food. I hadn't known I needed her approval. It was the feeling of tripping in the road – as I'd done in Hackney once, and after managing to stand, strung out with shock and embarrassment, started walking again, until a stranger put her hand on my back and said, *Are you okay? That looked terrible* – and that was the moment when I collapsed and wept, with a total stranger patting my shoulder, aghast. Haneen met my eye as though she was going to say something to appease me. I waited. She didn't say anything; she looked weary. Maybe she didn't feel it was necessary. Maybe she had other things, other than me, on her mind.

I set off for Ramallah the following day. I'd neither driven Mariam's car before nor driven at all on either Israeli or Palestinian roads. I spent an over-caffeinated hour and a half on Highway 6 following the GPS to the Qalandiya checkpoint, at which point the GPS mysteriously stopped functioning, and the voice kept telling me to turn around and rejoin the route. I dragged the map across the screen with my fingertip; the route was a road into an Israeli West Bank settlement. Cancel Route. The checkpoint into the West Bank was unmanned, although I could see, over the way, a line of cars jammed at the checkpoint leading out. Soldiers loitered, taut green uniforms against green fields. I drove on into Beitounia and, passing a store with a bright apron of fruit, considered stopping for figs. My mind hung back among the soldiers. I thought about Wael pretending to be one, and wondered if there was something especially subversive about that here, in a military state, where the soldier is a sacred figure, an image in their ideology as olive trees are in ours. When they look at their soldiers, they see sons and daughters. When we look at their soldiers, our hearts also beat harder, although it is for different reasons.

16

Without cuts, *Hamlet* can take up to three and a half hours. Our version lasted two. Even so, the more we ran the play top to bottom the more both the length and the darkness of the action weighed on us. At night we slept like the dead.

We had two weeks left until dress and tech. The stage manager, a rangy tattooed woman named Dunya, and our dreadlocked lighting designer, Motaz, became regular features of our long days. Props accumulated, so that we held objects instead of shapes in the air, and we wore pieces of costumes, strips of muslin with suggestions of regalia. At this point we should really have been working on Acts Four and Five but our priority was to fit Mariam as our new Hamlet into the show.

The news about Dawud – or Yunes, as we were starting to refer to him – had still not persuaded Wael to come back. It did, however, unify the rest of us, and while it was hard to tell if Amin's solemnity was real remorse or just an extended sulk, no one felt like chastising him any further. According to Mariam, the guys at the theatre who'd hired Yunes as Dawud hadn't even asked him for reference letters, and didn't know he was from '48. She said this with indignation, as in, Look at this level of incompetency; this is what we have to deal with!

Salim's suspension had lately fallen out of the news, ousted by the events in Jerusalem, although the investigation was ongoing. The Shin Bet had searched his house twice, and apparently he'd been instructed to refuse media requests about the Al-Aqsa protests. But if Yunes had been sent to collect information about him then at least it was probably a fruitless mission: I couldn't remember much chat about Salim in the rehearsal room beyond the occasional reference to funding. The discovery of the Yunes plot settled nothing, at any rate, it only pointed at further unknowns, it might be just the tip of an iceberg and we wouldn't know. And yet there wasn't anything we could do about it except continue rehearsing as though nothing else was going to stop us.

But without Wael, and without Salim, the scale of the production kept shrinking, which put even more pressure on the quality of the show. Mariam leaned on me in private, sifting her fears aloud on the living-room sofa. The cast's anxiety was at an all-time high. Scenes that had been set with Wael felt unfamiliar with Mariam and required reorganising, sometimes with Faris at the helm, sometimes Amin, sometimes me, sometimes a couple of us, conferring. Without Mariam as our pilot we were like a ship steering itself, unwieldy, recalibrating slowly as a team the moments when tension peaked, scrutinising old decisions, relocating turning points, taking a vote when we disagreed.

Mariam also devised an exercise in which we improvised certain scenes in dialect. I wondered if this was a modification of her previous idea of me trying the willow tree speech in English. Without the crutch of our written lines, we groped for language, and words came at once too easily and not easily enough. The exercise was taxing, and shone a spotlight on the tenuous point between being and not being, reminding us how difficult our task was, to summon something from thin air and believe in it. Hardened patterns broke open and the story became strange again. Returning to the text, we then blended in the new spokenness, and this stopped the classical register getting too lofty.

Relieved of the burden of Ophelia, I was obsessing over Gertrude, over the rhythm of her few lines, her speechless maternal reactions, and my onstage rapport with Mariam as Hamlet centred on a vicious, grief-laden love. Our closet scene was physical in a way we'd never achieved with Wael. Really, it felt like she was assaulting me, her anguish and her anger battling inside her, while I, Gertrude, was tormented to see her so tormented.

'Don't forget,' she said, switching into director-mode while half-straddling me, having spontaneously pushed me to the turf, 'there's a dead body over there. I've just killed Faris.'

Faris, eating a sandwich nearby, looked up at the sound of his name. Mariam reverted into Hamlet and considered me, gravity pulling her lips down. Then, gently but firmly, she pushed my face to one side and rubbed my cheek into the grass.

'Oh shame, where is your modesty?' she said.

'Horrible!' I said, through my squished cheeks.

'Yeah?' said Mariam, releasing me.

'I think so. Amin?'

'It's good,' said Amin. 'But do it on this side so we can see it.'

On Tuesday, the Israelis started removing the gates around Al-Aqsa. By the end of the week, all the gates were gone. The emotion that permeated the rehearsal room and the streets of Ramallah was not quite elation, though. The loss of Al-Aqsa had been staved off, yes, but it was hard to call that a victory. Just as suddenly as everything had erupted it disappeared again, and judging from the television and what Majed was telling us, by Saturday life in Jerusalem was already returning to what Jerusalemites considered a normal level of unease, and Muslims of all ages were allowed to enter the mosque without being harassed by the police. So it went. The day-to-day struggle of an oppressed people had briefly ignited the interest of the world, until that interest was extinguished by the turnover of the next news cycle. I had little faith that people who were not here would remember those thousand-strong street prayers in a few months' time.

Advertising for *Hamlet* began. Flyers, posters, Facebook events, email invitations. Mariam decided on an unannounced performance in the town centre as a publicity stunt. She insisted on big headpieces, which were not part of the costume.

On a windy morning we walked in single file to Al-Manara Square, our faces painted like commedia dell'arte characters, backs straight to balance the items on our heads. Mine was a headdress with tall plumes dyed navy blue, Mariam's was a big black top hat; the others wore colourful architectural pieces cobbled together by Wardrobe, secured with thread beneath their chins. None of this had anything to do with *Hamlet*. George carried a boombox. Stepping between traffic we paraded once around the lion statues and returned to Clock Square, which was marginally quieter, and stationed ourselves around the blue tiles of the emptied fountain encircling the statue of a man climbing a pillar to hoist the Palestinian flag. The boombox radiated Majed's voice, a murmur magnified, interspersed with an extended whine like furniture creaking. Shopkeepers peered out with confusion and some dismay. We caught the attention of a few loitering shabab, some teenaged girls, elderly men, people shopping or taking narghile in the windows of Sindyan Café. A guy selling hot sweetcorn from a metal cart took quick advantage of the gathering crowd to ply his trade, even shouting over us as we began the scene. This wasn't so far from flyering at the Edinburgh Fringe Festival, in costume on the Royal Mile, albeit the Royal Mile was also crawling with hundreds of other desperate performers, and the feeling of degradation there was more acute.

We did a stylised version of the scene with the Players, ending with a formal dance around the statue. After her exchange with Jenan, Mariam passed handbills to onlookers, running off a rapid sales pitch to a few suspicious young women. On the edge of the fountain, Jenan was coming into her own. Her voice, fine but strong, carried even better with an audience. Once the scene was over, we walked back to Mariam's house in Al-Masyoon carrying our headpieces under our arms. Everyone was talking loudly, with the sun breaking through. I said to Jenan: 'Hey, that was awesome.'

She gave me a shy smile, blinking against the light. Her eyelids were sweating off their cobalt paint and she had smudged an eyebrow. Our line broke around a corner and I fell behind, beside George. His face was striped black and white like a badger.

'She's doing well,' I murmured.

'Yes,' said George. 'It was a good decision, after all that.'

'All what?'

In motion, silences are easy to gloss over. I saw George calculate how to dodge me, and caught his arm before he could slip into an adjacent exchange between Faris and Ibrahim.

'It was a good decision after all what, George?'

His brows, stiff with black paint, twitched. I could see he felt bad. We had reached the gate. Mariam brought up the rear, pulling keys from her pocket.

In the driveway, Dunya and Motaz were loading Anwar's car with lighting equipment: spotlights, scoop-lights, bolts and poles. Anwar appeared in the doorway, carrying a cardboard box.

'How was it?' he said to his sister, looking over our gaudy faces. 'We're about to go to Bethlehem for the installation, sorry it took a bit longer to get ready.'

'Can we help?' said Mariam.

'Wow,' said Amin, staring at his phone. 'The numbers.'

'Numbers of what?' said Ibrahim.

'People attending on the Facebook event,' said Amin. 'That's not because of what we did just now, in the square, right? That's not possible.'

Ibrahim peered over Amin's shoulder. 'Huh. Imagine how many would sign up if Wael was still in it.'

'Yeah,' said Mariam, lifting one side of a floodlight while her brother took the other. 'We need to change that.'

'It still says Wael?' said Ibrahim, rapidly stroking the screen with his forefinger.

'I should have done it earlier,' she said.

'Oh, Mariam,' said Ibrahim.

We waved Dunya, Motaz and Anwar off. Weighed down with equipment, the car wobbled slowly into reverse and turned down the road. Faris put his arm around Mariam's shoulders.

'It is a *great* play,' he said. 'You are *great*.'

Inside, we washed our faces and had lunch, and then we headed to the arts centre for the afternoon's rehearsal.

A few hours later, Mariam received a phone call from Anwar. He, Dunya and Motaz had found their route to the set in Bethlehem blocked by a row of crowd-control barriers, and as they pulled up, an army truck and ten soldiers came into view. Anwar jumped out, calling in Hebrew: 'What's going on?'

A bowlegged young soldier in a helmet with a torch ambled up to him. 'The area is closed.'

'The area of our stage?'

'The whole area is closed,' said the soldier.

'But the only area you have closed off,' said Anwar, pointing at the arrangement of metal barriers, 'is our stage.'

Two soldiers were climbing onto the stage itself. One mounted the white staircase, gun aloft. The other poked his muzzle at the curtain leading to the backstage ledge, affixed to the rear of the set. Their curiosity was so outsized it was like they'd never seen a theatre before – until the first one descended the stairs and kicked over one of the mock-up tables, and then the stage was just like another home they were raiding.

'Hey, don't touch that,' Anwar shouted.

The bowlegged soldier swivelled his boots towards him. One hand touching the gun, the other hand waving, he called in ugly Arabic: 'Go from here. Go.'

> MARIAM *hangs up the phone.*

MARIAM	The army have taken the set.
AMIN	What?
IBRAHIM	No.
MAJED	I can't believe it.

> Enter GEORGE, *who has been in the bathroom.*

GEORGE	What's happening?
AMIN	Well, I mean, shit. (*Pause.*) What are we going to do?
MARIAM	I don't know.
AMIN	Does it *have* to be in Bethlehem?
GEORGE	What happened in Bethlehem?

> MARIAM's *eyes flick over the dusty studio floor.*

AMIN	What about Nablus?
GEORGE	Something happened?
SONIA	They confiscated the set.
GEORGE	What?

AMIN *puts his hands on his hips. Desperation in his voice.*

AMIN	Nablus is not so far from Ramallah.
GEORGE	Kussokhthom.
AMIN	People from '48 can come through the Jalameh checkpoint.
MARIAM	I don't know.
GEORGE	I want to smash something.
AMIN	There must be a cool— wait, what about Sebastiya? On the Roman ruins, that would be, I mean that would be great.
IBRAHIM	This is unbelievable.
SONIA	Is it? Or is it actually very believable?

MAJED *removes his glasses, rubs his eyes with the heels of his hands, grasps the roots of his hair.* IBRAHIM *starts laughing.*

SONIA	(*In English.*) It's not funny.
IBRAHIM	On the contrary, I think it's very funny.
AMIN	(*To Mariam.*) Didn't you say, let them throw more in our way, we'll just climb over it?
MARIAM	(*Voice rising.*) They've confiscated our *whole set*. You think Anwar can just make a new one in a week? Do you understand how much work that required, how much money?
JENAN	(*Fiddling with a BIC pen.*) The only thing we really need is that chandelier.
AMIN	Which Anwar hasn't put up yet.
MARIAM	And the lights.
AMIN	Sure.
MARIAM	And everything else. The backdrop. The plaster. Our equipment. So much of our equipment.
FARIS	How about we do a smaller version of the stage? I always felt it was a *little* bit too large, the stage he made.

MARIAM *rolls her eyes.*

AMIN	Wait, wait.
MARIAM	Even if we move, what if they just announce that the new place is also a closed military zone?

Pause.

FARIS	We could try doing it spontaneous – secret, even.
MARIAM	(*Sarcastic.*) A secret play.
FARIS	We spread it by word of mouth. We'll get some audience. Maybe not huge crowds. You must *lengthen your mind*, my dear.
MARIAM	They'll find out.
FARIS	Why don't we try? What's the worst that can happen?

MARIAM *opens her hands at* FARIS, *as if to say: That is a ridiculous question.*

The new location was scouted by Dunya's aunt's husband's brother, who knew the guy who ran an organic farm on the outskirts of a village west of Ramallah. The land was in Area B, under joint Palestinian and Israeli control, and the village was renowned for weekly Friday protests against a nearby settlement, and against the soldiers who protected the settlers, who often terrorised the villagers, particularly around the olive harvest. I took this to mean that the location ticked one of Mariam's mental boxes, sending a message along the lines of *We are on this land*, which wouldn't have felt so much the case had she opted for somewhere in Area A, like a theatre in Ramallah or at one of the universities, although that certainly would have been easier and less risky.

The road there was so bumpy that a string of beads hanging from the rear-view mirror leapt from side to side. Half of the team was riding in a yellow minibus that we'd hired along with its driver, Abu Hafez, whom the boys subjected to the singing mood that came over them when the well-known intro to a George Wassouf song came on the radio and the minibus erupted into a dramatic ensemble rendition, splintering into laughter when our George stood to click his fingers and fell immediately across the tiny aisle into Majed's lap, on account of a crater in the road that Abu Hafez may or may not have deliberately failed to avoid.

'You should tell your friends to come,' I heard Mariam say. She was in the front seat. I was sitting directly behind her.

Abu Hafez's mirrored eyes shuttled over the rest of us. 'Come to your play?'

'Now you'll know where it is. Maybe your colleagues, other drivers – you could drive people over from Ramallah. Opening night is next Wednesday.'

Abu Hafez looked dully at the road ahead, where three boys playing football jumped out of our path. Through my window, I met the eye of the tallest, holding the ball to his hip.

'What is the play?' said Abu Hafez.

'*Hamlet*,' said Mariam.

'*Haaam-let*.' Abu Hafez began to laugh, booming from his gut. He lifted a hand from the steering wheel. 'To be or not to be!' he yelled.

We burst into applause.

Abu Hafez parked on a hillside. The earth was dry underfoot but night rains had left the air smelling soily.

'Is everything still on hold,' I asked Mariam, 'all your plans with Salim, while they investigate him?'

Mariam opened the trunk. 'One step at a time,' she said, her voice straining as she dragged out a suitcase labelled PROPS from under the heap of our overnight bags. 'First, the show.' Over the hill we climbed and there, below us, stood the stage. Like a half-built house, its gappy planks rattling in the wind, unpainted. A black tarpaulin flapped on the ground beside it, held down with rocks and buckets of quick-dry ceramic. It was a makeshift echo of the Bethlehem set, still with a peaked roof, but more modest, without a second level or stairs. Faris would be pleased. Instead of the separation wall, the backdrop was now one of fields, stones, the regular white buildings of the village, and, if you turned your head, the nearest settlement. Two of Anwar's workers bent over the base of the stage, hammering into the wood. Two others stabilised a stepladder while a third rigged a spotlight onto the scaffolding. Anwar was twisting light bulbs into a panel of sockets. They'd been at it all week, said Mariam. She also told us that we were only metres from Area C, pointing to a vague area in the grass. In Area C, building any structure required an Israeli permit, which no one ever heard of any Palestinians being granted. Permit-less structures were demolished by the army. Most of the West Bank was Area C.

Some hundred metres in the other direction stood the farm, a stone building with a corrugated roof, which we now approached. A barefoot man with yogic posture was cooking coffee in a big tarnished pot at a stove, talking to Dunya. A tiny snake was inked onto each of his big toes. 'Welcome, guys,' he said, peering out at us.

'Hey, everyone,' said Dunya. 'This is Mo.'

We said hello and recited our names, and Mo nodded at each of us in turn, trying to commit them to memory.

'You have a cute place,' said George.

Like many rehearsal days at this point, it was a day of waiting around. I set up camp on a rocky outcrop with my coffee and watched Anwar's team carrying boxes and objects from cars, unravelling and connecting thick black cables. Abu Hafez stood smoking with some of the guys. He didn't seem in a hurry to return to Ramallah.

'Taxi drivers,' said Mariam, sitting near me, 'are the key to everything.'

I sipped my coffee and got a mouthful of grounds. I thought about how her brain worked. 'Strategic' was a word that sprang to mind.

'Anything that's going on,' she said, 'they'll know about it. They're the ones to ask.' She leaned her broad smile close to mine. Crow's feet shaped the tops of her cheeks.

Once everyone had used the toilets at the farm, Mariam drew actors away in small groups to run scenes. Others practised speeches and dialogues together in patches of shade. Farm workers tossed straw over the soil to protect it from the sun. Eventually Jenan and I took our bags into the village to meet our hosts, an elderly couple who greeted us with enthusiasm. I presented them with a carton of coloured macaroons, Jenan a box of dates. Our bedroom had twin beds with twin red bedclothes and a little balcony. They trapped us with lunch before we could escape, with grape leaves and small talk and anecdotes about their daughters and grandchildren until Mariam called me three times and sent a text saying, *Where the hell are you? Anwar and I are going back to Ramallah for Emil.* Night was falling. We returned to find the stage covered in tarps, and Motaz building a fire in a ring of stones. Anwar's car was gone; so was Abu Hafez's. *Sorry,* I texted Mariam, sitting beside the flames. *See you tomorrow.* The farm workers had cooked a vegetarian stew, which they shared with us, ladling portions into bowls, their fingernails darkened with grit, faces flushed with exercise and satisfaction, reddened by firelight. Someone else handed out blankets made of synthetic jersey. The thickening darkness created the interesting illusion that the fire trapped our voices inside the circle of light and held other sounds at bay. Shadows pulsated unevenly. Something in me was being sated, looking at the faces of my colleagues, my friends. Sated and saddened: soon this would be over. I tilted my head up away from the fire and felt the cold, beneath the pale flaming of the stars.

'Sonia.'

Ibrahim stood near me clutching his emptied bowl at an angle. His tracksuit bottom had torn just below the left knee.

'What's up?'

He crouched. He didn't say anything.

'How are you feeling?' I asked.

'Ready. I think. You?'

Ahead of us, one log seemed to rise, wrapped in flame, while another fell, blackened, and crumbled into pieces.

'It was amazing that they took the gates down in the end,' I said.

Motaz was tossing more logs onto the fire, freeing sparks into the darkness. He pushed in a metal pole to curate the arrangement.

'Do you think,' I went on, 'that the reason it didn't get so much attention in the news was because it wasn't very violent?'

I tried not to let Ibrahim's continued silence perturb me. After a while, he said: 'You realise they did a deal with the Jordanians.'

'Who?'

'That thing at the Israeli embassy in Amman?'

'The shooting?' I asked, recalling the news items we'd read during my last weekend in Haifa.

'The Jordanians returned the Israeli guard who killed those two guys,' said Ibrahim. 'In exchange, the Israelis took the gates down.'

'Are you sure?'

'Yes – are you okay?'

'Surely,' I said. I released air from my lungs. 'That's a bit upsetting actually.'

Ibrahim touched my shoulder kindly. 'This is the way it works, baby. Gotta be realistic. The diplomats are way more important than us little guys.'

'Maybe we still had some effect.' I was struggling to conceal my disappointment. 'Even if it wasn't so direct.'

Ibrahim pushed out his lower lip. 'Maybe.'

I stared into the brightness, which kept flaring unexpectedly, tickling the air.

'I have something to say,' he said.

'Okay.'

'I'm sorry.'

His tone was so throwaway that I didn't immediately register this apology as the something he had to say.

'Sorry for what?'

He laid a palm flat on the ground to lower himself. The sinews in his jaw were moving, his skin orangey in the light.

'I'm sorry I suspected you.'

'*Suspected* me? Of what?'

'I don't know, I – something George said.'

'Oh, for heaven's sake.'

I located George across the fire. He was on second helpings, gripping a spoon.

'It's nothing,' said Ibrahim. 'It was stupid – I'm sorry I just, I knew I had cooled off with you and I wanted to explain.'

I took a deep breath and released it, counting. The phrase that came to me was: Get outside the frame. This was just the play, bleeding. Everyone is suspicious of Gertrude. Everyone is suspicious of each other.

'What did he say?'

'Nothing, just about a feeling he had – look, don't be angry with him, we were all on edge, remember? Amin . . .'

Was it bleeding, though? Or was it, in this case, a real-life hostility justified by the shape of a suspicion? Why *did* George dislike me?

'He's not on edge any more,' said Ibrahim.

Staring over the fire at George, I ran through the wording of a possible confrontation, sizing up the risks and benefits in the context of opening night.

'Listen,' said Ibrahim, 'I really like you.'

I looked back at him. We had arrived at the main thing he wanted to tell me. Once he knew he had my attention, he put his elbows on his knees and looked between them. I said his name. I wanted to say something like, I don't think you like me really. Or, It's natural when you're in a play with someone.

After a while, I said, 'I just got out of a shitty thing.'

He shifted round, examining my face. The light licked his dimples into shape, casting shadows near his mouth. His eyes were a little wide.

'When are you going back?' he said.

He meant London, not Ramallah. I caught an image of myself stirring in his mind.

'I don't know. Next month, probably.'

I didn't know just then what stopped me from encouraging him. I did know that blaming Harold was a coward's escape. Harold was already fairly stale in my mind. Yet he occurred to me in that moment as a kind of useful ghost, a reminder to be gentle with someone else's feelings. Parting from Harold in the mornings had been like turning from the glow of a fire into the heatless air. Cynicism is easy in hindsight, to say, Oh, but it wasn't real. I don't know what makes a feeling real. All I knew was that at the time it felt like flying, even if I looked terrible in my evening dress, and the holes in my sense of self were widening, like a cheap coat's lining, ripping out of sight.

I put my hand on Ibrahim's warm hand, pressing it into the blanket. He didn't look at me. I released him.

We let the fire die around midnight, setting the remaining logs side by side, and then used the torches on our phones to guide our feet into the village. Jenan and I let ourselves in with our spare key. This was the first time I had been alone with her indoors and the first time I'd seen her without her hijab. Her hair was shoulder-length and thick. I lay awake for hours, listening to the soft measure of her breath from the other bed.

I thought about Ibrahim, shiny and foolish like a young man, even though he was only a couple of years younger than me. He seemed so unafraid of rejection. I smiled, looking at the window, at how silly he was. Then I thought: Sonia you are such a bore. There was nothing foolish about Ibrahim. I was the one unable to accept affection from a kind person who I found attractive.

Already with these thoughts I could feel myself thawing dangerously. I recalled the weight of Ibrahim's hand on my shoulder. Anything solid between us carried implications of a certain magnitude, that was the problem. For one thing, it might mean a commitment to this place, to coming here and being here. And that was too much, at the moment, for me to think about.

Jenan made a snuffling noise and shifted in her sleep. I didn't dare check the time. I was going to be exhausted in the morning. Why did I have this feeling that no one was to be trusted, not even Mariam? This business of Ophelia – I'd never cared about playing that part; I'd cared about what Mariam thought of me. *After all that*, George had said. In the darkness my fears were swelling, I saw my ego daubing everything with an ugly obvious paint, like something garish on my fingers that wouldn't wash off. I shut my eyes hard as though to make myself disappear. I was envisioning the end of the play and the return to my loneliness. Sleep crept up when I stopped looking for it. Eventually, the sun rose.

OPENING NIGHT

Intro oud music.

Enter into the audience: HAZEM, EMIL, THREE STRANGERS, AMIN'S BROTHER 'THE RIFLE' *and* THREE FRIENDS, MAJED'S WIFE NINA *and* TWO CHILDREN, *and* SEVEN MORE STRANGERS. *They settle largely in the front and the back of the seating area, leaving an empty swathe in the middle.*

THE CAST *stand in a circle behind the stage. From her position in the circle,* SONIA *can see round the left side of the set at the gathering* AUDIENCE, *who are talking loudly.*

MARIAM	Tongue twisters. Start with the mishmish.
THE CAST	Haada lmishmish mish min mishmishkum haada lmishmish min mishmishna.
IBRAHIM	A silk thread on Khaleel's wall, yalla.
THE CAST	Khayt hareer 'ala hayt Khaleel. Khayt hareer 'ala hayt Khaleel.
AMIN	My cow's neck.
THE CAST	Maraqet raqabet baqartee ahla min maraqet raqabat baqartak. Maraqet raqabet baqartee ahla min maraqet raqabat baqartak.

Enter RIMA *into the front row*

SONIA	(*To no one.*) Oh.

> *followed by* JAD, *very slowly, on walking sticks.*

JAD	(*Audibly.*) Look at that chandelier.

THE CAST *begin stretching.*

IBRAHIM	Sonia, could I speak to you?

298

SONIA   Sure.

IBRAHIM   I want to say I—

DUNYA   (*Holding out a waistcoat.*) Brahim, can you check this fits you?

> IBRAHIM *puts on the waistcoat.* DUNYA *buttons it, pulls the bottom edge flat, snips at a loose thread.*

> *Enter into the audience* HANEEN, SALIM MANSOUR, UNIDENTIFIABLE BLONDE WOMAN *and* THREE MEN IN SUITS.

SONIA   What were you going to say?

> *Enter into the audience* THE MAYOR OF RAMALLAH, THE MAYOR OF AL-BIREH, THE PALESTINIAN MINISTER OF CULTURE, MO *wearing a porkpie hat, followed by various employees of and interns at the* BRITISH COUNCIL *and the* RAMALLAH GOETHE-INSITUT.

> DUNYA *takes the waistcoat away.*

IBRAHIM   I don't want to pester you about it. But I want to be honest. I haven't felt this strongly about someone since I met my wife.

> *Enter* ABU HAFEZ *and his wife* UM HAFEZ.

SONIA   *What?*

IBRAHIM   You know, Sonia, sometimes you speak with a very cynical tone.

MARIAM   Okay, everybody. Positions.

> HANEEN *and* JAD *have caught sight of one another. They wave.* JAD *reaches for his stick, slowly standing;* HANEEN *hurries over, flapping at him. She kisses her aunt and uncle in their seats, then crouches in the aisle to talk to them.*

SONIA   What's that supposed to mean?

MAJED *begins to pray.* DUNYA *adjusts the swords on the props table. The music is getting quieter. Strings of a single oud. The lights start to go down.*

IBRAHIM   It's my cue.

THE AUDIENCE *is larger than expected – about a hundred people. In the moment before the stage-lights rise, the* CAST *look at each other in the gloaming. There is an end-of-days feeling. Let the struggle begin on the rim of the well. Stage-lights up.*

Enter onstage IBRAHIM *and* GEORGE.

IBRAHIM   Who's there?
GEORGE   No, answer me. Stand and reveal yourself.
IBRAHIM   Long live the King!
GEORGE   Barnardo?
IBRAHIM   Indeed he.
GEORGE   You came on the appointed time most exactly.
IBRAHIM   It has struck twelve. Go to bed, Francisco.

From the rear, SONIA *listens to their voices, watching the shadows from the lights. She leans against the crane supporting the chandelier. When* MAJED's *shadow appears on the stage wall, the Ghost's voice booms from the speakers. Gasps and some laughter from* THE AUDIENCE.

Scene Two. Enter onstage SONIA, MAJED, FARIS *and* IBRAHIM *dancing, followed by* MARIAM *dressed in black. Music dies.* MAJED *begins to speak.*

We conferred backstage over how it was going. The play was a machine and we kept going out to touch the parts. Generally the impression was that it was going well. Despite the recorded instruction before the show to please turn off your mobile phones, a couple of ringtones and loud 'Allo's occurred but none at crucial moments and the attention continued to feel quite pure. Praise was due to Motaz's lighting design, which was precise and spectacular. There were also some great moments like when Mariam said *The time is out of joint, oh damned spite / that ever I was born to set it right* where you could practically hear audience members grunting with satisfaction and agreement.

Then, in the middle of the second act, Jenan lost her lines. An awful quiet followed during which she breathed loudly into her microphone. Ibrahim and I met each other's eyes in horror. *Hamlet raised his other hand like this*, she began saying, and then silence. Oh shit, I whispered. Someone prompt her.

She got there herself, and actually this was a point where I think Mariam's scriptless exercise may have been both partly to blame for Jenan's stage fright (although blame in these cases is hard to measure) but also part of the remedy, since Jenan knew where she had to go and could feel her way there in dialect, saying, He shook my arm up and down! And then the poetry flooded back in, and her wheels returned to the rails. Behind the stage, we were all sighing with relief. Ibrahim shut his eyes and pursed his lips, blowing out his cheeks like a cartoon of the West Wind.

MARIAM   Welcome, good friends! How are you, Guildenstern, and
            you, Rosencrantz? How are you both?

I peered round the base poles at the audience.

MARIAM   In the private members of Lady Fortune? By God you
            are truthful, she is a loose whore. What's your news?
GEORGE   No news, sir, except that the world's become virtuous.
MARIAM   Then Judgement Day is close. But this news is not true.
            Let me be specific: What is it, my kind friends, that you
            have done to offend the Goddess Fortune so that she has
            sent you to this prison?
IBRAHIM   Prison, my lord?

In the front row, Jad wore a look of approval. Yes, this is a prison, his face seemed to say.

MARIAM   Denmark's a prison.
GEORGE   Then the whole world's a prison.
MARIAM   An excellent prison, with halls and cells and dungeons, and Denmark is among the worst.
GEORGE   We don't think so, my lord.
MARIAM   Well, she's not a prison to you. For nothing's good or ugly except thinking makes it so. To me, this country is a prison.
GEORGE   Then your ambition makes it one – it is too small to fulfil your mind's needs.
MARIAM   God! I could be confined to a walnut shell, and count myself king of space unlimited

                                   were it not that I have

                                                     bad dreams

In the dark beyond the audience, something was stirring. I heard a car and saw headlights flash on and off. Typical, I thought, that people would be late. At least many of the best scenes were yet to come. We still had To be or not to be, and Hecuba was about to start. The stage was emptying, leaving Mariam alone.

MARIAM   What a coward I am. What a peasant slave.
          Is it not a disgrace upon me that this actor,
          in a fiction, in a dream of passion

SONIA   Brahim

MARIAM   forces his spirit to wear his illusion
          so that it blazes, his countenance goes pale entirely
          tears in his eyes, frenzy in his features

SONIA   Brahim, are those soldiers?

MARIAM   his voice breaks and trembles, and all function of his body
               wears that illusion . . . and all that for the sake of nothing?
           For the sake of Hecuba!
           What is he to Hecuba, or Hecuba to him

           Eight ISRAELI SOLDIERS *enter the perimeter of the stage's glow.*

           that he should weep like this for her?

IBRAHIM   Oh God protect us

MARIAM   And what would he have done
           had he the motive and tormenting passion
           that I have? By God, he'd drown the stage with tears,
           split the ears with terrible speech,
           push the sinful into madness. Frighten the innocent,
           amaze the ignorant, terrorise
           the very ears and eyes.
           And in spite of that, yet I

Mariam's voice broke and I wondered if she'd seen them. Then she
carried straight on.

                       I stupid wretch, from mud my meat and weft
               steal a look, like a dreamer-idiot, un-full of my motives
               unable to say anything

           Silence. The SOLDIERS *approach the left flank of the stage. Some
           members of the* AUDIENCE *have seen them, a few heads turn.*

                       not even for the sake of a king
               upon whose dominion and dear life an evil defeat was
               made. Am I a coward?
               Who calls me villain? Breaks my skull?
               Plucks my beard and throws it in my face?

                                                                    303

It amazed me that she was still going. Neither speeding up nor stumbling.

> Rubs my nose, calls it a lie in my throat
> or even in my lung? Who does that to me?
> *Ha!*
> I must submit, by God: my liver is but the
> liver of a pigeon, there is no gallbladder in me
> to make my oppression bitter, or I'd have
> fattened every kite in the universe
> with the intestines of this slave, this obscene criminal
> villain,
> this immoral traitorous villain that
> exits the laws of nature without conscience.
> *Without any vengeance!*

Four of the SOLDIERS *get closer to the stage. They look young. Two are women.*

MARIAM   (*Suddenly much quieter.*) What an ass I am.

The AUDIENCE *laughs.*

MARIAM   What a beautiful sham,
               that I, the son of a dear murdered,
               I whom heaven incites – and hell as well – to vengeance,
               break open what is in my heart as prostitutes do with words
               and go cursing like a whore
               an adulterer
               but damn it! Ouff.
               Come on, my brains. Ah—

Now she had seen them. Ibrahim, Jenan and I were pressing ourselves up at the planks of the backdrop to peer through the gaps. I watched Mariam adjust her position so that she seemed to be addressing the soldiers. I wondered if any of them could understand her.

MARIAM   I have heard
           that criminals

At this point she actually half-gestured at the soldiers, which made
my stomach drop.

                        sitting in a theatre
           have been so struck by the skill of the scene in their souls
           that they have straightaway
           declared their offences.
           For murder, though it lacks tongue, yet it speaks
           sometimes
           with an extraordinary, miraculous—

SONIA   (*Whispering.*) Shall I tell her to stop?
IBRAHIM   No.

MARIAM   I'll make those actors perform something resembling the
           killing of my father
           before my uncle. I'll observe his features,
           I'll pierce his core to his very last breath, and if he winces,
           even a single wince,
           I'll know my way with him. For the spirit I saw
           might be a devil, and the devil can
           put on a pleasant appearance – and perhaps
           deceives me to drag me to ruin.
           I'll find firmer evidence than this. The play is the thing
           by which I'll catch the conscience of the King.

           The SOLDIERS *remain standing in two rows but don't come closer.*
           Members of the AUDIENCE *look unsettled. It dawns on* SONIA
           that the soldiers are standing on the patch of earth that marks the end
           of Area B and the beginning of Area C.

SONIA   Do you think they realise there are two mayors in the
           audience?

| IBRAHIM | They won't care. |
| AMIN | (*Gleeful, coming up behind them.*) Did you see they're watching us? |

By the end of the second act, the soldiers seemed restless, moving back and forth, conferring. A couple of times a blast of static erupted from one of their radios, but they never attempted to stop us. Eventually they returned into the darkness, to their vehicle. After that, my main fear was that settlers might turn up, maybe even with arms. I realised Ibrahim was thinking the same thing when he asked me which way the nearest settlement was again? The soldiers felt like a premonition.

AMIN	(*To Sonia as she comes offstage.*) Are they still here?
SONIA	I don't know.
JENAN	They're in their car. Can you see it? Look.

Following Jenan's hand, we could just make out the nose of the military truck in the darkness. So they were continuing to watch us. I wondered if they were waiting until the end. And if so, why?

The rest of the show ran fast and taut. The audience sat uncannily still. They were clearly aware that *they* now had an audience, too, and this was binding them to us. Together we were a team, determined to continue, spurred on by a blend of fear and defiance.

Then, in the closet scene, something peculiar happened to me, which may or may not have had anything to do with the Israelis. First of all, Majed entered as the Ghost and Mariam reached for his hand. My nerves were incredible, which was unusual, and in my effort to contain them I was moving with a smoothness that verged on robotic. At least that's how it felt. Later, Mariam would deny having noticed anything.

| SONIA | You focus your eye on vacancy |

Mariam looked up at me, crumpled, babylike, vulnerable.

and discuss with the air that has no body

At this point, my engine split in two. I felt a touch seasick, like the set was tilting beneath me. I was entering a fugue state. I watched myself being Gertrude.

MARIAM   On him! On him! Look how pale his glare is.
         (To Majed.) Do not look on me, lest with this act that breaks the heart you
         alter my stern deeds. What I've decided to do will drain of its proper colour,
         it will be made of tears instead of blood.
SONIA   To who do you say this?
MARIAM   You don't see anything there?
SONIA   Nothing at all.

Mirror-me gestured at the empty space in which Majed was standing.

                    And everything that is there I see.
MARIAM   And you don't hear anything?
SONIA   Nothing, except for ourselves.

As I said this I heard the wings of something enormous shuddering on the air.

MARIAM   How strange. Look there. Look how it sneaks away from us.

Majed crept offstage. Terror of the Ghost coursed through me. Was it terror of the Ghost? The difference between this and the normal embodying of staged emotion was basically, I think, one of degree and duration. My fear was like a child's play-fear, it had that prolonged innocent intensity, blending the unreal with the real. The way the body rehearses for danger. I was having the flight reaction I would once have had, a long time ago, to shadows in a bedroom. Now I was both the child and the shadows.

SONIA   If words be of breath

I gasped for breath.

> and breath of life, believe me, there is no life in me
> to breathe what you have said to me Hamlet.

When I came off I slipped out of it, returning to myself.

An air of mortal seriousness reigned backstage. The cast and crew looked steely. On balance our performances were probably enhanced by the soldiers, although had they tried any harder to disrupt us I don't doubt that balance would have careened. Preserving the play's illusion felt even more vital. The audience must not crack. Acts Four and Five were galvanic, treacherous, as Hamlet's situation deteriorated and the deaths of the other characters piled up. The heat of the fire stayed on our faces. The set was half-destroyed, shards of the quick-dry ceramic that had been broken off the back lying like white gravel over the stage-floor.

At the very end, Amin said the final line: *Go, bid the soldiers shoot*. I looked reflexively at the spot where the military car had been parked. There was no sign of it. They had left in silence.

The audience gave us a roaring ovation. Anwar turned the floodlights on. I could see Hazem and Emil, I could see Haneen. I was sweating with relief, bowing again, again, through the whistling and stamping. There was the distinct, if illogical, feeling that our mettle had kept the army from the stage. After the fourth bow we started laughing. I applauded Amin grinning beside me and thought, with a burst of mental fireworks, Oh I could probably do this forever. Ibrahim hugged George. After applauding our tech team we separated and moved to the stage edge to applaud the audience. So we were all applauding each other, making a massive sound with our hands up to the heavens. Two women approached the steps to present Mariam with a bouquet of white flowers. A couple of PA ministers wanted to talk to her, apparently. In the second before we descended into the crowd I glimpsed a little sad look on her face, which she wiped off with a smile. Uncle Jad had brought me yellow roses. They were hidden in a plastic bag under his chair.

*

Over the course of the next few days, neither Ibrahim nor I mentioned what he had said to me at the start of opening night. At first, the play outshone all declarations. Then I took his silence as a response to my silence and thought, Well, I won't be the one to bring it to a head. Despite this, his presence continued to have a calming effect on me. He stood unchanging in the corner of my eye. I tried not to look too closely at what this might mean.

The audiences at the remaining three shows were sizeable if never quite so large, and the soldiers didn't come again. Certain schoolchildren from the village returned nightly, trundling over for a shy hello after curtain call, wearing expressions of love and awe. On Thursday, two foreign journalists interviewed Mariam and took press shots of her with Anwar. On Friday, a representative of a Swedish organisation expressed interest in funding a tour, with the caveat that we must display English subtitles on a screen. Mariam gritted her teeth and Anwar said in Arabic, Don't be hasty, let's discuss it next week. I don't want European funders! she said with a mismatched smile at the Swede, before thanking her, thank you so much for coming, we'll be in touch. A cast-and-crew meeting was set for after our return to Ramallah, in which we would discuss next steps.

That night, the Friday, while the general mood was soaring during our post-show fireside meal, I saw Ibrahim walk towards me. Here we go, I thought. I could fend him off with something hazy and philosophical and possibly condescending about how being in a play bound you in a way that felt eternal and revelatory but always passed. Instead, he said: Try not to be so sad all the time, it gets me down. I'm not sad, I said defensively, and he responded: What you and Mariam have onstage is amazing, there are all these things under the surface, you can really feel it. I was struck by how brazen he was being, trying to read me. In a new voice, I said that it would be a shame not to tour, whether or not I took part. Four shows was nothing. Oh, but of course we'll tour, said Ibrahim. We both fell silent.

On Saturday I became thirsty during Act Four and ducked beneath the stage for water. A single yellow light bulb illuminated an area for equipment and supplies; an adjacent, darker section, marked off by boxes, was used by the boys as a changing room if the designated curtain was occupied. Ibrahim was climbing back over the boxes in his Laertes robe as I ripped the plastic carton to extract a bottle. I thought he was trying to pass me so I moved aside, and then he picked up my left hand and met my eye with a quite hilarious sideways glance, awaiting my reaction. Above us, the stage trembled with the weight of the other actors. I was going to make a quip about his seeming rather optimistic, but there was something so chaste about the hand-holding, I ended up smiling in a way that was obviously sincere. He didn't even try to kiss me. He laughed and dragged me out into the fresh air, saying, Come on, stop wasting time.

We woke early to strike the set before the sun got too hot. Dismantling is always poignant. It was also hard work, and entailed climbing back and forth over the hillsides carrying planks, boxes of wires and lights. Everyone dropped off on the way back to Ramallah, and occasionally I woke and cast an eye over the sleeping bodies around me jiggling with the road. The future was hanging over me. I needed to return to London in a few weeks, minimum. I had teaching responsibilities, bills to pay. My income from playing Gertrude was not covering my mortgage. Beside me, Ibrahim had twisted his head away. I put my forehead on his shoulder and sensed him wake, aware of me, his breath deepening.

Haneen arrived at Mariam's that evening in a patterned sleeveless shirt and jeans, hoop earrings and lipstick. To my surprise, she was the one who initiated the dancing, shaking her shoulders in front of the fridge, drawing George into a contest over who could move more extravagantly – the winner, predictably, was George – which got everyone hooting. Majed made a speech, we ate pastries drenched in sugar syrup, drank beer and wine. The alcohol hit me fast. At a certain point there was an outbreak of dabke, naturally. I noticed Mariam had vanished and went outside to find her alone on the garden bench.

'Budge up,' I said, sitting.

I was barefoot and the grass was cool and rough between my toes. She rested her head against me and lifted it again in lieu of saying hello. Inside, Majed howled with laughter.

'I wish we'd had someone from Gaza in the play,' said Mariam. 'I wish that had been possible.'

I tried to watch her. Lights blinked in my eyes. 'Maybe you still can have someone from Gaza,' I said. 'If you tour, abroad.'

She didn't respond. My thoughts were slow and kept slipping.

'Is that why you're disappointed?' I asked.

'I'm not disappointed.'

'You were fucking great. You're such a good actor. I mean really you could have been an actor, no problem. You played Hamlet.'

She laughed. 'Are you drunk?'

'It may not have been perfect but it was really good. Is that you, Anwar? What are you doing there, you scared me.'

'Sorry,' said Anwar, emerging from the shadows. 'Hey.'

'We should turn the music down,' said Mariam.

'I can do that,' I said. 'I guess I'll go and find, er, you know.'

'Find what?' she said.

'Oh, no one.'

Anwar took my place on the bench. 'Just go and talk to him.'

'Talk to who?' I said.

Anwar shook his head. Inside, Ibrahim was sitting on the arm of the sofa, cracking his knuckles. I sat on the opposite end beside my sister, who immediately stood to get a drink. The gesture confused me. Did everyone know? Ibrahim hesitated, then swung his socked feet onto the vacant sofa cushion until he was facing me.

'I'll see you in another ten years then, will I?' he said.

'Let's have this conversation when I'm sober.'

He sat back upright, moving away. 'Okay.'

'I didn't mean to be sharp.'

The portcullis was descending; I needed to stop it. I breached as much of the gap between us as I could in one casual motion, which considering my loss of motor control probably didn't look very casual. I refrained from touching him, even though his leg was right there. The music switched to a quieter acoustic song and I remembered, at a lag, my mission to reduce the volume. Haneen was singing along. I looked down at my lap.

'I hate my hands,' I said.

'Don't hate your hands,' said Ibrahim. 'You have nice hands.' He picked one up and turned it over.

I looked at my hand inside his. 'There's time,' I said.

'Is there time?'

'Tomorrow, the day after. I can't think right now. But I do want to talk. Just, in a little while.' I looked up at him. 'Don't roll your eyes at me.'

'I didn't roll my eyes. This is my face when it's relaxed.'

'You're awful.'

The party ended before midnight. Majed and Jenan faced long routes home and waiting families, and once they announced they were leaving everyone else seemed to remember how tired they were, and in a matter of minutes the whole party had been unpinned. Weighed down with imprecise feelings of regret, I hoped Ibrahim would loiter, but he only kissed me on the cheek before following George out the door.

Mariam set up her bed for Haneen and said goodnight to me from the doorway of Emil's room. Moments later, in the violet light of my own room, I saw I had an email from Harold.

Hi Sonia. New auditions for the Cherry Orchard. Are you interested? I think you would be a wonderful Ranyevskaya. Details and audition speeches attached.

Thinking of you,
H

I felt nauseated with dread. Or maybe it was just nausea. I slept without dreaming and then the sun, rising and stretching into my room, scratched my eyes. My headache was mild. I crept through the kitchen mess to locate my shoes and drink a glass of water and stepped outside to find the day already hot, and as I wound my way towards at-Tireh with a particular upmarket bakery in mind, I couldn't recall the name or exact location only that I would know it when I saw it, Harold's message floated up again through the murk of my hangover. I hadn't even replied to his last two emails. You had to give credit to the man's persistence. I ran over it again in my head. I knew what I was going to say, I just needed to be in the right frame of mind. Beyond the supermarket, I noticed a figure in a leather jacket, outlined by the fogging sun, kicking up dust.

'Wael!'

He turned. He didn't move. Then: 'Sonia.' The empty street carried our voices. I took his stillness as an invitation and approached.

'You look, you look sad,' I said uncontrollably, as his face came into view. I pulled him into a hug. 'Hey, I missed you.'

'How is the play going? I heard it was amazing.'

'It's been fun – who did you hear that from?'

'My mother.'

'What did she say?'

'She said Mariam was very strong.'

'She is. I wish you'd come to see it. I wished you'd been *in* it. We missed you at the party last night.'

'Shwaya,' said Wael. Finally, a trace of a smile. Then he clouded.

'What's happening, huh?' I said.

He shrugged.

'How's your family? Is everything okay?'

The muscles of his face quivered, answering the flow of his thoughts. I waited for him to find the words. Then he said, only: 'I miss everybody,' seeming deliberately to miss the mark.

'How's work? Have you been singing? Writing songs?'

'Yeah. I think I'm going to tour a bit. There's a concert in Abu Dhabi, and stuff, I think.' He paused. 'Then I'm going to move to Dubai.'

'Oh?'

'I'll take my mother with me,' he added.

I wondered why my response to this news so resembled the sloping feeling of loss. Why shouldn't Wael move to Dubai, if he could and wanted to? Also, what did it have to do with me?

'Good for you. That's great, I'm happy for you. Actually, you know, I'm leaving too. I have to go back to London.'

We still hadn't moved from our spot. I thought about suggesting a walk, or inviting him to breakfast. I didn't want to scare him off.

'How old are you again, Wael?'

'Twenty-four.'

I looked at him, my sweet boy, and he glanced back at me in shy discomfort. Or maybe it was guilt. I threw caution to the winds; I said: 'Why don't you come back and join us?'

He looked me straight in the eyes and I saw I'd hit something.

'Yeah,' I pressed, gently. 'Why don't you just come and do one more performance? Just one. For fun.'

'I don't think they want me back.'

'But they do!' I said, grasping on. 'I promise you, they do.'

'Mariam is Hamlet now.'

'We're all Hamlet now. She's Hamlet, you're Hamlet.'

'*You*'d be a good Hamlet.' He chewed his lower lip, pausing. 'I heard she was really convincing. People in the audience cried.'

'Don't be jealous of her.'

'Not jealousy,' he said, indignant. 'I'm happy about it.'

I grabbed him by his leather sleeve and said, 'Let's walk. I need your help carrying the breakfast anyway.'

Hi Harold.

I hope the run went well. I appreciate this offer, and I'm sure the show will be terrific. However I won't be trying out for the part. As for your other messages, I don't want you to read my silence as anger or bitterness or anything, or as an invitation to write. Yes, it's true, you did behave pretty badly. So what? You seem to want me to express something, some strong feeling either way. But I don't have one any more. I'm happy to say, I'm free.

Sonia

17

Exactly whose idea it was, I already can't recall. Only, since it was suggested, everyone has egged each other on, which means that any individual fits of doubt have been staggered, and there's always an adequate level of confidence at any one point to carry us forward. Since playing Hamlet, Mariam seems to have relinquished her leadership over us, and we continue making decisions as a team, instinctually. There hasn't been much time to dither, anyway, and we've agreed it will be like a stunt, or an experiment. I'm nervous about the younger men with West Bank IDs, and have made the case, which I have won, that Wael and Amin should only join us at the very last moment.

In the car on the way there, Mariam looks unusually serene. I ask her what she's thinking about.

'This sense I have,' she says, 'that I'm finally letting the play go. Mentally. You know?'

I'm not sure why, but hearing her say this aloud makes me thrum with nerves.

'And that feels okay?'

'Yes. I set it in motion but now it has a life of its own. It can fail or it can succeed.' She briefly lifts her palms off the wheel, to illustrate this. I wonder, but don't ask, what she means by fail or succeed.

It takes two hours for fifteen pairs of hands to build the stage by the checkpoint, on our side of the wall. Pedestrians funnel past us, buses clog the passage, little boys shuttle between car windows offering chewing gum and plastic kitchen items for sale. The patch of separation wall behind the set is adorned with a huge mural of Marwan Barghouti waving his chains. To the right stands a scorched lookout tower. One of the windows has been smashed in and it looks, mercifully, empty. The final piece of the puzzle is raising the chandelier on the crane: Dunya does the honours, Anwar steadying the glass pieces as it lifts off the canvas. Some of the baubles have been lost in the transfer but it's still magnificent, glittering in the afternoon sun, shivering and flashing. Around us the traffic dwindles, and then, after sunset, it begins to thicken again. Cars park off the roadside, young people loiter, watching us. Ibrahim comes over to give me a bottle of water and I touch his arm. He says, I guess the news is out about Wael, then.

Wael himself has been caught in the traffic that he has, indirectly, caused. When finally he springs from his BMW in sunglasses, clicking his car key, and jumps onto the stage, the street behind him whistles and calls his name. Car doors open, windows slide down. He lifts one hand at the crowd and flashes a grin before disappearing behind the set. Some drivers are bellowing about the congestion, they are actually commuting, what the hell is this – and Majed and Anwar become traffic wardens, directing cars this way and that. Motaz has started the floodlights, which catch on clouds of exhaust fumes. A conspicuous group of young hipsters appear from a minibus to our left, and approach sheepishly, smiling. I assume they are foreigners, and wonder if someone has invited them, or if they were passing by chance. Then I hear two of them speaking Hebrew.

'Oh my God,' I say to Mariam, who has also noticed them, and looks perplexed.

'Some of Wael's Israeli fan club, I guess,' she says.

I can't dwell any longer on what this might mean because I'm distracted by the sight of Amin and Wael among the chairs by the wall. They're hidden from the crowd by the stage, and Mariam and I are to the left, carrying some of the props over from her car. I set the bag I'm carrying down at my feet. Wael reaches out his hand, and Amin shakes it, coolly. There's an exchange of nods. Ibrahim, who has opened one of the costume boxes, makes a face at me to the effect of, Well, would you look at that. Then, as though he has just recognised me, he straightens up and beams. I've recently put my dress on and have plaited my hair. I turn shyly from Ibrahim's attention and catch sight of the moon, low and bloody, hanging above the wall. George jogs round the back towards us with his arms full of khaki fabric, brandishing two pairs of army boots and a helmet.

'Where the hell did you get those from?' says Mariam.

'It's an experiment.'

'What? Are you kidding me? George, this is risky enough.'

Ibrahim takes a pair of the boots and measures one against his foot. He glances up for my reaction, an eyebrow lifted. I'm trying to think it through.

'You can't do this,' says Mariam. 'You're going to confuse them. We're *at* a checkpoint.'

'They won't think we're actual soldiers,' says Ibrahim in a silly voice. He draws a stiff khaki shirt from the pile and holds it against his torso, checking the sleeves.

There's no time to debate the issue because it is already eight o'clock, the lights are going down, and George has pulled a pair of army pants on over his jeans. They are a little large, gathering under the belt.

Mariam shakes her head. 'You're out of control, all of you.' But she's smiling. 'Fine. What the hell.'

'At least they don't have guns,' I say, and Ibrahim raises a finger and beckons Faris, who passes over a long black rifle. 'Woah.'

'It's not real,' he says quickly.

'Why does Faris—' I begin.

Stage-lights up. George enters, dressed as a soldier.

Actually, the audience is not confused. There's an initial jolt, some intakes of breath, but then the dialogue starts and everyone recognises that the uniforms are costumes. The effect is interesting, actors-as-soldiers on-stage-beside-checkpoint. Like seeing adjacent shades of paint communicate on a canvas, each colour drawing out hues in the other. The soldier costumes are a gesture at the context. They hold no particular meaning. They are, also, funny and daring. Although I wonder if it's only funny in the way that fear sometimes produces laughter. Backstage, Mariam says to me: Yeah, it kind of works, I guess.

The end of the scene is close and I'm about to go on. Lights down, set change, lights up. Majed and I, King and Queen, bow at the crowd. There's a festival atmosphere and the audience of cars, pedestrians and street-sellers greet our appearance with wild applause.

I'm downstage when Wael makes his entrance. People actually scream. He raises his arms and there's instantly an air of off-script. Looking at my other cast-mates I can see I'm not the only one to break character and smile. The audience has really grown, now; buses and taxis extend down the street, we keep acquiring more traffic. People are sitting on their roofs and bonnets, passengers alight to cram into the gaps between vehicles, pushing down to the front. Wael closes his eyes at them, puffs out his chest, and begins to sing. I expect an anthem, something to rouse the crowd, wheel their kuffiyehs in the air, but instead he goes for an old love song. The moment he starts, we all sigh. His voice is like a liquid, pouring over us, smooth and easy, flowing from his mouth. It trembles in his throat, sliding on the minor notes. His head quivers with the vibrato. I feel euphoric. Everyone knows the words.

There's another round of jubilant applause and we melt back into the scene. *It seems to you, Madam?* says Wael to me. A synthetic echo trails his lines. To compete with the traffic noise, our mics have been adjusted to double volume, and this is costing our dialogue some intimacy. The crowd is still growing, and when Ibrahim and Jenan are left alone onstage, I can see people straining for a glimpse of Wael at the back. We're being filmed on dozens of mobile phones. I imagine this moment being streamed across the world. It also crosses my mind that a precedent has been set and this audience are now going to expect more singing from Wael than the play will viably allow for. Another part of me trusts Wael to trust his instincts. There is a special providence, and so on. *His imagination spurs him on into contempt for death*, Amin is saying onstage. He, too, has now donned army fatigues.

I believe in the compulsion to repeat. I think we are always doing it. Not one of us has given a name to this, our collective, unspoken decision to recreate some of the conditions of opening night. But even though on some level we must be expecting it, when the thunderous monotone finally breaks from the loudspeakers of the checkpoint behind us, we jump to our feet with terror. At first, the actors onstage keep going. Someone – Ibrahim – grasps my hand. We stand at the rear of the stage and see George frozen in his mock-up uniform. The whites of his eyes glow back at us, then he turns his head and carries on saying his lines, loudly. Members of the audience are yelling now, they are scattering, cars are trying to move, they honk: they see what we cannot yet. Doom crashes into my chest as the soldiers come streaming around the corner. One of them fires a shot. A few stones hurtle through the air. Tear gas expands like dry ice. The chandelier rocks precariously from the crane. The recording of Majed's voice begins to boom. *Mark me, I am thy father's spirit.*

Enter Ghost.

Explanatory Notes

'48: A term referring to Palestinian land taken during 1948. This territory is today considered to comprise the modern state of Israel, although Israel has never officially declared its borders and the West Bank and Gaza also remain under Israeli control.

'The inside' (in Arabic, 'al-dakhil'): another term referring to the 1948 territories.

Fida'i, fida'iyeen: a general term for militant revolutionaries; in the Palestinian context it specifically refers to nationalists committed to armed struggle in the mould of other anticolonial movements such as in Vietnam, China, Algeria and Latin America. The Palestinian fida'iyeen were most active from the 1950s up until the first intifada in 1987, and largely based outside historical Palestine, in Syria, Lebanon and Jordan.

The version of *Hamlet* I used is the Arabic translation by Jabra Ibrahim Jabra, which I freely translated back into the English language.

In Chapter 1 I adapted the first scene of Gordon Witty's translation of *Al-Moharrij* by Mohammad al Maghut, drawn from *Modern and Contemporary Political Theater from the Levant: A Critical Anthology*, eds Robert Myers and Nada Saab. With thanks to Sham Maghut, Gordon Witty, Robert Myers and Nada Saab for their permission.

Acknowledgements

Thank you everyone who shared their experiences of working in theatre in Palestine with me, especially Emil Ashrawi, Vera Tamari, Dia Barghouti, Bashar Murkus, George Ibrahim, Tania Nasir, Mohammad Hajj Ahmad, and members of The Freedom Theatre. Thank you also to Sabri Jiryis and Shukri Abed for their insights.

For their thoughts on various parts and versions of the text, and/ or for answering technical questions, thank you Allison, Andrew, Georgia, Joe, Kathy, Liz, Maan, Margaret, Melanie, Nana, Rabea, Ruth, Saad, Suhail, Tareq, Yara and Zena.

Thank you to the wonderful teams at Grove Atlantic and Jonathan Cape, and a big thank you to MacDowell, the Lannan Foundation, and Emily, Annemarie and Aline at Dar Jacir for their support while I was writing this.

ALSO BY ISABELLA HAMMAD

The Parisian

ISABELLA HAMMAD

Isabella Hammad is the author of *The Parisian*. She was awarded the Plimpton Prize for Fiction, the Sue Kaufman Prize for First Fiction from the American Academy of Arts and Letters, the Palestine Book Award and a Betty Trask Award. She has received fellowships from MacDowell, the Rockefeller Foundation and the Lannan Foundation. In 2023, she was named on *Granta*'s Best of Young British Novelists list.

9030 00008 7774 9